PRAISE FOR JOE GORES AND
MENACED ASSASSIN

"It takes some nerve to ~~~~ ~~~~ ~~~~ ~~~~polo-
gist and a maniacal ~~~~ ~~~~ ~~~~ ~~~~ores
has the nerve—and ~~~~ ~~~~ ~~~~ His
inventive narrative, w~~~~ ~~~~ ~~~~ cop
drama, mob caper, a~~~~ ~~~~ ~~~~, takes its theme
from a mesmerizing lecture on the innate brutality of men
and apes."

—**Marilyn Stasio,** *New York Times Book Review*

O

"A fine, tense crime story."

—*Houston Post*

O

"A multidimensional thriller that engages the reader on
two levels . . . a fast-paced trip through the shadowy world
of stalking and murder. . . . Gores, the consummate plot-
ter, pulls it off."

—*Rocky Mountain News*

O

"A taut suspense thriller, MENACED ASSASSIN transcends
the label 'murder mystery.'"

—*Library Journal*

O

"Gores has mastered the hard-boiled Hammett irony . . .
taut, colorful, stylistically convincing and satisfyingly complex."

—*Detroit Sunday News*

O

"A tough, taut writer who views his subject matter
unsparingly and unsentimentally."

—*Washington Post*

O

"This is one author who can write with a vengeance."

—*New York Newsday*

more . . .

MENACED
ASSASSIN

By Joe Gores

NOVELS
A Time of Predators
Interface
Hammett
Come Morning
Wolf Time
Dead Man
Menaced Assassin

DKA FILE NOVELS
Dead Skip
Final Notice
Gone, No Forwarding
32 Cadillacs

COLLECTION
Mostly Murder

ANTHOLOGIES
Honolulu, Port of Call
Tricks and Treats
    (with Bill Pronzini)

NON-FICTION
Marine Salvage (1971)

SCREENPLAYS
Interface
Hammett
Paper Crimes
Paradise Road
Fallen Angel
Cover Story
    (with Kevin Wade)
Come Morning
Run Cunning
Gangbusters

TELEPLAYS
Golden Gate Memorial
    (4-hr miniseries)
High Risk
    (with Brian Garfield)
"Blind Chess"
    (B. L. Stryker)

EPISODIC TV
"Kojak"
"Eischied"
"Kate Loves a Mystery"
"The Gangster Chronicles"
"Strike Force"
"Magnum, P.I."
"Columbo"
"Remington Steele"
"Scene of the Crime"
"Eye to Eye"
"Helltown"
"T.J. Hooker"
"Mike Hammer"

JOE GORES

MENACED ASSASSIN

THE MYSTERIOUS PRESS

Published by Warner Books

A Time Warner Company

MYSTERIOUS PRESS EDITION

Cover design by Jackie Merri Meyer
Cover illustration by Jeff Fitz Maurice

The Mysterious Press name and logo are registered trademarks of Warner Books, Inc.

 Mysterious Press books are published by
Warner Books, Inc.
1271 Avenue of the Americas
New York, NY 10020

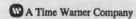 A Time Warner Company

Printed in the United States of America

Originally published in hardcover by The Mysterious Press.
First Printed in Paperback: December, 1995
10 9 8 7 6 5 4 3 2 1

For DORI

Heaven's last, best gift,
my ever-new delight

Author's Note

The geological eras and time frames on the part-title pages refer to notable mass-extinction events during which 60-85 percent of all life on earth disappeared, with its ecological niche then promptly being refilled by new life-forms.

Man is now destroying other life-forms at the rate of one every twenty-four hours. Their ecological niches are not being filled with new species, because the niches themselves are being destroyed. Once a species and a niche are gone, they are gone forever.

I am your dwarf.
I am the enemy within.
I am the boss of your dreams . . .
the kindred of blackness and impulse.
See. Your hand shakes . . .
It is your Doppelganger
trying to get out.
Beware . . . Beware . . .

Anne Sexton
"Rumpelstiltskin"

PART ONE

End of the Cambrian

510 m.y. ago

Death be not proud, though some have called thee
Mighty and dreadful, for thou are not so,
For those whom thou think'st thou dost overthrow,
Die not, poor death, nor yet canst thou kill me. . . .
One short sleep past, we wake eternally,
And death shall be no more; death, thou shalt die.

John Donne
Holy Sonnets

CHAPTER ONE

Listen to Raptor, *mon vieux*. Don't take this life so seriously,
you'll never get out of it alive.

I kill. Oh, I know. You expect me to add, Therefore I am.
But that is nonsense. I do not kill out of any inner compul-
sion to give what that fool Hemingway called the gift of
death. If killing is a gift, it is a gift to the killer himself, during the ritual frenzy of the hunt. Whoever considers Proud
Death a gift to a healthy animal has no imagination and is already half in love with his own *finis*.

I am not. I kill—without pity, compunction, emotion or
moral qualms, to be sure—but not because killing obsesses
me. Just because, well . . . it is what I do. Previously I have
done other things, perhaps in future I will do other things
again. But for at least a few hours more, I kill. After that . . .

After that, well, tonight Will Dalton plans to give a lecture. A lecture on the nature of man in hopes of exposing, no
less, the roots of man's endless violence, perhaps man's evil,
and to draw some sort of inane conclusions from it.

No, no, my dear women, lower your knitting needles. I am
sure he will not exclude the Fair Sex, the Better Half, the Little Woman, from his overview. *I* would not. When I say Man
I speak not of gender, but of my own kind *sui generis,* as a
class by itself apart from all else in Nature.

Separate, let me hasten to add, only in the way that a dog
is separate from a stork. Not separate as the fallen angel of

Religion (with an immortal soul breathed into it by God) is separate from the beasts of the field. And not separate as the risen ape of Science (last best result of evolution's efforts) is separate from those same angels set twirling by Aquinas on the head of a pin.

Rather, I speak of man as *fallen ape,* of whatever sex he might be. Baser than heaven, baser than our primate stock, baser even than the slime from which both Science and Religion insist all life springs.

I admit that I speak to you now out of my own base pride in my own base actions, because I am vain enough to want to give you my version of events—small things make base men proud, you can appreciate the reference. And also, by showing it in action, my version of man's nature to set against Dalton's pitiable attempts at exculpation and justification for mankind.

But I grant poor fool Will life enough to air at least some of his views. Grant? Of course—*I kill,* remember? Before this night is over, Dalton will have joined the other dead, and my work will be done. Or I will be.

Does that give you pause? The assassin facing his own assassination? The policeman Dante Stagnaro will be at the lecture, peeping behind the arras and beneath the chairs for that murderous wraith Raptor, that mocking evil fellow who has haunted his dreams for lo these many months, yea, verily and forsooth, even *moi,* your humble servant. Shoot-out at the O.K. Corral.

But you have seen through my façade already, haven't you, *carcajou mauvais*? You know that despite the front I put up, the easy amiability and the desire to please, I am self-centered and selfish and self-righteous. That I love wrangling and the utter bleak tension that goes with it. That I love to pile lies upon lies, thus justifying and excusing my own actions. That the self-lie is always preferable to other lies, because when one lies to oneself one need never confront naked truth.

But if I lie to you tonight, *mon brave,* and then die, my truth will never be known. So contrary to my own dark nature, I must be totally honest. I must make you privy to my thoughts, memories, feelings, and reactions to those other deaths, seething in the dark of my brain during these past fifteen months.

So my story—like any good fairy tale—begins with
Once upon a time . . .

CHAPTER TWO

Once upon a time, in the twenty-ninth year of her life and seventh year of her now-failed marriage, Molly Dalton sat at her desk in the Atlas Entertainment corporate offices, staring out across deserted lower California Street at the lighted apartments and raised walkways of San Francisco's tony Embarcadero Center. She chewed her lower lip, strangely breathless and not a little . . . probably *frightened* was not too strong a word.

So. Frightened. What she had accessed in the corporate mainframe had made no sense at first, but being very bright, and with an attorney's inquisitiveness besides, she'd transferred the data to a 3.5″ floppy and taken it to her penthouse apartment and for the past few days had played with it off and on during her free time. And suddenly it *had* made sense. Too much sense.

It had angered her at first—this was her career, after all—then suddenly it had scared her. So now . . .

Moll—short for Molly, short for Margaret—was a platinum blonde with very large blue eyes, a tip-tilted nose and small chin, high cheekbones and narrow cheeks, arched, slightly thick brows, and a dazzling smile that just naturally gave men very specific erotic notions. Her hair was a golden halo around this innocent angel face, her full-bosomed body was kept rounded yet taut by fanatic devotion to Nautilus and the stairs (on the chart she could climb the Empire State Building without getting winded).

Naturally, starting with her daddy when she was an infant, almost every man she ever met told her she was beautiful, and she had believed them all. Mirror, mirror on the wall. But that wasn't quite enough for her, because she was also smart, whiplash smart, and wanted to be told that as well.

One of those proclaiming her beauty had been a rawboned grad student named Willard Dalton. Will was finishing up his Ph.D. in paleoanthropology at Cal-Berkeley while she was finishing her senior year in psych at the same school. They had met in a drama class—inevitable for her, given her background, just fun for him and a place to meet pretty girls, although he showed a fine flair for playacting and an unexpected satiric wit in improv. Perhaps in Will the stage lost a fine actor to science.

He quickly began to tell Molly that she was not only the most beautiful but also the most intelligent woman he had ever met, which was what she had been waiting to hear. So it was Will for Molly; and what Molly wanted, Molly got.

Too bad. Because Moll's daddy was an entertainment attorney with a plush suite of offices in Century City, and she went to Beverly Hills High with the spawn of movie stars. She was deflowered in a hot tub by her best friend's older brother—second lead in a sitcom on CBS—at age thirteen. Physical beauty was the only measure any man ever judged her by, so sex became the only coin with which she could confirm her value. By the time her daddy gave her the expected cherry-red high school graduation Ferrari, Moll already was finding a fortnight without a fuck like a year in a convent without a door.

Will, on the other hand, was from Wyoming, the son of a rancher, a childhood dinosaur freak who, before he'd moved from *T. rex* to *H. habilis* at Cal, had done a lot of amateur digging. While growing up he'd even unearthed a nest of maiasaur eggs that Jack Horner himself had called "significant." He was an excellent naturalist, hunter, tracker, used to vast spaces, solitary thoughtfulness, self-reliance, voluminous reading, and spending all his spare time alone out in the field. Thus he didn't lose his virginity until his second year at Cal. He quickly became adept as a hunter in those sexual jungles as well, but just never found it any hardship to go without.

Major culture clash in almost every area of their lives. And when he and Moll got married before she started law school the September after her bachelor's degree, her daddy as a matter of course picked up the tuition. That didn't set well with Will, who felt paying for his wife's advanced degree was sort of his responsibility. But he was starting his post-doc work, money was tight, and he was dementedly in love with Moll. If that was what she wanted, that was what she should get.

Will paid her father back by working multiple night jobs, but by then they'd had their first real fight: Moll had gotten pregnant and an abortion without telling Will about either one.

"Will," she said when the tattletale medical bills came in, "we just don't have the money. And there's lots of time."

"But dammit, we can never have *that* one again."

The argument ended in bed, so he never discovered her real reason for the abortion: an almost irrational dread of ruining her figure, reducing her seductiveness to men.

Many men. Her first affair as a married woman followed an international conference in Paris on australopithecine locomotion the second summer after Will's Ph.D. The conference led to an invitation for three weeks in the field at Hadar, Ethiopia. The Lucy site. Heady stuff for Will, the lowly postdoc, but since her daddy happened to be in Paris on business, Moll elected to stay behind in the City of Light rather than grub around with her husband after old bones out in the arid African bush.

Will agreed, never dreaming she'd be fucking the brains out of a French film director before his plane left the ground at Orly International. Her daddy, who had mean feelings about Will, had made the introduction with malice aforethought: he'd been most unhappy when she'd gone and married a real-life replacement for him, and a strong man to boot. *Au fond,* he wanted her always to be Daddy's little girl.

At Hadar, Will found nothing of significance in the ground. But when the focus of their endless campfire discussions became the visionary Jesuit Teilhard de Chardin, with his heretical notions of moral evolution in man, Will found himself faced with conundrums he'd never had to bother about before. He'd always considered himself a scientist concerned only with phenomena rather than meaning, but these people were asking, Where did we come from? What are we? Where are we going?

On one level it was easy; since primitive beliefs had been thrown out long ago as fairy tales, legends or myths, there were only two games in town. Religionists said we were some variant of your basic fallen angel, come from Eden by way of Adam and Eve, due for heaven or hell when our span was done. Darwinists said we were your basic risen ape, come from African-savannah primates by way of the hominids like *A. afarensis*—Lucy—through *H. habilis* to *H. erectus* to us, *H. sapiens sapiens,* destined for dust and dust alone when we fell off the twig.

Lying on his back in the moonlight on those ancient eroded sun-baked hills, staring up into the same star-choked African night that Lucy, old *A. afarensis,* had stared at 3.5 million years before, Will had to ask himself, Was there really so much to choose between the two? Either way there was a sort of fall from primitive grace into culture; and who had Adam and Eve been, anyway, and what the hell had they really looked like?

Besides, it seemed to him that something basic was being ignored. The latest studies showed that only about 5 million years separated Lucy from the gorilla, and a mere 1 to 1.5 m.y. from the human/chimp common ancestor. Now Jane Goodall had taken a good look at chimps, and Dian Fossey had taken a good look at gorillas. But neither had undertaken her empirical field studies from Will's specific viewpoint: was it possible that where we came from wasn't as important as what the great apes had passed on to us through those so-recent common forerunners?

Then and there, he realized he would have to remain a paleoanthropologist while giving himself impeccable credentials as an ethologist (one who observes and analyzes animals in their natural environment), through an intensive study of the great apes. Just as Darwin had given himself impeccable credentials as a naturalist through his intensive study of barnacles.

Thus when he started publishing the conclusions he hadn't yet formed about what mankind had brought with it from its primate base stock, no one would be able to challenge his basic data. His conclusions, perhaps, but not his data.

But of course his studies couldn't start right away. First he had to return to Paris, to be met by a laughing, loving, rowdy Moll, who had missed him terribly and fucked *his* brains out in their Paris hotel room before their return to America. He never thought of the possibility of French movie directors. He was, after all, crazy in love with Moll, and as a son of the Old West actually believed all that sweet outmoded stuff he'd got from his folks about love, honor, and obey, 'til death do us part, amen.

Moll, in turn, loved him in her fashion, because she knew he loved her, really *loved* her, all of her, not just her beauty of body but her beauty of mind also. And Moll, with her multiplying neuroses not even her psychiatrist could charge enough to keep in check, really *needed* that rock to cling to.

Ancient history now. Moll squared her mental shoulders and punched SPKR on the phone and autodialed Will's office number over in Berkeley. In this moment of crisis and indecision she called the husband from whom she was estranged rather than the daddy who had always doted on her; something about inner strengths, perhaps?

"Yep, Will Dalton," said the phone in Will's voice.

"Honey, when are you ever, ever going to learn to answer your phone as a full professor should?"

"Short clipped vowels? British accent?"

Probably only Moll could have discerned the lingering hurt and bewilderment in his voice. It had been extremely gross. Not only what he walked in on, but what she had done and said then.

"How . . . are you, Will?"

"Busy." But then he immediately added, "The Institute is getting up a fund-raising exhibit covering their new directions, and it's using up all my free time." He stopped, said abruptly, "Moll—why?"

"My analyst says—"

"*Fuck* your analyst!" Will burst out, then quickly recovered himself. "Listen, Moll, I just . . . can't . . ."

The trouble was, when she had finished law school and passed the bar, through her daddy's connections she had gotten this tremendous position as corporate counsel with the San Francisco arm of the newest L.A. conglomerate, Atlas Entertainment. It had a lot of money said to be Common Market, and was wildly grabbing small independents in a whole slew of areas—features, syndication, cable movies, a sound studio, special effects, a record company, a couple of comedy clubs, interactive—just about the whole entertainment package. They boasted they'd be challenging the majors within three years.

Moll had ridden that pony and ridden it hard. She was smart, tough, hard-driving, soon indispensable. More and more, while Will the dreamer was off checking out apes and monkeys in places where they had just invented the wheel last week, she was doing hard, focused work in the corporate boardroom, wanting both husband and daddy to be proud of her, wanting to show everyone she was more than just a beautiful face and an available body.

On the phone, Will was saying, "So, Moll, if you just called to say hello, ah, Hello. But if—"

"Not just that," she said quickly. "I want to see you."

There was a long silence. Will finally said, in tones of a coldness and finality that were chilling, "I don't think that'd be a very good idea right now, Moll."

"I *need* to see you."

More silence. Stretching out, attenuating itself like spun glass at the end of the blower's tube.

She had only herself to blame. Moll had discovered that what she needed more than anything else in this world was to fuck power. It was her ultimate aphrodisiac. And while Will was in western Sumatra for six months observing orangs, she had developed an almost hysterical passion for Kosta Gounaris.

Gounaris was tall and dynamic, had created a Greek shipping line that had made him rich, and was now president of Atlas Entertainment—hence, nominally Moll's employer. A beak-nosed, muscular, well-conditioned fifty-five, Kosta had a great deal of black body hair that really turned Moll on, and all that power that turned her on even more.

Will's life changed forever when the monsoon arrived early and he came home from Sumatra a week ahead of time, without telling Moll because he wanted to surprise her. Surprise her he did, and himself besides, by walking into her San Francisco penthouse to become that universal figure of fun, the cuckolded husband.

Will found Moll in the bed where he'd been planning they should make long and tender love, half-lying between Kosta Gounaris's wide-spread hairy legs, sucking his cock.

They both heard the door open, Gounaris turning to look lazily over his shoulder, Moll able to see past him to Will's shocked and astounded face. Gounaris turned back to Moll.

"Here it comes, baby," he told her with sudden urgency, "a real gusher," and came in her mouth.

And Moll, even though horrified for Will to see her this way, was at that moment totally, completely in thrall to Kosta Gounaris and his power. So she paused only long enough to raise her head and wink at her husband and say, "Welcome home, honey," before returning to her work.

Gounaris threw back his head and roared with delight at such pungent wit, as Will was staggering from the apartment and across the hall into the still-waiting elevator, his skin red and mottled, his face full of nausea, his chest heaving as if he were having a heart attack. Those horrific visual images had burned away all thought of defending his manhood or his marital bed.

Half an hour later he was sufficiently recovered to return, deadly of purpose, but by then the apartment was deserted. And by the next day he had convinced himself he wasn't a true son of the Old West after all, where blood was the ransom of betrayed manhood, but rather was just another civilized modern urban wimp.

Moll hadn't seen her husband since that night, and he hadn't been returning any phone calls. A month ago, an eon ago, for both of them. Tonight she'd caught him, but Will's silence had become positively thunderous.

"Need to see me," he finally repeated in a flat voice.

"*Need* to," Moll affirmed.

At least he hadn't hung up. Oh God, she thought, if only she hadn't hurt him so. If only she'd just . . . just clung to his strengths, asked him to stay home with her. He would have. He was the only man who had ever truly loved her. Now . . .

Now she said in a rush, "Please, please, meet me, Will. I need to talk . . . to ask . . ."

"When?"

"Tonigh—" She checked herself. "Tomorrow night, seven o'clock? That Italian place on Jackson where we used to . . ."

He sighed. "All right, Moll. Tomorrow at seven. But I could be there tonight in thirty min—"

"Tomorrow," she said quickly, almost sharply.

She hung up almost ashamed of herself, because she knew why she hadn't made it tonight, right now, as he had offered, as she had intended when she had called him. In twenty minutes she wanted to be at the penthouse with Kosta's cock buried in her up to the hilt. *Needed* to be at the penthouse.

And maybe Kosta would have an explanation. Maybe . . . maybe she was misinterpreting the data she had run across by accident in the computer. Maybe . . .

No. She was too smart to kid herself *that* much. She had

found what she had found, and even though she would ask Kosta about it, she still had to tell Will about it too. At the last minute she put the disk she'd made into a mailer, addressed it, and dropped it down the mail chute in the hallway beside the elevator on her way to the penthouse and Kosta.

CHAPTER THREE

In the penthouse, Kosta had mounted Moll from the rear in the dog style that was an unconscious preference from his early years as a *koritsopoulo,* a girl-boy in a Turkish brothel, thrusting into her with long slow almost lazy strokes. Over forty years before this night, his ticket out of that Istanbul slum had been the aging Turkish pederast who ran the brothel and kept his strongbox under the floor. Kosta had waited his chance.

After they were finished, lying side by side on the bed, Moll panted out something about a "thing" in the computer she didn't understand.

Kosta asked, in an amused voice, "You sure it isn't my thing in you—or did the mouse get off the pad and into the hard disk?"

"No, in the data there was a . . . a sort of chart . . . A breakdown of percentages . . . names and figures . . . banks . . . all in a sort of code . . . I found it by accident, got intrigued, started playing around with it on my own time . . ."

"What do you think it means?" he asked as if fascinated instead of feeling sick to his stomach. "You know I am an idiot with that demented little electronic jack-in-the-box."

"I think it means that the money behind Atlas Entertainment comes from organized crime, not the Common Market."

"*What?*" he cried, sitting bolt upright on the bed. "My God, what are you telling me?"

"Finally, that was the only way I could interpret the entries." She was delighted with his reaction; if Kosta had been involved himself, had started making excuses . . .

He swung around to face her, took her hands in his.

"I sold Gounaris Shipping, my Molly, because I was tired of being a playboy. I didn't take your father's offer to head Atlas Entertainment to become a pawn of the . . . what should I say, the *mob*." He was off the bed, pulling on his clothes with manic energy. "I'm going to start finding out about this right now. If there is dirty money in Atlas Entertainment, they will have my resignation on their desks immediately." He paused in zipping up his pants, frowning. "You haven't told anyone else about . . ."

"Of course not, not until I had a chance to talk with you."

"Good, good," he said. "To be fair, I don't think either of us should mention it until we're sure that's what the file really means."

Moll felt terrible. She had made that call to Will . . . Her voice stopped him as Kosta pulled on his shirt.

"Sweetheart . . . I . . . made a date with Will for tomorrow night at Bella Figura. I was going to . . . talk with him about it, but now I'll cancel it—"

"No no no, my love." He gestured expansively. "I will be back from Los Angeles with all the facts before then. If it is true, we will shout their perfidy from the rooftops. If I find there is a reasonable explanation . . ." He shrugged and finished buttoning his shirt and smiled. "Then you will just have a pleasant evening with another man." He leaned down to take her chin in a lean brown hand and gently kiss her on the lips. "But no fooling around with your husband, you understand? Kosta Gounaris is a jealous lover."

After he was gone she remembered she'd mailed off the disk, but it didn't matter since Kosta was not implicated.

Outside in the corridor, he leaned against the wall beside the express penthouse elevator, weak as a baby, in much the same state as Will a month before but for very different reasons. He wiped the sweat from his forehead. Being a ruthless and powerful man himself, he knew the almost unspeakable ruthlessness and power of those to whom he had sold himself so many years before.

How could he have been so unutterably stupid as to leave the original setup file in the computer when they had been working out the organization of the company? Once deciphered it was absolutely damning, naming names and estimating what each department could be expected to produce, and how much each could launder without the IRS suspecting that offshore millions were being funneled through this legitimately profitable shell.

And how could she have uncovered it and broken their code so easily? Too damned intelligent for her own good, that was her trouble. The elevator came, he stepped aboard. Greeks liked their women smart, but she was too smart to live. He didn't mean that literally, of course, but *tou Theou*, he didn't look forward to the phone call—*pay* phone call— he would have to make to his spiritual godfather, Gideon Abramson, in Palm Springs.

Gid Abramson was seventy-four years old, a diminutive gnome in loud aloha shirts and $400 plaid slacks and $900 shoes and a Dodgers cap, smoking a stogie the length of his arm, peering benevolently at the world through clear-rim trifocals. He was a grandfather eight times over, slept nine dreamless hours a night, swam ten laps in his pool every morning before his juice, dry toast, and decaf, and played golf or tennis five days a week like a man thirty years his junior. Gid was going to live forever.

This evening he was sitting out the hand as dummy in his foursome at the country club's bridge night, telling one of his usual infamous jokes.

"So this guy is chewing out the *shadchan,* see, the marriage broker, for lying to him about this woman he had been planning to marry. The *shadchan* says, 'By you, she didn't graduate from Brandeis? By you, she's not as beautiful as

Julia Roberts? By you, she doesn't sing like Barbra Streisand? Where did I lie?'

"And the guy says, 'You told me her father was dead—but she told me he's been in prison for ten years!'

"'*Nu,*' says the *shadchan*, 'you call that living?'"

Under the dutiful laughter, the club steward whispered in Gid's ear there was an urgent phone call from his nephew. He left the table feeling smug. He was up nearly $700 for the evening, and Charlie Hansen was looking a little green across the table. Gid had heard his Mercedes agency hadn't sold a car in two weeks. Good.

Let the bastard sweat a bit before suggesting a loan. Strictly legit interest, of course, because you didn't shit where you slept—but he would end up owning 51 percent of the agency. Before his retirement he had controlled the rag trade loan-sharking on Manhattan's Lower East Side, and Gid just couldn't seem to help making money.

When he was in the manager's office with the door closed, he picked up the private telephone and chirped into it, "So speak to me, *bubela*!"

"Uncle Gideon, I'm in a lot of trouble!"

Kosta did indeed sound scared over the phone—and it took a great deal to scare Kosta. He'd been the kind of dashing, adventurous kid none of Gid's own *nebbische* sons had been. When Gid had run across him in the late fifties, Kosta, just a teenager, was using an Arab dhow with black sails and no outboard to run American cigarettes from Greece into Turkey, and opium out.

Once, drunk on ouzo, he'd told Gid he'd slit a Turk's throat in Istanbul for the money to buy the boat. Gid had never seen any reason to doubt him, so he bankrolled him through bigger and better boats to his first freighter. Then he'd taken 51 percent of Gounaris Shipping for the Family, finally had recommended Kosta for the presidency of Atlas Entertainment.

And it was this man who now sounded scared. Just to test the waters, Gid said, "You hear the one about the gorilla walked into Goldman's delicatessen and ordered a pastrami on rye with a pickle to go?"

"Uncle Gideon, there's no time for—"

"Goldman says, 'That'll be six-fifty. And I gotta say, I never expected to have a gorilla in my store ordering a pastrami on rye!' The gorilla says, 'At those prices, you never will again!'" He paused. *"Nu.* Tell me *your* story."

Kosta did. It left Gideon shaking his head at the phone.

"You're right, Kosta, that was really very stupid of you to leave the file in the computer. If any word of your doing that should get back to Martin Prince . . ." He paused for a moment, thinking. "I tell him the woman had been snooping around, asking questions, suspecting something, we had to move very quickly . . ."

"But nothing about me leaving the file in the computer?"

"Our little secret, Kosta," he said gravely but with a wink in his voice. "Now, there's one thing I want you to do . . ."

"I already did, Uncle Gideon. Even before I called you. I erased the file and tomorrow will have a new hard disk installed and all the other files transferred to it individually so this file can't be brought up later if the feds should ever come snooping around with one of their tame computer geniuses."

"Good, it sounds as if this woman has not totally addled your wits. In your opinion, has she spoken to anyone else?"

Kosta told him about Moll's date with her husband the next night, and what he had told her to do about it.

"Very good!" exclaimed Gid with delight. "The perfect way to keep her quiet until we can talk to her."

"You think she'll believe what I tell her when—"

"We'll *make* her believe it, sonny boy—I think you got nothing to worry about. You just let me handle this."

Before hanging up he told Kosta just what he should say and do the next evening, and also casually got from him the name of a corrupt Frisco cop, Jack Lenington. He would ask Otto Kreiger to contact Lenington—no use burdening Kosta with any of that. The *goyische* woman was obviously still leading him around by the *schlong.*

Tapping out the number of Martin Prince's safe phone in Las Vegas, Gid Abramson rolled his cigar between his lips and thought with delight, Intrigue! Threats! Danger! These were what kept a man young, made life worth living!

Bella Figura was a lot of glass and stainless steel and designer chairs and elevated prices in the low-number high-rent end of Jackson Street. They put too much garlic in the sauces and you had to fight for your pasta *al dente,* but their drinks were generous and the service was good. And at Bella Figura, because of the high ambient decibel level, two people could put their heads together and talk without being overheard.

Not that there was any need of that now. Moll would tell Will about it, of course, but it had all become academic. When she'd been getting dressed to come here and meet him, Kosta had burst into the penthouse with his black eyes snapping like firecrackers, tremendously exhilarated.

He'd been in L.A. having it out with those bastards down there, he said, and she was right, Atlas Entertainment *was* just a fucking Mafia front! Tomorrow, by God, they would go to the FBI with what they knew! Until then, Moll should keep quiet about it, because they knew about Kosta but not about her. She might be in danger if they knew the information had come from her.

Meanwhile, tonight . . . tonight he'd roughly shoved her forward over the back of the couch, pulled up her Laura Kiran skirt, jerked down her Victoria's Secret panty hose, and rammed all that excitement into her from behind, the way they both loved it best. She exploded within ninety seconds, but he wasn't done yet. He tumbled her onto the couch and went down on her, something he'd never done before, not once.

He finished off by crouching over her face and coming in her mouth immediately, without ceremony or tenderness, snorting like a bull. Then he jumped off her as off a horse hard-ridden, zipped up, chuckled, kissed her cheek without love or passion.

"Now I send you to see your husband, my little tart—now that I know you will think only of me as you do it with him."

So here she was in Bella Figura drinking her second Midori sour and thinking that Kosta knew her all too well. She indeed was planning, with a nasty little frisson in her soul, to get Will into bed tonight. Kosta had hurt her a little and scared her a lot with his wildness; she needed Will's tender loving strength to restore her.

The stranger in the light topcoat and tinted glasses came up behind her at 7:39. Expecting Will, Moll turned on her stool with a welcoming smile just as his gloved hand pressed a .22 pistol against the bridge of her exquisite nose and pulled the trigger. During the nanosecond of searing pain as the bullet passed between her wide, beautiful eyes, she knew *That's why he was so wild, he was excited by*

Moll thudded to the floor, a brain-splattered bundle of ruined designer clothes. The assassin put the coup de grâce into the base of her skull before staring around at the surrounding patrons frozen on their stools.

"Dead men tell no tales," he said. "Live men too, if they got any smarts."

He laid the empty .22 on the bar beside Moll's purse, and strolled out stripping off his topcoat. As he rounded the corner into Front, he handed it to a homeless man poking around in a trash barrel at the edge of green block-square MacArthur Park.

Back in Bella Figura the screaming had begun, after several long moments of silence during which they all had looked at one another and then guiltily away. By the time the police arrived, no one had seen anything significant.

Live men tell no tales. Nor, of course, dead women.

Will had been held up on the Bay Bridge by a four-car crash blocking all lanes on the upper deck into the city. He got to Bella Figura just after the first black-and-white. When

Homicide Inspector Tim Flanagan arrived, Will was cradling Moll's ruined head in his arms and crying all over the crime scene.

"Who the fuck is he?" Flanagan demanded of the uniformed team who had answered the original squeal. "The fucking Pope?"

"The husband."

"Whyna fuck ya let him near the body?"

The black patrolman said, with exaggerated courtesy, "'Cause we couldn't come up with any way to keep him away from her, Inspector, short of shooting *him* in the fuckin' head too."

Flanagan, who had a heavy round red face and a swag belly and pink tightly waved receding hair, looked and sounded like every casting director's concept of the beefy, stupid, venal Irish cop with his hand out. He had, however, a degree in criminology from USF and was totally devoted to police work. His dumb act was strictly professional.

He told them to secure the crime scene—and he did mean getting the fucking husband away from the corpse—and went to call Dante Stagnaro at home even though Dante wasn't Homicide and Tim was, so this was his beef entirely.

It was just that this looked professional, just the sort of homicide that Dante, with his surprisingly moralistic stance toward crime and murder in particular, especially professional murder, loved to get in on early.

CHAPTER FOUR

That was fifteen months ago, and Lieutenant Dante Stagnaro, head of SFPD's Organized Crime Task Force, still didn't have anyone in the cage for Moll Dalton's murder. Oh, he had a self-confessed assassin who called himself Raptor and left messages on his phone machine, and he was pretty sure he knew who had hired the guy—but he was as far from an arrest as when he had started.

Dante drove around the block because the parking lot for the Institute of Human Origins was off Euclid just north of the Cal-Berkeley campus. Will Dalton's green 4Runner with its license plate HABILIS was parked in the lot: the damn fool had shown up. On his own car's bumper was a sticker put there by his sixteen-year-old son, Antonio, that he hadn't had the heart to scrape off: BAD COP—NO DOUGHNUT.

Organized crime in San Francisco didn't mean the Mafia as it did in New York—traditionally, the mob didn't have a strong enough presence in the Bay Area to merit a task force. What he and his two inspectors investigated was organized criminal activity in San Francisco of any sort—drug trafficking, chip theft and sales, car thefts, alien smuggling. Even murder, if there was a demonstrably organized conspiracy behind it.

A sign directed him through a gate and along a walk to a doorway and the basement of the Graduate Theological Union. Dante found it either ironic or touching—he'd never made up his mind which—that IHO was housed with the Union. Some of the Union's vocally Christian primates just had to be appalled by the Institute's strictly Darwinian view of life. Tight budgets made strange bedfellows.

On a stage, students and a faculty director were rehearsing a drama with song and modern dance that said something about God, man, and the human soul. At a desk alongside the stage, IHO was taking money and checking in attendees— $3.00 for members, $5.00 for non—for Will Dalton's lecture in the next room on similar subjects from a very different perspective.

Dante laid down five bucks and went into the lecture hall, checking the possibilities for ambush with a professionally careless glance. Behind a lectern and a stand-up mike was a slide-projector screen on a round raised box. Off to the side was a video camera to record the lecture. Several feet behind the lectern and screen, curtains. The wall on the right was a plasterboard partition with a couple of bright watercolors on it; the other three were brick, the windows in the left one recessed and covered with drawn drapes.

Rows of folding chairs in the body of the hall were filling up. In the rear were tables for hawking books, brochures, Institute T-shirts, calendars and the like.

The audience was students and adults ranging from the mid-twenties to old white heads, wearing suits, dresses, sweatshirts and jeans. Dante knew the type from other lectures; most of them were vocal, well spoken, self-possessed. A university crowd, very unlike the students at his community college over twenty years before.

Rosie said he had a better mind than any of them, but Dante always felt inferior in such gatherings. A sham. As if he had come in with a hick grin and mud on his shoes, tugging at a shoulder strap of his Can't-Bust-Ems.

Anyway, danger points: the curtains behind the lectern; the recessed windows. He casually wandered around behind the lectern. No exit. Raptor would never risk boxing himself into such a dead end. And the window drapes were pulled back.

A shot from outside through the glass? No. Raptor had never endangered innocent bystanders; in that he adhered to the largely abandoned values and traditions of the Mafia when they only killed each other. But Dante was sure that his code could not exempt the dead Moll's living husband. Dalton just had to be Raptor's prime—indeed, final—target. Nothing else made sense. And if he was wrong?

Then Tim Flanagan would get a few more belly laughs. Tim had the belly for it.

The windows would be safe enough unless someone closed the drapes so Raptor could slip behind them. Checking them, he caught his own fleeting reflection in one of the panes. Early forties, medium height, an athlete's body under slacks and jacket, narrow jaw, high cheekbones, black hair generously shot with silver, brown eyes under heavy brows.

He turned away; Dalton had come in with a knot of other scientists; they had paused near the tables.

Dalton hadn't changed much during the fifteen months he'd been gone—five-eleven, 180, brown eyes, brown hair, still something of the real West about him, very tanned and fit, the brown hair shorter than when he'd left, almost brush-cut, the brown face leaner, harder than before, more closed.

Dante's grasp on a forearm cut him out of his confreres. He came along with a wry shrug back at them.

"Good evening, Lieutenant."

"Welcome back, Professor. But tell the truth, I don't like seeing you here in the target area. I spent half the day trying to reach you at home or here at the Institute to tell you not to give this lecture tonight."

Dalton grinned; it momentarily wiped the sadness from his eyes. "Why do you think I was dodging you all day?" His face changed; a bitter irony replaced the pleasure in his eyes. "I've been gone for fifteen months. If you haven't been able to find Moll's killer in all that time, what makes you think he's going to show up here tonight?"

"To take you off."

"And why would he want to do that, Lieutenant?"

"You tell me."

He shook his head. "Always the same tune with you, isn't it? I take it Gounaris is still out of jail."

"As of this afternoon, yes," said Dante stiffly. He wasn't going to go into his own history with Gounaris. "In California they don't jail you for sleeping with another man's wife. And Gounaris isn't the point here. I know damned well that you lied to me about not knowing any reason for your wife's murder, and that you changed your plans and went away so abruptly because you were afraid you'd be killed too if you didn't leave the country."

Will gave a wry bark of laughter. "I see. I was a coward who fled with no thought of helping get my wife's murderer—"

"You said it, I didn't."

Will took a deep breath, sighed. "Moll's still dead, whatever we say here. I'm not comfortable with you in this gathering, Lieutenant, but I can't make you leave. So . . ."

He started to turn away; Dante thought, What the hell, go for the throat. "You could say that Moll's dead because you left her alone here for long periods of time, so she . . ."

Will tensed as if to swing at him, but a long-faced man with laugh lines but a worried expression tapped the mike.

"Hel . . . Hello? Yes. It gives me great pleasure to start our spring lecture series in January this year." He chuckled at his own wit. With his black fanny pack over his belly, he looked about as much like a scientist as Dante's teenage son did. "Will Dalton is no stranger to this Institute, having spoken to us at various times on his work with the great apes in Rwanda-Burundi, the eastern Congo, and northern Sumatra. Before Dr. Dalton's talk, I would like to briefly outline the Institute's aims and accomplishments for the many new faces I see in the audience tonight."

Dante grabbed Will's arm with sudden urgency.

"Goddammit, if you're going to make a target of yourself, before you go up there at least tell me what your wife left with you that . . ."

The look on Dalton's face stopped him. The deep-set brown eyes were deeper than they had been, as if used to looking through things to truths they had been unable to see before.

"After I buried Moll I just felt damned fortunate to have a funded foreign research field project already set up to give me two years of rough, exacting, solitary work away from the memories here. Now here you are, stirring them all up again."

· The damned man always had been able to put Dante on the defensive. All those years in university, perhaps, all those graduate degrees, as opposed to Dante's two years of community college before he had quit to go to Vietnam? Or maybe just the fact that Dante was used to dealing with mob types who, although now often college men, still showed brass beneath the veneer.

Dalton had changed his stance again. "I don't really care what happens to me, Lieutenant, so maybe I'm not being fair to you. Stay for the lecture—we can chat afterwards. Who knows—maybe you'll even find my talk instructive."

He went up past the windows as Dante slid back behind the sales tables, where he could watch both doors and see everything going on between him and the speaker. He couldn't even give himself the luxury of a folding chair as he suffered through a lecture on some scientific subject in which he had no interest and probably wouldn't understand. ·

The man with the fanny pack was still at it.

"Dr. Dalton has just spent fifteen months observing the forest chimpanzee of western Uganda, and tonight we will hear the first report of his findings. Dr. Dalton began his career . . ."

At the front of the room a short well-fed man with gold-rimmed glasses and a black ponytail down the back of his neck leaped to his feet. Dante went into a half-crouch, his right hand sweeping toward the gun on his belt. He checked himself, glanced about, embarrassed. Hardly the stone killer Raptor. A member of the Institute about to videotape Dalton's speech.

Dante made himself slouch back against the wall, eyes busy and a hand near his gun in case Raptor might want to take Dalton out right now, before he had a chance to pass anything on. The hitman's physical presence was almost palpable, but Dante was here first, ready . . .

So why did he still feel he was just another bit player in Raptor's latest scenario?

Take Dalton out. As Raptor had taken out Dalton's wife. One thing Dante was damned sure of, if someone killed Rosie he wouldn't run off to Africa for fifteen months. But that was unfair. He was a cop, with a cop's training and experience, a cop's familiarity with guns and violence, a cop's Old Testament *eye for eye, tooth for tooth* idea of justice.

While in uniform he'd killed an armed robber in a 7-Eleven holdup; fifteen years later he still lost sleep over his memory of the man's face as the arterial blood pumped out on the dirty floor. That killing was why he had jumped at the chance to head up the Organized Crime Task Force ten years later.

Yet he knew he would kill again in the same circumstances.

And if it was Rosie who was at risk, or worse, Rosie who had been slaughtered as Moll Dalton had been slaughtered . . .

Unbidden, Dante Stagnaro's mind returned to that first night, fifteen months earlier, when his involvement with Moll Dalton's murder had begun.

CHAPTER FIVE

At night, Clown Alley at Lombard and Divisadero had the lonely, small-town, just-passing-through look of the all-night cafe in Edward Hopper's *Nighthawks*. Even the counterman looked as if Hopper had started to sketch him, then said to hell with it: unmoving in his stained white apron in front of his blackened and smoking grill, his arms folded, his cigarette lisping motionless smoke as he waited to flip a burger, his face unfinished, the features somehow merely suggested.

Hopper could have done plenty with the only other patrons in the place, a pair of easy riders in stomp boots and black leather cut off to show arms made tree trunks by endless hours of pumping iron in some jailhouse yard. Their Harley hogs, agleam with chrome, were illegally parked at the curb outside.

The two cops sat down and studied the menus brought by the dark slim intense waiter. Flanagan suddenly guffawed loudly.

"Hey, check out your horoscope. You're a Christmas baby, ain't you?" Before Dante could answer, he started reading. "'Capricorn. You are conservative and afraid of taking risks. You don't do much of anything. There has never been a Capricorn of any importance. Capricorns should avoid standing still too long as they tend to take root and become trees.'"

Flanagan roared with laughter again, but Dante was checking the back of his own menu.

"'Scorpio,'" he read. "'You are the artistic type and have a difficult time with reality. If you are a man you are most likely queer. Chances for employment and monetary gains are excellent.'" He looked at Flanagan over the menu. "Wait 'til Internal Affairs hears about that." He looked down again. "'Most Scorpio women are prostitutes. All Scorpios die of venereal disease.'" He nodded solemnly. "And wait until Maureen hears about *that*."

"Up yours, chief," said Flanagan as the waiter returned.

"Just coffee for me." Dante sighed and jerked a thumb at the pay phone and said to Flanagan, "I've put it off too long, I've got to call her father in L.A."

"I always have one of the detectives do that for me."

"That's why I make the big bucks, Tim," Dante said sadly as Flanagan burst out with his big braying laugh once again.

Skeffington St. John ("Pronounce that Sinjin") was on the phone with talent agent Charriti HHope when Dante's call came in. Sinjin put Charriti on hold; after all, his business with her and her clients was long-standing and not in the strictest sense business. On the other line was someone who identified himself as a Dante Stagnaro of the San Francisco Police Department.

"Mr. St. John, I have some rather—"

"Please. It's 'Sinjin.' The British pronunciation."

A pause. "I see. Your daughter Margaret Dalton . . ."

"We prefer Molly Sinjin, Officer."

Another pause. "Yeah. Well, your daughter, Molly Sinjin . . ."

"How'd St. John take it?" asked Flanagan when Dante got back to their table. He had a huge cheeseburger and fries in front of him, with a side of rings and a green salad. At this time of night all Dante could stomach was black coffee and a couple of Tums.

"It's 'Sinjin'—British, you know."

"Yeah?" Flanagan nodded wisely. "An asshole."

Dante sighed, trying to wash St. John's unexpected sobs from his mind with the thought, *It's just a game, pieces on a board*. But he knew it was starting again, that intense involvement with a case that robbed his sleep and soured his gut.

Flanagan bit hugely, wiped away beef juice with a paper napkin, gestured with the ruins of his burger.

"Sorry I called you in on this one, chief. It's the fucking husband did it." Flanagan shook salt on his onion rings, belched, amended, "Had it done, anyway."

"What did I miss?"

"He was *too* broke up."

"He explained that, Tim. He got held up on the Bay Bridge or he would have been there before the hitman. He was feeling guilty because—"

"Because he wasn't there to take one up the snout himself?"

"I checked with the bridge cops. A four-car pileup closed down all westbound lanes just about the time Dalton said—"

"See? You were bothered by him, too."

Dante nodded abstractedly, sipped his coffee. He should have asked for decaf. He'd be up half the night.

"There was *something* with him . . . maybe what you say, *too* upset . . . or maybe he was holding something back."

"Yeah, like who he hired to do the dirty deed."

Dante took out his notebook and checked it, even though he needed no refreshment as to what was written there.

"Just take a look at it for a minute, Tim. He's a professor at Cal-Berkeley in paleoanthropology. His wife is—was—corporate counsel for some big entertainment conglomerate. No kids, he does a lot of field world out of the country . . ."

Flanagan looked up from his meal. "Yeah. So?"

"So where does this guy find a professional hitman?"

"Some of them perfessers might surprise you. Hell, he just cruises the Tenderloin bars, waves a few C-notes around—"

"And gets mugged and wakes up in an alley with a

headache and no C-notes." Dante shook his head again, decisively this time. "No way, Tim."

"So you're buying it as big-time all the way."

"All the way." Dante marked off his points on his fingers. "One. The hitman walked into the place knowing she'd be there and what she looked like. Two. He used a Jennings J-22 that you can buy anywhere for seventy-five bucks but, amazingly enough, is still a hell of a reliable pistol. Even so, you have to be sure of yourself to know you can make a clean kill with a .22. Three—"

"He shot her in the back of the head to make sure."

"I'll get back to that in a minute, I've got a theory." He paused, eyes almost dreamy. "You know it was Hymie Weiss back in 1922, working for the Dion O'Banion mob out of Chicago, who invented taking a guy for a ride? Invented the shot in the back of the neck with a .22 to finish him off, too."

Tim stuffed in french fries. "Yeah? Fucking fascinating."

"Anyway, three. He leaves the gun behind, serial numbers intact, which means he knows it's clean, can't be traced beyond some gun shop robbery. Four. Only two rounds in the gun—confident he isn't going to need more than two. Five. The gun had been sprayed with Armor All, even though the witnesses say he was wearing gloves. You've got to admit that's a pro's touch."

"Or a Hell's Angel's."

"They're not pros?"

Dante finished his coffee as Flanagan dabbed the last of his fries in his ketchup. Dante started over with his little finger again.

"Six. No elaborate disguise, just tinted glasses that hide his eyes and make a lineup identification virtually impossible. Seven. He *walked* out of the place. No running, no guilty looks over the shoulder. Delivering the mail. Pro hit all the way." He leaned closer. "I'll even tell you who he was."

"A beer on league bowling night you don't. But I gotta admit you could almost convince me the guy was pro. Except . . . "

"Except?"

"Pro hitters using guns do the old H and H—the head and the heart. But these days, most of 'em like to work close—a knife is so much more personal. Or they use ropes, garrotes, explosives . . . But *this* guy—"

"That's why I know who he is. You ever hear of 'Popgun' Eddie Ucelli?"

Flanagan thought. "Back east, right? Jersey, like that?"

It was things like that made Dante like and respect Tim Flanagan, and work with him whenever he could. He nodded.

"He runs a legit meat wholesale business—as legit as anything a wise guy owns is ever legit. But the story is there's sections of the Jersey Turnpike didn't need any rebar—the bones of Eddie's victims were enough to reinforce the concrete."

"What makes this one Ucelli's work?"

"The Jennings J-22—it's a trademark of his, since the Colt Woodsman became a collector's item, it's why they call him Popgun. Other trademarks: One up the nose into the brain. Lightly tinted glasses. Armor All on the gun because he knew he would be leaving it. Walking out afterwards. I bet he gave his topcoat to the first guy he saw—Eddie always does. And he prides himself on never needing more than one shot to complete his contract."

"This guy used two," Flanagan pointed out again.

"That's where my theory comes in. I think he was supposed to take out the wife *and* Dalton. Dalton wasn't there so he used the second shot as a coup de grâce on the wife only to empty the gun, because he didn't want some hero picking it up while he was on his way out the door and shooting him in the back with it."

Flanagan drained his coffee, was silent for a long moment.

"That's a pretty flaky theory you got there, chief."

"But mine own."

"You got that right," said Tim with his big laugh.

The bikers turned and looked at him, hopeful of an excuse

to use their stomp boots, but saw cop in the bleak looks both men returned to them and hastily went back to their fries.

Flanagan got serious again. "Somehow, Dante, it just don't scan. Same question you asked me a few minutes ago about her husband—where does the woman tie up with the wise guys?"

"She was a lawyer, what more do you need?"

"Yeah, what's the difference between a spermatozoa and a lawyer?" Dante shook his head. "The spermatozoa has a one-in-400-million chance of becoming a human being."

Tim guffawed loudly at his own joke, wiped his mouth with a fistful of napkins, and squealed his chair back.

"Okay, you go start drawing another one of your fucking flowcharts on your blackboard in the task force office, and I'll track the husband and wife back to when they were wearing didies. Then maybe, a day or two depending what I find, we'll go toss hubby around a little, see what falls out. Somehow I still favor him for it." He gave another of his guffaws. "Either he was protesting too much, which means he hired it done and I don't like him, or he meant all that pissing and moaning—which means he's a sissy and I don't like him."

"So either way you don't like him."

"You think?" asked Flanagan in a mock-surprised voice.

Will had bought the old boxy two-story Victorian in the Berkeley flats at a bargain price after one of the periodic riots that bubble up to keep the area so volatile and alive. He spent little time there anyway, what with Moll so much at her penthouse in the city (down payment by her father), and his frequent field trips, and most of his research material being at his office. But here he was, staring out the living room window at the drizzly autumn afternoon.

Moll's penthouse in the city.

Oh God, if only he hadn't gone there that day. Or had called her from the airport. Or, once there, had thrown that bastard Gounaris out and talked it through with Moll, shouted it through, screamed it through, anything to get through it with her and out the other side.

Because adulteress, alive, dead, she was the only woman he'd ever love. Like a swan, he'd mated for life. And he knew she'd loved him too. Loved him, needed him—nobody could fake that kind of emotion . . . Yet she'd slept with Gounaris.

He felt a rage inside himself, felt it froth over even as he snuffled and realized his face was wet with tears.

Outside, the cold wind blew three female coeds down the gleaming street like autumn leaves. The phone started to ring. The women's laughter tinkled distantly like icicles on fir boughs. There was a rattle and thunk at the front door as the mailman slid that day's delivery through the slot. Will made no move to get it or the ringing phone.

He fought his anger. Gounaris was the one to blame for Moll's infidelity, not Moll. She had always been ambitious in her career, he'd cut her out of the herd, focused all that power on her, made her feel important, unique, seduced her . . .

Hell, Will was as guilty of her death as Gounaris was. If he'd insisted on going over to the city as soon as she'd called him . . . or allowed enough time coming across the Bay so he wouldn't have gotten held up on the bridge . . . Then that crazy guy with the gun would have had to find some other single woman to obsess on, and Moll would still be . . .

How in God's name would he get through the funeral two days hence? Just three days ago Moll had been alive, vital . . .

The phone quit ringing. And he was sniveling again, for Godsake. He hadn't done that since he was five years old.

Will Dalton wasn't answering his phone at home, but the people at the Institute said that's where he'd probably go when he'd finished with the funeral arrangements, so they drew an unmarked sedan from the police pool. Flanagan turned left into one-way Harriett Alley from the garage under the Hall of Justice, made another left into Harrison, both men trying to talk at once.

"Ucelli was off somewhere on a—"

"Your fucking Professor Dalton—"

Flanagan made yet another left, into Eighth, stayed in the left lane for the final ring-around-the-rosie left into Bryant and the on-ramp for the Skyway. Once on their way to the Bay Bridge, he gave his big laugh and made a courtly hand gesture.

"Okay, you first, *mon capitaine*. Whatever you got is gonna look like shit when I get through talking."

"Don't be too sure," said Dante. "I checked with the Feebs—they've had a tap on Ucelli's phone since Christ made corporal. They never get anything, but at least they know he was out of town for four days and just got back this morning. You have to admit, Tim, being gone like that spanning the time of the hit makes him look awful good for it."

"'Cause he went fishing or something? Hell, if he was burying guys in the Jersey Turnpike, he must be old as water."

"Made his bones with a barbershop hit in '52," said Dante with something like pride of race in his voice.

Flanagan hit the horn at a slow car in the fast lane on the bridge's lower deck, then passed him on the inside. He always drove as if responding to a silent alarm; Dante was used to it.

"Fifty-two, huh? Over forty fucking years ago!"

"It was his sixteenth birthday."

"So he's pushing fucking sixty now. The old hand-eye coordination's gotta be going—"

"According to the feds, the mob uses him for jobs where they need someone with the balls to do it up close and right the first time. You don't need an Olympic marksman for that."

They came out from under the top deck to the broad apron, nearly a quarter of a mile wide, where the tollbooths for traffic going the other direction were located. Water hit the windshield. Flanagan turned on the wipers, turned up his hand.

"Don't scan, Dante. You know the Mafia don't do shit around here, it isn't like Vegas or L.A. So what the hell would the woman know they'd need to kill her over? Atlas Entertainment sure as hell isn't Mafia, it's big Eurobucks. I got their brochures, financial statement, prospectus—not a sniff of mob. European money from Luxembourg or somewhere. I had a good reason to make a pain of myself, her murder and all, so I talked with the secretaries, the peons—finally went up against the big boss himself."

"Kosta Gounaris," said Dante. "Former Greek shipping tycoon. Sold his shipping line four years ago. Kids grown, Greek wife he divorced when he sold his company. Gives a lot to charity, he's in the papers a lot."

Flanagan was in a left lane so he could angle into the northbound traffic on I-80. They were a half hour before the main body of the rush hour started; the drivers sending up sheets of water ahead of them were mostly timid souls who treated the posted speed limits as hard fact instead of fiction.

"Okay, lemme tell you what I found out. Past few years, Moll Dalton's been sleeping with half the power brokers in San Francisco."

"You sure?" asked Dante, surprised. "The way Dalton—"

"Way I see it, Academy Award all the way. None of the secretaries at Atlas liked her, she was just too fucking bright and too fucking beautiful, and her boss had been dicking her for three months."

"Gounaris himself?"

"He didn't want to talk to me at first, so I got a little nasty . . ."

He wiggled his eyebrows, and Dante burst out laughing. He had seen Tim in action, many a time, and *nasty* was too kind a word for what he did. Tim swelled up and got as red in the face as a turkey wattle, his voice became a bullhorn. But what turned men's guts to water was that he looked like a very big and extremely stupid man dangerously out of control.

"What'd he say after he changed his underpants?"

"Not this guy, Dante." He was getting into the right lane for the Ashby Avenue turnoff. "He talked to me only because he knew he'd have to talk with someone sooner or later. Said, and I'm sorta quoting now, we're all going to miss her terribly here at Atlas Entertainment. She was a very special person, an indispensable attorney, and a wildly inventive lover."

"Just like that, huh?" asked Dante, feeling a sudden deep antipathy toward Kosta Gounaris. Even if the dead woman had been just a sexual convenience, he had held her in his arms and entered her body and now she was dead in an ugly, violent way.

"Just like that—I got the rest of it from the typing pool. Seems Dalton came home unexpectedly from Borneo, Sumatra, like that, he's studying those fucking apes. Anyway, he catches Gounaris and his wife playing hide-the-salami in her penthouse."

"Somebody was watching through the keyhole?"

"It gets better. She's sucking Kosta's knob, and *she finishes him up* and then says to hubby, 'Welcome home, dear.'"

Dante turned very quickly on the seat to look at him. They were stopped for the light at Adeline, and Flanagan was waiting for the look, grinning slyly at him.

"Yeah," said Flanagan. "Gounaris told it as a funny story in the locker room. One cold fuck. Here's Molly Dalton crazy in love with this guy who don't give a shit about her, here's Dalton crazy in love with his wife who don't give shit about *him*—and he walks in on them."

"So he stews about it for a month—"

"You got it, chief. Then goes out and buys himself a shooter and gets stuck in traffic on the Bay Bridge."

"Only one thing bothers me about your neat little package, Tim. Why didn't he take out Gounaris instead of his wife?"

"Sure he'd be pissed at Gounaris, but Christ, Dante, she's the one who betrayed him."

"I don't buy it. I think he was too much in love with her to kill her, no matter what she'd done to him. He's a guy who digs up old bones, for Chrissake! A guy who watches chimps in the jungle. That's patient, contemplative work. That sort of man doesn't lose his head and go crazy with a .22 pistol."

"No, he hires himself a hitter to go crazy for him."

Dante shook his head stubbornly. "Pro hit and Popgun Ucelli was out of town. I just don't think Will Dalton is our man."

"Let's find out," said Flanagan, braking in front of the old brown two-story Victorian. "His 4Runner's in the drive."

CHAPTER SIX

It was a beautiful April Sunday with towering cumulus clipper ships unusual for California. He and Moll had gotten a couple of beers and two poor boys and some potato chips and gone from the campus up to Tilden Park behind Kensington for a picnic. They'd hidden their bikes under some greasewood and climbed up a fire trail to the green brushy crest where they could spread out their blankets and see for miles across the Bay to the gleaming towers of the city.

Even then, Will had worshipped her, adored her, she was the most beautiful creature he'd ever seen, like some exotic wood duck or Chinese pheasant, too glorious to be real.

But when she had come into his arms, she had been stunningly real, the most real woman he'd ever known. He didn't hold hard, physical details of their first mating in his memory, just fragments of an almost unbearable poignancy. The apple-sweetness of a nipple between his lips, the vulnerability of a white flank as her panties came off, the heart-stopping moment when he entered her, he, Will Dalton, actually *inside* her, *her*, Molly St. John, the woman he would love and cherish for all . . .

Knuckles on the door thudded him to earth like a wingshot mallard. They kept on. He opened it red-eyed and stone-faced, teetering on the edge of hatred for these men who had dropped him from the sky to the bitter reality of *Molly gone, Molly dead*.

"No," he said, and started to shut the door.

A foot was in it. The men were holding up leather cases with gleaming shields. Recognition dawned.

"Oh. Sorry. I didn't . . ." He stepped back, nodding to the bulky one. "Inspector . . . Flanagan, isn't it? And—"

"Lieutenant Stagnaro," said the lean-faced taut-bodied one, vaguely remembered. A hunter, this one. Good. Moll's murderer needed to be found, punished, even if it would never . . .

Will stepped aside so they could come in. "You have news?"

"News?" asked Flanagan in a surprised voice. "Yeah, you might say we got news." He half turned to look back at his companion as they went through the archway into the living room. "Right, Dante, might say we got news?"

"And a few questions," said Stagnaro in a tired voice.

Will, who had paused to pick up the mail in the hallway, tossed it on the coffee table and sat down, suddenly wary through his grief. He was a keen observer not only of action but of nuance; any student of primate behavior in the wild had to be. For some unfathomable reason, these men were not his friends.

"I can make some coffee if—"

"This ain't exactly a social occasion, Perfesser."

Flanagan, pretending a stupidity not really his own. The other, Stagnaro, could never make even the pretense. Too much lively wit and intelligence in those deceptively soft brown eyes. Rage, love, hatred, sorrow, joy, delight—but never stupidity.

"Then what sort of occasion is it?" Will asked with deliberate coldness. Steady. Hang on. Don't give them any satisfaction. "My wife is dead, if you have no news about her murderer then why are you intruding on my grief two days before I . . . have to bury her . . ."

"Intruding on your grief? Hey, that's very classy, isn't it, Dante?" Flanagan's mouth hung open ever so slightly after he had spoken, a look of remarkable stupidity. "I got a question maybe relates to her death, like. What'd you feel like when you walked in on Moll givin' Kosta's dick the old mouth massage?"

Will realized he was on his stomach on the floor with his arms pulled painfully up into the small of his back and a man's knee keeping them there. Flanagan was sitting slack-legged under the window holding a red-splotched handkerchief to his nose. Will must have knocked him right off the couch.

"You have to admit you asked for that one, Tim," Stagnaro said from Will's back. Will raised his face off the dusty rug.

"I'm all right now. You can let me up."

After a moment, the weight went away from his back. He got quickly to his feet, in case the fat cop wanted some more. But Flanagan now was standing by the window with his back half-turned, gently dabbing at his swollen nose.

"The bathroom is down the hall on the left."

Flanagan looked grumpy but not terribly vengeful. His nose was red and puffy. He nodded and shambled off down the hall.

Stagnaro sat down, took out a notebook and ballpoint.

Will said, still sore, "What the hell was that all about?"

"He was looking for a reaction." Stagnaro chuckled. "He got one." He leaned forward, serious now, his elbows on the chair arms, his hands resting on the notebook in his lap. "I'm head of the SFPD Organized Crime Task Force—three guys working out of a cramped little office in the Hall of Justice. Any sort of organized crime, that's our meat."

"Organized crime? I don't understand." His bewilderment was real or he was damned good. "Some madman shot Moll—"

"A madman who coolly walks into a crowded restaurant and does his business with a .22 target pistol that's been sprayed with Armor All? A madman who then leaves the gun empty on the bar, warns people about seeing anything, then walks out?"

"Armor All?"

"Stuff they put on car finishes to seal—"

An impatient gesture. "Why put it on a gun?"

"The Hell's Angels started using it in the sixties when they knew they had to leave the gun behind at a hit. Armor All prevents the metal from picking up the shooter's body oil from his fingers. No oil, no fingerprints. Nowadays most pros who still use guns spray them before even handling them, even if they will be wearing gloves. Just a bit of added insurance. Your average crazy isn't going to know that, or go to that much trouble even if he does know it."

Will wasted no more time on needless objections. Sketched out that way by a man concerned with organized crime—did that include the mob, the Mafia, whatever they called it? Anyway, it made the point. It was just that the point made no sense at all.

"There's very little Mafia activity in the Bay Area," Stagnaro was saying. "But I know of a meat wholesaler back east in New Jersey who moonlights as a hitman and fits the . . . parameters of the case. Eddie Ucelli—they call him Popgun. Only Ucelli never used more than one bullet for a hit, and this killer had two. Now, why do you think that might be?"

"I never heard of anyone named Ucelli, Lieutenant."

He seemed to say it rather sadly, as if even this slight connection would be better than the bewilderment his wife's death must be to him right now. If he wasn't faking it, of course.

"Even so, I need whatever your wife said to you before . . ."

"She told me she wanted to see me and we made a date for the next night. We hadn't spoken for a month, not since . . ." He made a vague gesture in the direction Flanagan had gone.

"So no reason at all for the man to want to kill you too?"

"*Me?* Why in God's name would anyone want to—"

"Why your wife?" To Will's bewildered silence, he added, "Two bullets in the gun—if it was Ucelli, of course, or some other pro using his M.O. One for your wife, one—"

"No hard feelings, Perfesser?"

Flanagan's nose was red and swollen, but it had stopped bleeding and obviously wasn't broken.

"Not on my part."

Will asked, in a voice so low he could barely be heard, "How did you . . . learn of it?"

"Gounaris."

"In that sort of detail?"

Flanagan cleared his throat again and sat back down.

"It, uh, seems to be common knowledge at Atlas."

The men were silent for perhaps as long as a minute. Dante couldn't remember when he had seen such a bleak look on any man's face, no matter how devastating a loss he might have suffered.

Will sighed. "So you thought that because I'd . . . found Moll with him, I'd brooded and finally had hired someone to—"

"We have to check out every possibility," said Dante soothingly. "It's just routine, Dr. Dalton. Nothing personal."

"Maybe a little personal with me." Flanagan's voice was thick. He touched his damaged nose. "So I'm gonna hit you with something else you ain't gonna like, Perfesser, and I hope you don't try to take another poke at me because if you do I'll break your fuckin' arm and then take you in for assaulting an officer. We clear?"

"Clear."

But Will was staring at the mail he had put on the coffee table. Suddenly he wanted the policemen out of there. Moll's unmistakable back-slanted handwriting was on that small flat padded mailer on top of the stack.

"Okay, here we go. From the time you were first married your wife has been almost continually promiscuous."

Will was on his feet again, all the blood drained from his face. It was a lie, a goddamned lie the fat cop had . . . Then he saw the look of pain for Will's pain on the other policeman's face. Endless infidelities by Moll over the years would explain so many things he'd steadfastly ignored. Ignored because . . .

"Is this true?" he asked Dante softly.

Both cops relaxed slightly. Dante sighed, nodded.

"So Gounaris was just the last . . . the worst . . . of a . . ." He took in as huge a breath as he could, held it until colored spots danced before his eyes. He let it out softly. "I don't believe I can answer any more of your questions right now. Perhaps after the funeral . . ."

Dante paused to write on the back of one of his business cards, laid it on the edge of the coffee table as he followed his partner toward the foyer.

"I've left you my card, Dr. Dalton. With my home number on the back. If you think of anything . . . or just want to talk . . ."

"Thank you, Lieutenant."

Going down the old wooden steps to the sidewalk toward their car, Dante asked Tim, "So, what do you think?"

"A very short fuse as regards his wife."

"Which means if he was going to do her . . ."

"Yeah," Flanagan said sadly, seeing the easy solution to the murder slip away, "he wouldn't wait no friggin' month."

Will sat with the mailer in his hand, almost afraid to open it since Flanagan had taken the lid off his life and let him peer down into the murky depths of his marriage, his wife, their love—*love*? The images of Moll with Gounaris rolled quickly before his eyes like the picture on a badly adjusted TV set, except the man now was faceless. Could Moll love him and . . .

Yet what had changed so much, really? One man or five or fifty or five hundred, what did it matter when the central fact was infidelity? And a woman like Moll, looked at logically, how could his sole love have been enough for her? He knew about the hot-tub deflowering at thirteen, had seen the way her father looked at her, knew how many men had pursued her at Cal . . .

But logic had little to do with it. He realized he was damned mad at her—enraged, in fact. He'd loved her—did love her—with such intensity, such single-minded devotion, and she was fucking everybody in town . . .

No. He was who he was, Moll had been who she had been. He knew, despite everything, she had loved him as hard and as constantly as she was able. He, with his studies of primates and hominids, knew better than most what cold atavistic winds blow through the human psyche. *Pneuma,* the ancient Greeks had called it, the great wind of Nature, of the gods, of creation.

Female chimps in estrus copulated thirty, forty, fifty times a day, with all the males of the troop they could find. And a woman's genetic code was over 99 percent the same as a chimp's, but she didn't have to wait for estrus, could copulate every day with . . .

And down below everything, below the massive human brain's neocortex, was the much more ancient mammalian limbic cortex, and deeper yet, at the very base of the brain stem, was a reptilian core called the R-complex, which programmed basic sex, fear and aggression. The overlap between brains was not seamless; the lizard brain's ancient neural impulses sometimes bled through to the higher control centers. Perhaps . . . with Moll . . . those atavistic urges . . .

He blew out a long breath, picking up the packet, and with resolute fingers opened the folded flap she had stapled shut.

It was four in the morning when Will finally made sense of the data on the disk Moll had sent. So simple yet so profound.

If she had only seen him the night she had mailed this, when, he knew now, she had been frightened—but also still in thrall to Gounaris. So she'd delayed a night, to ask Gounaris about it, tell him she was going to see Will the next night. And if Will was interpreting the disk's data correctly, he'd had to act fast. A phone call back east to . . . what was his name, Popgun Ucelli. Allay Moll's fears so she would divulge nothing until she could be . . .

If Gounaris had ordered Moll's death, was Will Dalton

ready to kill him? Oh, hell, of course not. Maybe it hadn't
been Gounaris at all, just someone he told about the discovery. Or maybe Stagnaro's insinuations were wrong, maybe
the floppy disk had nothing at all to do with her death.

Stagnaro had said there was almost no mob activity in San
Francisco; but he had also said, two bullets in the gun. If
Will had been there with her, would he now be dead, too?
Then why hadn't they done it since? Because it was too soon
after Moll had been killed? Both at once, okay, but serially it
would look suspicious. Eventually, when the case had gone
into the open file—which meant closed, he'd read somewhere—a hit-and-run . . . a fall down the steps . . . a random
mugging . . .

For the first time since it had happened, Will had something to think about besides his loss. The loss of himself. He
was no hero, he didn't want to die. He would give the disk to
Stagnaro, tell him it had come from Moll, that its data was
meaningless to him, but since it had been mailed on the night
before her death he'd wanted to turn it in.

Stagnaro already suspected a professional hit, so give him
the disk, let him do the rest. He knew his job, Will was sure,
would be good at it. Just as Will was good at his, studying
wild apes. Until Moll's death, he had planned two years in
Uganda with the forest chimpanzees, even had his grant; so
why not now? Going to the rain forest would give him a
sense of purpose. The time to stick around would have been
when Moll was still alive; now it was just an empty gesture.

On the other hand, give the tape to Stagnaro and eventually everyone in the SFPD would know about it. That's just
the way bureaucracies worked. Since the tape had told him
about a crooked cop on the force, Will might very well find
himself worse off than he was now no matter how well Stagnaro did his job.

There was the smart thing to do and the professional thing
to do. The obviously heroic thing to do and the perhaps cow-
ardly thing to do. Through the long night they merged and
separated and paired up again in unlikely combinations in his
mind. He wrestled with them until dawn was lightening the

room through the lace curtains, but he finally made a tentative peace with his options and with himself.

Dante went to Moll Dalton's funeral, Tim Flanagan didn't. Tim had no interest in an innocent Will, and he didn't share Dante's belief that Will had been slated as a second target for the hitman. Even if true, they'd be nuts to hit him this soon.

There was a tense moment when Gounaris showed up at the closed-casket service in the mortuary chapel. Will sat stony-faced in his pew staring straight ahead. He did the same when Moll's father entered. Interesting, thought Dante. Even more interesting, Moll's mother wasn't there. Most interesting of all, neither were Will's parents.

Afterward Dante went up to offer condolences as the others filed out for the cortege to the cemetery.

"You thought any more about what I told you, Dr. Dalton? About the possibility that you were a target yourself?"

"A great deal," said Will. He was different today, lower-key, subdued. "Is there anything I can do to help with the investigation?"

"Yes." Dante was a bit surprised, but seized his chance. "There was a padded mailer on top of the other letters you brought in from the hall the other day. From Atlas, looked sort of like your wife's handwriting. If she sent you something before her death . . ."

The two men stared at one another; something electric passed between them, though neither would acknowledge it.

"Tell me one thing candidly, Lieutenant. Is there any real hope you'll catch whoever did this—assuming you're right and it wasn't just some nut?"

"Possibly, if you help me out."

"Possibly? I don't hear a lot of conviction in that. Even you don't believe you'll get them. No, I have nothing to tell you." Will gave a slight shrug. "I'm grateful for your concern about me, but I'm leaving shortly on a two-year grant to study a troop of wild chimpanzees in an East African rain forest, where I'll be out of the way of any possible danger."

Dante realized he had been outmaneuvered. He hadn't known how much he'd counted on learning the contents of that mailer until he found out he wasn't going to.

"I can't stop you, of course. But before you go, please have the courtesy to stop playing goddam games with . . ."

He paused. They were the last ones left in the room, but the professional pallbearers who would take the casket to the cemetery had entered, and his voice had been rising.

"I have no games to play, but I do have professional obligations that don't depend on your approval." Will added, in a parody of his western background, "Anyway, Lieutenant, I reckon the danger'll still be here when I get back."

That evening, the first of the series of phone calls Dante would receive from the man called Raptor was waiting on his answering machine when he got home from the funeral. The voice was heavy, guttural, a parody of Arte Johnson's *Laugh-In* Nazi.

"*Ich bin* Raptor, Herr Policeman. I haff taken care uff de voman. Who iss next? You vill be hearink from me again, *nein*?"

Raptor. Wasn't that some predatory bird, an eagle, a hawk, something like that? And "Ucelli" meant bird—an odd name for the superstitious Sicilian *mafiosi* to trust their hits to, wasn't it? Birds sang, after all.

This Raptor was singing now, but not telling him anything. Trying to make Dante think he was Ucelli?

Maybe something like this had spooked Will Dalton; he'd have to ask. Probably just a kook; but even though he didn't take it too seriously, he was just as glad Rosie was at her Greek dance class and fourteen-year-old Antonio was out in the kitchen scarfing down the pasta Dante had made for their supper. In the organized crime squad, he dealt only with the scum of the earth; he didn't like it coming into his house, touching his family in any way.

He erased the tape and went out to the kitchen to eat pasta and garlic bread and talk basketball with his son.

PART TWO

End of the Ordovician

439 m.y. ago

About two weeks after you die,
your phone calls start tapering off.

Johnny Carson
in monologue

CHAPTER SEVEN

Here is Raptor, all those deaths later. My revels now are ended—or will be in a few hours. Looking back, I can only think of how succinctly Willy the Shake once put it:

> *O proud death,*
> *What feast is toward in thine eternal cell,*
> *That thou so many princes at a shot*
> *So bloodily hast struck?*

Enough erudition. Let us consider the humble gene: a chloroplast will make a symbiotic attachment to a cell, and the cell will not eat it. How altruistic, we think. But no. The cell does not deny itself a tasty meal because it holds warm feelings toward chloroplasts. It refrains because in the history of unicellular life, cells that ate their chloroplasts died out while those that nurtured their chloroplasts survived.

You see? Even at this submicroscopic level, altruism is only long-term selfishness. Self-interest is the norm for all life on earth. To wit: inside your body at this instant, legions of white corpuscles are rushing through your veins to slaughter in their tens of millions some army of invading bacteria which, unchecked, would kill you.

What is life but the prelude to death? Nothing animate can live without killing something else. Did I say animate? Among plants, the competition for nutrients, underground water, and sunlight is equally fierce. Darwin found that on a two-by-three-foot plot of ground, 295 out of 357 sprouted seedlings were destroyed before they could mature.

The creosote bush poisons the ground for fifty feet around it, so no other bush can live near and steal moisture precious for its existence. Pine forests lay down hardpan so undergrowth cannot crowd in below them and share their nutrients. Overstory trees keep sun and rain from the lesser trees beneath so even if they do not wither and die they will be stunted. Colorado aspens drop a poison on their own offspring around their boles to kill off eventual competition.

The carnivore plants are even more ruthless. Venus flytraps *et al.* tempt insects into their brightly colored abdomens, slam their jaws shut, and digest the hapless insects alive without remorse for the prey's slow agony as it turns to aspic.

Now, I know that despite what the rest of Nature does, it is no small matter for us to take from another human being the one thing irreducibly his or her own. But is the killing of another person a difference in kind—or in mere degree—from taking the life of a wolf who I mistakenly believe has been killing my stock? Of a rabbit whom I wish to have for supper? From swatting a fly that is trying to lay its eggs in my food?

Enfin, these others participate in life as fully as we, is it not so? And even as you and I, are they not just trying to live out their allotted span in whatever joy, sorrow, delight, and pain is given them? Do you know that perhaps as high as 50 percent of all human beings start out as twins, and that the twin who lives does so by subsuming and absorbing its own sibling in the womb, much like the Venus flytrap digests the insect?

Ma foi, we humans do often abide killing our own kind through self-delusion. Every day women who speak words of nurture to their plants murder the unborn children in their wombs, on the scientifically unsound and morally specious argument that these little tailed people are not yet human beings. How convenient! But do they not enjoy life at least as much as the philodendron enjoys Bach?

I kill, but I do not kill indiscriminately. I kill those marked down to die, those who merit death, those who *must* be excised, like a brain tumor bent upon your destruction.

That comic cop, Stagnaro, did not believe me or my comic German accent right after Moll Dalton died. But he soon did . . .

And now, before the night is out, I will have my terminal bit of business with that dead woman's living husband. *La ronde.* A wonderful circularity. Closure, in current argot. A grapefruit in the puss to you, Stagnaro! Top o' the world, Ma!

Dalton had fled me down the labyrinthian ways, but now one of us must die. I have promised you that he shall be allowed to strut at least some of his little hour upon the stage before I give him quietus: you and I are in for a long boring evening, aren't we, as we listen to the speech that will be the final act of his meaningless little *commedia*.

CHAPTER EIGHT

"'Not in innocence and not in Asia was mankind born. Our ancestry is firmly rooted in the animal world, and to its subtle, antique ways our hearts are yet pledged . . .'"

Will Dalton looked almost challengingly around the conference hall. His gaze fell on Dante, leaning against the back wall, held his for a long, ironic moment.

"That is the opening of Robert Ardrey's seminal work, *African Genesis,* which caught the popular imagination, discomfited the scientific world, and in the years since 1961 has been dismembered and disemboweled by the pacific-minded with a ferocity that does more to support Ardrey's beliefs about innate violence in man than anything he ever wrote.

"Until I read *African Genesis* as a high school senior, I was going to be a paleontologist and solve once and for all the riddle of the extinction of the dinosaurs 65 million years ago at the K-T boundary. Ardrey fired me with a new purpose, because he set us squarely in the natural world and then said we are a 'bad-weather animal'—implying that we forge ourselves in the crucible of disaster, that whatever man has become occurred after a changing environment drove him from the trees out into the savannah. Even then I had a sort of instinctual disagreement with Ardrey on that point— why *driven* out by bad weather or other animals? Why not *adventuring* out—because it was a fun and exciting thing to do?

"But even so, Ardrey stole my heart from the dinosaurs and gave it to man. I would become a paleo*anthropo*logist and find *the* moment our line parted from that of the great apes. It was as a budding paleoanthropologist that I was first invited to Hadar nine years ago, after a hominid conference in Paris.

"One night during dinner—corned beef hash mixed with rice, washed down with Lemon Squash laced with a capful of rum, many here know the gourmet delights of living in the field—a *gamin*-faced French fellow post-doc introduced me to the vision of a renegade Jesuit named Pierre Teilhard de Chardin. She lent me a book in French of his writings; it was heady reading by lantern light in a white nylon tent on the site where our Institute's Don Johanson and his team had discovered those multiple *Australopithecus afarensis* remains they dubbed Lucy and the First Family.

"Heady reading indeed! 'Everything is the sum of the past,' Chardin wrote. 'Nothing is comprehensible except through its history.' He claimed that man was spiritually as well as mentally evolving. Science couldn't ask *why*—it could only ask *how*. Chardin was asking why; myth and story asked why; suddenly I was suffused with a need to do the same.

"Lucy and the First Family were left to tell the tale, but what tale? Questions concerning their understanding of life would not even be a legitimate scientific inquiry. Only storytellers, artists, and mythmakers could consider such unscientific questions. But I was a scientist.

"From the time of scientism in the nineteenth century, science had been preaching that nothing is real that is not palpable. Well, after all of this concern with the *real*, with matter, what did we, divorced from our animal nature and at war with our planet, have to show for it?

"We had the facts. Did we have the truth?

"By chance, on our way back from Paris we took a two-day stopover in Boston. At the Museum of Fine Arts I saw the original Gauguin Tahitian painting he called, *D'ou venons nous? que sommes nous? ou allon nous?*

"All the way back here to San Francisco, I couldn't get that painting and its title out of my mind.

"'Where do we come from? Who are we? Where are we going?'

"Science alone couldn't even *ask* these questions, let alone answer them. Yet modern man's nature was bound up inextricably not only with our genetic heritage and the strange twisting ways of extinction and evolution from much earlier times, but also with the myth and ritual of our early *Homo sapiens* years.

"I was going in the wrong direction, asking the wrong questions. *When we parted* from the great apes was not nearly so important as *what we brought with us.* Our carbon-dating and argon-dating techniques for fossil-associated strata had come of age; we had not parted from the chimps 8 or 9 million years ago, the break was less than half that ancient. Our direct ancestry started at least 4 million years ago, not a million.

"The chimpanzee, our closest living relative, was so close we could not call him cousin, but had to think half brother, half sister. Even the baboons, way off on the side as far as direct descent goes, gave us a hierarchical organization that eerily foreshadowed the Zulu *impi,* the Greek phalanx, the Roman legion, the British infantry square.

"I realized I would have to study not only the stones and bones to learn about our early hominid and human ancestors, but the living creatures that most resemble what we were then. The great apes, who can tell us much about the primate genetic input we get from the ancestors we all have in common.

"So I've studied gorillas in Rwanda-Burundi, orangutans in Borneo, and now wild forest chimpanzees in the Kibale Forest. When I accepted the Institute's invitation to speak on my work, I was still in Uganda doing the ethological fieldwork and taking the slides I expected to show you tonight. Vital stuff, because any discussion is teleologically, whether stated or not, a prelude to the understanding of *Homo sapiens sapiens.*

"Well, tonight I have to beg your patience as I reverse the procedure. I want to examine some aspects of human nature as a prelude to our discussion of the Kibale chimps. I want to do this because, as most of you know, shortly before I left for Uganda my wife, Moll, was murdered."

Dante's head jerked back in such surprise that he banged it against the wall. He rubbed his hand over the spot, watching the surprised stirring in the audience. This was not what they had come expecting to hear.

"Because of her death, it is perhaps not surprising that I went seeking insights into the chimpanzee's understanding— if any—of death. Conventional wisdom holds that such knowledge first appeared with Neanderthal, some fifty thousand years ago, but tonight I hope to place it much earlier.

"To do this I'm going to have to ride two horses, because this is not the material of hard science. I don't scorn science; it is my life. But science has made some mistakes. It has tried to put death and chaos on hold. It has given us permission to explore anything, do anything, take anything, destroy anything, until we have exploded the natural world and strewn its dying guts around us for all to see.

"It has the power to do this. Does it have the right? It can tell us *how* to make the *bang!* but not *when* to make it. Or whether we should make it at all. But it has the facts on its side. A human being exposed to too much radiation will die whether he believes in radiation or not.

"But I want to explore the other side also. If we cannot scorn science, we cannot scorn myth and legend, either. That guy I just mentioned, who is trying to avoid his fatal dose of radiation, stole the fire at which he cooks his meats from angry gods. It is that same fire, nurtured carefully but used carelessly over the millennia, that has gone from catapult to cannon to missile to smart bomb to megaton that will destroy him because he forgot who he is and where he came from.

"The tragedy is not that we want science to tell us what to love and what to hate; it is that science isn't designed to know the difference between them. So we have to look elsewhere. That is what I want to do here tonight . . ."

Listening, Dante thought, Love and hate. Life and death. His mind swooped back unbidden to the time when Dalton's staying alive seemed a day-to-day, even an hour-to-hour thing . . .

CHAPTER NINE

It was ten days after Moll Dalton's funeral, and to Dante's relief her husband was still alive. And about to depart for East Africa. But Dante was leaving nothing to chance, so here they were on their way to SFO, Will's stuffed duffel bag and backpack on the backseat of Dante's car.

Whatever Molly had sent him must have thoroughly terrified Will; he had followed Dante's safety precautions to the letter. Leaving his distinctive 4Runner in the driveway and renting a nondescript compact under a name not his own—a trick used in protecting federal witnesses. Varying the times and routes by which he left his office. Changing motels every two days. Monitoring his answering machine until he knew who was calling.

Dante was still a little sore at him for holding out—but during these ten days he had come to respect the scientist as a careful, moderate, committed, and very bright individual. And even at this last minute he hoped Will might finally trust him enough to talk about the contents of the padded mailer.

"Where's all your safari gear or whatever you need?"

"My kind of work doesn't require a safari or very much in the way of equipment. I've got an old Land-Rover in Nairobi; beyond that, a camera, film, notebooks, all the books I can carry—the rest is perishables I renew every couple of months."

Dante glanced over at him. A strange peace emanated

from the man, as if he had come to terms with his mourning. Just on impulse, Dante sought to disrupt it.

"On professional hits, I collect information, collect information, until suddenly something from over *there* comes together with something from over *here,* and I have a toehold."

"You seem damned sure Molly was . . . murdered professionally."

"I am."

Switching grounds, Will asked, "Information like what?"

"Why wasn't your wife's mother at the funeral? Why weren't your folks? I snooped around a little, found her mother's still alive, found out you're real close to your parents."

"Her mother, I don't know. I've never met her. My folks, I asked them not to come. They love me, I love them, they knew that Moll and I loved one another, but they didn't think she was the right woman for me. So I couldn't handle their being there."

"Fair enough. Why don't you like your wife's old man?"

"Did you know there's a strong incest taboo among most bird and animal species, Lieutenant? Dian Fossey saw only one silverback gorilla mate with its daughter in all her years there. Gorillas are strict vegetarians, but when the offspring of that match was born, the troop killed it and partially ate the body."

"You're telling me that you suspect St. John of sexually abusing Moll when she was a child?"

"Once I was able to accept the idea, things began to fall into place. I think that fucker . . ." He stopped, got control. "I think he also pandered for her, introduced her to people and got some erotic pleasure out of imagining her with them—with anyone but me. In Paris . . . maybe L.A. . . ."

"Palm Desert," said Dante. To Will's suddenly dense silence, he added, "Her old man comped your wife and Gounaris to a long weekend at a resort near Palm Springs called the Desert Spa to celebrate her getting the position as San Francisco corporate counsel for Atlas. Legend says Al Capone—"

"The Desert Spa," said Will in a low, flat voice. "That's where Moll and I had our honeymoon."

Dante had dropped in the Desert Spa hoping to jar Will into showing his hole card: all it did was make him fold his hand. He said nothing more until they arrived at the USAir terminal. Dante wasn't about to leave him alone and unprotected at the gate; if there was going to be a hit, he wanted to be there, take down the fucker who tried it. Then Dalton would talk, by God!

His eyes swept the unloading area; nothing suspicious. Armed with Will's flight numbers and times, even his contact number in Nairobi, he showed his badge to the airport cop in front of USAir so his car wouldn't be towed, used it again to follow Will through the metal detectors with the gun on his belt.

At the commuter gate, Will said abruptly, "Do you think Kosta Gounaris had anything to do with Moll's death?"

"What do *you* think?"

"That he's a rich, powerful, manipulative, sadistic son of a bitch who seduced my wife."

"Which doesn't make him a murderer." Dante added, almost grudgingly, "But if I come up with anything definite on him or any aspect of the case, I'll call you."

"*Call* me? Once I leave Nairobi, not even mail will reach me for at least three months, until I go to Fort Portal for supplies." He paused. "Maybe I don't want to know anyway."

And Will Dalton walked through the gate and down the ramp to the plane without shaking hands or looking back. Dante stared after him, irritated again. Will Dalton wanted . . . *something*. Help, maybe. But he wouldn't give anything. Maybe Moll had felt that way, too. Dante owed the bastard nothing, except the pleasure of the case, but unexpectedly he had gotten something: Dalton actually suspected Gounaris of being directly involved in his wife's death. He hadn't actually said so, but . . .

Did he have something beyond the obvious wishful thinking of revenge for his sexual humiliation? Something that might have been in that padded mailer—assuming it really had come from Dalton's wife? If Dante had voiced his own suspicions of Gounaris, would Dalton have talked to him?

Dante returned to his car, started the long loop around the departure gates to get back onto 101 North to the city. How would he have acted in Dalton's place? Probably no better, maybe worse. And he had gotten the man safely on the plane to L.A. for the British Air flight over the Pole to London and then on to Nairobi and his chosen jungle.

Everyone chose a jungle of sorts in his life. A place of solitude where pain could be taken out and looked at. Maybe it was simple as that with Dalton. His synapses fusing, he had to get away to get sane again.

Or maybe not. Will Dalton was a very smart man. Maybe he knew more than he was telling. Maybe his wife had left him something that let him know organized crime might be involved in Atlas Entertainment. Maybe he thought it would take Gounaris down while he was gone. Dante was no stranger to that sort of thing. Secret witnesses dying, months of work coming unraveled just because the wrong person overheard a single careless word. Because he knew cops who were stupid, casually venal, and frankly corrupt, his own work was one long secret from everyone but Rosa.

Cops corrupt like Jack Lenington, as he was soon to learn.

Kosta was getting jumpy. Ten fucking days after Moll's funeral, her husband was still alive, and no word from Jack Lenington. He'd put on a bland face for the fat cop, Flanagan, during the questioning following Moll's . . . death—but he didn't know if he could do it today.

He'd been almost crazed when he found out she'd been hit. He'd called up Gid, who'd told one of his fucking Hebe jokes, then added, "You knew damn well what would have to be done about Moll," and hung up. But Kosta *hadn't* known. He'd been crazy about Moll.

Of course the night they'd killed her, he'd told her Atlas Entertainment *was* dirty as Gid had told him to do, knowing she'd run to her husband with it. What did he *think* they'd do to the two of them? And he'd been crazy wild with her, even going down on her—he who never went down on anybody, not once since Constantinople and the fat greasy Turk. He must have known, somewhere deep inside, what was going to happen to her. But whoever pulled the trigger, it was her husband's fault she was dead, right? You don't walk off and leave a woman like that.

Why didn't Uncle Gid eliminate that fucking Dalton so it was over and done with? "Patience," he'd said, and Gounaris had replied, "No loose ends," because he wanted Dalton off the face of this earth forever. He contemplated the idea with great personal satisfaction, but told himself that the real reason was just what he'd said to Gid, Dalton alive was a constant danger.

Martin Prince had bought Gid's explanation of why Moll had to be hit, but Kosta knew he couldn't trust even Uncle Gid if the FBI started an active interest in the case. And if Martin Prince even dreamed he'd been so stupid as to leave an incriminating file in a computer, Kosta's own life would be on the line.

So right after the hit, despite Gideon's admonitions of caution, Kosta had got hold of Jack Lenington and had told him to keep an eye on Dalton's comings and goings. Ten days ago, and not a fucking word since. Maybe it was time to bring in some wrecking crew of his own. The Organization had probably used that guy out of Jersey—Ucelli, that was it—but he needed somebody Prince and the others didn't know about. Somebody as expert with accidents as Ucelli was with a .22.

Hell, there wasn't anybody. He'd have to do it himself. He'd done the Turk in Istanbul at fourteen, he could do No-Balls Dalton at fifty-five. But first he had to know what was going on.

Ten days was long enough. He needed to see Lenington.

Sergeant Jack Lenington of the SFPD Vice Squad thought, Maybe fucking Kosta Gounaris wasn't so hard-nose as everybody said: he'd let the silence go ten days before asking for a meet. So Lenington would push it. He had a hard, lined face and doleful blue eyes that tipped down at the outer corners like a bloodhound's, with none of the bloodhound's sweetness of disposition, however: rage was his central metaphor. Whether forcing a hooker to go down on him in his patrol car or knocking her pimp around for a little rake-off of the profit, anger was his drug of choice.

Anger with caution. His suit was never quite expensive enough to raise Internal Affairs eyebrows, his boat was fiberglass with a 30-horse Evinrude, just possible on his department income, his home was a Sunset District stucco row house a few blocks from the similar house in which incorruptible Tim Flanagan lived.

But just wait until he had his twenty in. Then he'd dump his cow of a wife and head over to the Bahamas to his nice little offshore account. Buy a boat, get an all-girl crew . . .

He was almost smiling as he entered one of Vince O'Neill's porn palaces on Mason Street in the Tenderloin. The garish red and yellow sign over the door read: HOT STUFF!!! XXX ARCADE!!! PHANTASY IN THE PHLESH!!! Covering the walls inside were intimate photos of women wearing only pubic hair, if that, and facial expressions seldom seen in full daylight. The middle-aged woman reading *The Wall Street Journal* in the raised change cage monotoned, "The-hottest-show-in-town-have-a-good-time," without raising her face from the page. AT&T was down an eighth, but now that they were going into fiber-optic TV transmission . . .

Mobile masks of light flickered over male features from the eyepieces in the labyrinth of coin-operated peep-show machines, set up so each patron had his back turned to anyone passing by, thus assuring him a modicum of privacy. Perfumed disinfectant gave the place a county-jail smell.

Kosta Gounaris was at the end of the many-angled corridor, the only place where two machines stood relatively side by side. His eyes were glued on some unrolling endless loop of tape; throughout their discussion he seldom moved except to feed in coins when the machine clicked and went black.

Lenington jammed a fistful of quarters into the slot as fast as his machine would swallow them, ignoring what was behind the eyepiece. He was a hands-on, dick-in kind of guy; watching someone else do it did not interest him at all.

"You called," he said to Gounaris in his flat angry voice. "Tell me everything happened that night."

He was instantly defensive. "There a fucking problem?"

"You're here to answer questions, goddam you. Everything that happened that night."

"Okay, okay."

Lenington worked through Vince O'Neill since he was Vice and Vince was who he was supposed to be stamping out, and was a hardcase, so he'd been planning to push it with Gounaris; but now he wasn't sure. The whisper was the tall, hard Greek had been a life-taker in his time. And he looked ready to do it again.

"Guy was supposed to have come in from JFK on a one-stop through Dallas, but I met him in the main concourse so I didn't actually see him get off the plane."

"You make him if you saw him again?"

"You think I'm fucking nuts?"

Gounaris nodded as if this were the right response, and fed in another quarter. "Go on."

"I gave him the overnight bag, Naugahyde, some shit, I'd wrapped a pair of gloves around the handle like I was told, inside two photos, a man and a woman, the address of Bella Figura, street map with the route marked in yellow highlighter, gun, overcoat, spray can of Armor All. He put on the gloves before he touched anything else, then went in the men's room. I went to one of the airport bars, gunned a couple drinks. You wanta know which bar—"

"No."

"Couple hours, he's back, hands me back the overnight bag without the overcoat. The gun was gone, too. He was still wearing the gloves. He caught the next shuttle to LAX. I returned the rental car, dumped the overnight bag. Next morning I read all about it in the *Chronicle*."

Another quarter. "What about the husband?"

"Nothing."

"What do you mean, nothing? I directed you to—"

"Listen, you and me haven't worked together before," said Lenington, taking a chance. "I know you draw a lot of water, but I don't eat *too* big a ration of shit from anybody, okay? I'm telling you there was no way I could keep tabs on him. Dante Stagnaro was in on this from the git-go."

"I don't know any Stagnaro. Just Flanagan."

"Yeah, well, Flanagan's just a cop, but Stagnaro's a fuckin' snake. You don't see him, you don't hear him, don't know he's near you, all of a sudden he's lighting your fuckin' cigarette. He heads up SFPD's Organized Crime Task Force."

Gounaris had returned to his machine. His voice tightened. "Organized Crime? And he's been on it from the beginning?"

"Flanagan called him from the crime scene." Lenington's mouth twisted into a secret, angry smile. The fucker was worried, you could hear it in his voice, see it from the corner of your eye in the tension of his stance by the machine. "It looked like a pro hit to Tim, and they're close, so he called him in. Anyway, Stagnaro on the scene I walk light, believe me. Day after the funeral, Dalton dropped out of sight."

"I don't understand."

"No answer on his phone, just the machine. Never seen going to or coming from work. Not going home at night. Car in the driveway . . ." He paused for his secret angry smile again. He'd shake the fucker up good. "Until today."

"What happened today?" Gounaris was again tense, alert.

"I sat near Stagnaro and Flanagan in the caf at the Hall this morning. Late yesterday, Stagnaro drove Dalton to the airport. He was flying to fucking East Africa—"

"*East Africa?*"

"For two fucking years. To study monkeys or something."

Yeah, a goddamned bombshell. Gounaris was over there feeding in quarters like a fucking degenerate, and he didn't say anything for over a minute. A full fucking minute.

Lenington finally said, "So what do you want me to do now, Mr. Gounaris? Try to find out where in East Africa he—"

"No. Don't do anything else."

"Nothing? I thought—"

"Don't think, either." After a moment, Gounaris said in an abstractedly impatient way, "Go on, get out of here. Go beat up a pimp or something."

Kosta stayed behind for almost ten minutes, feeding in the rest of his roll of quarters, watching the filmed action through the eyepiece. He was better hung than the guy the girl with the pimples on her butt was blowing.

Any killing he'd have to do himself. Not just because of Martin Prince. Why the fuck hadn't Lenington told him about Stagnaro ten days ago? He wasn't sure what the Organized Crime Task Force did, but it had been in on the investigation since the very night of Moll's death! Lenington was one stupid son of a bitch. Or else he was jerking Kosta's chain . . .

Okay, okay, calm down. Africa wasn't the moon. Send a man in after Dalton? Hell, he probably wouldn't even be able to find the bastard out there in the jungle. What about lining up one of those game poachers on Channel 9, chop him down, bury him? Nothing was impossible, but the logistics were appalling.

On the other hand, with Dalton somewhere even the Mafia couldn't reach him, any threat he had posed was also gone for two years. And maybe Moll hadn't told him a damned thing. Or maybe she had, and her getting wasted had scared him so bad he'd chickened off to Africa. Yellow bastard. Well, Kosta could wait two years. What was that thing he'd heard? Revenge was a dish best eaten cold? Yeah. Dalton had killed Moll, sure as if he'd held the gun to her face himself.

Meanwhile, Kosta would order all surveillance off him and let Uncle Gid pass the news on to Martin Prince. And even if Stagnaro could get subpoenas, with the file Moll had seen gone from their mainframe he wouldn't find anything.

Moll. He realized he had an erection from thinking of her while watching the action on the tiny screen. He missed her, but it was time to think of his own future. Time to hang on to this power that was his own. Yes! It was good to be thinking independently again, like when he was a kid in Constantinople. He felt powerful, even invincible.

And his new British secretary, Miss Pym, with the horsy upper-class face and manner, already was letting her breast brush his shoulder when she leaned over him from behind to hand him some papers. Time to score again.

CHAPTER TEN

Dante hadn't expected to score so soon, but Danny Banner, the black inspector who liked to say things like, "Don't be dissin' my 'do, Lou," and was half of his task force and was on Gounaris, knew Lenington by sight.

"Gounaris in at ten-eleven A.M.," said Danny. "Lenington in at ten-fifteen. I didn't want to go in to see if they ended up together, but Lenington was out at ten twenty-seven, Gounaris at ten thirty-six."

"Lenington have any legitimate reason to be in one of Vince's places?" Dante had always avoided Vice and had a remarkably sketchy knowledge of its modus operandi, although he knew or suspected enough about Lenington to turn his stomach.

"Oh sure, check out the action, make a presence—you know. But it could also mean . . ."

"Yes," said Dante in crisp comprehension. "And Gounaris had no reason to be there whatsoever. I think you can drop the Gounaris surveillance for now, Danny, but drop a word to I.A. about Lenington at the same time. It won't do any good, I just want them to make a run on him to keep the bad guys confused."

If there were any bad guys, of course. He might be looking under the beds in Atlas Entertainment for Mafia bogeymen who weren't there. As Tim was fond of pointing out, Popgun Ucelli might just have gone fishing.

                    *   *   *

Diana Pym had a long face but lovely chestnut hair and
very blue eyes and a touch of hauteur that Dante had a hunch
Kosta Gounaris would soon take out of her. She served
Dante an excellent cup of tea and was quite cosy this morning as they waited for Gounaris to show up. Dante made no
attempt at all to pump her about Atlas Entertainment affairs.
Tim Flanagan liked gossip, innuendo, coffee shop specula-
tions, but Dante thrived on the half-heard word, the oblique,
surprised glance, the shift of the eye, the dryness of the lips,
the break in the voice.

It was after 10:00 A.M. when Kosta Gounaris finally arrived. Four thousand dollars on his back, three times that on
his wrist. Tall, whipcord, distinguished, a slight glint of silver here and there in otherwise coal-black hair. Thin black
mustache. Disturbing eyes because they were full of life, intelligence, and wit instead of being the dead BBs that Dante
had come to expect from connected men.

"Good morning, Miss Pym."

Good, deep, masculine voice, a little of Zachary Scott in
his *Mask of Dimitrios* role, maybe a pinch of Gregory Peck's
bluff, deep-voiced, sly elegance in *Roman Holiday*. Rosa
often sat up watching American Movie Classics while waiting for Dante to get home on late nights, and they usually
stayed through to the end of whatever film was on before
going to bed.

"There's a Mr. Stagnaro waiting to see you, sir."

The head turned, those intensely alive eyes met Dante's.

"That's Lieutenant Dante Stagnaro of the Organized
Crime Task Force, isn't it?" said Gounaris. He waggled
beckoning fingers over his shoulder as he headed toward his
inner office. "I can give you . . . Miss Pym?"

She swept Dante with suddenly frosty eyes. "Mr. Taylor at
ten-thirty."

"So. Twenty-one minutes."

Everything designed to put him at a disadvantage. Knowing his name, rank, affiliation; zinging him for not so identi-
fying himself to Miss Pym; giving him a precise twenty-one

minutes as if he were a job applicant. Elegant. Impressive. A worthy opponent. Gounaris wouldn't rattle easily; this first crossing of swords would be rapier work, thrust and parry, no slash and hack of sabers. A feint or two and Dante would be gone.

Twenty-one minutes would be more than enough. He only had one fact that would surprise, maybe shake Gounaris, and he wasn't yet sure how to play that one to maximum advantage. If at all.

The office was at the top of the building, windows on three sides. Directly behind the antique desk that Gounaris claimed while waving Dante to a chair was a wonderful view of Yerba Buena, Treasure Island, distant Oakland. The day was clear, the air sparkled with sunlight, the cars on the Bay Bridge span clever moving toys in a master artist's diorama.

"You've got an incredible view, Mr. Gounaris."

"It is wonderful, isn't it? That's why I decided to work out of San Francisco rather than L.A. Being Greek, I need my mountains and water. Or at least hills."

"I'll get right to the point. The death of Mrs. Dalton."

"Ah yes. Moll. Tragic." Gounaris stood, turned to the window as if studying the tragic dimensions of her demise.

"Also very professional," said Dante. "Which is what brought me in on it and is still puzzling me."

Gounaris turned to frown at him. "Professional."

"As in hitman professional." Dante shrugged, making himself as Italian as he could. "As in Mafia, Mob, Outfit, Organization, Cosa Nostra, the Family, Our Thing. But our task force looks into *any* organized criminal activities that would come under the RICO statutes. Which means it could be linked to Mafia-controlled operations in other parts of the country." He leaned forward earnestly. "The trouble is, Mr. Gounaris, no matter how hard we look, we just can't find anything in Mrs. Dalton's private life that would account for anyone hiring a professional killer to murder her."

"You come to me because I was sexually involved with—"

"Not at all," cut in Dante heartily.

He caught it in the eye, the flicker of surprise, maybe even annoyance, as if this stupid copper wasn't sticking to the script Gounaris had written in his head for this interview. Because Dante wouldn't, he'd have to make the obvious connection.

"It is true that Dr. Dalton was very upset . . ." He lowered his voice. "He walked in on his wife and myself, you know."

"I know. *Flagrante delicto,* as they used to say. But even if he wanted his wife dead, he could never have found a killer of that caliber. And he hardly would have stopped with her." Dante chuckled and spread his hands, a typical wop enjoying a good joke. "But here you are, safe and sound, and there Will Dalton is, in Africa." He paused. "Safe and sound."

Gounaris chose to get angry. "Are you implying—"

"Nothing at all, Mr. Gounaris. It's just that nothing's happened to you, nothing's happened to him . . . the two principal players. So—nothing to do with her personal life."

"I see," said Gounaris, then added, "Leaving, to your literal policeman's mind, just her professional life." He spread his hands in turn. "There I can't help you, Lieutenant. Moll was an excellent attorney, very independent, so I have very little knowledge of what she was working on at the time of her death. If you—"

"Bed and board strictly separate, as it were," said Dante.

"Strictly." His tone was dry as British toast. "But if you feel it would help in your investigation, Atlas Entertainment would be perfectly willing to put at your disposal any papers she was working on when she was killed."

Meaning the papers would be worthless. "Thank you. I'll have someone pick them up." Dante was on his feet. "You have an appointment in a few moments . . ."

And the brass showed through, as he had hoped it would. When Gounaris spoke again, Dante *knew* he was right that Atlas Entertainment and its president were somehow, someway, dirty.

"You are of Italian blood, are you not, Lieutenant?"

"As they say in Italy, Mr. Gounaris, *Romano di Roma.*"

"That's what I thought. So I wanted to ask you, did you

get into the investigation of organized crime because you are so sickened by the vicious things men of your blood habitually do?"

Dante smiled. "Organized crime is no longer essentially Italian, Mr. Gounaris. Equal opportunity employer. Irishmen, Jews, African-Americans, Latin Americans . . . *Greeks* . . ."

"Just what do you mean by that?" demanded Gounaris quickly, either angry again or faking it again.

Dante would give his fact away, but he would turn it around first. He was suddenly confidential.

"Let me make a suggestion, Mr. Gounaris. You might be wise to stay out of Vince O'Neill's porn palaces for now. I imagine your sex life must be . . . somewhat curtailed since Moll Dalton's death, but even so . . . they're in a pretty rough part of town."

He saw the tiny flicker of alarm mixed with anger in the dark alive eyes, instantly quelled, and spoke even more softly.

"Some unsavory sorts hang around there. Corrupt vice cops under secret investigation by the Internal Affairs Division . . ." He turned from those again-startled eyes, tossing *"Ciao"* over his shoulder as he strode out.

And almost just walked out into the bright San Francisco October sunshine. Instead, thinking about the vile bug juice dispensed at the Hall of Justice, he decided to get a decent decaf at the lobby's tiny afterthought of a coffee shop.

Kosta fretted at his desk for ten minutes, trying to sort out exactly what he had learned and what he had given away. The damn cop was good, all right; he'd needled so skillfully that Kosta had lost it for a moment, had gotten personal.

He strode from the office, curtly telling the surprised Miss Pym that Taylor should go into a holding pattern until he got back. At the lobby pay phone bank he placed a call to Gideon Abramson in Palm Springs, caught him on the links. Gid kept a cellular phone in his golf cart, so the call was transferred direct from the clubhouse.

"Kosta!" he exclaimed in a delighted voice. "So these two married guys are talking, one of 'em says, 'You mean you been married twenty-five years and your wife still looks like a newlywed?' '*Cooks,*' says the other guy in a sad voice, '*cooks* like a newlywed.'"

Kosta was finally able to tell him the latest problem: how he'd been chatting with Jack Lenington the day before, how Will Dalton was safely out of the country, and finally how Stagnaro had visited him that morning.

"I agree with you about Dalton—we can just file him and forget him, he poses no threat," said Gid in his high, chirping voice. "As for Stagnaro, I know him by reputation, he's highly thought of by Rudy Mattaliano in New York, which probably means he's a very dangerous man. But what can he do you?"

"He told me Lenington is under surveillance by the Internal Affairs Division, and wanted me to know they saw him and me going into the same porn place. They didn't see us together, but that's got to be the end of Jack fucking Lenington."

"I agree," said Gid thoughtfully.

"Do we have to tell Mr. Prince?"

"Just that Jack should be eased out." In a more hearty voice, he added, "Be well, Kosta. I'll handle it from here."

Gounaris hung up, feeling better as he always did after he had shifted some dangerous burden to Uncle Gideon, and turned away from the phone.

And stopped dead: sitting in the coffee shop not ten yards away was Dante Stagnaro, smiling and nodding at him like one of those idiotic toy dogs in the rear windows of automobiles.

CHAPTER ELEVEN

It was a week before Jack Lenington had his first—and, as it developed, last—interview with Internal Affairs. In the interim, Dante had been busy. Checking phone company records for long-distance calls from the lobby pay phone bank in the Atlas Entertainment building had turned up three calls to the same country club in Palm Springs, one of them placed the night before Moll Dalton's murder at Bella Figura.

Suggestive but not really indicative, because Tallpalms Country Club had no record of the calls, so of course they could not help with who the calls had been placed to.

Probably not Bob Hope.

Probably not Sonny Bono.

Probably not even Spiro Agnew. There were not as many retired mobsters in Palm Springs as there were in Vegas, but the number was not negligible. And by some strange chance, all of them happened to belong to Tallpalms.

Dante, the eternal optimist, hoped to winnow the possibles for a short list of probables he could work in earnest.

He had also called for everything LAPD might have on Moll's father, Skeffington St. John, who had arranged her employment with Atlas Entertainment. That was just facts, but for himself he kept returning to the question of whether St. John had molested Moll as a child. Quite a heavy accusation for a man as bright as Will Dalton to level at his father-in-law unless there was something more than an intuition to back it up.

He kept wanting to ask Dalton more about it, but Dalton was in Africa: he faxed a request to Interpol for any facts on Gounaris instead. Then there was Lenington, corrupt in all the small ways a vice cop could be corrupt, from shaking down pimps to free sex from the hookers, but Dante hadn't thought of him as involved with organized crime.

Jack was an angry and careful man. All they had was him entering and leaving one of Vince O'Neill's legal porn palaces at about the same time that a man under investigation for possible organized crime ties had entered and left. Not illegal; merely suggestive.

The I.A. lived on that sort of suggestion, but Dante wasn't watching through the one-way glass in the adjoining room when Lenington was brought in by the shooflies; he knew a transcript of the interrogation would be on his desk the next day.

I.A.:	Hello, Jack. Come in and sit down.
SUBJECT:	Hello, Simon, you fucking weasel.
I.A.:	No need to take that attitude, Jack. We're all cops here. Somebody's got to keep the department clean—
SUBJECT:	Yeah, somebody has to look up assholes for a living, too. You don't have to be a cop to do it.
I.A.:	You know this is being recorded, Jack—
SUBJECT:	You gonna edit out all the dirty words afterwards, Irv?
I.A.:	You understand this is just a preliminary investigation, Jack, so we haven't asked you to have your attorney present—
SUBJECT:	What I got to tell you guys, I don't need an attorney.
I.A.:	Okay. On the twenty-second of last month—
SUBJECT:	Uh-uh. Somebody wants to go after me for

<table>
<tr><td></td><td>dereliction of duty or some shit, that's my watch commander or the Chief. Not you ass-holes. You wanta charge me with a crime, my lawyer's here fast as you can jerk each other's wienie. Which leaves you miserable fucks with my bank account, my mortgages, my spendable income.</td></tr>
<tr><td>I.A.:</td><td>We told you, Jack, this is just a prelimi-nary—</td></tr>
<tr><td>SUBJECT:</td><td>I got like thirty-seven cents in my bank ac-count, couple CDs worth one, two K. Mort-gage on the house's got maybe thirteen years to run. My boat, another two years. The car, I paid that off last June. Four years. Neither of my kids are in college—they're working stiffs, I couldn't pay the freight. So fuck you guys very much. Take two nine-millimeter pills up the ass and call me in the morning.</td></tr>
</table>

Sound of slamming door. Dante flipped the transcript onto his desk and chuckled despite himself. He'd been through the academy with Lenington, and knew him as a mean-minded man and a corrupt cop, but he'd also been on the street long enough himself to enjoy seeing the shooflies eat a little shit from another street cop. Lenington didn't deserve the name. But he was tough, it would take a lot to bring him down.

Internal Affairs never did bring Jack Lenington down, or even back in for another shot. Jack knew they'd gone through his personal affairs with a vacuum sweeper, had found nothing because there was nothing to find. When he had gone to the Bahamas to set up his offshore numbered ac-count, he'd done it by a small-plane commuter fight from Fort Lauderdale during a family vacation to Florida. Left the wife and kids—small then—at Disney World believing he was in the Keys angling for bonefish.

The I.A. turncoats didn't worry him. What worried him was that his meeting with Kosta Gounaris must have been under surveillance. The I.A. hadn't had a tail on him, he knew that; but did Stagnaro have a loose tail on Gounaris? Just like the fucker; and he would have tipped I.A. to the meet.

He'd better tell somebody about it, so they wouldn't think *he*'d worn a tail to their meeting. They didn't take kindly to having that sort of dumb fuck on the pad.

So he went to see Otto Kreiger. The I.A. probably knew Kreiger was his lawyer; what they didn't know, what nobody knew, was that Otto Kreiger, through Vince O'Neill, king of the Tenderloin porn dealers, was also his mob contact. O'Neill had obliquely approached Jack, many years ago, about doing a couple of things for a couple of bucks for a couple of guys he knew. Kreiger was one of those guys, and it had grown into a lucrative proposition that carried, however, its own built-in risks.

He felt he was at risk right now.

Kreiger had offices in the old Hunter-Dulin Building at the foot of Sutter Street, an ornate art nouveau cakebox from the 1920s. Kreiger's office was an unpretentious suite with windows looking down on Market Street; a far cry from the fifty acres in Woodside where Lenington knew the attorney raised horses. He didn't know, nor could he have imagined, that Kreiger's cheapest mare, a purebred Arabian, had been a steal at $758,000.

Kreiger had a brutal, booming voice that was extremely effective in court when carping about violations of his mobster clients' civil rights. He used it now on Jack. "I hear you had a little chat with the I.A."

Jack rattled the ice in his bourbon, asked in his angry voice, "Those peep-show machines have fucking mikes in them?"

Kreiger shook his head and chuckled.

"You're not the only man gets an envelope each month, Jack. I appreciate being alerted to the interview, even after the fact, but if you've been reasonably prudent—"

"Woulda looked bad, calling in my lawyer before I'd even had my first interview. I'm not worried about the I.A. It's something else."

"Indeed." Kreiger was a large man with a square face and heavy lips and the coldest eyes with the palest lashes Lenington had ever seen. He interlaced beefy hands in front of him.

Jack said, "I had a meet with a certain guy—"

"I know."

"I think we were clocked in and out." To Kreiger's narrowed eyes, he quickly added, "That's why I had to see you. *I* wasn't followed there—Gounaris was. And—"

"How can you be sure?"

"Jesus, Mr. Kreiger, I been a cop for—"

"Yes. Of course. The wolf knows its own excreta. So your feeling is that Mr. Gounaris was under surveillance."

"Or it was just by accident, but who the fuck knows who he is unless they're already watching him? I got plenty of reason to hang around one of Vince O'Neill's jerk-off shops anytime I want, shit, I'm Vice. But Gounaris is just a john, so why would anyone notice him—"

"Dante Stagnaro," said Kreiger abruptly. There was almost admiration in his voice. "That would be quite like him—a loose tail on the Greek." He nodded. "Yes. Then you going into O'Neill's place at the same time suddenly gets important."

"You know Stagnaro?" asked Lenington cautiously. Frankly, Kreiger scared the hell out of him. A phone call, he was meat. Just like Moll Dalton had become meat after a phone call.

"Not socially, of course." Kreiger waved an arm. "He's that most dangerous of men, an idealist smart enough not to be corrupted by his own obsession. Which is our destruction. He visited Gounaris shortly after you two talked."

"There you are," said Lenington in angry vehemence. He was damned glad he'd come in and told his side of the story. Then he paused, suddenly hesitant. But it had to be said; it was what he was here for. "I wanted to tell you about it, Mr. Kreiger. And I, ah, wanted to ask you . . . there hasn't been . . . I mean, I wouldn't want anyone to think *I* had led . . ."

"I can assure you that your reconstruction makes sense to me," said Kreiger.

"So there's no . . . uh . . . word out that—"

"I can assure you, Jack, none at all."

He was on his feet, moving around the desk. Jack stood up, took the huge callused palm that was offered to him. He spoke as Kreiger put a hand on his shoulder to walk him to the door.

"I mean, if they want me to take an early retirement so the I.A. can't keep—"

Kreiger chuckled to silence his plaint.

"Jack, Jack, quit looking under the bed. I have had absolutely no word about you at all. Everyone feels you have done an excellent job, you handled the matter of that visiting fireman very well indeed, he even remarked on your efficiency. We may not ask anything of you for a while, until this I.A. thing has passed, but don't read anything into that, my friend. Not a rebuke, just a general precaution."

"I was going to suggest the same thing myself, Mr. Kreiger," said Lenington with relief in his angry voice.

When he was gone, Otto Kreiger sat down at his desk and thought for several minutes. In the middle of it he got up and poured himself a schnapps. You could compute the geometry of Jack's revelations in only one of two ways.

So he called Abramson in Palm Springs. Since Gid was having people over, he made Otto wait while he took the call in the den. Kreiger could picture the old kike there among his worldly possessions like one of the Seven Dwarfs in the gem mine. He preferred real wealth. Horses. Clean, outdoors, *manly*.

"So, Otto," chirped Gid's birdlike voice, "why did God make the *goyim*?"

"Why did he?" asked Kreiger in ill-disguised impatience.

"*Somebody* has to buy retail."

Into Gideon's chuckles, Kreiger said heavily, "Abramson, we seem to have been told a conflicting pair of tales in the

Atlas Entertainment matter. You know Mr. Prince does not want that connection made public, so I think we'd better bring the matter to his attention."

When the phone rang, a relaxed and reassured Jack Lenington—going to see the fucking kraut yesterday had been the thing to do, all right—was two-fingering a report while trying to remember if counselor, as in attorney, had one "l" or two. His spelling was atrocious but his reports, when he couldn't get out of writing them, always managed to say what he wanted them to.

He grabbed up the receiver and barked, "Vice, Lenington," into it. And heard for the first time the high-speed, high-pitched delivery of the man who never called himself anything but Burkie.

"My name is Burkie you got something I want sweetheart and I got something you want, cash."

He stopped there as if he had said something significant.

"Yeah, Madonna's got a red-hot snatch I want, too," said Lenington in his angry voice, "but I ain't liable to get it."

He hung up. The phone rang again immediately.

Lenington picked up, snapped, "Vice, Lenington," into it, and the same high-speed high-pitched almost-falsetto almost-fag voice began, "We got cut off I want—"

Lenington hung up on him again. When the phone rang a third time, again immediately, he snatched it off the hook. Some fucking guys never learned.

"Listen, asshole, I—"

"No, asshole, *you* listen," said the voice, sounding suddenly not faggy at all. "Five large just to listen."

This time the man calling himself Burkie hung up.

And then didn't call again. Goddam him! Had he played the guy wrong? Jack already had started to think of those five dimes as *his* five dimes he didn't have to do anything for except just *listen*. But how could he listen if the fuckhead didn't call?

Couple of evenings later, Jack was gunning a few in Liverpool Lil's, a neighborhood pub cattycorner across Lyon from the Presidio gates. It was a dark narrow place with red brick floors and wooden walls covered with photographs, and shiny wineglasses hanging upside down over the bar, and a good steak-and-kidney pie on the menu.

But he was here after making his monthly dual collections—gash and cash, Jack liked to call them—from a discreet high-price call girl who lived just up the street on the Presidio Wall. They'd have a drink, Jack would warn her if anything bad might be coming down, she'd take him home to lay him and pay him.

"Hey, Jack," said the bartender, "telephone for you."

Even though off duty, Jack had conscientiously left the number with Dispatch. Never knew when one of his other little arrangements might need servicing.

"Lenington," he said in his hard, angry voice.

"Jack-baby—Burkie!" Then the familiar high-speed delivery began. "That secondhand store fronts a treasury book on Mission off Fifth near the old Remedial Loans around the corner from the Mint in the phone booth one hour."

Dial tone.

Five large, just to listen. Against that, a setup. The mob? The kraut had assured him he had a plus ledger with them for his efficient handling of his part in the Moll Dalton hit.

The IAD? He takes the phone call in the booth, he gets five large, the bills are black-light or paint pellet, the numbers recorded, dirty money, he's on his way to the slam. Trouble with that scenario, obvious entrapment by Internal Affairs. With the kraut as his attorney he would walk away laughing, and they'd know it.

Stagnaro?

For it being him, he was a sly fucking fox, Jack had been through the academy with him and never met one slyer. Maybe he wanted to catch Jack dirty, force him to roll over on Gounaris, or worse, the mob. And the tidbit about the treasury book in the secondhand store would fit Stagnaro. Guy got around. Shit, even Jack hadn't known about that one, or he would have been leaning on the guy himself. Right around the corner from the fucking Mint! Somebody had some balls. Or a sense of humor.

Against it being Stagnaro? Much as Jack hated to admit it, he wasn't that kind of cop in the first place, and was a hell of a lot brighter than the IAD in the second place, which made him too bright to try that sort of cheap shit in the third place.

So who did that leave who might be trying to get something on him? And meanwhile, seventeen of Jack's sixty minutes had evaporated.

Should he go there or not?

CHAPTER TWELVE

Fifty-nine minutes after Burkie's call, Jack Lenington was leaning against the wall of the secondhand store on Mission Street, arms folded, the width of the sidewalk away from the phone booth. At 11:00 P.M. there wasn't much foot traffic, only a few cars. As his second hand hit twelve, the phone rang. Lenington got it on the second ring.

"Yeah."

The same rapid-fire high-pitched voice. "What you listen to is this phone ringing every night at eleven o'clock don't pick up unless it stops ringing and then starts again then pick up on the third ring and answer like you did tonight."

"What will you want to know?"

"I'll ask specific questions about Stagnaro's investigation when I have them to ask and when I do you get ten large if you can answer them or not."

This guy was really fucking desperate, thought Jack. He started, "Do you know . . ." then stopped. He'd been about to use the kraut's name, for Chrissake! "You said something about—"

"Oldest gag in the book, envelope under the phone tray."

Buzz.

Jack looked around as his hand found the envelope, his fingers felt around it for wires. Nothing. Just masking tape to hold it to the metal.

Nobody coming by right at the second except the goddamnedest white nigger you ever saw. Everything was black except his face, and sixties black at that! Fucking dreadlocks down to his ass, stacked heels made him six inches taller, floppy wool green, white, and purple beret, one of those vari-colored robes, dashiki or some shit, shades, bopping down the street with a cellular phone pressed to his face.

"My man!" he was shrieking in a high skinny black voice as he went by, "the key is G sharp and the beat is dum-dum-dum-dee-dee-dum-dum-dum . . ."

He was gone in a cloud of reefer, and Jack had his envelope in hand, into his pocket, was walking away from there.

Jack did everything to the envelope except zap it with X rays, but he couldn't find anything suggesting a letter bomb. Finally he put it in a pail of water in his postage-stamp back-yard overnight. Next morning the manila envelope had disintegrated and the pail was full of soaking greenbacks. A few hundreds, a dozen fifties, the rest twenties, none new, none consecutive. No dye. Wearing gloves, he dried them out with his wife's hair dryer, took them to Hymie the Handler at the Crime Lab as evidence in a case. Hymie loved to handle evidence of any sort from any source, hence his nickname.

"I want you to subject these to every fucking scrutiny known to man and have them ready for me this afternoon."

Hymie was a hairy bear of a man in his mid-thirties, muscular and handsome if you liked hebes, not at all like his name. He looked mildly astounded that Jack finally had brought him some evidence, any evidence, of anything whatsoever.

"And for Chrissake keep it under your hat, Hymie. I don't want *anyone* to know about these bills except you and me."

"For you, Jack, anything," he said wryly. "I'll even give away my lunch hour to commemorate the day Jack Lenington actually brought in evidence to be analyzed. Must be your first bust, huh, Jack? Congratulations!"

"Go to hell" was Jack's only comment, so mild because Hymie was, after all, doing him a favor.

The bills were clean as Christ's conscience.

That afternoon at 3:00 P.M. he mailed them off to the Bahamas, the zip code of the phony return address his account number instead of 94122, and that night at 11:00 he was back in the phone booth ready for more of them. What he knew about Stagnaro's investigation you could cram up a gnat's ass, but if Burkie had specific questions maybe he could find out . . .

The phone rang, went silent, didn't ring again. Just as well, too many people going by on the sidewalk, made him nervous. So he scanned everybody, damned carefully. No familiar faces. No easy place for a shotgun mike to be set up, record whatever he said, either; but just the same he'd request a face-to-face on *his* turf if he had any information to give when the time came.

Next night, the same. Nice thing was, he was only at the phone for like twenty seconds. Minimum exposure.

On the fourth night there were no pedestrians on the street at all except the white nigger, who came bopping up as Jack waited out the preliminary rings. This time the beret was cherry red, otherwise he still had his splayfoot nigger walk, his stacked heels, his dashiki, his smell of grass, his cellular phone. Guy sure did a nigger good. Maybe he was a mulatto, not a white man at all.

The phone rang. As Jack turned back to it, the white nigger brought out of the sleeve of his dashiki an already-cocked short-barreled revolver, a .357 Magnum loaded with 125-grain hollow points and wrapped in a plastic supermarket bag. He pressed the muzzle against the back of Jack's head and blew Jack's brains all over the inside of the booth and beyond.

The assassin shook the gun out into the gutter, retaining his fingerprints only on the plastic bag, and kept on bopping. The first pedestrian by lost her dinner and the first black-and-white pulled up four minutes later, but the assassin was boarding a bus for the Outer Mission by then.

At three minutes before midnight, Raptor, his bebop persona safely stuffed into a Salvation Army bin in a Safeway lot a few blocks away, walked into the all-night Standard station on Army Street. It was a clean, sharp night, crisp as a new-crop Gravenstein. His gloved hands laid a fan of five twenties with a note clipped to them on top of the pump. The bills bulged the eyes of the night man, a husky African-American kid of seventeen. The note was typed, all in caps.

I WANT YOU TO MAKE ONE MORE PHONE CALL. YOU WILL GET AN ANSWERING MACHINE OR A MAN'S VOICE. EITHER WAY, JUST SAY THE WORDS ON THE BACK OF THIS INTO THE PHONE AND HANG UP.

Dante didn't monitor the answering machine down in the living room overnight because duty calls always were buzzed through on his beeper. But he was never a heavy sleeper when involved in a complex case, so the midnight ringing downstairs had jarred him awake and kept the rest of his night fitful. He was up at six, slurping instant and wandering through the house as he waited for the *Chronicle* to thump against the front door. The machine's blinking green light reminded him of the call.

He ran the tape back, listened to it. The voice was husky but immature, obviously black or faking it, nervous and hesitant. As if reading the words when reading came hard.

"Uh—this is Raptor. Uh—I gave the, uh, gentleman the message. It, uh, really blew his mind."

Raptor! A Raptor had called in a comic German accent after Moll Dalton had died. And Dante had erased the tape . . . He listened to this new one again, then ran the tape back and removed it and put in a fresh one—which he should have done with the first Raptor message, even though he was sure the hit had been made by Ucelli. But Ucelli didn't leave cute messages on cops' answering machines. Eddie delivered the mail and got out of town.

Even though he hadn't told Tim, hadn't told *anyone* about that first erased Raptor message—a crank call, right?—he wasn't going to make the same mistake twice. Not even if he now had *two* crank calls. He'd go see Hymie the Handler.

At six-thirty in the morning the drive in to the Hall of Justice from North Beach was an easy one. It was not even seven when he went up the wide concrete steps of the Hall, winked at the fat black cop manning (womaning? personing?) the metal-check monitor, and crossed the lobby to the elevator bank.

Just before the doors started to close, two black hookers and a pudgy white lawyer with garbage eyes got on. The hookers wore stretch body stockings, one black, one white lace, the lawyer a suit off the rack at Mervyn's, a purple tie with BAM! WHAM! and ZOWIE! on it in neon-red letters. Purple and red. Dynamite.

"Where's Marlene been keeping herself?" he asked.

"She broke her foot," said the short wide hooker.

"Yeah, I know how, too," the lawyer said sadly. "Kicking her attorney in the nuts."

"Wouldn't break no foot that way, Clyde," said the taller of the women with an exaggerated slap on his arm. "Squirrel run up a lawyer's leg, he'd starve to death fo sure! Kick a lawyer in the heart, *that'd* break a girl's foot. Great big rock, a lawyer's heart."

Both girls were giggling as the threesome got off at the court floor where the Organized Crime Task Force had its makeshift office. Dante stayed on, got off at four. He went down the hall and around the corner to a plain wooden door with CRIME LAB on it. Inside, a mild-faced overweight man in chinos and a plaid lumberjack shirt nodded from behind the desk.

"Dante."

"Norb. Hymie in yet?"

"Got here a little before six." Norbert, who was thick and slow and hefty, talked exactly like the lean and snaky movie actor Bruce Dern, even to the timbre of the voice, but was totally unaware of it because he never went to movies and didn't own a TV. "And Tom said the guy left after midnight last night. Glad *I* ain't Hymie's old lady."

"So's Hymie," said Dante as he was buzzed through the waist-high gate.

He started down the interior corridor, then turned back to shut the door of the room where all the dope confiscated from dealers was stashed. He shook his head in mock disapproval.

"Norb! What if Al Fatah or somebody stormed the building and came busting in here—"

"Fuck 'em, Lou. Let 'em have it."

They both laughed and Dante went on down the corridor past the deserted forensics rooms. In the open doorway of one lab was a shopping cart full of confiscated semiautomatic weapons, some with scopes, others with banana clips, all flat black in color and heaped in the cart like cordwood. He crossed another hallway to the larger lab where forensic chemists analyzed fibers, cloth, dust, hair, semen, and the like after the fact of murder.

Hymie the Handler, in white smock and thin physician's gloves, was alone at a counter halfway down the room, snipping fibers off a stained automobile floormat. He looked up to grin at Dante coming down the deserted laboratory toward him.

"If these fibers match those caught in the panty hose of the dead woman, my dear Dupin, Mme Guillotine shall drink the blood of another murderer."

"I think on the contrary, my dear Watson, they shall prove to be the hairs of a monstrous hound."

"*These* hairs?" demanded Hymie in apparent astonishment.

"No, I refer to what you have mistaken for the panty hose of the murdered woman. I said *monstrous*."

Hymie laughed and put the hairs he had clipped on a slide, put another slide over it, laid it on the counter and stripped off his rubber gloves, began moving toward the back of the lab.

"Coffee?"

"Unless it's from the stomach of a corpse."

"This is the Crime Lab, not the Coroner's Office."

They sat in straight chairs on either side of a table that held a Mr. Coffee, cups, spoons, sugar and Equal, Pream. At this time of day the lab smelled rather pleasantly like Dante's high school chem lab where he had once blown up some peanut brittle made with something besides baking soda, he couldn't remember what it had been. Miss Tchinin had been furious . . .

"What would you substitute for baking soda in peanut brittle that would make it explode when you broke it?"

"Why ask me, I just work here." Hymie's intelligent black eyes sought Dante's, and he sighed. "Okay, hit me."

Dante laid the answering machine tape on the table.

"I need the call on this tape voice-printed."

"Sound-spectrographed," corrected Hymie automatically. "You have anything to match it with?"

"Not yet. I hope never."

Interest sparked the dark eyes. "A call from a killer?"

"Or a hoax. Could you just file both the tape and the voice print here so I don't have to worry about them?"

"Sure. What name for the file?"

"RAPTOR. And could you not mention this to anyone else?"

"You and Jack Lenington," mused Hymie as he dug out an accordion file folder. Dante, who had started to turn away, stopped abruptly.

"What do you mean by that?"

"Three, four days ago Jack brought in five K in old, small-denomination, unsequenced bills for analysis for black light, impermeable dyes, like that. Said it was evidence, asked I didn't tell anybody about it. But since the guy's dead—"

"Dead?"

"Yeah, last night, eleven P.M., a phone booth on Mission Street. Somebody blew his face off with a .357 Magnum. Looked professional—no prints, the gun immediately dropped in the gutter. Funny thing, it had been sprayed with Armor All—"

"Jesus Christ," exclaimed Dante under his breath.

Uh—this is Raptor. Uh—I gave the, uh, gentleman the message. It, uh, really blew his mind.

Dante laid a hand on the bearlike technician's arm, then laid a finger to his lips. "Hymie, my lips to your ear only on this phone tape, okay?"

"Sure," said Hymie. When Dante was gone, he added, "Interesting," to the tape in his hands, and starting making up the RAPTOR folder. That was it: he had the most interesting job in the Hall of Justice.

CHAPTER THIRTEEN

It wasn't until three mornings later, after Lenington's departmental funeral, that Dante finally went to see Tim Flanagan about the case. He'd had to organize his thoughts first, uneasy thoughts about Lenington's execution inspired by the second Raptor phone call.

The call had come in before the media'd gotten hold of Lenington's death—he'd checked. If it was genuine, did that mean Eddie Ucelli hadn't hit *either* Lenington or Moll Dalton? Could he ask the Feebs about their phone taps on Ucelli again? Whoever had hired Eddie could be a nutcake, leaving phone messages for Dante once he was sure Eddie had made the hit. And so many of the characteristics of Moll Dalton's murder had fit the Popgun's M.O. . . .

Or what if Tim had been right all along—that it was some psycho Will Dalton had hired to kill his wife? And what if Dalton had set up a second murder for when he was out of the country with a perfect alibi, just to confuse the issue?

Dante hadn't told Tim, hadn't told *anyone* about the first erased message from Raptor because he'd thought it was just a crank call. How could he now tell Tim about this second? But maybe he could pick Tim's brains about the Lenington hit.

Only Tim wasn't too cooperative; besides Lenington, he had a gambling murder of a small boy in the Vietnamese community—probably to show someone that someone else meant business—and a hotel arson fire in which two pensioners had died. So, the best defense being a preemptive strike, Dante asked Tim why he hadn't been memoed on the Lenington investigation.

"Why would I think you'd be interested in a corrupt vice cop getting gunned down?" asked Flanagan patiently.

They were on either side of his desk in Homicide. The desk was as messy as Tim was, which was very messy indeed. Dante shoved aside enough paperwork, empty coffee cups, report forms, pizza boxes and doughnut bags to make room for an elbow.

"He was observed having a meeting with Gounaris, that's why you should have thought I'd be interested."

"Now, you see, I didn't know that," said Flanagan mildly. He took a big bite of sugar doughnut, spilled white sugar down his tie. The tie looked as if it had been used to mop up soup.

"You didn't know that because I didn't tell you about it."

"Not surprising I didn't know." He brightened. "Besides, I doubt it has anything to do with this case you don't have. What I hear, they're gonna proclaim Hooker's Holiday in the Tenderloin, everybody half-price for a day in honor of Jack's passing. The pimps figure their net'll go up 10 percent without good old Jack there to take his cut off the top."

Dante's elbow slipped off the desk, and he demanded irritably, "Couldn't you stack a little more shit on this desk?"

Flanagan leaned back in his swivel chair and on the corner stacked his size 13 shoes, one on top of the other.

"How's that?" he asked sweetly.

There was little sweet about the phone conversation going on at the same time between Kosta Gounaris and Gideon Abramson.

"Mr. Prince is *very* upset, Kosta, and for once I have to agree with him."

"Mr. Prince is upset?" demanded Kosta. "What about me? I thought we said nothing would—"

Gid, talking at the same time, was saying, "When you said that was the end of Jack Lenington, I didn't think—"

"Wait a minute, are you saying—"

"Of course. Are you trying to tell me . . ."

They both fell silent at the same moment. Then Gideon said precisely, "You're telling me you had nothing to do with Jack Lenington."

"I am. And you're telling me Mr. Prince didn't either."

"He did not." There was another long silence on both ends of the line with the scramblers on either end. Then Gideon added, "At least not through me."

"Do you think he went around you?" asked Kosta. He was pleased he was able to make his voice sound as though a little icy finger had just been run down his spine.

"Ummm . . . no. He would have no reason to do that." Positive now. "No. I think definitely not."

"Then who *did* order it?" asked Kosta.

"And who would dare to carry it out?" mused Gideon.

"It might have been Clint Eastwood," said Flanagan, his shoes still on the corner of the desk but a frustrated look on his face. "This *was* a .357 Magnum. But I still prefer some badass from the Tenderloin that Dalton paid before he left."

"You've got Dalton on the brain," said Dante quickly. Because he'd had the same unwelcome thought himself since the second Raptor call, he wanted to argue Tim out of it. "First of all, there's no way he could know about Lenington being associated with Gounaris, and second—"

"Remember *your* favorite theory, chief? That his wife mailed him something that contained clues about what she was involved in that then got her killed?" He reached for the final doughnut, this one jelly-filled. Dante hadn't eaten any of them. "What if she did, and Lenington's name was there?"

"He still would have hired the hitter to take out Gounaris, not somebody on the fringes like Jack Lenington." Dante leaned across the desk as much as its littered surface would permit. "He didn't think *Lenington* had been sleeping with his wife."

"Never can tell—she sounded like the town pump to me."

But Dante had convinced himself by now: for Dalton as mastermind to work, it would have been Gounaris who had been killed. Back to square one. Popgun.

"I think it was Popgun Ucelli on behalf of somebody in the mob. Even the same M.O.—a shot to the head."

"Sure," sneered Tim. "Her in the face, Jack in the back of the skull. A .22 and a .357 Magnum respectively. Her twice, him once. Her in a crowded bar, him on a deserted street." He gave his big braying laugh. "Identical."

"Close enough," insisted Dante.

"Maybe it was Dalton *himself* both times," said Flanagan doggedly. "Did her, left, sneaked back into the country . . ."

Dante was sick of that game. He dug around in his pocket for his notebook, found his page, threw it open across the desk to Flanagan.

"There's his contact number in Nairobi—the Kenya National Museum. I don't know what the time difference is, but maybe you can catch him there."

"I thought he's supposed to be buried deep in the bush."

"He was going to be in Nairobi for a month doing studies at the museum before he left." He baited Flanagan some more. "Worth a try maybe, huh, Tim?"

And damned if Flanagan, with that same dogged look, didn't take him up on it! He direct-dialed, with country and city code, and got the museum as easily as calling his wife out in the Avenues. He winked at Dante as he put it on speakerphone.

"Do you have a Will Dalton there at the museum?"

The crisp African voice, whose English had a lilting singsong and the elongated vowels of East Africa, said, "Dr. Dalton? I believe I just saw . . ." The voice receded. "Dr. Dalton?"

As Will started across the glass-walled lobby of the museum, the pert African receptionist began waving a hand at him. She had the telephone in her other hand. Through the tall floor-to-ceiling windows he could see the hot bright African sunlight outside. Inside the modern museum building, it was dim and cool.

"You have a telephone call . . ." As Will came up, she added into the phone, "Caught him on his way out. He's been reviewing some of the Koobi Fora data . . ."

"Who is it, Miranda?" Will asked as he took the phone.

She shrugged. "Not British."

"Will Dalton here," he said into the phone in the British manner. There was a very long silence on the other end. Then Dante Stagnaro's unmistakable voice came bouncing down from a communications satellite a thousand miles above.

"Dr. Dalton, this is Dante Stagnaro in San Francisco. You've just struck Tim Flanagan dumb."

"You got him!" exclaimed Will in a voice full of reprieve.

"The . . . Oh. No." Genuine regret came over the wire. "I'm sorry. We . . . There's been another murder . . ."

"Gounaris?" demanded Will in a hopeful voice.

"No. A policeman named—"

In a flash of insight, Will interrupted, "And you thought I wouldn't be here. You thought—"

"Did you know a San Francisco vice cop named Jack Lenington?" Flanagan's voice had the hollowness of tone peculiar to cheap speakerphones.

"No." His voice was angry now. "What does this have to do with . . . with my loss?"

"Nothin'," said Flanagan bluntly. "Not in my book."

Will stood there in the cool dim museum by the reception desk, dressed in safari gear, a pained look on his face, trying to decide what he wanted to say. He finally burst out, "Goddam you people, I'm leaving for Fort Portal in the morning, I'm trying to get beyond . . ."

He slammed down the phone, stood beside Miranda's desk, breathing deeply, almost panting, as if he had been running. She started to raise a hand to touch his arm, then let it drop to her desk again. He found a small smile and a wry shrug for her.

"All the way from San Francisco," he said.

"Where little cable cars reach halfway to the stars," she said in her lilting voice, as if anxious to help him from his black mood. "Is there anything I can . . ."

"No, thank you. Just . . . policemen having silly ideas."

"Policemen usually do," she said precisely.

He shook hands with her formally in the British way and went out of the museum. Mirinda stared after him with brown wounded eyes full of unprofessional thoughts about the rugged, handsome widower. Since she had never met Mrs. Dalton, she had felt no urge to grieve when she learned of her death.

Outside, Will unlocked his beat-up old Land-Rover on the museum tarmac parking lot, hoping that phone call was the end of it. Maybe now they would let him get to Fort Portal, then off into the rain forest, and would forget all about him so he could get to work in earnest. All he wanted was to do his work.

And start forgetting. Maybe then the nightmares would start to ease up. He didn't really believe they would, but all he could do was immerse himself in his work and . . . hope.

It would be so good to sleep without bad dreams . . .

"Got all the egg off your face, Tim?" Dante asked in an overly solicitous voice.

"Get the fuck outta here, lemme work."

"Maybe I can find a map of East Africa around here somewhere, you can look up Fort Portal, find out what country it's in. Maybe they'll have a store there or something along the road that has a telephone, you can call them up and ask them to have somebody stand in the doorway with the phone in his hand for the next few days, see if Dalton happens by—"

"Okay, okay, go fuck yourself, chief."

He began ostentatiously burrowing into the paperwork that

littered his desk. Dante dropped a final comment on his way out.

"I think you owe me another beer on bowling night."

It was the measure of Flanagan's demoralization that he didn't even argue the point. But back in his own office on the court floor of the Hall, Dante stewed and stewed, and then, realizing he should have done it earlier, spent the rest of the day calling all airlines for the name of Will Dalton on any passenger list in or out of Nairobi during the past week.

Nothing. The name was on no manifest. So, finally, he could let Dalton go out into the rain forests with his chimps for good, and start trying to make sense of the Lenington hit.

Which actually made almost too much sense.

Lenington is all but seen conferring with Gounaris and is hauled up to I.A. at Dante's instigation. Dante tells Gounaris about it—and almost immediately, Lenington is whacked.

What didn't make any sense at all was the obscure game being played by the man who called himself Raptor, and what he could possibly have had to do with the two killings.

PART THREE

Late Devonian

362 m.y. ago

A man is the sum of his ancestors;
to reform him you must begin with a dead ape
and work downward through a million graves.

Ambrose Bierce

CHAPTER FOURTEEN

Dread naught, devoted fans, it is I, Peregrine Raptor, Esq., that extraordinary assassin, that bird of prey, that sardonic quipper of quips, who made strawberry yogurt of the Lenington brainpan and arranged the call to Stagnaro about it afterwards. Why does that silly policeman have so much trouble accepting me? Well, it is early days yet. Perhaps he has not had time to fully appreciate what a grand killing machine I really am.

But enough of that. I want to chat about the Lenington kill with you, *hypocrite lecteur,* because in his murder I was faced with a problem of great delicacy and finesse: how does one get close enough to fog a veteran police officer who is also wary and thoroughly corrupt?

What difference does the corruption make? Aha, that is what gives him his extraordinary wariness. By being always on the watch for someone watching him, he becomes as difficult to track as a man-eating tiger that out of sheer animal instinct loops back to check its own backtrail.

I turn to my advantage the fact that I can only observe him from afar, can only, as it were, touch his life as lightly as the most gossamer of spiderwebs. Thus I arouse no slightest fear in him of the hunted for the hunter, because he is unaware of any hunter behind him. Also, this way I am able to see him in the round. The whole man.

Who is this whole man I see? Someone vicious. Someone

sexually corrupt. Someone consumed with money hunger. Someone racially prejudiced. Someone cocky. And angry. Oh, so angry. Why? I soon figure it out. Because life has screwed him. Yes, *semblable, frère,* he is *owed* the good life.

Having penetrated his psychology, I begin my stalk. He aids me by being observed in his meeting with Gounaris. This brings great pressure on him. I myself watch him go to the attorney appointed for him by the Family—he must be thinking, Will they blame me? Should I run and hide? So he is subconsciously attuned to a quick-getaway stake; a stake he would otherwise examine much more carefully from the outset.

I assume a breathless style of speech with a disarming homosexual cadence when I call him, talk wildly of $5,000, to get which he needs do nothing except listen, then I hang up. This arouses all of his cupidity and only a minimum of his cunning—and by leaving him stew for a few days, I assure that he will come to feel the money is already his. It is *owed* to him, just as the good life is owed to him!

See his anger work for me? And then I give him a sudden short deadline to get this money he deems to be rightfully his.

Ah, the moment of truth. Has the wind shifted, has the tiger caught scent of the hunter sitting up over the staked-out goat? No. He goes to await my call at an open phone near an apocryphal bookie joint on one of San Francisco's major streets.

Safety, you see. How can he feel anything but safe there, with no easily apparent ambushes from which he can be stalked? And with the subconscious assurance that an illegal book is operating there with impunity, thus implying like immunity for his own illegal bribe-taking?

I use a cellular phone so I can walk by him as he takes the $5,000 bait, after I have given him silly instructions of how to get $10,000 more, and perhaps another $10,000, and another . . .

Thus I can see how he stands at the phone, can monitor

pedestrian traffic up and down the street. And I can do it in total safety, because I am invisible to him.

Invisible? How can this be when I am made up in the most bizarrely eye-catching charade possible? Because he sees me only as a white man trying to be black—thus, beneath contempt, beneath notice, because black is the last thing this violently prejudiced man would want to be.

Thus, invisible.

Each night as I walk by, waiting for that moment when no other pedestrian is about so I can do my delicious deed, the boy at the all-night gas station on Army Street is placing the 11:00 P.M. call to that phone booth, letting it ring, and hanging up, touchingly delighted to get $20 each time he dials. And after Jackie-boy is no more, even more delighted to get the $100 bonus to call Stagnaro and relay my little Raptor message. Of course I get back my note from him and destroy it.

Why this slightly cumbersome charade? Because this way I leave Stagnaro my Raptor call in a voice he can never connect to me through voiceprints should he ever get one of mine. I doubt he taped the first one, which was me; why would he? At that time it was merely an isolated crank call. Am I not clever?

In closing I must tell you, since my promise is to be honest with you, that I am surprised by a rather rotten dream the night I kill Jack Lenington. I am Pharaoh's executioner in ancient Egypt, I have died, and my *maat* (the orderliness and justice of my life) is being weighed in judgment by Osiris in Dat, the Egyptian underworld. Found just, I will be given eternal life. Found lacking, I will be forever dead.

All of my deeds, I argue, were from the noblest of motives. Ordered from on high. But to my terror the scale in which I am being measured tips heavily against me. How can this be?

Mighty Anubis says sadly, "You are self-righteous, O falcon-man. All of the horrors you perpetrate are for the highest of motives. But these are really the basest of motives. Selfishness, self-aggrandizement through being 'noble' at all times. This way you can justify any action, no matter how base. Go to eternal death, O falcon-man."

As I fade into nothingness I wake from my dream with sweat standing on my brow. What can this mean? Bah! Humbug! It is only some ploy of my little brown walnut of a man, my gnome, my Rumpelstiltskin who crouches down at the hinge of my subconscious and denies me access to . . .

Enough of that nonsense! My fitful sleep since Lenington's death will pass when I begin plotting the next assassination. The next one. Ah, *that* will require time, cleverness, dissimulation. I must locate, then plan, then stalk . . .

But I am getting ahead of myself again. Behind myself? This playing with time can be so confusing. So can playing God, but—no matter. It is what I do. While there is yet time, let us listen to more sentimentalized drivel about man's capacity for violence from poor Will—if he would ever get to the bloody *point* of it all . . .

CHAPTER FIFTEEN

Will Dalton said, "So, in sum, I will be speaking as much from speculation as from observation, as much from surmise as from scientific thesis. I will be radically interpreting many facts already in evidence, which might not be too acceptable to many brilliant and knowledgeable colleagues in the audience; *mea culpa* in advance, ladies and gentlemen.

"Ironically, it is science that is starting to bring us back from the edge of the pit it dug for us, trying to return us to an ordered view of our universe and our place in it.

"Most of us here are 'historical' scientists concerned with classification of ancient, already-extinct species, rather than experimentation, thus have never been guilty of misusing Nature or trying to take man outside his rightful place in the universe. Paleontologists try to understand what Nature has already done, not try to change what she is doing currently. So we don't need power, we need sturdy knees, sharp eyes, nimble fingers, and much more generous grants than we currently get.

"Recently, theoretical subatomic physics has joined us by shifting ground from materialism to idealism, by hinting we can almost do without this material world, since it is just a by-blow of energy. Quite different from scientism's 'matter in motion' theorem, and surprisingly close to the ancient animism modern materialist man rejected long ago—the animism which says everything that exists has the wind of life blowing through it.

"Wind of Life. Energy. The ancient Greek concept of *pneuma*. Not really much to choose among them, is there?

"At the same time, biologists and ecologists are now telling us there are limitations built right into the cosmos concerning how much we can misuse and how badly we can mistreat Nature. Because we are destroying the ecosphere, the shadow of that nonbeing science thought it had banished five centuries ago now looms over us again with empirical evidence to back it up. And the ancient word 'pollution' is being used again in its original religious sense by—science.

"To every primitive culture known, pollution means the same thing: the bad breath of God striking man. *Pneuma* on a bad day, perhaps. Infection, contagion that requires quarantine, ritual cleansing, purification of anyone exposed to it. Which is what modern science says about our modern pollutions, be they toxic waste, corrupted water supplies, AIDS, or the numerous other infections plaguing mankind with their deadly presence.

"Can we count on science to handle our modern pollutions? Unfortunately, no. Through no fault of its own, it isn't up to the job. We cry to science, 'Author! Author!' but we are shouting in an empty theater. We demand a lineage, a legitimacy to answer ethical and moral questions about our place in nature. We demand solutions to our problems, but science can't tell us what to do because it can't tell us who we are, where we came from, or where we are going. *It doesn't know*. It was never designed to know.

"Leaving us who, exactly, to legitimize our existence? Nature? Science, walking in religion's footsteps, has demythologized Nature, robbed her of reverence, treated her as a blind whore who will spread her legs for any passerby. The great religions? God, not Nature, is their measure. Science itself? Science's mosaic shows *us* as the measure of things, because we are the creature, quite literally, who can measure them.

"Since this is hubris so horrific it sets the teeth on edge, we realize we need a very different kind of knowledge from that which science offers us, a knowledge that cannot uncover scientific facts but *can* uncover their meaning. Because science has a hard time with the beginning of our story. With beginnings in general. With the intersection of the known and the unknown. With the moment of being or of nonbeing.

"What scares science is the idea that *something* begins only where *nothing* ends. Science can't start its stories with 'In the beginning' because, being experimental, it can't admit to a time when there was nothing material upon which to experiment.

"But myth's stories start with 'Once upon a time.' Myth *needs* to know what happened 'in the beginning,' because primitive man always needed the gods' permission to tell our story. And he needed a *place* to tell it, some particular time and space that had to be consecrated for this purpose. Outside this holy place was chaos in which to wander was to die.

"It is this, finally, that marks the difference between myth and science, 'fiction' and 'fact.' Science banished 'nonbeing' five hundred years ago and only recently had to reinstate it. We don't have a pantheon of gods to tell us about nonbeing any more, but we do have 'fiction'—which concerns itself with the shadow of nonbeing. To think about death is to think about what is there and is not there.

"Science doesn't know, doesn't care, about things that might not be there. *Can't* know or care, because science deals only in 'facts.' It *must* fail in this endeavor, because facts can't tell us how or where to begin or end. Yet having a beginning and an end tells us we are alive. It takes the poet to point that out to us. The philosopher. The mythmaker. The purveyor of fictions.

"Robert Ardrey, all of the above, used science's facts to show that by Precambrian times there was life, but there was not death. Not as we know it. Organisms were immortal in the sense that they merely divided. They were alive but they didn't know they were alive, and life seemed set to go on this way forever.

"But Nature was also using what Stephen Jay Gould calls

contingency, a two-tined fork of accident and chance. Accidents of variation—sometimes the two sides of a newly divided ameba did not exactly mirror one another—and accidents of chance. Meaning, here, mutation. Mutation, that always sudden, always unforeseen, sometimes radical differentiation of an organism from its parent. A change that is inheritable.

"Sometime during this ongoing process, some mutation by some organism introduced the capacity to reproduce rather than merely divide. With reproduction, the individual became possible. As Ardrey says, the hen no longer needed to split in two, she could lay an egg. An individual egg.

"With the individual egg came the possibility of variation. Infinite variation. Infinite selection. And . . . infinite death. By choosing evaluation, life chose death. Only with death came the consciousness that we are alive, and, for man and probably many other animals, the consciousness of death. With *that* understanding came everything that self-aware beings think of as life. It's scary, but only death gives life value and meaning.

"When did all of this happen? The geological demarcation about 570 million years ago between the Precambrian and the Paleozoic eras marks what is called 'the Cambrian explosion'—the first appearance in the fossil record of multicellular animals with hard as well as soft tissue. The Burgess shales, named after fine-sand fossil beds in western Canada that preserved soft-bodied fossils in exquisite detail, date from about 40 million years after that. Too soon for 'the relentless motor of extinction,' as Gould puts it, to have eradicated very many of those new multicellular species.

"The Burgess shales suddenly make the idea of man as the measure of all things silly indeed. This unparalleled fossil record of soft-bodied sea creatures destroys any illusions we might still cling to that evolution is a stately progression of life from simple to complex structures to that unbelievable apex—*Homo sapiens*. Chance, not design, rules.

"This is Gould's *contingency*—which borders on the chaos theory of the subatomic physicists. Had the weather been a bit different in the Precambrian . . . had a certain dragonfly not died in the Mesozoic . . . The point is that the species which survived the Cambrian's catastrophic extinction—species without whose survival we could not have occurred—was no more fitted to survive than hundreds of other primitive species that didn't.

"Wild, wonderful species such as *opabinia, anomalocaris, aysheaia, waptia,* and *hallucigenea* died out, and their fossils were persistently misclassified as early versions of phyla that did make it through: trilobites, brachiopod crustaceans, sea cucumbers, polychaete worms, jellyfish. Because no one, not even scientists, wanted to admit we came into being only by chance.

"What does this leave us with? Despair? To find meaning, must we shut down our minds and posit some sexist patriarch in a long white beard who created all of this in six twenty-four-hour days, then kicked back with a burger and brewski on the seventh?

"Gould regards the whole process of contingency with breathless wonder at its beauty. He feels the same moral responsibilities he would if he believed that God or a pantheon of gods and goddesses had planned it all. Here we are, after all, all sensibilities intact, even if by blind chance.

"Probably no one in this room believes that evolution, or creation, or both, occurred just to place us at the center of the universe. The fact that we have lived on an insignificant piece of dust circling a minor star in an inconsequential solar system for not even a single tick of the clock of life is not our central concern. But we are here, we are *somebody,* we mean *something,* and who we have been is important at least to us.

"I have gotten ahead of myself with the Burgess shales, but they do set the stage for a short review of life's earliest beginnings, before the carnage starts in this room . . ."

Carnage in this room. Jesus, thought Dante's policeman's mind, he did come back to the States knowing a hitman was waiting for him! Dante had to . . .

Then he almost blushed. Dalton's carnage was the expected rejection of the audience to many of his theories of man's origins and nature, not a fear that a hitman named Raptor was going to whip out a big pistol and start blazing away at someone unexpected.

CHAPTER SIXTEEN

Skeffington St. John was nursing a massive depression in his posh Century City office—temperature-controlled, furnished with antiques—careless shoes up on one corner of the hand-polished mahogany desk. Two hundred coats of the thinnest of oils, each hand-rubbed into the wood until it glowed like distant fires reflected in still water.

Outside, L.A. was being washed away by the pineapple express. This particular sort of storm system is created when a strong winter low born in the Gulf of Alaska dervish-swirls off the coast of Washington State to drag warm, waterlogged clouds up from the tropical Pacific. It explodes over Southern California, the L.A. storm drains overflow, electric power shorts out, and million-dollar houses slide off their hillside stilts to end up as kindling on the canyon floors below.

But here, high in his ark above the raging waters, St. John suffered at a perfect 72 degrees F. He looked more like a film idol than a film attorney, with his piercing blue eyes, beautifully coiffed and gleaming gray hair, impeccable clothing. Now a touch of sadness on his stern, angular, clean-cut features as he daydreamed of his lost daughter, Molly St. John—he would never think of her as Moll Dalton, not ever, never.

Oh Molly! Molly! You beautiful child who at age five would have put Shirley Temple to shame! On the particular afternoon he was remembering, Daddy had just bathed little Molly and somehow had gotten so splashed in the process himself that he had stripped to towel off also . . .

Thus was born Horsy, the little secret game between just the two of them. St. John naked on his back on the big round bed made popular by *Playboy* centerfold shoots of those days, tiny naked Molly astride his bucking-bronco hips, riding the horsy, hanging on for dear life, shrieking with delight. Gripping horsy's pommel with her little hands as it got bigger and bigger and stiffer and stiffer, the bucking bronco bucking harder and harder and faster and faster, little Molly hanging on tighter and tighter with both little hands as she shrieked with laughter . . .

What an explosion, on that first dim afternoon with the shades drawn against the searing LaLa Land light! Shrieks and tears, of course—totally unexpected hot and wet and sticky stuff all over her little hands and Daddy's lean belly . . .

But a week later, Daddy volunteered another half-day home from the office just to take care of adorable little Molly. Bath, splashing, naked, toweling off, big dim bedroom . . . This time it didn't surprise little Molly when Daddy's big stiff pommel suddenly spurted all white and sticky. By now it was just part of the game of Horsy . . .

The intercom buzzed. St. John got his feet on the floor, his mind back inside his head, and answered. "Yes, Angelle."

"A Lieutenant Stagnaro from the San Francisco Police Department, Mr. St. John. He wants to talk with you about—"

"I don't recall any appointment. But . . ."

But he recalled Stagnaro. That officious phone call that hideous night that his darling Molly . . . And, more recently, St. John's letter threatening legal action to make him back off Atlas Entertainment . . . Better to get it over with now.

"All right, five minutes, and he's damned lucky to get it."

He expected the sort of bullying bureaucrat who turned timid the moment he was jerked out from behind his official shield. He got Fonzie grown-up with gray in his hair. The epitome of every ballsy Italian stud hanging around a street corner in the Bronx, moving easily, in terrific shape, with a mobile face and alert eyes that St. John was sure missed nothing.

"Mighty nice of you to give me these five minutes, Mr. St. John," he said in a voice that wasn't at all grateful.

"Say your say and get out, Lieutenant," said St. John coldly, fighting down his surprise at the man facing him across the desk. "I am an attorney and I know my rights."

But Stagnaro merely settled back in a costly designer chair as if for a long stay, hooking one leg over its arm and swinging his foot idly.

"I just bet you do, pal," he said. "As for being an attorney—things like that can change."

"I take that as a threat, Lieutenant."

Stagnaro waved a hospitable arm as if this were his office, not St. John's. "Take it any way you want." He got a notebook from his pocket and set it open on his knee, then didn't refer to it or write in it at all. "I have a few questions."

St. John sighed in a long-suffering manner.

"Go ahead, then, Lieutenant."

"You ever molest your daughter?"

It was exactly as if someone had kicked him in the scrotum. He felt his face get pale and knew his mouth was gaping, but there wasn't a single thing he could do about it for the moment. Scant minutes ago he had been daydreaming about sweet Molly and himself and Horsy, and here was Stagnaro asking him . . .

"How . . . " He'd almost blurted out *How did you know?* but his attorney instincts took over. "How dare you—"

"Seeing as how you pimped for your daughter several times during her marriage to Dr. Dalton, I get the feeling you either didn't value her enough or valued her way too much."

It had to be bitch Gloria's work, trying to hurt him even more by . . . but maybe, he thought, seeing a ray of light at the end of this particular horrible tunnel, maybe that abrogated the terms of the agreement under which he was paying

her those ghastly alimony payments and she kept herself
hard to find. She had put in writing that she would not divulge anything about . . . about him and Molly. So if she had
gone public now, even a quarter century after the event . . .

"Such a disgusting accusation does not deserve the dignity
of a reply," he snapped belatedly. Perhaps too belatedly.

"Exception noted, Counselor—isn't that what you lawyers
like to say? So we'll stick to the public record: the hard-core
porn-film company you set up back in '72."

St. John's name had appeared nowhere on those incorpo-
ration papers, and this hadn't come from Gloria; she had
walked off by then. His association with Mr. Prince had
come about *because* she had walked off—with infant Molly
and every dime he owned.

"Benny the Bullet—you remember Benny, don't you,
Counselor? He was looking at twenty-to-life for one of his
little peccadillos, so he decided to fill us in on everything he
knew about anything, even when he got toilet-trained. Verbal
diarrhea, tell you the truth. Freedom Films came up."

St. John rallied again. "If I did give free legal advice to
some acquaintances in setting up a small corporation, there
was nothing illegal about it. And in the early seventies—"

"A quarter of a mil and points to set up the fuck-film company is the way I heard it." Stagnaro winked at him across
the desk. "Never declared, Counselor. I haven't talked with
the folks over at the IRS . . . yet. But I bet they'd love to try
to make a net-worth case out of it."

He'd owed the shylock a lot of money and that Benny person had come around talking about electric drills and
kneecaps. All that bitch Gloria's fault, she'd stripped him
naked and he'd had to borrow from the leg-breakers because
nobody else would lend him enough to keep his nascent legal
firm afloat . . .

"Why . . . are you here?" he asked hollowly.

But Stagnaro said, "My five minutes are up, Counselor."
He stood, leaned across the desk. "Atlas Entertainment," he
said. "Kosta Gounaris." He dropped his voice lower. "Martin
Prince."

St. John jerked back as if Stagnaro were a viral infection. "What . . . "

"Maybe you have the impression that I'm a homicide cop, Counselor. I'm not. I head up the SFPD's Organized Crime Task Force. Anything organized, not just the mob; but the thought of dropping on somebody like Martin Prince gets me so excited I have to go buff my nails. And you're gonna help with my impossible dream, pal, 'cause you got short eyes."

"Short . . . eyes?"

"Old penitentiary term for your kind of pervert. You like to do it with little kids—short people. But the big people you're dealing with, they don't like pedophiles."

He turned back at the door, spoke quietly, almost sadly.

"Your daughter is dead, St. John, murdered, and you just don't seem to give a fuck who did it. But I do. And when push comes to shove . . ." He made his hand into a pistol with the thumb cocked, the forefinger a gun barrel pointing at St. John. "I push you for information and I get it, or . . ." His cocked thumb fell onto the firing pin of flesh at the base of his forefinger, and the finger shot St. John dead. "They shove you right off the edge of the world."

Then he laughed, a chilling laugh that hung in the temperature-controlled air long after he was gone.

St. John sent Angelle home early, poured himself a brimming snifter of Paradis, sat back down behind his desk with the bottle. The $350-a-liter cognac tasted like wormwood.

He knew these men were hard, he knew they could even be brutal, but not . . . not *Molly*! Kosta had even come to her funeral, the others had sent flowers and cards . . .

Kosta. Gid. Martin—yes, he was one of those permitted to call Mr. Prince "Martin" to his face. They knew how proud he was of Molly. He had boldly demanded she be made junior corporate counsel overseeing the San Francisco operation as a condition of his setting up the complicated deal on Atlas Entertainment. They had said yes, and he had told

them how to take over the shell of the existent entertainment
corporation for their own purposes.

They would never order Molly's death. Kosta himself was
in love with her, for God's sake. Had been shattered by her
death. Had felt it had been one of those tragic senseless
killings where Molly had died because she was *there,* and for
no other reason.

He felt salt tears on his cheeks. Sweet Molly . . .

The policeman had made it up to shake him up, that was it.

Through the tears his eyes moved around the office. All of
this was because in those lean years after bitch Gloria had
taken sweet little Molly away from him, he couldn't meet the
vig on their loan to him, and they'd become his silent partners. They'd kept him alive with their referrals. If the busi-
nesses were a little . . . well, grungy, those early contacts had
led to bigger and better work. Now he had seven attorneys
under him, none of whom knew anything about his . . . *affiliation* with Mr. Prince.

He shivered slightly as he finished his cognac. It tasted
better going down by now. He seemed finally able to let his
mind think the unthinkable. And in that instant he knew—
knew—that Mr. Prince had ordered sweet little Molly's
death; and if Kosta hadn't been in on it, at least he'd known
or suspected it might happen.

Then why hadn't he himself suspected it? These were
ruthless men, he'd always known that. And he'd always
known, in his secret soul, that he'd been valuable to them because of, well, his breeding, his manners, his appearance of
impeccable class. He'd even had the sense, occasionally, that
Mr. Prince coveted those qualities himself, qualities mere
money couldn't buy. He had always been flattered by Mr.
Prince's attention.

But now, thought of that attention made his long tapered
hands tremble. What if Mr. Prince had his office bugged?
What if they knew Stagnaro had been there, were listening to
a tape of their conversation right now? Would they . . .

For one pitiless moment he saw himself as they must have
seen him all through those years: his Anglo-Saxon good

looks empty, vain, a straw man for Mr. Prince, the real power behind his law firm. A soft man, not as sharp as they. A man who got along with everyone because he feared to offend anyone. A man who loved little children . . .

He was almost scrabbling for the phone, calling Charriti HHope, whose talent agency he had used for many years.

"Charriti? I need a blond female, about four foot six . . ."

Charriti HHope's voice said, with a trace of asperity, "Short notice." He almost heard a sigh over the phone. "How young does she have to be, sweetie?"

"About ten—if you have one who is . . . convincing."

Charriti gave a throaty chuckle. "Pretty soon you'll be telling me you want 'em for diaper commercials."

St. John hung up, sat there unconsciously rubbing his hand forward and backward over the surface of his hand-rubbed antique desk. Contemplating the little girls wearing jumpers that rode up off their naked chubby thighs as they clung to his pommel playing Horsy. And how at the ultimate moment, just as he had planned to teach his beloved little five-year-old Molly to do on that magical afternoon bitch Gloria had ruined all those many years ago, they lowered their sweet little heads to . . .

What had become of them now?

He knew, only too well. When a bit shopworn, they were graduated to porn flicks, then were passed on for stable work in Miami or Vegas and, as their bloom faded, ended their useful days under fat, sluggishly thrusting government officials in one of the less appetizing hot countries to the south . . .

And Molly, Molly was dead. Oh God. Nothing in his life was going to work for him ever again. And if he wasn't very, very careful, he might soon be dead himself.

Unless . . .

CHAPTER SEVENTEEN

Martin Prince, like so many great football players in the NFL, had come out of one of the small, desperately poor steel-puddling towns of western Pennsylvania. He had been an Honorable Mention All-American in college, but had been too smart to go into the pros even if he had been heavy enough.

Now in his mid-fifties, Martin Prince was dynamic, corrupt, kept fit by massages, saunas, and heroic avoidance of the richly sauced pastas he loved. He had a wedge-shaped head, heavy jaws, and a chin that one could imagine jutting out over the thousands in Piazza Venezia. Prince's rise had not been so meteoric as Il Duce's—but for the past five years, he had reigned supreme in Las Vegas.

It was to Martin Prince that the other capos came when they needed a neutral city in which to iron out their differences. They trusted him because he was quicker of mind, more decisive and more ruthless than they. Today he was cautious.

"Gideon, my good friend," he said into the scrambler phone five minutes after he had hung up from Otto Kreiger, "how would you like a weekend in Vegas? We are opening our new golf course here at Xanadu and it would not be right if you didn't hit the first ball down the fairway. Otto will also be here—I believe he wants to try to sell you one of those racehorses of his."

"The man can always try," Gideon chirped, then added before Prince could hang up, "You'll like this one, Mr. Prince. This sexy young woman comes to a dinner party with this rich, ugly old man. She's wearing this huge diamond, and the woman sitting next to her says it's the most beautiful diamond she's ever seen. So the sexy young woman says, 'Yes, but this is the Plotnick diamond. It comes with a curse.' The other woman says, 'What's the curse?' and the sexy one looks over at her ugly companion and whispers, 'Plotnick.'"

They shared a chuckle and hung up with mutual assurances of regard. Martin Prince was well pleased. He found Gideon, unlike the BB-eyed Nazi Kreiger, always Old Worldly and full of respect even if a bit boring.

As it should be. Respect. He beckoned, they came. Good men, strong men in their own right—but men who recognized him as the *capo di tutti i capi*—not that anyone believed in that Mustache Pete stuff anymore. Not in *his* organization. Though he had come up through the ranks in the traditional way, he had abandoned as many of the trappings of the Mafia as he could.

But he had never forgotten where he had come from and where his interests, talents, and allegiances lay. His old man had been a waiter in a wop restaurant, sweating and scrimping and saving for countless hours to send his kid first to parochial school and then to college; Prince had shown his appreciation for his education by murdering his first man for profit the night after he had thrown a winning touchdown pass against Penn State—who would suspect last night's hero?

He had killed twice more, but only to show he had *coglioni, quello!*—big enough balls for the Pittsburgh underworld. After those three, he had never personally killed again, which meant his brains were as big as his balls. Martin Prince had never spent a night in jail, and had made a solemn vow to himself that he never would.

That was why he was phoning certain specific invitations for purposes having nothing to do with the mini crime summit he had decided St. John's phone call demanded. Should the FBI be somehow listening this fine day, they would get nothing useful.

After speaking with Salvador Madrid, whom he had opposed for the council but had been overridden, his last call was to Enzo Garofano, one of the old-timers whose advice he valued and who still ran his own quadrant of the nation at the age of eighty-two. A little frail, perhaps, but only of body, not of mind or will.

Enzo's passion was Italian opera, so Prince said, *"Don Enzo, vi aspetta una cosa favolosa nel Showcase Lounge del casino. Abbiamo una nuova cantatrice."*

"Martin, io le cantatrici le sento ogni giorno."

"Non come questa, vi assicuro. È meglio di Callas."

"Meglio di Callas non c'è."

But Martin Prince knew he had the old Mustache Pete in his pocket. Just *in case* the girl in the Showcase Lounge was as good a singer as Maria Callas the fiery Greek had been, Don Enzo would not be able to keep himself from coming to Vegas. Prince switched to English.

"That is why I implore you, Don Enzo, come and hear her for yourself. I insist on sending my jet to pick you up."

Enzo agreed. Prince hung up and went to the window and looked out at his city. *His* city. Bugsy Siegel might have built it, but Martin Prince ran it—and would have called Bugsy "Bugsy" to his face if the *stronzo* had been around today.

Prince's name had once carried extra syllables; after his father had somehow scraped up enough money to send little Marcantonio Princetti to St. Paddy's across the river, *rhymes with spaghetti* had been the schoolyard taunt of the predominantly Irish lads at the school.

Sweeney.

Kiley.

O'Malley.

He'd never forgotten these ringleaders of the taunts during his formative years, so just about the time the extra syllables had been dropped to make Marcantonio Martin, faith an' bejaysus, and those poor Irish boyos each had a wee drap o' bad luck.

Martin Prince had never called to gloat. He'd never had to. *They* knew. At least Sweeney and Kiley did. O'Malley didn't know much of anything anymore except how to piss down his pant leg. None of them could ever do anything about their misfortunes, but they would *know*.

Respect. Enzo Garofano still held his important meetings in the back room of an Italian restaurant, but he got respect. Martin Prince demanded it too. But on a much grander scale and with great personal pride in the safety measures that were his secret passion. He believed in careful evaluation and planning, and had a great deal invested in Atlas Entertainment; the company's continued profitability depended on its connection with the Mafia remaining secret.

He met the four undercapos in the executive boardroom on the top floor of his Xanadu Enterprises hotel, casino, sports and entertainment complex. The three who were associated in greater or lesser degrees in the Atlas Entertainment affair, and the fourth, Spic Madrid, who was not involved but would serve as protective coloration should the feds belatedly realize these men were in Vegas for more than pleasure. Others might meet in a drafty warehouse or upstairs over a pizza joint; Martin Prince had flown in an interior decorator from Via del Babvino to furnish the suite with exquisite appurtenances from declining Roman estates and a lighting system developed in Cine Citta.

Prince had imported San Francisco's most famous private detective to oversee the security arrangements. The place was swept twice daily for bugs, and waves of electronic vibrations washed inaudibly across the surfaces of the windows during meetings, so the latest laser mikes couldn't pick up voice-shimmers off the glass and turn them back into human speech through a complicated electronic process.

"Enzo, mio caro amico. La cantatrice è brava, no?"

The old man nodded his seamed and shrunken head. Even in Las Vegas he wore a wool suit, vest, tie, polished shoes.

"Maria Callas—*mai!* But a good opera singer . . ." He shrugged and made a gesture of approval with the fingers of his hand pinched together at the tips. "You should encourage her."

"Perhaps, Don Enzo, you would like to tell her personally how much you enjoyed her singing . . ."

By the look on Don Enzo's face, he knew he had made the perfect suggestion. He would make a couple of suggestions to the *cantatrice,* too. What the hell, he owned her contract.

He turned to Salvador "Spic" Madrid, who controlled street drug sales in four upper Midwest states and had recently been elevated to the board after winning a rather messy internecine war on his own cold northern turf.

"Salvador—you find the floor shows pleasing?"

Spic couldn't quite keep the gleam out of his eyes.

"Magnifico!" he exclaimed. "Last night . . . there was one blond showgirl . . . she looked seven feet tall . . ."

They all carefully laughed with him, not at him. Martin Prince nodded sagely. "I believe she might be waiting in your suite when this meeting is over."

Spic tried to look man-of-the-world, but his eyes had gone round at the prospect of feasting on a woman two feet taller than he, one who outweighed him by fifty pounds and carried no extra flesh at all except where it counted.

To give Spic time to recover his poise without anyone seeming to be overtly aware he had lost it, Gid Abramson chirped up, bright as a bird.

"Martin, that golf course! It is a dream, a treasure! I almost had a hole in one on my first round!"

"And your stud farm is impeccable," said Otto Kreiger. He sincerely meant it—and lusted after it. If Martin should ever stumble, Kreiger would pick up the pieces. If he stuck out a foot for Prince to trip over, Kreiger wondered, would he have any allies on the board to help him take over?

After the waiters had brought drinks and had departed,

Martin Prince pushed a button to play back his phone conversation with Skeffington St. John.

"Mr. . . . Mr. Prince, this is Skeffington St. John—"

"Skeffington! Always a pleasure."

"I thought I should notify you—that policeman from San Francisco was here yesterday. Dante Stagnaro. Trying perhaps to enlist me by suggesting that the Organization might be involved with Atlas Entertainment and also . . . also with . . . Molly's, ah . . . my daughter's, ah . . ."

"With the death of your daughter? My God, man, I felt about Molly just as I do about my own daughter!"

"Oh, yes, Mr. Prince, I understand that totally! But I felt you should know so appropriate actions could be taken."

"Well, Skeffington, I want to thank you, and tell you again how keenly I feel for you in your loss. I hope to get you over here to Vegas soon, cheer you up a bit."

"Then you don't think—"

"That this Stagnaro is anything to worry about?" Martin Prince chuckled. "He knows Gounaris is connected to Atlas Entertainment, and he knows you are. But he doesn't know any of you are connected to *us*. And he won't know."

"But the things he said about my daughter—"

"He's just manipulating you, Skeffington. Shaking the box to see if anything rattles." He added, with malice too delicate to be identified, "Unless you can think of something in your personal life that makes you vulnerable . . ."

"Oh, no, no, there's nothing like that, Mr. Prince."

"Then don't give him another thought," said Prince heartily. The tape clicked off. There was a long silence.

"This is a badly frightened man," chirped Gid finally.

"Too frightened," said Kreiger.

"On the other hand," said Prince, "he called me when Stagnaro came to see him. He told me that Stagnaro told him we had been instrumental in his daughter's death. It takes a certain strength of character to make such a call."

"Or cunning," said Spic, who'd had a brandy and felt himself an expert on cunning. With a sudden dazzling certainty, he knew that someday he would own this whole thing that was Prince's. "He knew we'd hear one way or another about Stagnaro asking him questions."

"But perhaps too frightened to handle our affairs?" persisted Kreiger. His tone was deferential, but he wanted to establish his position as contrary to Prince's, without doing so strongly enough to make it obvious that was what he was doing. Prince caught the subterfuge, but said nothing.

"This guy is too frightened to live, perhaps?" suggested Spic Madrid.

"First the daughter, then the father? Both associated with Atlas Entertainment?" Enzo Garofano shook his aged head.

Fortunately, thought Martin Prince, Enzo didn't know about that troubling hit on their bought policeman, Lenington. Also, indirectly, associated with Atlas.

Garofano continued, "And with this organized crime cop, what's his name, turncoat wop bastard, Stagnaro, with him snooping about . . ."

"Yeah, what about doing *him*?" asked Madrid. "He's the guy who's scaring this St. John and pressuring Gounaris."

"Hit a policeman? Very chancy," said Garofano.

"I think we are going astray here," said Prince.

"How'd the woman find out about it in the first place?" asked Spic. "This Gounaris was fuckin' her, was he stupid?"

"She was a computer whiz," said Gid very quickly but with a relaxed chuckle. This was dangerous ground for Kosta, he wanted to deflect the attention. "As we have been able to piece it together, she was looking not so much for something in the computer as for the space where she thought something should be in the computer if there was anything illegal going on." He looked around the room. "If that makes sense to any of you.

"It made sense to my computer man, that's good enough for me," said Martin Prince. He held up a hand to forestall further discussion. "Our immediate problem is the demoralization of Skeffington St. John, which I do not believe to be acute. He has been a very fine attorney for this organization. He set up the Atlas Entertainment deal in the first place. He got an injunction that stopped the pressure Stagnaro was putting on Gounaris."

"He's a sexual degenerate of the worst kind," broke in Kreiger. Prince knew he didn't really care if St. John was a deviate, he was cautiously stalking out a position counter to Prince's. "That makes him susceptible to the pressures a man like Stagnaro can bring. Promises of immunity . . ."

Otto was getting hungry, looking for a way to move up. Probably seeing Prince's stud farm for the first time had done it. So much better than Otto's, his horses of such better bloodlines. Not that he cared much about horses himself. Martin Prince tapped on the side of his water glass with his pen. Everyone fell silent.

"Let's put to a vote whether Skeffington St. John is still a reliable part of this organization. Any seconds?"

"Second the motion," said Enzo Garofano.

"Thank you. I believe a show of hands will suffice."

But then Otto Kreiger came out into the open. "I would also like a show of hands on the question of the policeman Dante Stagnaro."

"Second," said Spic Madrid quickly.

Bene. These two lusted after Martin Prince's domain, and might align themselves together against him. Martin Prince was stimulated by the challenge. He smiled benignly.

"One motion at a time, gentlemen, please," he said. After the vote, he signaled Enzo Garofano to stay on after the others had left. "You heard, Don Enzo?"

"The tinkle of a distant goat bell."

"It will get louder."

Garofano nodded judiciously. "Perhaps send a message . . . *Si!* We can trust Eddie Ucelli to take his time in finding the right moment. He will do it right. He and I go a long way back, I will call myself."

Martin Prince bowed his respect and admiration.

"*La cantatrice*—she is waiting in your room to discuss her career, Don Enzo."

Garofano nodded in turn, a sudden lustful gleam in his faded octogenarian eye.

CHAPTER EIGHTEEN

That same evening, out in San Francisco, Dante Stagnaro was having a high old time of his own. He had taken Rosa out for pizza on Columbus Ave a few blocks from the small bungalow in the steeply slanted 500 block of Greenwich Street where he had been brought up. Theirs now, his parents had moved down to the Valley near Modesto to raise walnuts. Dante and Rosa always went out for pizza when they wanted to celebrate something. Often, like tonight, the celebration was just Dante being willing to take a night off, and them being alive, and together, and still in love.

When Dante had fallen in love with Rosa Benvenuto, he had been nineteen and in his first year at community college, she had been seventeen and a high school senior. A thin quick Italian girl with a round face and great dark flashing eyes and clouds of curly black hair down her back. Pert, proud breasts under soft sweaters, a tiny waist, sweet flanks under tight jeans. He had asked her to marry him after his return from Vietnam two years later, on the day he had entered the police academy.

Motherhood and the relentless tug of gravity had made the breasts heavier, the years had thickened that tiny waist, good Italian cooking had widened those sweet flanks. But to Dante, she was only more beautiful now than she had been on the day he had taken her down the aisle at Saints Peter and Paul two blocks from the house he took her home to—Joe DiMaggio's church, some of the old-timers still called it.

The thickening and softening of the body, the laugh lines at the corners of the eyes and mouth were to be treasured, for they spoke of living, of two wonderful children borne and being raised, of hard work and the wisdom only women can attain.

Rosa was not feeling wise tonight. She was feeling, truth be told, giddy from the wine—it didn't take very much. She hated to admit it, it was such a cliché—like an African-American who loved watermelon—but a sausage/pepperoni with extra cheese and a bottle of Chianti in a straw basket were Rosa's idea of absolute gastronomic heaven. Dante knew it, and whenever he was feeling really good he took her out for such a feast. And afterward, when they got home . . .

Right now he was regaling her with memories of pizza joints once known—when he was a tiny kid, to be exact.

"There were these two brothers down the Peninsula, Monte and Renato. Monte's place was on the old Bayshore before it was a freeway, just across from Moffett Field in Mountain View when the Navy still had it. Just called Monte's. Renato had his place in Redwood City on El Camino Real, called himself 'Renato, King of the Pizza.'"

He started to laugh at the memories the very names evoked, and she loved him passionately at that moment, his fine Italian eyes squinched up with laughing. He took a big gulp of Chianti.

"Thing was, they wouldn't speak to each other. Family picnics, holidays, like that—one in each end of the room. It was wonderful!"

"What's so funny about a brother-brother feud?" asked Rosa, but also laughing just because he was.

"The feud was about pizza crusts! Monte was a thick crust man, Renato was thin crust. Each thought the other was a fool, a charlatan, an imposter!"

They laughed together over this, ate pizza, drank wine. Finally he got down to his interview with Skeffington St. John.

"He pronounces it Sinjin."

"As in unholy drink?" giggled Rosa. She was on-her third glass of dago red, and her eyes shone like the candles on the tables, like the stars in the heavens.

"S-I-N-J-I-N. Unholy genie out of a bottle, maybe."

"We agree on unholy," said Rosa. She pointed at the last slice on the big round tin scored by countless pizza cutters through the years. "Anybody want this more than I do?"

Dante waved a hand, leaned forward across the table as she scooped it up. "Thing is, Rosie, I *have* that guy." He closed his hand into a fist to show how he had a particularly vulnerable part of Skeffington St. John in his grasp. "He's a degenerate and he's falling to pieces. The people he's associated with don't like people who know a lot about them falling to pieces."

"Can he give you what you want about Atlas Entertainment?"

"That's the question," admitted Dante. "He was the lawyer who set up the purchase of the corporate shell for—this is speculation—Martin Prince in Las Vegas. I don't know how much he knows about what they've done with it since they bought it. If they *do* own it and if they've done *anything* with it."

"Your obsession is showing again, darling," said Rosa with a little chuckle.

"What? It's an obsession to hate the bad guys?"

"You hate the bad *Italian* guys who screw up our good Italian name in this country," she said, "so you just have to think Atlas Entertainment is a mob front."

"That's what I think," he admitted with a wry chuckle. "I just can't prove it. There's no obvious illegality that would let me get inside their operation and look around. I can't get a search warrant, I can't get phone taps. I think they had Moll Dalton murdered—but I can't prove it. I think they had Jack Lenington murdered—but I can't prove that, either. I don't have a motive for either killing—but hell, who needed one for Jack, you knew him from our academy days, he even made a pass at you, remember? A sleazeball even then. But Moll Dalton . . ."

"You're projecting again, darling. Moll Dalton wasn't corrupt, I grant you, but from what you tell me she was no maiden in distress. She was an ambitious, hard-driving woman who habitually cheated on her husband and would do anything to get to the top. You say Gounaris was using her sexually—well, maybe she was using him sexually, too. Maybe she overestimated how much power he had, and maybe that's what got her killed."

"He couldn't protect her?" Dante nodded almost grudgingly. "Not bad, sweetie. But the point is that maybe I don't have to prove the mob killed Moll Dalton. Maybe somebody will tell me. Her husband thinks she ended up being promiscuous the way she was because St. John had molested her as a little girl."

"His own daughter? And you believe Dalton? Without any facts to back up his supposition?"

"Yeah, I believe him. I talked with Beverly Hills Vice, there's rumors around St. John gets little girls for sexual purposes from a low-life talent agent." He gave another chuckle. "Calls herself Charriti HHope." He spelled it. "She's a known—let's say alleged—procuress, but she has a lot of powerful friends in LaLa Land so she's never been busted."

Rosa's eyes flashed. "She gets little children for—"

"Yeah. For guys like Moll's father, if the rumors are true, and I think they are. So Dalton was probably right about the molestation of the daughter as a little girl."

"And this puts this St. John in your hand?"

"He's juggling a dozen balls and he's going to start dropping some of them. When he does, his playmates are going to decide he's expendable. Then he'll have to come to me."

"Unless they kill him first."

Dante sobered. "There's that. But . . . a few months after his daughter is professionally hit?" He shrugged. "I'm almost ashamed of myself, but I told him his buddies had put out the contract on her even though I don't know for sure that they did."

"Did he believe you?"

"I'm banking that eventually he will. Whatever he did to her, I think he loved her. He was sure broken up when I told him she was dead. I'd love to put more pressure on him, but—"

"How long ago were he and his wife divorced?" interrupted Rosa with a thoughtful look in her eye.

"Um . . . twenty-five years ago, like that."

"And you think he might have molested his daughter when she was a little girl? About four, maybe five?"

Dante leaned across the table and kissed her.

"You wonder why I love you? Of course. The *wife*. If I can find her and she confirms it . . ." He paused for a moment, then said uncomfortably, "Sweetie, there's something else. I think I screwed up. After Moll Dalton was murdered, I got a message on the phone machine. From somebody doing Arte Johnson's Nazi from *Laugh-In* and calling himself Raptor."

"Raptor like in bird of prey?"

"Yeah. He said he was the one who'd killed her."

"In a comic German accent?"

"That's why I thought it was a crank call. So I just, uh, erased it off the tape."

She met his eyes, held them with her own. Her face was serene and beautiful in the candlelight.

"And it wasn't a crank call," she said softly.

"I'm not sure. I got another call after Lenington was killed. This time it was a black talking, but it was a message from the same guy. He called himself Raptor again."

"And you haven't told Tim."

"I had a hell of a time telling you, Rosie—that first call was probably Raptor himself. Now he's using other people to make his calls so I'll never get a voiceprint of him."

"Don't be too sure," said Rosa. "These men have egos. He'll call you again."

"You think so?"

"I would." For a moment, her black eyes penetrated his

soul, then she gave her chuckle that was almost a giggle, and stood to start putting on her coat. "Haven't I always?"

She led him back, hand in hand, to the house in Greenwich Street where he had first dreamed of her.

In Vegas, Enzo Garofano had been seduced into his first dribbling orgasm in almost two years by the *cantatrice* Martin Prince had sent up to his penthouse atop Xanadu. Seduced as much by the memory of her fiery rendition of Carmen's "Habañera" as by suckling like an infant at her magnificent *meloni*.

She had departed with his promise of getting her into a good opera company back east, and Enzo, after he had recovered from his sexual labors, had set out to honor his private arrangement with Martin Prince.

Mae's Place had started life in the thirties as a roadhouse on the way to the Columbia turnpike, with good steaks on the first floor and high stakes on the second. Just "the Roadhouse" then, a rambling white frame building set in a nice grove of eastern white pines, plenty of parking. From her late teens Mae had been the hostess with the mostes' in the downstairs lounge, and after legalized gambling in Atlantic City made the Roadhouse a losing proposition, bought in and changed the name to Mae's Place.

Mae made the steaks even thicker downstairs, closed the unprofitable gaming rooms, and started running a different kind of beef on the second floor. Her girls were Grade A, some were Choice or even Prime, scrupulously clean and low-cholesterol. And her local protection was firmly in place: the county sheriff came out every Friday night for a thick T-bone and a thin blonde, on the house; and Mae had an excellent video of the reform mayor serving as the high-price spread between two of her girls, one whole wheat, one white bread.

Mae was now forty-nine, still flame-haired with a little help from her hairdresser, heavy-hipped and heavy-breasted, rings on every finger, expensive musk dabbled deep in her sensational cleavage, pink and voluptuous as a Rubens nude, randy as a goat. She indulged herself freely with a few old friends: if you were fortunate enough to be offered Mae, you didn't pay.

One of her oldest friends was Eddie Ucelli. His company supplied her steaks, but he himself usually only came around when she called him, because she was his contact for the nowadays rare hits he was asked to perform. But sometimes he would come out for a sirloin with his wife, and Mae would sit down at their table to chat about the old days. And Eddie would get all steamed up.

So on nights such as this, Eddie would see his wife home, leave her in front of Jay Leno, and loop back for a little stroll down memory lane. Mae's memory lane.

Because even though Eddie was fifty-seven years old, a little too squat, a little too wide, and naked a little too hairy, ah, good Christ, Mae could remember him when. Eddie had popped her cherry for her on a rooftop with a view of Manhattan across the East River when she was just entering her teens and he just leaving his. Even now, Mae could coax him alive as no other woman could—and most nights he needed a lot of coaxing even from her.

The phone call caught him on his back under Mae, who wore only her push-up bra pushed up so one of her enormous breasts was in his mouth seemingly by accident—Mae was inventive in ways like that. When she leaned back to take the call, Eddie slid a thumb into her luxurious bush and began rolling her clitoris because it took him a long time to get one of his partial hard-ons and he hated to lose his rhythm. Stifling a moan of pleasure, Mae leaned down to wedge the phone between his shoulder and chin.

"Ucelli," he said into it.

He listened. His thumb stopped moving inside her. Mae didn't mind; she could always get herself off if Eddie couldn't do it for her. She sat placidly astride him; this was not the first of the many such phone calls that Eddie had taken himself here at Mae's Place. He always came around to celebrate with her after he had completed his contract, but by then his sexual fervor inevitably had ebbed.

Now, before he hung up he said, "I understand. The Feebs got a fuckin' tap on my line, I gotta duck 'em but it's no problem." He added in a guttural voice, "When the time's right, I'll do it right."

At that same moment Mae felt something thick and heavy pressing up against her belly as it hadn't in years.

"My God, Eddie!" she exclaimed in amazement. "You're as hard as an iron bar!"

She quickly impaled herself on it, and then, ever so slowly and lasciviously, slid down the pole and started rolling those ample hips as if they were on oiled ball bearings. As she started to breathe very quickly, Mae knew they were both in for the fuck of a lifetime before she would let him die the little death.

CHAPTER NINETEEN

Salvador Madrid was *muy borracho*. Shitface, in fact.

Spic was drunk because this night he'd had to put out a hit on Manuel Monteluego, one of his wife's many nephews, and it made him sad and nostalgic at the same time. The hit was to be disguised as a drunken Saturday night stabbing outside a rural dance pavilion in Coates, a tiny crossroads place a score of miles south of the Twin Cities on Minnesota 62. Spic had rented the barnlike wood frame building for a *baile* following a wedding that afternoon only so that he could logically send Manuel down to Coates to pay for everything. And there be made to die.

"Can' let her know," he explained in drunken seesaw English to his bodyguard Alejo. He took another hit of tequila. They were alone in the shabby little bungalow on Robie Street that he used as an office. "She keel me dead she fin' out."

"*Es verdad, jefe,*" agreed Alejo obediently; he knew Spic was referring to his wife, Maria. Alejo was another nephew, but that was all right, he was from Spic's side of the family in Guadalupe, Nuevo León; the soon-to-be-dead nephew was a *hijo de puta* from Sonora and there was little love lost between them.

Normally none of Spic's people would be caught dead (pardon the pun) at Coates. But few of these would have green cards, so they would all melt away at the discovery of the body soon to be lying on the frozen ground between the dance hall and the gas station. Anyone *estúpido* enough to be picked up by the county sheriff would *no tengo, no entiendo,* and would soon walk—or be deported as an illegal alien. Either way, no loss.

"Tol' 'em to do eet while I am here at th' offeece," Spic explained. When he was *borracho,* his English became the slurred wetback English of his youth. "Tha' way Maria, she gonna know I deent have notheeng to do weeth eet."

Since Maria would eventually learn there had been friction between husband and nephew over missing receipts, Spic had arranged that she would hear of Manuel's death almost as quickly as he would. She would call him here to wail over the phone; and later, learning of the estrangement, she would remember her husband had been nowhere near Coates when Manuel had died.

This was necessary because the only person on earth Spic Madrid feared was his wife. Not Maria as Maria, short, wide, mother of his five children. Rather, he feared her spiritual powers, renewed daily at mass. Family was *muy importante* to Maria; if she knew he'd had her nephew killed, she would put God's curse upon him, and Spic would surely wither and die.

Por Dio, where was the call? In his mind he could hear the Mexican band (originally from Chihuahua) he'd hired for the wedding. Horns, guitar, bass, accordion, fine-tuned Peavey cranked to the max, bowing out the dance hall walls with "Las Mariposas." He was nodding his head in time to the unheard music. Stamping feet, whirling bodies . . . flashing knife . . .

The phone rang, an unknown voice said, *"Es muerto."*

Spic hung up. So. It was done. Now Maria's call.

She would be at their rambling frame house on Marshall Ave in St. Paul, far from the west side where he did his business. When they had married twenty-two years ago, she'd been tiny and skinny; during their wedding dance, he in his rented black suit, she in her rented white wedding gown, she had clung to him as if she were an appendage of his body.

He had been the strength she had needed, the realization of her dream of El Norte.

In turn Jose, their two-year-old son, had clung to her white skirt with both his little brown hands as they had danced. At the time of his conception and birth, they had been afraid to get married lest they be caught in the system and deported.

Three years before that, at seventeen, Spic had been a *mojado* muling kilos of raw heroin taped to his ribs across the Tortilla Curtain at El Paso, until one night some *maricón* pusher tried to pay him off with a switchblade. He left the man dead under a mesquite bush, minus his head, which Spic left in the middle of the road with the tongue sticking roguishly out.

He fled north all the way to St. Paul where what he now termed "a shit job the *gringos* wouldn't take" was arranged for him by a man named Cisco Monteluego. For his new life he took the name Madrid because Madrid was in Spain, not Mexico, thus had no echoes of his *pachuco* past.

During his two years washing dishes in the restaurant where Cisco cooked, he had met Cisco's niece, Maria, and their son had been born. After he and Maria had married, he started calling Cisco "Tío," and together they started selling tacos at county fairs during the summers. The next year, they opened a taco stand on Concord Street in St. Paul's mostly Latino west side, and during the next few years prospered in a modest way.

Awaiting Maria's call, Spic shut his eyes and remembered . . .

It was three-thirty in the morning, and the tiny four-stool place was deserted with the door open to let out the hot grease smell of deep-frying taco shells. The sign over the door said TÍO'S TEXAS TACOS. Tío Cisco was sweeping the floor and Spic was in the minuscule storeroom opening a hundred-pound sack of corn flour. A man dressed in black, with black gloves, and wearing a Porky Pig Halloween mask, came in and took a stool.

"We are closed, sir," said Uncle Cisco in his invariably courteous way. "If you come back tomorrow . . ."

But Porky Pig took from his pocket a gun with a silencer screwed onto its muzzle. His voice was distorted by the mask.

"You want to be closed forever, or you want to pay us a hundred dollars a week so nobody comes around bothering you?"

"Señor," began Uncle Cisco in a terrified voice, staring at the gun, "a hundred dollars a week will take all of our profits."

"That's one," said Porky Pig.

Spic was drawn to the storeroom door by the voices. Porky Pig turned his stool to give the short skinny Mexican a measuring look, swinging the lethal silenced gun Spic's way as he did, then turned back to Uncle Cisco as the main man in the equation.

"That's two," he said.

"We will pay, we will pay," said Uncle Cisco very quickly.

"No, no pagamos," muttered Spic sullenly.

But Porky Pig must have understood Spanish. He said, "That's three," and the silenced gun said *pfft pfft pfft,* like that. But not at Spic.

Instead, Uncle Cisco seemed to leap backward, his feet coming up off the floor, the broom flying from his hand. He caromed off the end of the counter to sprawl facedown on the faded linoleum, his limbs jerking and twitching, then still.

Porky Pig stood up and began unscrewing the silencer from the gun. Death had loosened Uncle Cisco's sphincter so the smell of shit overrode the hot grease smell in the little room.

"Whew!" he exclaimed in his muffled pig voice, "smells like something crawled up there and died." He chuckled. "Must be all that hot Mexican food." Spic hadn't moved from the doorway of the minuscule storeroom. To him, Porky Pig added, "Remember, beaner, one hundred dollars a week, starting Friday."

Then he was gone, leaving Uncle Cisco dead on the floor.

Before calling the police, Spic took all the money from the cash register and from the body and hid it under the floormat of Uncle Cisco's dilapidated Chevy. That way the cops would treat it as a simple robbery and would not look very hard for the killer.

Uncle Cisco, dead upon the floor.

Tonight, Uncle Cisco's son Manuel, dead upon the sere yellow grass and frozen ground beside the Coates Pavilion.

Spic felt tears hot behind his eyelids. Leadership was a stern mistress. He opened his eyes, looked at his nephew Alejo across the scarred and battered wooden tabletop. The tequila bottle was empty, his limes and salt were gone. His drunkenness had passed. He wanted to be alone to mourn the death of Tío Cisco's son at the hands of unknown assassins.

"Go get me another bottle of tequila, Alejo."

"I s'posed stay with you, guard you, *jefe*."

With a chuckle, Spic made the sign of the cross over him. "I absolve you." He threw money on the table. "And more limes."

Spic had paid protection for five weeks, always leaving the cash drawer ajar with a single hundred-dollar bill in it, staying in the storeroom until Porky Pig had come and gone. Then he began closing the store to follow Porky on his rounds, finally to the house where Porky lived under his real name of Alex Jones. One night after the wife had gone to bed, Spic cut off Porky's head and set it on top of the TV set, tongue protruding, for Mrs. Jones and their two children to find in the morning.

Spic took over the collection route. When the Organization sent a man to kill Spic and thus reclaim the route, Spic killed him and buried him in a patch of woods overlooking the Minnesota River near Fort Snelling. He sent the killer's head, packed in dry ice, tongue lolling, to the killer's fag boyfriend.

The local capo realized Spic had no compunctions about killing anyone whatsoever, for any reason, at any time, and that he would be harder to kill than to absorb. So Spic became a made man, always moving up by killing the man above him, always just before that man realized he was in Spic's way. Now, at forty-two, he controlled illegal drug sales in four northern states.

His wife called. She sobbed and wailed in Spanish about the death of Manuel, her favorite nephew. Spic consoled her, crying too, promising to come home right away to pray with her for the salvation of poor Manuel's immortal soul.

While they talked, he heard Alejo behind him, returning with the tequila and limes. As he turned, phone in hand, the muzzle of the Jennings J-22 was pressed by the gloved hand against the bridge of his nose, and he just had time to think, *Maria knows that I*

As Alejo got out of the car with the tequila, shivering in his sports jacket in the freezing drizzle, the bulky man just coming down the front walk from Spic's business bungalow tossed a new, heavy overcoat around the skinny Mexican's shoulders. Alejo dropped tequila and topcoat to run up the walk into the house. As he was doing that, the assassin U-turned his rental car to get back onto Minnesota 3 South which would take him to 494 and, eventually, the Minneapolis–St. Paul International Airport.

Because of the M.O., Dante Stagnaro got word of the Madrid hit off the FBI wire and was on Northwest flight 350 at 6:45 A.M. He was met around noon by Bob Carman, Agent in Charge of the Minneapolis FBI office. Carman was caricature FBI—blue-black hair, blue eyes, blue suit, blue tie, blue sedan.

"Thanks for bringing me in on this," said Dante.

Carman chuckled as they shook hands, smile lines creasing his lean cheeks, tanned even in a Minnesota winter. Dante wondered if a sunlamp was involved.

"It was actually Rudy Mattaliano, your federal prosecutor buddy in New York, who gave you a good report card, Stagnaro. The car is this way. The incident occurred over in St. Paul."

The freeway took them east and then north toward the

tract bungalow on Robie Street where Spic Madrid had been a few hours before becoming an incident on an FBI report form. The skies were gray and cold; pockmarked snow lay on the banks flanking the freeway.

"New York feels this ties in with something you're working on out in San Francisco," said Carman in an insinuating voice.

"I wouldn't see Madrid associated with my case in any way, except that he was in Vegas last week at the same time as some of those who might be involved. So . . . maybe. And from what I heard of the M.O.—small-caliber weapon, one up the nose . . ."

"Professional hit all the way," agreed Carman sternly.

He got them off the freeway on Concord, drove a few blocks north and doglegged over to Robie. There was slush in the gutter; frozen footprints between street and sidewalk made walking precarious; Dante got a wet foot.

The frost-crazed walk was slippery with new ice; the February thaw had ended with drizzle and then a freeze the night before. The house, like most of the others in the block, was probably from the 1920s, white frame, squat and narrow, with a veranda and peeling green shutters. A small jet shrieked by overhead on its takeoff from Holman Field beyond the freeway. Their breaths went up in white puffs. Dante was shivering inside his inadequate San Francisco topcoat.

The two men acknowledged the uniformed cop on duty outside the house in greatcoat and gloves, ducked under the yellow crime scene tape; the seals were not yet fixed to the door, so they entered, switching on lights in the early afternoon. The only room used was the living room, its only furnishings a table that had served as a desk, a swivel and two straight-backed chairs, a broken-down couch. Table lamp, telephone with two lines, TV set. The heat was off, it was cold.

"Classy," said Dante. His wet foot was freezing.

"Local cops tell me Madrid used it only to coordinate the street sales. Just a few years ago this was mostly Latino, but a lot of Hmongs from the Laos highlands have diluted the mix."

"Did Madrid deal to them, too?"

"Maybe," said Carman without too much interest. "But word is they made him nervous, so the only people who ever came here were his direct lieutenants. Not so dumb, at that."

"Until last night," said Dante.

The body had been removed and the place dusted for prints and vacuumed for fibers, but otherwise was untouched. White tape outlining a hologram of someone sitting in the swivel chair tipped backward over the desk. There was quite a lot of black-dried blood puddled around the taped outline of the head.

"He was talking with his wife on the phone when he got it. And his bodyguard probably met the hitman coming down the walk."

Dante looked sharply over at Carman. "Courtesy absence? Warned off by the killer?"

"The locals don't think so. He's Madrid's nephew and was devoted to him. Madrid was drunk, sent him out for tequila and limes. Another nephew also was killed last night a few miles south of here in a little town called Coates."

"Open season?" mused Dante.

"That one looks like a simple knifing after a wedding dance, but you could be right—a straight power play by other locals. Madrid was a vicious bastard, climbed over a lot of widows and orphans on his way to the top of the pyramid." He stopped with a short, almost bitter laugh. "Allegedly."

Dante was trying to visualize the hit from the taped outlines on chair and desk. "Anything else odd about this one?"

"The killer left the gun behind—no fingerprints on it."

"Jennings J-22, maybe? Only one round in it? Sprayed with Armor All? And he gave his overcoat away afterwards, maybe?"

"Yeah, Armor All. And yeah, he gave the overcoat to the nephew." He added sternly, "Okay, Stagnaro. Give."

"Popgun Ucelli out of Jersey. Either him or someone who

knows his M.O. and is using it. Your Organized Crime people have a running tap on his phone . . ."

Carman was already turning away toward the phone. Another airplane shrieked by low overhead, rattling the windows in their shrunken frames. A taped X on the edge of the desk marked where the killer had set down the murder gun after using it.

"He's sitting at the desk, talking on the phone, hears something behind him," Dante said aloud, more to himself than Carman, "and thinks it's the bodyguard coming back. He turns, the pistol is pressed against the bridge of his nose, whap! he's dead meat." He shivered with the cold, looked over at Carman. "How many shots?"

Carman held up one finger, then opened his hand, palm toward Dante, in a *stop* motion as he listened to the phone. He grunted a few times, said thank you, and hung up shaking his head.

"They didn't have an eyeball surveillance on Ucelli. They'll send somebody out to see if he's in town, but . . ."

"Yeah. If he *was* here he'll be back in Jersey by now."

Dante spent the day reading the papers they'd found in Spic's office. *Nada.* Dinner was with Carman and the homicide cop in charge of the investigation, a thick-bodied German named Heidenreich. Ucelli was in residence in Jersey but could have been away for as long as a week before the Madrid hit. They'd had no eyeball of him during those seven days, hadn't picked him up on any of the voice-activated surveillance tapes.

The next day with Heidenreich was fruitless. That night Dante caught the 10:15 Northwest nonstop to SFO. In-flight, in a *New York Times* the flight attendant brought, he read about the murder he had just been watching being investigated.

This one would go into the St. Paul Police Department open file. No one would bust his butt on it. Local slaying of local slime, no connection between Madrid and Atlas Entertainment, the parallels with the Moll Dalton and Jack Lenington hits genuine coincidences. They happened.

Dante spooned up behind the sleeping Rosa in their double bed and went hard asleep, so it wasn't until he got up the next morning that he saw the blinking light on the answering machine. He rewound the message without the slightest premonition.

The voice was obviously Latin, slurring the English words in that liquid south-of-the-border singsong now becoming so familiar to anyone living in California.

"Hey, señor, thees ees Raptor. I bushwack heem in the arroyo. Cure hees postnasal dreep. *Mucho diversión, verdad?*"

PART FOUR

End of the Permian

245 m.y. ago

A man can die but once: we owe God a death. . . . let it go which way it will, he that dies this year is quit for the next.

William Shakespeare
Henry IV, Part II

CHAPTER TWENTY

Much diversion indeed!

But listen; you want to know why I kill, I will tell you.

It is the summer between my junior and senior years in college, and I am seeing this great nation of ours firsthand in an old red Ford Falcon with one blue fender from a junkyard in Phoenix, Arizona. I work two weeks at a job, any job I can find wherever I am, then I move on: I wash dishes in Salt Lake City, I unload boxcars in Elton, Illinois, I pack corn in Rochester, Minnesota, where the canning factory has a water tower painted like a huge ear of corn, kernels, husks and all.

The night I leave Rochester I end up in a small, old-fashioned, midwestern bar in Austin, where Hormel has its headquarters. Long and narrow, with dark wood booths along the right wall, the bar along the left, a few tables down the middle, shuffleboard, in the back a golden oldies country-western jukebox—"Good Night Irene," "Your Cheatin' Heart."

But the evening's real entertainment is two very drunken Great American Working Men with thick arms and beer bellies out over the tops of their Levi's (Raptor's rule: Wealthy American males of a like age have pear-shaped guts up over which they wear tailored slacks). These men don't have tax consultants, but they do have their Detroit tin, their washer-dryer, their outboard motorboat on a trailer in the backyard.

Tonight they are drunk in a bar near Hormel's, heads together to chuckle over one another's dirty stories. Then the one with hair rears back on his stool, almost falling over.

"You summitch, ya can't say that to me!"

"Say anything I wanna say, shitferbrains!"

They are off their stools, wild-eyed, lump fists faking jabs. Nobody moves to break them up. The Hairy Man's round-house swing at the Smooth Man's bald pate misses. The force of his own blow whirls him around so he knocks over two stools and lands on his *derrière*, startle-eyed.

"Get up'n fight!"

The Smooth Man shuffles like a trained bear. The Hairy Man rises. The Smooth Man swings at him, misses, spins, falls. Twice more each. They assist each other, ascend their stools.

"Onliest frien' I got inna worl'."

"Can't count on nobody but you."

They embrace, and weep upon one another's shoulders. Quaff their beer. Heads together, they chuckle once again.

"Rotten bassard, can't say that 'bout my wife!"

"You summitch, you said it 'bout *my* wife firs'!"

In almost an hour, neither lands a solid blow.

Sitting beside me through this floor show is a lanky sandy-haired man with large knuckly hands scrubbed red and raw-looking. He thrums like a high-power line as he sprinkles salt in his beer to raise the head, drinks, wipes his mouth with the back of his hand. His change and cigarettes are in the wet puddle left by his glass.

"Every fucking Friday night," he says. He has a low, hoarse voice that makes me want to clear my throat.

"Better than TV." I gesture at the bartender for refills of his glass, my own. "Any work at the packing plant?"

"You don't want to work there. I'm a plugger and . . ." I do not know what a plugger is. He starts to roll up his left sleeve. I do not know what he is doing. Stitched up his fore-arm is an orderly row of white dimples. "Gook AR rounds in 'Nam."

I clear my throat, but there is nothing in my throat except the sound of his voice. I wish I had been old enough to go to

Vietnam, see who I was, what I had. He nods as if I have spoken.

"Agent Orange," he says. I have never heard of Agent Orange. I am nineteen years old. "Why I got me this voice." He raises the beer I have bought him. "Dead gooks," he says.

We drink to dead gooks. He puts his glass down.

"We pack hogs. Cut their throats and hang them upside down on a conveyor. The bristles don't get used for brushes any more, so we take 'em off with acid. Whole hog except the head gets dipped in the vat."

He waits as the bartender brings us our beers. He is nodding to himself and drumming on the bar with the fingers of both hands the whole while. He drinks beer.

"If the acid gets under the skin, it'll ruin the meat."

"But if the head doesn't go in, how could the acid get—"

"The other end does."

I sit for a long moment with him, then, as I assimilate what he is telling me, I drain my beer just as he drained his.

"Yeah," he says. "For eight fucking hours a day I shove corks up the assholes of dead pigs."

Late as it is and drunk as I get before the 1:00 A.M. bar-close, I drive on out of Austin. I pull off the road somewhere on the way to Albert Lea, throw up the night's beer into a clump of willows, and sleep in my sleeping bag beside the car.

I do not know if his story is true, but in the casual hour of our acquaintance he does not strike me as a fanciful man. A proud man, with nothing in his life to be proud of—back then, Vietnam vets are denied their public due—but not fanciful.

So you see, I kill for existential reasons—if you can intuit the deductive validity of my argument.

I grow as long-winded as Will. You wish only to know why I kill the Mafia underboss the newspapers call the Spic.

What can I tell you? It is mere butchery, anyone could do it, not really my sort of thing at all. I have had no bad dreams about it, so my nightmare after Lenington was naught but aberration. Perhaps I et a bad oyster—remember that line by a drunken and delicious Kay Kendall in *Les Girls*?

But I digress. Two days after the Spic's assassination, I chance to read a one-inch piece about it in the *New York Times*, one of those much thinner editions distributed outside the five boroughs. Reading of it after the fact makes me feel strange—no, I am not going to tell you in which city or hamlet I read it. I do not wish you to know where these feats might take me; and tonight, after I end Will Dalton's miserable existence, it will be, as Stepin Fetchit used to say, Feets, Do Yo Stuff.

Since Spic Madrid is Chicano, an Hispanic voice sings my song of death to Stagnaro's answering machine. I discover the voice at the mission church five miles down the road. He is happy to read my little note into the telephone. He thinks it harmless fun. He thinks payment inappropriate, so I make a donation which I believe makes him happy. But who knows when dealing with a man of God?

Perhaps Will Dalton, still droning on, is also, as the Latin has it, *dis manibus sacrum*—sacred to the gods of the underworld. I hope so; because soon he will join them.

Do you really believe they will be there to welcome him?

CHAPTER TWENTY-ONE

"'In the beginning God created the heaven and the earth,'"
said Will. Looking around the hall, a fleeting pause at Dante.

"Pretty familiar, isn't it? Genesis, chapter one, verse one. I
want to contrast that story, spanning six days, with the same
story told by science, spanning 6 billion years. The Bible
representing myth, science representing the rational mind,
and here is the moment of intersection. Religionists might
object to calling the Holy Bible myth; but certainly Genesis
is the creation story (remember, myth can be more true than
mere fact) best known to our Western minds.

"Myth can tell us *who* we are—science, *what* we are. And
here is where the attempt to equate creationism with evolution—to present them both as authoritarian belief systems—
is bound to fail. Evolution is science; should it claim to be a
belief system, it would make a lousy one. When creationism,
a belief system, claims to be scientific, it makes lousy science. Here tonight, we seek not exacerbation, but intersection between the two systems. Is it possible, with science and
myth telling two such wildly different stories?

"Or do they? Genesis first: 'And the earth was without
form, and void; and darkness was upon the face of the deep.
And the spirit of God moved upon the face of the waters.'

"What says science of this birth? Science would go back
before the making of the heavens and earth, to the making of
the universe. Most astronomers today accept the Big Bang

theory: an immense explosion 15 billion years ago that flung energy and pulverized matter out as far as space stretches. Carl Sagan and Ann Druyan start the story of our earth 10 billion years later in *Shadows of Forgotten Ancestors:*

" 'There was once a time before the Sun and Earth existed, a time before there was day or night, long before there was anyone to record the beginning for those who might come after. . . . An immense cloud of gas and dust is swiftly collapsing under its own weight.'

"Almost 'in the beginning,' almost 'once upon a time'— but not quite. In their version, matter already exists. And they take pains to point out, 'Nothing lives forever, in Heaven as it is on Earth. Even the stars grow old, decay, and die.'

"In the Bible's account, only God is eternal. 'And God said, Let there be light: and there was light. . . . '

" 'And God divided the light from the darkness . . . And God called the light Day, and the darkness he called Night.'

"In the beginning, God was already here. The God, the Baltimore Catechism tells us, Who 'always was, and always will be, and always remains the same.' In other words, God's nature is *to exist*. It's what He does, all by Himself. There never was *nothing*, there always was *Something*—God. Self-creating. Self-sustaining.

"Thus Genesis would say, nothing *material* lives forever. Would say, science's immense clouds of gas and matter weren't there until God created them, because it was not their nature *to exist*. Would perhaps say that the Big Bang was merely God's hand-clap to create matter, and would ask, Where else *could* gas and dust come from—*in the beginning*?

"Science is usually silent on beginnings—remember?— and only says this swirling mass of gas and dust, whatever its origin, soon collapsed under its own weight. The chaotic cloud became a thin disk, glowing a dull red in its exact center. During the next 100 million years, the central mass got whiter, more brilliant, until finally, some 5 billion years ago, it burst into sustained thermonuclear fire. The sun had been born.

"'Let there be light: and there was light.'

"The two accounts don't differ much after all, do they?

"Inside that cloud, milling around that central fire, were a million or more small worlds, with a few thousand larger ones that eventually would collide and fuse together. All of this was occurring in a vast sparsely mattered intersteller vacuum within our galaxy, the Milky Way. Which, by the way, is only one of a hundred billion similar galaxies in the universe—where solar systems such as ours are being formed about one hundred a second.

"As the dust settled, a vast array of little worlds made up of those colliding atoms and grains began revolving around our sun in a variety of slightly different orbits. Inevitably, they started ramming into one another. If the meeting was head-on, goodbye, worldlets. If it was a matter of gently intersecting trajectories, however, one larger world could be born from the fusing of two smaller ones.

"Before long in astronomical terms—200 or 300 million years—just a relatively few larger bodies were left in established orbits around the sun, having escaped destructive collisions and having grown as smaller bodies hit them and were absorbed. They had become large enough, indeed, for their own spinning to have smoothed their irregular shapes into rough spheroids. One of them, third from our particular sun, had shaped itself into our earth about 4.5 or 4.6 billion years ago.

"Meanwhile, back in Genesis, God was also busy creating the earth; but we need some rearranging to illuminate the parallels between the two accounts. So let's for the moment move day four in Genesis ahead of day three.

"'And God said, Let there be lights in the firmament of the heaven to divide the day from the night; and let them be for signs, and for seasons, and for days, and years. . . .

"'And God made two great lights; the greater light to rule the day, and the lesser light to rule the night: he made the stars also.'

"In science's story we have already seen the birth of the sun—'the greater light to rule the day'—and of planet earth, and of those other countless planets and asteroids and small worlds Genesis calls stars. In both accounts we now have sun, earth, and stars all in place. In Genesis, too, the moon: 'the lesser light to rule the night.'

"So let's hear science on the creation of the moon.

"Despite it being now pretty much a sphere, earth was still colliding with smaller earths. Craters were gouged, debris flung up, ice became steam, and vapor shrouded our spinning world. The vapor trapped the heat from these continuing collisions, until the earth's surface became a sea of molten lava.

"From one such collision, a huge one, a sizable hunk of this molten magma was sent juddering off into space. Earth's gravitational pull was so strong that this drifting chunk couldn't escape, but began circling the earth in its own orbit.

"When it cooled down it was the moon. In its circling, in turn, its gravity set up tides of molten magma on the earth's surface and in its molten core, slowing its spinning and lengthening earth's day from a few hours to something nearer the current twenty-four."

Will paused, took a drink of water. Dante came off the wall with a start and looked guiltily around, realizing that for the past few minutes he had been standing there literally openmouthed, the threat of Raptor's attack forgotten. Hearing things he'd never heard before, totally absorbed, caught up. *Seeing* it all as if it were an animated reconstruction of the birth of the world on *Nova* or something. He heard it with a sense of wonder, something always in short supply in a cop's life.

And Will was going on. "So now we have the sun. We have the moon and the stars. We have the earth. We have the Bible's years and seasons (says science, our orbit around the sun), and days (says science, our rotation on our axis).

"Back to Genesis: 'And God said, Let the waters under the heaven be gathered together unto one place, and let the dry land appear; and it was so. And God called the dry land

Earth; and the gathering together of the waters called he Seas.'

"Science says that by this time our galaxy had been pretty well swept free of gas and dust and debris and rogue worldlets running around smashing into everybody. The explosions of collision were disappearing, with them the vapor that held their heat in, and the earth was starting to cool down. For a time, indeed, it literally froze—after its ocean of surface magma had solidified but before the bombardments had quite ceased—because the dust kept sunlight from reaching the surface.

"But as the sun got through we warmed up, and had several million years of rain—yes, H_2O as we know it today. With the dissipation of the dust atmosphere, a secondary atmosphere of outgassed water vapor was squeezed up from the earth's interior. The sun shone fitfully through this new atmosphere, making more water by vapor condensation, water that trickled down to fill the lowlands of the no-longer-quite-frozen surface.

"With this warming, history's biggest hailstones, huge boulders of ice that had formed in the earth's atmosphere, came raining back down to vaporize on contact. With them came many millions of years of torrential rain to form vast oceans.

"Bringing us, in both versions of earth's creation, to that vital moment when there suddenly was . . . *life*."

Life. The word brought Dante out of his trance again. Life and death. And he remembered.

CHAPTER TWENTY-TWO

Remembered being royally pissed off because Salvador Madrid was dead in Minnesota, unconnected to Moll Dalton's death in any way Dante could imagine, yet Raptor had found another voice in which to send his third mocking message, four months after the first one last October. None of it made any sense. But he was still bugging Hymie about this latest tape.

"Got my voiceprint yet, Hymie?"

Hymie gave him a pained expression. "Sound spectrogram," he corrected. "Yeah, I've got it—for what it's worth."

"Hell, Hymie, if they're as individual as fingerprints—"

"A gross oversimplification." Hymie opened his folder of printouts to jab a hairy-backed finger at the squiggles that looked like seismograph readings of earth movements. "This is a record of the frequency and strength of the voice signal through time. If the spikes and patterns don't match, that means they contain frequencies not present in the target spectrograms."

"And these don't match?"

"Even you can see they don't, even with the shitty samples you got me."

"Shitty? They're the originals right off my machine."

"I need at least ten common words of exceptional clarity from each tape for a visual comparison of spectrographs.

What have you given me?" He made a disdainful gesture. "'Raptor' and a mittful of conjunctions."

"Despite all the bitching, they're two different people."

"Two different people."

"Any way to tell nationality or racial stock?"

"Just the obvious stuff—one *sounds* like an African-American, one *sounds* like a Latino."

"Thanks, Hymie. Just hang on to them for me, will you?"

On the way to his office he stopped at Homicide to pick a fight with Tim Flanagan. He caught Tim behind the littered desk in his corner of the office, near a window looking out on the cold, gray, rainy day; the cars in the under-the-freeway parking lot gleamed like the arched backs of sounding dolphins.

Tim shoved a pink cardboard box of doughnuts toward Dante. "So I suppose now you want me to investigate that homicide back in Minneapolis for you." He chuckled. "When I was a kid, I used to think it was Many-apples, Many-soda."

Dante slid low in his chair, braced one knee against the edge of the desk and said in a disgruntled voice, "St. Paul."

Without changing tone, Tim said, "So I suppose now you want me to investigate that homicide back in St. Paul for you."

"I'd settle for you investigating my two homicides right here in your jurisdiction."

"You think all I got to do is chase around after your nutty theories? I got too much stuff to handle as it is—"

"Yeah. Doughnuts. Pizzas. Week-old Chinese take-out."

"Fuck you, chief." Tim leaned forward across the desk, the weight on his elbows, bunching his open-collared dress shirt around his meaty armpits. "Remember that Chinese kid they found shot in Golden Gate Park?"

"Sure. You figured it for being gambling-related."

"I figured wrong. The mother ran a Chinese gambling house, right enough, but her boyfriend, unbeknownst, as they say, to her, took out a big life insurance policy on the kid.

With himself as beneficiary. Anybody can do that, you know."

"And then had the kid snuffed?"

"Yeah. Insurance agent smelled a rat, came to us, we went after the guy, hard, he split open. I'd like to see the ratfink fucker fry, and he might just. But . . ." He shrugged, reached for a doughnut. "Fuck 'im. So you can't connect Madrid in St. Paul with Dalton or our own Jackie-baby?"

"Madrid was in Vegas last week with three, four other mob figures who *could* be connected with Atlas Entertainment, but . . ." Dante shrugged in turn. "One was in for a new golf course opening, one to look at horses, one to hear an opera singer, Spic to ogle the showgirls . . ."

"They all stay at the Xanadu?"

Dante nodded. "And a few days after they leave, Spic gets wasted with Popgun Ucelli's trademark M.O.—only the feds can't get Popgun out of Jersey at the time of the hit. I think he knows they're tapping him." He stood up, started pacing. "If it's a power play inside the mob, why Moll Dalton? Why Jack Lenington? If it *isn't* mob-related, why the mob-style hits, why Spic Madrid by the same M.O.?"

Flanagan leaned back and put his elbows on the arms of his creaking swivel chair and tented his fingers in front of him.

"Maybe your givens are fucked. Maybe you gotta get some fresh data. See it in a new light. You ever check out that Interpol material on Kosta Gounaris you asked for?"

"Tim, sometimes you aren't entirely stupid."

"Yeah, I think you're a great guy, too."

Dante's Organized Crime Task Force office was in a converted storage closet between two jury deliberation rooms on the court floor. To get there, a visitor had to go by the monitored desk from the public corridor to the private back hall connecting the judges' chambers, and even then had to know precisely how to find him. No windows, but he liked it. It held three desks, four chairs, two three-drawer file cabinets with good locks, and a blackboard with the preliminary findings he didn't mind being made public drawn neatly on it in red chalk.

In sharp contrast to Tim's cluttered desk, Dante's held a computer and screen, a Laserjet IIP printer Rosa had given him two Christmases ago, IN and OUT files squared on different corners, and a family portrait taken by a professional photographer for the church yearbook: Rosa, himself, and the kids when both of them had still been home.

Neither Danny nor his other inspector, Jamie Fraser, was in, so he started methodically through the Interpol response to his request for information on Gounaris.

Born of Greek parents in Istanbul just before World War II (no birth record available). Reputedly a child prostitute at the age of twelve in a brothel run by a Turkish pederast called Mustapha (last name not known). (Probably) disappeared from the brothel and Istanbul at age fifteen, just when Mustapha (maybe) was found in his bedroom with his throat slit (perhaps) and (rumor stated) the floorboards pried up to get at something hidden underneath.

Three years later, a teenager (reputed) to be Gounaris was in Greece, running cigarettes and booze into Turkey, raw opium back out. Was befriended (unconfirmed) by an American businessman (name unknown), who (supposedly) was in Athens to set up the importation of Greek cloth to the United States . . .

No birth record available . . . last name not known . . . probably . . . maybe . . . perhaps . . . rumor stated . . . reputed . . . unconfirmed . . . name unknown . . . supposedly . . .

The dossier didn't become factual until the 1960s, when twenty-one-year-old Kosta Gounaris bought a single rusted old British tramp steamer and began hauling putatively legitimate cargoes in and out of the Levant. After that the file was mostly media coverage as he expanded, buying freighters and tankers, becoming Gounaris Shipping as his fame and wealth increased along with the inevitable Onassis comparison. The file ended with his sale of Gounaris Shipping to a consortium of other Greeks.

The portrait of a tough survivor who dragged himself out of the slums and ended up president of a huge multinational company. The American dream played out in a thousand American ghettos and exported all over the world ever since World War II.

Dammit, *something* of use had to be there . . .

Who did he know was Greek might help him out with Gounaris? There was the man's discarded wife, of course, living in a suburb of Athens called Maroussi; but Dante spoke no Greek, could never get departmental approval to go to Greece and talk with her, and knew it was useless to ask the Greek cops to interview her for him. If *he* didn't know the questions he wanted to ask, how could he expect them to?

He needed someone who might have been involved in Greek shipping after the war, might have known Gounaris firsthand, might have heard some rumors about him. There were Greek cops on the San Francisco police force, but he couldn't go to them; his habitual M.O. and his cop's paranoia made it essential that his informant be unconnected with the department.

Dante was sort of helping Rosa with the dishes—she washed, he dried what didn't go into the dishwasher—when he got his idea. He'd already poked into Gounaris's business life at Atlas Entertainment; maybe he could poke into his private life a little also, in ways that would shake him up without bringing another stinging letter from St. John as head counsel for Atlas.

"You know that Greek movie festival over in Berkeley at the Pacific Film Archives you were talking about? Who goes to something like that?"

Rosa laughed. "Me, for one thing. Maybe you—have you forgotten you said you wanted to—"

"I mean, do a lot of Greeks go?"

"Mostly Greeks."

"Prominent ones?"

She looked at him shrewdly. "Okay, big boy, what's going on? When you start treating me like a witness to a murder . . ."

So they sat on the couch and talked. Through the wall from the bedroom where Tony was supposedly studying came the beat of an album called *Rembrandt Pussyhorse* by an obscure vile punk band he had chosen to shock his folks with, the Butthole Surfers. The Surfers actually weren't too bad, but Dante always objected very conscientiously to whatever band Tony chose; he didn't want to deprive him of the joy of blowing his parents' minds.

Dante told Rosie about the Interpol reports.

"Gounaris had to get investment capital from somewhere to buy his first freighter, then to expand. He wasn't going to get it from the World Bank, that's for damn sure."

"So if the American cloth buyer was Mafia . . ."

"I'd have the connection I'm looking for. It's so thin that if it turns sideways you can't see it, but it fits the other facts I have right now. If Atlas Entertainment is a mob front, there has to be some earlier point of connection between them and Gounaris—they didn't pick him off the street."

"Will he be at the Greek Film Fest? Probably, at least for some films. The Greek community is pretty cohesive, and this is a big event." She clapped her hands. "Of course! *1922!* He'll *have* to go to that one. He's a Greek from Turkey, and *1922* is a film about the extermination of the Greek colony in Smyrna after the Greek Army was withdrawn. Those who didn't get on the boats were sent on a death march through Asia Minor. Almost all of them died. It's showing this weekend."

The theater at the Film Archives was intimate, its banks of seats steeply angled so there was no trouble seeing the screen over the heads of the people in front of you. Also no trouble seeing the people coming in through the curtained doorway to the right of the screen

They sat with Anna Efstathiou, who taught Rosa's dance

class, and Nikos Xiotras, Anna's lifelong friend and associate in Greek dance instruction. Anna was a tall, quick-moving woman with utterly black hair and huge, beautiful, penetrating eyes in a strong and unforgettable face. She and Nikos were almost constantly waving, calling, laughing, chatting over the recorded *bazouki* music.

Then Gounaris was there, moving easily through the entering throng, shaking hands and flashing white teeth in his dark face in a practiced smile. Dante, seated on the aisle, stood up abruptly.

"Be right back," he said to Rosa.

He angled his way through the patrons coming up the stairs, and was right in front of Gounaris as the tall Greek was about to move down a row of seats.

"Mr. Gounaris! Pleasant surprise," Dante said in a totally unsurprised voice.

Gounaris started back, a startled look on his face. He had been scanning the crowd for faces he knew before taking a seat.

"Our attorney sent you a letter about harassment—"

"This is just social." Dante winked at him. "Hope you took my advice about those porn houses in the Tenderloin."

He went back up to his seat, Gounaris's stony eyes on him for a long moment before the Greek turned away to find a seat the others in his party were holding for him. Rosa was regarding Dante with shrewd disapproval.

"Gounaris, I take it."

Dante grinned, pleased with himself. "In the flesh."

"You had to do it, didn't you?"

"Yeah."

"Handsome devil," she said, and gave her little giggle.

The houselights went down and the film started before he could respond. It was powerful and wrenching, leaving the audience drained. Greek memories of Turkish atrocities were long, their lists of dead relatives longer still. At the end of the film, Dante looked for Gounaris, but he had slipped away during the film. Ruined your evening, thought Dante exultantly.

Afterward the four of them strolled across the avenue to

Henry's in the Hotel Durant for ice cream sundaes and coffee. The talk drifted to Greece. Almost every year Anna leased a yacht to take a group of Americans on a guided tour of the Greek islands.

"Usually the Aegean is very kind to us, very smooth, the food marvelous, the weather great, the people wonderful, the yacht terrific." Her voice was soft with memory, but then her black eyes snapped like firecrackers. Her mother had fled Smyrna by boat just before the withdrawal, so the film had aroused a lot of memories for her. "But one year we stopped in Smyrna. We went into a Greek barbershop, and the man made us speak to him only in English. He said if the Turks knew we were Greek, we could get into a lot of trouble."

"Even though you were American citizens?" asked Rosa.

Anna spooned more hot fudge over her ice cream. "Just speaking Greek would be enough."

"The Armenians were killed first," said Nikos. "Then the Greeks. Men, women, children—you were killed or you were marched out. Kill the men, rape the women, then kill them too."

Nikos was a short, strong-looking man with a mustache and curly gray hair; like Anna, he was American-born but Greek-speaking. He had been in the American Navy during World War II, and American, Greek, and world history were his meat and drink. His blue eyes were filled with passionate outrage.

"When you think of all the gifts and talents destroyed! Doctors, lawyers, teachers—who knows, maybe one of them would have cured cancer or found the key to world peace!"

Rosa asked, "Are there many Anatolian Greeks in the Bay Area?"

"Certainly! A lot of them were in the audience tonight."

"Ari Onassis was from Smyrna," said Anna. "And Kosta Gounaris was from Constantinople."

"He was at the film tonight," said Nikos. "He left before the end of 1922. Dante seemed to know him." There was little that Nikos's quick eyes missed. Dante waved a dismissive hand.

"Interviewed him as a witness in a case a while back."

"I didn't see him," said Anna in an almost offended voice, as if anyone prominent in the Greek community who didn't greet her was not to be tolerated. Then she added, eyes gleaming with speculation, "I wonder why he would leave early?"

I could tell you, Dante thought; but he knew he wouldn't. He didn't want to involve them, even peripherally, in his case. And not just for him; for their sakes, too.

"A good-looking man!" said Anna with relish. "I remember him dancing the *zembeikiko* during the festival at our church in Castro Valley. He dances it like a Greek."

"He'd drop to the floor, then leap into the air like an eagle," said Nikos. "And he has to be over fifty years old!"

"Remember Georgios Stefanatos, used to come to dance class until his knees gave out?" asked Anna. "Didn't he captain a Gounaris freighter at one time?"

"Haven't seen him in years," mused Nikos. "I wonder if he's still living over in Marin?"

Anna laughed. "Do you remember the time he . . ."

Rosa joined in; Dante could tune out their reminiscences without being rude. Damn, he loved being a detective! There was a rhythm to it: he'd needed a window into Gounaris's early life; but not being able to find one, he'd settled for coming to the Greek Film Festival in hopes Gounaris would see him there and be jarred into doing something ill-considered.

Gounaris had left before the end of the film, so his departure was noted. But there was more. Because Dante was here tonight, he had a chance to maybe get what he'd needed from the beginning. And he hadn't had to abuse Rosa's friendship with Anna and Nikos to do it. It had just dropped into his lap. He wondered if there was some Greek god he could thank for this bounty—he'd have to ask Rosa.

Because now he had that needed window into Kosta Gounaris's life, if he was skillful enough to open it.

Georgios Stefanatos.

CHAPTER TWENTY-THREE

No phone, listed or otherwise, and Georgios Stefanatos did not show up on the Marin voter registration or property tax rolls. No car registered in his name, no driver's license. No wants or warrants. But when Dante checked public utilities, there he was: single-party utilities, water, and sewage hookups at the Kappas Marina on Waldo Point Harbor in Sausalito.

When it had been big with the bootleggers in the 1920s, Sausalito had been a sleepy little Italian/Portuguese fishing village facing Belvedere Island across Richardson Bay just north of the Golden Gate. Then, reachable only by ferry. The Golden Gate Bridge had changed all that, bringing auto traffic to Marin. Dante's fond Sausalito memories were from the seventies, when it had been a tourist town on the weekends but still wonderful midweek. Now it was jammed all the time, parking a permanent nightmare.

But Waldo Point was off Gate Six Road, the last stoplight on Bridgeway before the U.S. 101 North freeway entrance, thus outside the feeding-frenzy area. The sun was just setting behind dusk-purpled Mount Tam when Dante pulled onto the narrow blacktop behind the Marina Center, a sprawling gray two-story commercial complex. Fat wooden posts with loops of heavy chain slung between them separated the roadway from the stagnant little arm of Richardson Bay where the houseboats were moored.

He went through a gate in the fence and up a walkway of slanting planks to a locked and heavily barred metal gate. Yellow light shone down on twin banks of aluminum mailboxes, twenty-five to a side, with name slots on their fronts. No Stefanatos.

Beyond the locked gate, the pier stretched away like the railroad tracks in an art-lesson perspective drawing. From far down the dock a man was approaching. Up close he was lean and balding and black, with a round face and gentle eyes and wearing a black and silver Raiders windbreaker.

When he opened the gate to come out, Dante slid through.

"I'm looking for a houseboat owner, but he's not listed."

"I've been here sixteen years, I know just about everyone on the pier. I guess I'm about the oldest one around." He chuckled; he had a deep bass voice and *basso profundo* laugh. "*Both* ways, probably, it comes to that. If he's got a boat here, I'll know him."

"Georgios Stefanatos?"

"Georgie? The only guy on West Pier older than I am—by age, not by longevity on the dock." He gestured at the nearest houseboat. "You're almost standing on his deck."

The boat was some thirty feet long, built over a faded maroon metal hull with a somewhat upswept prow. The outslanting wooden superstructure had been built on top of that, vertical boards going up to a steeply slanted cedar shake roof with two miniature chimneys. Lines ran down into the water for electricity, gas, water and sewage. Dante expected Popeye to pipe him aboard.

"It's unusual compared to the rest of 'em—was a real boat before it was converted to a houseboat. Doesn't look like Georgie's home right now, but he never goes very far. I'm sure he wouldn't mind if you waited on his afterdeck."

A faded maroon awning covered half the boat's stern; there was a riot of ivies and ferns and herbs in clay pots or tattered woven baskets. Two of them rested on old wicker chairs. A pair of gulls swam around in the seaweed behind the houseboat; in the gathering darkness, the water was a dirty green.

Dante sat down gingerly in a sag-bottomed old canvas lawn chair, and promptly fell asleep. Georgios Stefanatos woke him up an hour later when he wheeled his ten-speed aboard.

"I was up at the Cafe Trieste in town, you know it? On Bridgeway." The old man chuckled. He was in his late seventies and had a gray beard and a blue denim Greek fishing hat smashed down on thick gray curly hair. His eyes were shrewd and dark and full of life. "I can bullshit about my seafaring days with the weekend sailors getting their lah-di-dah *lattes* up there."

"No Greek coffee?" asked Dante with a grin.

"Sure! But I had to buy it for 'em at a Greek shop in the city an' show 'em how to do it. Who the hell are you?"

"Dante Stagnaro. Anna Efstathiou and Nikos Xiotras—"

"Anna! Jesus, there's a woman for you!" Stefanatos clapped his hands together once in delight. "And smart! Marry her, she'd make you rich. And Nikos is good people!"

He leaned his bike against the railing under one of the hanging plants as he unlocked the door.

"I used to go to Anna's Greek dance class, had to quit when my knees went." He looked back over his shoulder and winked as he snapped on the lights. "Now I only dance the *zembeikiko* and only after so much ouzo I don't feel 'em 'til morning."

The *zembeikiko*—the same dance Anna had remembered Gounaris doing at one of the Greek festivals. From Rosa, he knew it usually was danced by men alone, when moved by music to sudden otherwise inexpressible emotion.

Inside, he found the little houseboat beautifully laid out. He said almost wistfully, "Looks like a nice life here."

"Oh, it is, it is." Stefanatos jerked his head at a narrow stairway leading down into the hull of the boat. "Got a little bedroom down there, so I got water slapping the hull beside me when I go to sleep."

Stefanatos went up to the prow, which had a tiny forward-looking bay window framed by black metal racks holding spices. The similar bay windows on each side of the living room held decorative brass ornaments, seashells, netting, things picked up at most of the world's ports during a lifetime at sea.

He brought back two brandy snifters and a bottle of Metaxas, poured without asking. They sat at a round wooden table beside a black iron potbelly stove. Like the other furnishings, it was miniaturized to studio apartment size. His pipe drifted aromatic smoke through the room. The bookshelves on either side of the kitchen doorway were filled with a seagoing man's library in Greek and English.

Stefanatos drank Metaxas, swiveled a sudden sharp eye at Dante across the table. "Real close friend of Anna's, you say."

"Met her once."

Dante stopped there; in interrogations, silence usually made the other person come to you. But Georgios Stefanatos merely stretched across the table to clink glasses.

"Yassou."

They drank. The Metaxas burned its way down into Dante's empty gut. He'd missed lunch and hadn't yet had supper. He broke first, finally saying, "Kosta Gounaris."

"Agio Nikolao sosete mas!" exclaimed a startled Stefanatos. He poured them each another tot, looked at Dante shrewdly. "Anna tell you I got my first blue-water command under Gounaris?"

Dante answered with a question of his own.

"You know he's now living in San Francisco?"

Stefanatos gestured at the big color TV with a VCR on top of it backed up against the starboard bulkhead. "Hell, son, I'm old, I'm not dead. Uncle Al hasn't come calling yet." Uncle Al. Alzheimer's. "You a real close friend of Kostas's? Maybe like you're a close friend of Anna's?"

Fifteen years a cop counseled caution, but this was not a man who would be a friend, even if he had worked for him, of the Gounaris Dante had built up in his mind. And if Dante's picture of Gounaris was skewed, now was the time to have it corrected.

"I'm a cop on an investigation. Routine. I'm not accusing him of anything, just—"

"Too bad," cackled Stefanatos. "There's a lot you could accuse him of. He slit the throat of a fat Turk for the strongbox under the floor when he was fifteen, you know."

"I read an unconfirmed Interpol report about it, but—"

"True report! He used to brag about it when he was drunk. That was early days, he had the one freighter then, the *Makedonia,* he was captain, I was first mate . . ." He trailed off with a faraway look in his eyes. "Half a lifetime ago, Kostas was twenty-one when he got that freighter."

"Where'd he get the money? From under the Turk's floor?"

"Naw, that just got him out of Constantinople, financed the *caïque* he used for his smuggling in and out of Turkey . . ." He cocked a quick inquisitive birdlike eye at Dante. "You prob'ly heard 'bout that too, didn't you?"

"Another rumor, yeah."

Georgie shook his head vigorously. "Also true. But he couldn't have made the down payment on the *Makedonia* from that. Once he got his second tramp, he made me captain of the *Makedonia* and opened an office on a dock in Piraeus. Never went to sea again until years later when he got that yacht of his."

"You sound like you've thought about this some."

Stefanatos rapped himself vigorously on the temple with fisted knuckles. "Greeks are smart. We talk to everybody and want to know everything. Course I've thought about it."

"So who *would* finance a freighter for a twenty-one-year-old kid with no history? Even just an old tramp steamer . . ."

Stefanatos nodded as if he'd made a statement rather than asked a question. "He wasn't making enough out of the *Makedonia* to finance it, was he?" He cackled and clapped his hands again. "You could barely trust that old hulk out of sight of land. Hell, you hit the hull with a sledgehammer, anywhere, an inch of scale'd fall off. No holystoning *those* decks, I can tell you. You'd of gone right through."

"You know where the money came from, don't you, Captain?"

Georgios stared at him a long moment, then heaved himself to his feet and went toward the staircase leading below.

"You just pour another tot for each of us," he said.

Ten minutes later, the old Greek captain slapped a beat-up logbook with a red-bound hard canvas cover down on the table between them with such triumph that it knocked over his snifter. He picked up the logbook, shook it, sending drops of Metaxas flying in every direction, then sat down with it.

"Log of the *Makedonia,* plenty of booze spilled on it in its day. Took it with me when I left."

Dante asked the expected question. "Why was that?"

"Kostas wanted to overinsure the *Makedonia* and her cargo, then have me scuttle her the first big blow came along. Said I wouldn't, said if he did I'd testify at the inquiry . . . Kostas wasn't a bad guy, just was crooked as a snake." He shook his head. "But you don't ask *me* to scuttle my ship."

Dante stayed silent. There were times to push your man, times to let him come to you.

"I got a command under Niarchos, when the *Makedonia* did go down in the North Atlantic I was at sea myself." He righted his snifter, poured himself another measured tot, held it up to the light as if the smoky liquid held answers to his inner distress. "But I never felt right about just letting it go."

"Not much you could do after the fact like that."

"Yep." He got a sly look on his face. "Y'know, Kostas was rich, but the richest man I ever met was a cloth buyer rode with me on a cargo run to Alexandria and back on the *Makedonia.* Right before Kostas got his second freighter." The logbook was closed against the finger he had inserted between its pages. He opened it, tapped the page with a blunt curved fingernail. "It's in here. In the log."

The logbook was written in Greek. Dante looked up at Stefanatos with arched eyebrows.

"Abramson," the captain said. "Gideon Abramson."

Dante got home in high spirits. Rosa was out, as was fourteen-year-old Antonio even though it was a school night. No note, which meant Rosa wasn't gone for long. He'd been starving in Sausalito, but now he just wanted a long shower to wash the rest of the Metaxas out of his system. Then, if Rosa wasn't home yet, he'd cook supper for everybody. But he was still sponging down the shower stall when the door opened and Rosa peeked in.

"You're home!" she exclaimed in delight.

"Unless you got another guy uses this shower."

"No one but you, alas."

She had obviously been shopping, and was dressed in jeans and a frilly white blouse with long sleeves and a scoop neck. He could just faintly smell her perfume, something flowery their daughter had given her for her birthday. When she leaned in to give him a quick kiss, he peeked down her blouse like a sex-starved teenager. He started to get an erection.

"You want something to eat, sweetie?" she asked.

He did a Groucho eyebrow wiggle. "What'd you have in mind, m'dear?" and faked a grab for her. But she was gone, the shower stall door drifting shut behind her. He yelled after her, "What kind of woman leaves a man in a state like this?"

The door opened again so she could stick her head back in.

"Anticipation is everything, sweet lips."

Gone again. Dante, chuckling, dressed in workout shorts and a tank top and floppy go-aheads, padded into the office he'd made of Giulietta's bedroom. In one corner he had installed a straight-backed chair and a desk he'd bought for a few bucks at a library sale.

Dante put the growing stack of files connected with the Moll Dalton murder on the pink bedspread of the frilly canopy bed where Giulietta still slept when she came home from U.C. Berkeley on weekends. He switched on the old-fashioned gooseneck lamp.

Hymie the Handler had given him the numbers of Lenington's $5,000 in small unsequenced bills, but none had shown up in circulation in the western states. Dante made a notation to circularize banks across the rest of the country also.

Nothing more on Spic Madrid. St. Paul cops and the FBI were writing it off as local; as a result the feds had turned down his suggestion that a tail be put on Eddie Ucelli for a couple of weeks to see if he went anywhere. The Bureau, they said, didn't have the manpower for it.

Even if he were willing to tell them about the Raptor calls they would just laugh. Hoax confessions were a staple of murder cases, and these were oblique and after the fact.

His request for a tap on Gounaris's home and office phones had been turned down. The same for a tap on the pay phones in the Atlas Entertainment building lobby. He hadn't really expected either one, but he'd had to ask. Ditto for a tap on Skeffington St. John's phones in L.A., home and office. Again, no surprise.

None of it high priority. High priority was his discovery of the American businessman who had been a guest of the twenty-three-year-old Gounaris aboard the *Makedonia* for a run to Alexandria and back in August 1962. Gideon Abramson. A Gideon Abramson was one of the four known Mafia bigwigs who had stayed at the Xanadu Hotel owned by Martin Prince, acknowledged *capo di tutti i capi* for the current Organization west of the Mississippi.

Scanning his case notes, Dante realized that the meeting had taken place just a few days after he had jerked around Moll Dalton's incestuous father. Cause and effect? Could be. It was hard to believe that if Atlas Entertainment was mixed up in organized crime, its chief counsel didn't know about it.

He went through the FBI reports. They already had photos on file for three of the four Gideon Abramsons—loan shark in New York's garment industry, retiree in Palm Springs, golf player in Vegas—and they were demonstrably identical.

Now that Dante had the passport number of the cloth buyer in Greece, the FBI could get his picture, too. He was certain the fourth Gideon Abramson would complete the chain between Gounaris, Atlas Entertainment, and the Mafia.

It was a connection that suggested reasons why Moll Dalton might have been murdered. If the Mafia was in control of Atlas, and she uncovered proof of that control, she would have become a lethal liability. Could Moll's father be part of the Outfit without her knowledge? Yes. But if she found out, and resentment of her childhood abuse still lived in her mind . . .

Nothing suggested that it did. And the scenario didn't tell him a damned thing about why Jack Lenington and Spic Madrid had been hit. They weren't his cases, but there were those damned Raptor phone calls. The calls tied the three murders together. If the calls weren't a hoax.

But his mind wasn't ready to let it go at that. He jotted down notes to himself. Try to find and interview Moll Dalton's mother, still presumably living somewhere in the L.A. Basin, for more leverage on St. John. Write or call Will Dalton's parents in Wyoming? No real reason to, except maybe they could tell him things about Moll that Will had been unwilling to do.

He realized with a start that it was nearly one in the morning, four hours since Rosa had brought him his dinner of *fettuccine con funghi* drenched in the dark mushroom sauce he loved. Rosa would be long since in bed, asleep.

But when he slid naked between the fresh fragrant sheets, as he always slept except for a T-shirt during the cold winter months, Rosa sighed in contentment and turned to him in silent hunger, still half-asleep, with open arms and hungry mouth, her tongue finding his, their hands finding each other's bodies as she drew him with her into the silken wonder of their love.

CHAPTER TWENTY-FOUR

Shady Lady was at it again. She was very obviously in estrus, the perineum around her genitals swollen into a great pink blossom. Will had named the chimp Shady Lady because when he had last seen her two years ago, she had been in the same state and methodically soliciting every stud in town for a quick wham-bam-thank-you-ma'am. Or rather, wham-bam-thank-you-sir.

"Town" for the moment was a giant *mucuso* fig spreading its great canopy arms over the forest floor in the middle of the Kibale Forest Preserve a lot of miles from any people besides Will. Fort Portal, the closest human town, was thirty miles of mud track away. The *mucuso* was crammed with ripe fruit, and first had attracted three male chimps, led by Randy Andy, a prime male with a sagittal crest more like a gorilla's than a chimpanzee's.

They had begun the haunting pant-hoot cries by which chimps communicate over long distances of forest, calling others to the feast, and soon nine males and three females were there, eating figs as fast as they could stuff them into their mouths.

Will shifted slightly in his uncomfortable perch two hundred feet away from the forest giant. He had bent African ginger and giant ferns down on top of one another to make a sort of nest offering partial concealment. The binoculars brought the troop of apes up to within a few startling feet of him.

He got a tremendous jolt, as always, seeing these forest people in their natural habitat. It was nothing like *Bedtime for Bonzo* or the chimpanzee named Cheetah in the old Johnny Weismuller Tarzan movies. These were wild animals and yet were so close to man in their actions, facial expressions, ways of moving and thinking and communicating, that it was like seeing your own slightly distorted mirror image, or looking down into the depths of your own being and seeing them crouched there.

The chimps had to use a close-by, smaller tree to gain access to the *mucuso,* which was smooth-boled, without limbs, its great crown spreading itself almost a hundred feet above the forest floor. It was a perfect scene of male bonding—the males were ignoring the females—until Shady Lady climbed up the egress tree to the feast from the wet, steaming jungle below.

Randy Andy, so named by Will because he was always ready for any quickie he could get, was the first to realize Shady Lady was in heat. Being a dominant male, he immediately began trying to monopolize her in what scientists like to call "possessive mating." This meant staring at her intently as she sashayed around the giant limbs of the fig tree, until he was sure of her attention, then flicking his relatively large erect penis suggestively with his fingers.

This was all poor sex-crazed Shady Lady needed. She turned to thrust her hugely swollen perineum almost into his face, letting her sexual perfume waft past his nostrils, then pushed back against him. He thrust into her with great speed, thirteen times to completion, and she screamed—Will didn't know if it was her own complementary completion or what—and moved away from him. Chimpanzees' matings, though frenzied, were of very short duration. Often only ten seconds from intromission—another one of those sexy scientific words—to completion.

Randy Andy swaggered after her to prevent any other male from mounting her. But a particularly juicy fig distracted his attention for a precious few moments, and Lefty, so named by Will because he had lost his right hand to a poacher's wire snare, managed to grab Shady Lady from behind one-handed and pump into her for seven seconds before Andy charged him, screaming threats.

Lefty fled to safety by leaping into the egress tree and plummeting like a stone eighty feet to the ground, somehow making do for holds with his single hand, then disappearing between the giant buttress roots of the *mucuso*. Andy followed him partway down, baring his fangs and screaming extravagant insults, even throwing a fistful of underripe figs after him. Then he started back up with self-satisfaction oozing from every pore.

A victory, but bad tactics. Will's glasses showed him that as soon as Andy had torn off in pursuit of poor old Lefty, Knuckles had sidled up to Shady Lady with his penis erect. She presented, he mounted her, thrust to completion. They uncoupled, turned away from each other as Captain Hook slipped up behind her to take his turn.

And to be charged by a roaring Andy, newly returned. But the Captain was no Lefty. He stood his ground for several seconds, jumping up and down and screaming insults in turn.

Long enough for Shady Lady to spot another as yet unseduced male eating figs behind a screen of foliage, and climb up to present. When he mounted her, Will saw that he was Zonkers, whose distinctively short, light hair showed his unusually well muscled physique to good advantage.

Will called him Zonkers because he was the first chimp crazy enough to take Will at face value when he had connected up with one of the troops in the forest. Zonkers not only tolerated him as a silent watcher, but by his nonchalance at Will's presence made the scientist at least partially forgettable and thus partially invisible to the other chimps.

Then Zonkers became as curious about him as he was about them. Zonkers would fake charges, rushing along a limb toward him, slapping the smooth bark with his hands. Will would scratch under his arm and exhibit other nonaggressive behavior, and Zonk would return to his fruit, his status raised among the other males by his daring maneuver. Sometimes, if alone, he would sit in a tree for a half hour just staring at Will fifty yards away, then drop down to disappear into the understory foliage and pant-hoot away into the distance.

Zonk didn't have his permanent canines yet, suggesting he was a couple of years from full adulthood—maybe thirteen years old. Since the chimpanzee life span, barring sickness or accident or fatal wounding, could reach around forty, he was a wonderful connection who could be a valuable asset for years to come.

But he was so much more than just an asset. After those first encounters, Will had seen him often enough that a sort of long-distance relationship had grown up between them. Then one day Zonkers had dropped out of a fig tree a hundred feet ahead and had strolled provocatively—if the chimps' rolling side to side knuckle-walking could be called strolling—down one of the tunnel-like game trails through the thick underbrush. And Will had followed, crouched and stealthy, praising himself on moving so quietly that Zonkers didn't even know he was back there.

After some twenty minutes, during which he never caught another glimpse of the ape, Will paused in a small clearing to stand erect and stretch his stiff back—he had to move through the tunnels bent over because he was so much taller than the chimps.

A dozen yards ahead was Zonkers, sitting on a tree limb that extended over the trail. He had his elbows on his knees and his chin resting on the backs of his crossed wrists, and was studying Will intently. When he met Will's eyes, he made a funny grimace that was surely a grin, stood, stretched himself, and melted into the understory foliage without sound or even apparent movement. He obviously had arranged the whole scenario.

An even more remarkable encounter came a month later, when Will was hurrying back to his hut at dusk, having kept vigil at a huge *dawei* tree where the chimps were feeding. He had stopped to pick a pocketful of figs to stretch his own dinner, and had no flashlight. Stumbling over a clump of twisted roots on the narrow footpath, he went down on one hand and one knee. When he started to push himself erect, Zonkers was sitting on the path only ten feet away, regarding him intently over one shoulder.

This was the sort of close encounter he had only dreamed of. Zonkers wrinkled his forehead and briefly scratched his left arm. His fingers sounded like sandpaper on his rough hide. Will immediately sat down and scratched himself vigorously in the same way. Zonkers didn't move away and didn't even look nervous, only unsettled. What further was possible?

Will slowly reached into his pocket for his figs. He had eight of them—which by chance was, observation had taught him, just about what a chimp could stuff into his cheeks at one time. Will held them in his open hand, then very very slowly leaned forward and even more slowly stretched out his hand and with a little flick of the wrist tossed the figs in a compact clump to the path about five feet from Zonk.

Neither moved for a full minute, although Zonk's eyes, more calculating than cautious, flitted continually from the figs to Will and back to the figs again. Then, ever so slowly, he leaned toward Will and stretched out one of his long arms, and his long flexible hairy-backed fingers closed around the figs. He only got seven of them, one was left on the trail. He stood erect, stuffing the figs into his mouth.

Then he gave a sudden yelp, leaped toward the last fig—and incidentally, Will—scooped it up, and in a second bound was gone into the undergrowth. Will blundered home wet and muddy and insect-stung long after dark, finding the hut more by accident than skill, but happier and more excited than he had been at any time since Molly had died.

And now here was Zonk again, getting laid, if dog style—chimp style?—could be called by that term. Will marked the time in his notebook—twenty-seven seconds. World-class for a chimp. But when he reapplied the binocs to his eyes, Shady Lady already was having it off with another, Old Blue. Six seconds.

So much for true love. Will busied himself with his notes, but he was feeling something . . . *wrong* about the observing. As if he didn't have the right. As if it violated something in his one-sided bond with the animals. So the next hour of Shady Lady's sexual activities came to him almost as *tableux*, when he would look up from his notes and raise the binoculars to his eyes for the quick observation the scientist in him made *de rigueur* no matter what his personal feelings.

At first, Randy Andy was successful in his possessive mating strategy. For nearly half an hour he was making it with Lady about every ten minutes. None exceeded fourteen seconds in duration.

Finally Randy was all through—he couldn't get it up any more. He returned to his figs. Shady Lady was of sterner stuff; she was insistent. He moved away, she followed; Will's binocs were tight on his face at that moment, and he could have sworn he saw alarm there. He was sure of it when Shady Lady began tweaking Andy's flaccid penis in hopes of getting a little action. Andy—Randy no more—fled, shrieking.

Will lowered his glasses, lowered his head, scribbled furiously in his notebook. He felt strange, had a choking sensation in his throat, a burning in his eyes.

When he looked up again, the other eight male chimps were lined up to take turns on the complaisant, indeed demanding, Lady in what scientists liked to call opportunistic mating. Will suddenly remembered a book by an apostate Hell's Angel he had read years before. The man had turned state's evidence against his former associates concerning a couple of cold-blooded murders, and had gone into the witness relocation program.

His book had been full of raunchy anecdotes about Angel activities in the swinging sixties, including that feature of every encampment, Angels lining up for a gang bang on some complaisant, indeed demanding, Mama. They called it pulling a train—because at the head of the line, on her back in some thicket, was the Mama taking them all on one after the other, puffing and chuffing like a locomotive.

Will was too far away from Shady Lady in her thicket of *mucuso* leaves to know if she was grunting like a locomotive pulling a train or not, but there were the males lined up with very little time between mountings, each taking ten to fifteen seconds for the act, then moving to the end of the line for another turn.

Will knew he was observing an extreme end of the chimp spectrum of sexual behavior in the wild; at the other end, as with humans, was pair-bonding. And unlike Shady Lady this time, most female chimps in heat would have a nursing infant doing his shrieking, biting, hair-pulling best to interrupt his mother's couplings—a new baby would take her attention from him, thus reduce his chances for survival.

Finally all were through—worn-out. Exhausted. Not Shady Lady. She put a move on the closest ape, Captain Hook, but he gave a shriek of alarm and fled at her approach. She stood looking after him, one hand between her legs in momentary, absentminded masturbation, then spotted Old Gray higher in the tree and took off after him.

Damn! Raindrops were hitting the pages of Will's notebook. Then he realized they were tears, not raindrops, and belatedly knew what the tightness in his throat and burning in his eyes had been.

For the second time in his adult life, Will Dalton was crying, silently at first, then sobbing aloud, shoulders hunched.

Moll. He had been seeing Moll there through his field glasses, Moll with a line of eager, raunchy men waiting their turn at her, Moll puffing and grunting and pulling her sexual train while he stood aside and watched, Moll whom he wanted and needed . . . Where was the difference?

And what difference did it make? He loved her, wanted her, craved her, lusted after her, needed her, no matter who she was or what she had done. And she was gone. Unfairly, undeservedly dead and gone and buried and he was still here.

So he cried, cried as if he would never stop, cried out of his grief and rage and loss and anger, cried there in his little crushed nest of ginger and ferns, cried at last for Molly as he had been unable to cry at her funeral. As he had begun to cry for her at his home until the two cops had arrived with their good-guy bad-guy routine to disabuse him forever of his naive delusions of their love together . . .

He realized that for some time a consoling arm had been draped across his shoulders, long fingers had been gently patting his upper arm. Will turned his head, slowly, unbelievingly. Zonkers was sitting beside him, his long arm around Will's quaking shoulders, offering silent comfort for his vocal grief. When, in his shock and amazement, he stopped wailing, Zonkers suddenly was gone, leaving only swaying branches behind him.

Will stood up also, almost overwhelmed by a great uprush of emotion. Chimps couldn't cry, couldn't possibly feel sorrow. Not as a human being did. Only Zonkers had. Had known those sounds Will Dalton was making were sounds of desolation, and had known, somehow, what desolation meant. And had offered comfort.

Will thought feverishly, he would stay here forever. His supplies were all but exhausted. So what? He would live as the chimpanzees did.

Better than that, he would make Edgar Rice Burroughs's fantasy creation of Tarzan a reality. He would join the troop. Live on fruit, maybe the occasional monkey or small antelope the chimps and him, hunting in unison, could catch. He would lead them through the forest, learn from them, teach them to avoid poacher's snares, would cut the snares that couldn't be avoided off their arms and legs before the limb could drop off from lack of circulation . . .

Meanwhile, his notebook was bulging with new observations that would have to be rerecorded and systematized, but Zonk comforting him would never be passed on to his colleagues. Few would believe it, but beyond that, it would be a betrayal of whatever had reached across 5 million years to bind them together in mutual distress and comfort.

So it was Will Dalton, ethologist, who dazedly gathered up rucksack, notebook, pen, binoculars, moving on automatic. This was crazy stuff, this was total emotional breakdown. Yet the bursting forth of his desolation and loss, and the ape's genetic understanding of it, had told him he had to complete his work. He had been wavering, vacillating; now he knew he had made the right choice. It was as Ardrey had said: our hearts were indeed pledged to the animal world's subtle, antique ways.

Meanwhile, he was down to a quarter kilo of coarse-ground white corn flour that he could cook with water to make *posho,* that standard of East African field cuisine. For now, it was time to leave.

He checked the *mucuso* one last time. It teemed with the two local monkey species, sooty mangabeys and redtails, gobbling the ripe figs left by the apes. The twenty-pound mangabeys wore their correct charcoal business suits, but the redtails, half their size, were dressed like clowns: long burnished coppery tails, white bellies and black backs, with a white spot on the end of their noses like clown makeup. Everyone chittered and called and scolded.

The chimps might never have been. So for now it was goodbye, Shady Lady and Randy Andy, Captain Hook and Brandy and Knuckles and Lefty. The vagaries of rain forest life, especially the poachers, meant any or all could be dead when he returned.

Robinson Jeffers's line from "Hurt Hawks" leaped into his mind: *I'd sooner, except the penalties, kill a man than a hawk . . .* Or a chimp.

The chimpanzees were his godparents, his uncles and aunts, his cousins, his nieces and nephews, and he loved them.

Especially Zonkers. Twin. Brother.

CHAPTER TWENTY-FIVE

Hey, brother, can you spare an apartment? Only kidding. The bothersome old man with the canary soon would be gone.

For some twenty hours he'd been defending what he'd called his "turf"—sitting on the sidewalk in front of Otto Kreiger's building on Sixth Street south of Market. On paper, of course, the building belonged to the bottom drawer of a file cabinet in a Cayman Islands real estate office.

Really quite a comical old man, resting his canary cage on one thigh and his butcher knife on the other. Runover shoes and a three-piece suit, a tattered Persian rug under his rocking chair, both chair and rug from the apartment he had refused to quit until he'd been carried down to the sidewalk in his rocker. There, smelling bad, he'd stayed, courtesy of a temporary restraining order on his behalf by Legal Aid. But the TRO had expired an hour before without being translated into a preliminary injunction.

The slightly rotund but pretty-faced black woman cop was being a hell of a lot gentler than Kreiger would have been, probably because TV news cameras were recording the event even though it was only eight-thirty in the morning. Kreiger was just there, one of the crowd.

"Mr. Kreplovski," the cop said, "won't you give me the knife? You don't want anyone to get hurt, do you, sir?"

Kreplovski just sat there looking bewildered. Kreiger hoped he would take a slash at the black broad, put himself in the wrong. But just then the morning sun touched the cage and the canary started singing joyously. The old man looked at the bird with his mad blue eyes, then handed over the blade.

"Thank you, Mr. Kreplovski."

Kreiger, standing in the crowd, said, "I bet she's from hostage negotiations. Smart move to bring her in."

"This fucking town," said the man next to him.

The woman cop was saying, in the same reasonable tone of voice, "You know we're going to have to remove you now, don't you, Mr. Kreplovski?"

"I know my Sarah died in that apartment. I know I want to die there, too."

"In a few days there won't be any apartment," she said brightly. Two burly uniforms were moving up on either side of her. Somebody jeered at them, but the presence of a black woman, though herself a cop, tended to dampen the crowd's hostility.

"Why can't they just let me die with the building?"

"Who would take care of your canary?" she asked in a reasonable voice.

That seemed to clinch it for the old man. The two burly blues crouched, got hold of the bottom of the chair and came erect with it, and Mr. Kreplovski, and the canary. They carried all three across the sidewalk toward the waiting ambulance.

"Clever," said Kreiger to the man next to him. "Ambulance instead of a paddy wagon. Good public relations."

"This fucking town," said the man, shaking his head.

Old Kreplovski turned to look up at the vacated apartment building as they put him and his canary into the ambulance. Tears were running down his cheeks from his startling blue eyes. The crowd started to cheer, then to applaud him.

Kreiger sighed, "Progress."

"You fucking asshole," the man next to him said, and stalked off.

Kreiger toyed with the idea of calling up someone to teach him a lesson; but walking back up to his office on Sutter

Street, he forgot about the fool. He had won. Kreplovski had been the last tenant of the run-down old apartment building. Now it could be torn down to make way for the offices and arcade Kreiger already had gotten the permits for from the city. He'd had to pay a few people off, but it was just part of doing business in a candy-ass town prizing environmental awareness.

Whether it made money or not was largely immaterial anyway: he would be washing large sums from the newly reviving heroin trade through it during demolition and after construction.

It had been three and a half months since the hit on Spic Madrid, and today, finally, Otto Kreiger was making his move. At first, truth be told, he had been terrified. Unlike the FBI and the St. Paul police, he had no doubts at all about who had ordered the killing, and no doubts at all about why.

He stopped for the light on the corner of Third and Mission; across the intersection was the Rochester Big and Tall that had been there as long as he could remember. In the early days he'd bought his own suits there, 50 long.

Obviously, Martin Prince had seen in Spic's muted opposition at the meeting of capos a direct challenge to his own authority. Kreiger had shown the same muted opposition. Spic had voted to have the baby-raper down in Los Angeles hit; so had Kreiger. They had been overridden, three to two, in the show of hands. Normally, that would have been the end of it.

But in this case, the end hadn't come until a week later, when Spic had been gunned down in his St. Paul headquarters.

Otto Kreiger hadn't been gunned down. Yet.

"Yet" was why, the day after Martin Prince had called with sadness in his voice to tell him of Spic's sudden end, he had gone to a private security firm and had hired around-the-clock personal protection for himself and his family.

It was degrading, but getting dead was even more degrading.

Two days after he had hired them, his wife came striding

into his study straight from her stables, still in riding boots and jodhpurs, anger in her wide-set blue eyes, slapping her riding crop in her gloved left hand.

"Otto, that new stablehand you hired has to go!"

"Stablehand?" He felt a sudden sharp anxiety. "I didn't hire any—"

"There was some large ugly man in ridiculous corduroy trousers and a tweed jacket and a cap hanging around the stables this morning. When I ordered him off the premises, he told me he was sorry, he couldn't leave."

"Good," said a relieved Kreiger.

"When I demanded to know what he meant he said to ask . . ." Belatedly, she broke off to demand, "What did you say?"

"I said, 'Good.' That tells me he's doing his job."

"You mean you *hired* him to stand around gawking at me?"

He said, with admirable mildness, "I'll have a word with him about being less obtrusive, my darling."

Like many Mafia wives, Tiffany had no real knowledge, only surmises, about what her husband did. She knew he was a powerful criminal defense attorney, and she knew most of his clients were not people she would ever invite to their Sunday afternoon pool party/barbecues. She also knew these clients did not explain his tremendous income, but she didn't question it because she liked to spend it—on her face, on her body, on her horses.

For his part, Kreiger liked indulging her. She was a very handsome thirty-four, kept her figure and most of the time her place, and was wise enough to service him sexually when and how he liked it. Since he would have considered anything beyond me-Tarzan-you-Jane unmanly and maybe degenerate, missionaries would have approved.

In mollified tones, she said, "I don't understand what he's doing around the stables in the first place."

"Well, actually, Tiff, he's sort of looking after you."

"What's the matter?" she exclaimed in alarm. "Is there danger for the children? Shouldn't we call the police or—"

"Nothing that troublesome, darling." He came around the desk to her. "Nothing we need bother the police about. Just a rowdy element . . ."

"I . . . I don't understand," she said weakly.

She was Woodside born and bred, educated at Sacred Heart in the city, then Stanford, she had never seen any of the rougher edges of life. He put his arm around her shoulders, walked her slowly to the door of the study. He could feel her tremble against him, could smell the horses on her clothing, could very faintly smell the perfume of perspiration from her exertions in the practice ring. It was physically arousing.

"Now don't you fret, my love. You know I've been buying some of those old fleabag rooming houses and commercial properties south of Market now that the Yerba Buena Center is up and running—"

"Well, yes, but . . ."

"There's some radical homeless advocates who want to see it all upgraded to low-cost housing rather than torn down for new, significant development, and they have made some silly threats. So I just thought it prudent to provide you with around-the-clock protection until the problem is solved."

There had been angry shouting matches in the Board of Supes over his permits, but the guards had really been to send Martin Prince the message that he was no stupid mark like the little beaner. A statement. A sort of deadly chess game.

He walked in the California sunlight down cleaned-up Market Street toward Montgomery, thinking that he liked the analogy. Almost poetic.

Down in Southern California, Dante was picking up his Avis rent-a-car at the Burbank airport. His elation at learning about the connection between Gounaris and the Mafia's Abramson had subsided. The bubble had burst. So all the Abramsons were the same guy? Even if confirmed it didn't prove anything at all about Abramson or anyone in the Mafia being involved in Atlas Entertainment, let alone the murder of Moll Dalton.

Even at ten in the morning, it was blazingly hot in the Valley; as soon as he got into the car he had the windows shut and the A/C cranked up. He drove in on Airport Way, thinking that in three and a half months he had accomplished exactly nothing to unravel the connection between the murders of Moll Dalton *et al.*

Not that he had been three and a half months idle. He had been so busy with the *real* business of the Organized Crime Task Force that if any leads had developed he wouldn't have been able to follow them up anyway. Rumors of a possible San Francisco link with the New York Chinese gangs smuggling freighters full of illegal Chinese immigrants into California. A goofy tip that an organized band of Latino ex-cons was extorting money from Valley farmers in some scam involving water rights, portable johns, bogus green cards, and reporting legal workers to *la Migra* as illegals.

He passed over the Ventura Freeway; directly ahead was the old Burbank Studios—now Warner Studios—with its distinctive old-fashioned tan water tower. Alameda merged with Riverside to carry him through determinedly quaint Toluca Lake.

Three and a half months, nothing further from Raptor, no more hits in the organized crime community. No further leads developing. Nothing on the slim leads he already had.

Dante cut over to Moorpark, which was faster than the Ventura Freeway it paralleled, drove west.

None of the used tens, twenties, fifties handed to Hymie the Handler by Jack Lenington had turned up at any U.S. bank. Not one. Unless Lenington had buried them in a fruit jar in the backyard—not likely—he had maintained an offshore numbered account. Which made his corruption more sophisticated than originally thought, but it didn't tell a damned thing about why he had been snuffed. Or if his death was in any way at all connected with that of Moll Dalton.

Dante turned south on Woodman, crossed Ventura's tacky commercial blare of fried chicken joints and Chinese take-out, at Valley Vista jacklegged uphill past bungalows, gardeners, and greenery irrigated so lavishly that Northern California water was running off in the gutters. Unseen smog stung his eyes.

Everyone had closed their books on the Spic Madrid killing, and Popgun Ucelli was staying home in Jersey, calling no one more exciting than a local steak house for occasional reservations, and his bookie for occasional bets. The Feebs monitoring his tap were eating well and having good luck following his ponies. No plane trips. No calls from a contractor offering him a hit.

Also, alas, no more trips to Vegas by the Mafia dons.

No corpses falling out of cabinets in locked rooms.

No bodies dead of exotic poisons.

No dogs doing curious things in the night.

No need for Dante's deerstalker hat and magnifying glass.

Benedict Canyon Lane was a dead-end offshoot up in the hills where, he had finally learned from SAG, Moll Dalton's mother was living as Gloria Crowley, a name she seemed to have picked out of a hat. He made the right turn into her street, seeing, up beyond the houses, the barren California hills where coyotes skulked that in drought times came down to dine domestic on pet pusses and pooches.

He began checking the house numbers painted on the curbs, squinting in the glare, hoping to talk to Moll Dalton's mother cold. No advance notice. If you connected, you got them fresh before they'd had a chance to start image-polishing.

He had better connect. Under the name of Green, he had made an appointment with St. John for three o'clock, the earliest he could get. He hoped St. John would be stunned by what Dante Stagnaro, alias Mr. Green, brought with him from his interview with dead Molly's living mother.

CHAPTER TWENTY-SIX

Over the ridge in Beverly Hills, three men were sitting down to lunch in Hubley's very swank Four Seasons. Dooley, with his back to the window, was a tall lanky writer who wanted to direct. He had a big nose and mean close-set eyes and a receding mane of hair that would have come down to his collar if he had been wearing a collar. Instead, he wore baggy fatigue pants, a rusty leather jacket, and a kelly-green T-shirt with HUNGRY? EAT THIS! in red letters across the lower abdomen. He had long arms and big basketball-player hands he used a lot when he talked.

"I've written three USA and Showtime originals this year, and script-doctored seven others, and I have to make an appointment to call my fucking agent," he complained. "Way he sees it, I'm stealing 90 fucking percent of his money."

Valli, the second man at the table, was a middle-aged actor turned producer; he had a high voice and a first-look production deal with Universal. His face was bland as mashed potatoes with a couple of rodent droppings stuck in them for eyes. His jeans were prestressed and his cashmere sports jacket had a red AIDS ribbon in the lapel. Between them the two men grossed close to a million dollars a year.

"You know what we call writers," sniffed Valli. "The first draft of a human being."

Dooley was buttering a roll with a lot of wrist action. "An empty cab pulled up and a producer got out."

"Now you boys see why you need me," interrupted St. John in a suave voice, eyes dancing with delight. "Both of you."

As host, he was dressed impeccably in a narrow-shouldered three-piece charcoal Shetland wool and a Sulka tie that had cost $200 on Rodeo Drive. He was ready for action.

It had been almost four months since he had called Martin Prince in Vegas and told him about Stagnaro's visit. Nothing had happened since then, nothing at all, yet everything had changed. His perception of who he was and what he was had changed. His perception of Prince and his minions had changed.

"I need personal management," said Dooley.

"Packaging," said Valli.

"Of course you do, dear boys," beamed St. John. "And a great deal more besides."

Since his realization that Prince and Gounaris had been involved in Molly's death, he had conceived a daring scheme in revenge: to set up a personal-management and packaging entity. It would give him clout and power in this town on his own recognizance, not something that was tainted with mob money. The daring part was that he hadn't told Mr. Prince about it. He had lain awake a lot of nights in a sweat of fear while planning it, but something had driven him on despite his terror. The only way he could hurt Prince was financially, and only in secret.

So he leaned across the achingly white tablecloth toward the writer and the producer, and spoke in his richest, most compelling courtroom voice.

"Let's look at the menu, gentlemen. Then, while we eat, I will tell you why you need us so badly."

Otto Kreiger's secretary buzzed him just as he ended a twenty-minute phone call with a drug dealer he was representing on First Amendment grounds.

"Mr. Ed Farrow from the San Francisco Redevelopment Agency is holding on line two, Mr. Kreiger."

Fucking Farrow again. The only possible hurdle to be cleared at Sixth Street, one that had surfaced only a week ago. This little nitpick, that little niggle, without ever saying exactly what was troubling him about the project. And despite anything the Planning Commission and the Board of Supes might approve, it was Redevelopment that had the final, life-or-death say-so on new development projects in San Francisco.

They hadn't even met in person, but this was Farrow's third call in a week. He wasn't going to just go away. Kreiger had a nose for corruption, dealing in it so much himself, and Farrow's voice reeked of it. The man had his hand out—Kreiger just didn't yet know why, or how, or for how much.

"I think we ought to meet," said Farrow suavely. "There are a few things we have to discuss. Not on the phone."

"The phone's been fine up until now."

"In person."

If the phones were tapped, or Kreiger was taping, nothing incriminating would be on record. When they got together was time enough for Farrow to show him the upturned palm.

"I have time free tomorrow at—"

"Today." The voice hardened, and Kreiger's features darkened. He never did like to be pushed. "In one hour."

"I don't have an hour this morning."

"How very too bad for your new arcade."

Kreiger mastered his anger: all he let be heard over the phone was his long-suffering sigh.

"One hour. Where?"

Farrow chuckled. "Kreplovski's apartment. Where else?"

"Ah." Farrow had style. Kreiger suddenly was looking forward to the meeting. "All right."

"Third floor rear. Apartment 333. The door will be unlocked but it sticks, you almost have to kick it open. I'll be waiting inside." The voice tightened. "I'll only be there once, Kreiger."

"Don't worry your little head about it. I'll be there."

*   *   *

"This house was built by Lou Costello," said Gloria Crowley. Her voice had a sort of throaty sensuality that seemed offhand and habitual. "Lou was the short fat one. Bud was the tall thin one."

"Who's on first," supplied Dante brightly.

He could remember an interview he had once seen on TV with Bud Abbott after Costello had died. The IRS had disallowed dozens of pairs of his shoes. It had depressed Dante, somehow. He had watched their old movies religiously on afternoon TV after grade school, and had split his sides laughing.

"Mrs. St. John—"

"Please. Ms. Crowley."

They were in the cool shadowy living room with French doors open wide to the apron of her pool. She had been doing laps when Dante arrived. The white filigree beach robe over her two-piece suit of bright harlequin colors was gray with wetness.

"His one-year-old son drowned in this pool," she said with an odd false brightness that was like the sound of chalk on a blackboard. "Legend has it that he heard the news and then did his radio show with his partner."

Dante didn't know how to respond. He finally just said, "I have a few questions."

She nodded, holding his eyes. She had the addicted swimmer's seal-like figure, and somewhat coarsened facial features, a little too much flesh under the chin as if the monthly alimony check didn't run to regular face-lifts. But Dante could see remnants of her daughter's remarkable beauty in her face and oddly provocative blue eyes.

"You were divorced almost twenty-five years ago?"

"That's right, Lieutenant. So I really know nothing at all about my ex these days." She focused another limpid-eyed stare on him, waved a hand. He realized she was nearsighted, which explained the come-hither looks. "After all these years . . ."

She squirmed around in the big leather chair like a fidgety child; her bottom left skid marks. She was having a very dark drink with lots of ice in an old-fashioned glass. Dante was having iced tea without anything. It was an iced-tea day.

"The ceilings are all just slightly lower than normal because Mr. Costello really was quite a short man."

She took another hit from the squatty glass; ice cubes tinkled. She waved a languid hand and gave a little laugh that did not tinkle.

"We have house finches nesting right outside the French doors, can you imagine? In the hanging fern pots. They're forever bringing disgusting things for the nestlings, and their droppings get all over the patio, but . . ." Another of the airy gestures with her free hand.

"I was wondering, Ms. Crowley, why such an attractive woman as you has never remarried. Obviously—"

"And let that bastard off the hook?" There was sudden clarity of eye and voice. "Once Molly was grown and the support payments stopped he would be scot-free and I could not abide that. I will not abide it."

Dante thought of a life wasted in getting even. For what? That's what he hoped to find out here today.

"So your ex-husband pays for all this?"

"Not nearly enough, but that bastard will keep on paying as long as he lives, I'll see to that."

She stopped abruptly, as if realizing she was saying too much too vehemently. In the plantings that hid the property fence across the pool, the male house finch puffed up his red chest to cheep at them. He had a loud voice. Dante leaned forward in his chair. The sun glinted off the pool. He wished he could shed his clothes and dive in.

"Why did you get divorced, if I might ask?"

"The usual," she said very quickly and airily. The dismissive hand again; it was her favorite gesture. "Growing apart. Incompatibility. Moving in different directions . . ."

"Nothing to do with your daughter, then."

"Of course not." Indignation now. Indignation he didn't believe for an instant.

"And what was your relationship with your daughter before her death, Ms. Crowley?"

"How can you ask such a question?" Her bosom quivered with indignation beneath its scanty covering. "We were as close as two women could be. The mother-daughter bond . . ."

"Yet you weren't at her funeral."

"The bastard never even let me know she was dead!" Tears appeared in her eyes. "I was in Maui with my friend Charles, and only learned of it two days after the service."

Dante put surprise into his face.

"But surely, as close as you and Molly were, her husband must have—"

"He . . ." She hesitated again. Took another hit of her drink; it seemed to loosen the reins of her caution. "He didn't know how to reach me." There was a long pause. "Will Dalton and I, well . . . we never actually met." A longer pause, but his silence compelled further revelation. "You see, once she was in high school . . ." She put her feet up on a hassock; her relaxed thighs were meaty but still shapely. She made the hand gesture again. "You know children have to rebel at that age . . ."

"But when she was in college . . ."

Anger burst through her watchfulness again. "By then the bastard had won her over, turned her against me! It started when she was thirteen, expensive gifts, school programs abroad during the summer months. Things I couldn't afford for her." Pain spasmed her features. "He was her father, she wanted to know her father, she was so strong-willed I knew any danger would . . ."

She stopped again, as if a curtain had descended.

"What danger is that?" Dante asked.

"Oh . . ." The hand wave, meant to be light and airy, was forced and static. "Corruption of values . . . materialism . . ."

"Child molestation?" he said in a tone to match her own.

She sat bolt upright as if wasp-stung.

"I didn't say that!" she yelped. She had her feet on the floor, was halfway out of her chair.

"Will Dalton did."

She paused, then sank back like a deflating balloon. All of the alarm and anger were leaking out of her.

"He said that?"

"He didn't know. Suspected. From the way St. John looked at her . . . acted with her . . . more like a suitor than a father."

"Just like that bloody bastard!" She caught herself again, looked over at him almost slyly. "Of course, that's just . . . just Skeffington's way with any woman. Like a tic, a reflex . . ."

"Will thought your daughter was unaware of whatever happened to her when she was a child, had blocked it all off . . ."

The idea seemed to disorient her and please her at the same time. For a giddy moment he thought he had her: there had indeed been something for little Molly to block off. Then she shook her head, almost like a fighter shaking off a punch, and again had control of herself. Lost her. It happened. She heaved a long, somewhat theatrical sigh.

"I'm afraid I have nothing to say about that, Lieutenant."

"Terms of the alimony payments, maybe? If you talk about something that . . . might have happened, he can cut you off . . ."

She stood up. There was an odd dignity in her stance.

"I suppose you think I'm one of these pathetic women who are willing to give up her own future happiness just to stick it to her ex-husband. It's not that, Lieutenant. The only way I could hurt him, back then, was financially. Nobody would have believed . . ."

"You hurt him by taking his daughter away from him."

"He got her back."

"And now she's dead."

A single tear rolled down her left cheek. She smeared it impatiently with the back of her hand.

"Yes, she is. Dead. And still the only way I can hurt him is financially." Her face puckered up, but no more tears came. "For what he did."

Dante made an instant decision. Sometimes you had to

give something away to get something you needed. She had what he needed, he was sure of it.

"I think he's mixed up with some very bad people. I think they had something to do with your daughter's death. I can't prove it yet. But—"

"Are you saying Skeffington knows they were involved and still has kept on with—with *them*?"

"If they were involved, I can't see how he wouldn't know it. And they're bad enough he'd be afraid to cut himself loose."

She started to curse in a low, hoarse voice. It was like the mindless swearing of soldiers under stress. Suddenly she demanded, "You think telling you will help to . . . to get them? Whoever they are?"

"I wouldn't ask you if I didn't think that. I wouldn't have told you what I have if I didn't need whatever you know to use as leverage on your ex-husband."

"All right."

Just like that. In the same low flat tones she had used to curse, she told Dante what she had walked in on that sunny California afternoon so many years before.

"I grabbed her up in my arms, naked as she was, and ran out of the house with her. I can still hear him crying out behind me." She paused. Her eyes were focused on the past. "Screaming, almost. As a woman screams." Her eyes came back to Dante. "I never saw him again without a lawyer present. I got uncontested custody, child support, alimony. He got no visitation rights, nothing. It was in the agreement that if I ever told anyone about . . . about that afternoon, I forfeited all rights to alimony. I would have had nothing to live on . . ."

"So when Molly was thirteen, you let her—"

"Damn you, I had to! I was afraid of losing her, not the money! Then I lost her anyway. Forever." Her face tightened, she began slamming her clenched fist on the arm of her chair and chanting through clenched teeth, "Bastard, bastard, bastard . . ."

Dante said quietly, "Thank you, Ms. Crowley."

There was no break in her litany. But as he walked out into the searing sunlight like a man leaving the dimness of a terminally ill patient's sickroom, she called after him. He paused, turned.

"They say that Lou Costello's radio show that night, Lieutenant, started, 'Heeyyy, Abbott—I just took a shower wit' my shirt, socks, and underwear on.'"

They stared at one another in the gloom; then Dante nodded at her, and was gone.

CHAPTER TWENTY-SEVEN

Otto Kreiger was in a cab going down Sixth Street. In those three and a half months, not a move, not a peep, not a whisper, from the vast network of contacts and informants he maintained in the criminal and law enforcement communities, about any moves planned against him. Tiffany's bodyguard had been reduced to carrying packages for her when she went shopping.

So he canceled the protection. Spic Madrid had been just a warning to keep his nose clean and stay in line. Sent to him from Martin Prince and, he was sure, ancient Enzo Garofano.

But he had been sick with terror—terror reduced to fear, fear to prudence, replaced by ire, elevated to anger, soaring to rage, and finally to full-blown fury. Now he was sending his own message, born of that fury at having been made to feel terror.

Kreiger paid off the cab, crossed the sidewalk where just two hours before old Kreplovski's tattered carpet had been. Gone now, to line some homeless person's shelter. He unlocked the street door of the deserted tenement and entered.

Probably as early as tonight homeless fucks would find ways to creep in, but now in daylight and still locked up it was deserted and echoing and shadowy, the stairwells still redolent of decades of cheap cooking and bad wine, not piss.

He paused to get his breath at the third-floor landing, went back to 333 at the end of the hall beside the fire escape.

"Farrow?"

Farrow didn't answer, which angered him further. A real games player, this boy. He would get his bribe money, all right, but also someday soon would get a couple of knees bent backward for his bad manners.

"Farrow!"

Angry now, he tried to open the door. It stuck badly, just as Farrow had warned. Enraged, Kreiger jammed a shoulder against it to make it open.

Tiny flames spurted from the match heads stuck between the edge of the door and the thin strip of flint paper fixed to the frame. With a whoosh, gas that had been seeping for over an hour from the ruptured kitchen line just inside the door ignited.

The explosion rocked the deserted building. Raptor, wearing a flowing bandido mustache, his bulky PG&E repairman's overalls draped with meaningless but picturesque tools and meters, had to duck back into the rear entryway across the alley to avoid being hit by one of the larger pieces of Kreiger.

He was two blocks away when the first emergency units arrived at the scene. They had received a call about a gas leak four minutes before Kreiger thrust open the door of Mr. Kreplovski's murdered home.

Dante ended up having a great cheeseburger at a place called Hamburger Hamlet on Doheney Road just above Sunset. They had a sort of sunporch overlooking the street with hanging plants and wicker-like furniture that gave it a sunny, leisurely feel.

As he ate, he tried to visualize St. John's face when he walked through the door armed with the wonderful new ammunition from the erstwhile Mrs. St. John. He remembered the phone conversation, setting up the meeting through St. John's executive secretary, with a great deal of almost vindictive relish.

"And what will it be concerning, Mr. Green?"

"Money," he had chuckled, "lots and lots of money."

"I beg your pardon?"

"Rightly so, young lady, working for a man like that."

Then he had added, "Three P.M. sharp," and chuckled again. "Time is money."

Money was what St. John was all about. He hoped the bastard would have to support his bitter ex-wife for the rest of his days.

At two forty-five, a quarter hour earlier than he had expected, St. John drove his glitteringly restored Maserati Bora coupe between Galaxy Way's artful emerald plantings in Century City. His briefcase was on the seat beside him, his suit jacket neatly folded on top of it. He drummed his fingers on the steering wheel, hummed a snatch of *"La donna è mobile"* from *Rigoletto*. He was superbly satisfied with himself.

Dooley and Valli—sounded like a dance team—had been pathetically eager to sign with his new firm. They had even shaken hands at the end of the lunch. He'd have them working together in no time. Which called for a very personal sort of celebration. A quick stop back at the office for his meeting with the mysterious Mr. Green, an hour of paperwork that would become four hours billable, then a call to Charriti HHope . . .

He turned down the ramp into the massive echoing concrete garage under the high-rise office building where *St. John Associates—Attorneys at Law* had their offices. His yearly rent could have housed the homeless of Long Beach, but front was more important in The LaLa than anywhere else on earth.

He slid his card into the slot, the gate went up on the monthly parker lane, and he drove down into the bowels of the building. His reserved floor was a huge low-roofed echoing concrete space filled with almost endless rows of high-priced cars, mostly foreign. The slot with his name on it was only a dozen paces from the elevator; he had been one of the first tenants after the building had been completed.

He parked, took his key from the ignition, then just sat there for a moment, savoring his day. Dooley and Valli would bring other dissatisfied creative people into the new enterprise—creative people were always dissatisfied, always looking for a change. He was well and truly on his way to freedom.

They always said, once in, never out: but it wasn't as if he was cutting Mr. Prince and his associates out, after all—they would still be silent partners in his very lucrative law firm. But he was branching away from them personally, to make a mint of money they'd never see a dime of. The perfect revenge. Sweet Molly would be proud of her daddy for doing something about her murder. Proud in the way she had been proud only of Dalton.

He opened the door and swung out his elegantly clad legs. A gloved hand touched the snout of a Jennings J-22 pistol to the bridge of his nose and the forefinger convulsed inside the trigger guard.

St. John died happy.

At five minutes to three, Dante drove into the underground garage of St. John's office building to hear an attendant yelling about some guy shot to death in his car. Goddammit! Without even knowing why, Dante jumped out and flashed his badge—who knew, San Francisco or L.A.—to get a look at the dead man sprawled halfway out of the car with the top of his head missing.

He was standing well clear of the open door of the Maserati when the first units of LAPD's finest arrived.

"His name is Skeffington St. John," he told the blunt-faced middle-aged plainclothesman who had beaten the blues to the site. "He's an attorney in this building who—"

"Who the hell are you?"

Dante showed him some ID. "I was on my way to see him in connection with a case I'm working up in San Francisco." He suddenly snarled, "Five goddam minutes—"

"Yeah. Tough tit but you gotta suck it."

Dante explained he thought it was an organized crime caper, thought it might have been a New Jersey hitman named Ucelli who had done it, if they hurried maybe . . . but cops don't like their jurisdictional toes stepped on, and who the fuck was he, anyway? Maybe he was tied up some way with the whacker even if he was a cop. It wouldn't be the first time.

Even after a few calls to Sacramento and San Francisco had confirmed he was some sort of supershit crimebuster from Baghdad by the Bay, it was over an hour before the first bulletins went out to the airports with Ucelli's description.

What with the paperwork and all, it was the final flight from Burbank that Dante caught to SFO. He spent the flight playing "what if" with himself. What if he had reversed his investigations, gone to St. John first? St. John wouldn't have been there. Literally out to lunch. Besides, he'd have had nothing new to pry at him with until after his talk with Gloria. But what if he hadn't had that second cup of coffee . . .

At Dante's urging, the FBI finally had called Ucelli's house in New Jersey. Nobody home. Not Ucelli, not his wife—the kids were grown, the two boys having graduated into the lower rungs of the Mafia like their father before them. Only a Puerto Rican maid whose English seemed to consist of "Not home" and "Leave *número*."

The Feebies would check back, of course, but all they'd get was an injunction from a mob attorney like the one that had recently come through to keep Dante away from Kosta Gounaris. No probable cause to harass Popgun Ucelli, that upright citizen.

But Dante *knew*. One up the snout with a $75 pistol in .22 caliber which had been dropped on the floor beside the car. Sprayed with Armor All. No topcoat given to a passerby, but there were no passersby in that garage, and who wore topcoats in L.A. anyway? He had tried to scare St. John with the possibility the mob might come after him; now it had happened.

*   *   *

Driving home on the 101 freeway from SFO, he heard a news report about the "shocking death" of a "prominent attorney" and in a momentary time/space warp thought they were talking about St. John. Relaxed when he heard the man had been blown up in a gas-leak explosion in a slum redevelopment project.

But then he heard the name. Otto Kreiger.

Otto fucking Kreiger? Known associate of Martin Prince in Vegas? Attorney of record for Jack Lenington, recently deceased? Now himself killed in an accident? On the same day St. John was hit down in Los Angeles?

Dante called Homicide right from his car to learn what time it had gone down. Before noon. Possible. Very possible. Lure Kreiger to his death, hop a shuttle to LAX, pop St. John, head out of town. And Tim wasn't at Homicide. Still at the Kreiger scene. So Tim wasn't so damn sure it was accidental, either.

But at Clown Alley for a postmortem, he was.

"We figured it *could* have been some crazy attaching himself to the radical homeless rights outfit that's been harassing Kreiger, so we wanted to take a real good look. Nothing there." He gave his huge openmouthed laugh, eyes ashine for the upcoming intake of fat and salt. "And then here you come again with fuckin' Popgun Ucelli! Popgun, planning an elaborate fake accident for Kreiger? Gimme a fuckin' break, chief!"

"So somebody else planned it," said Dante, thinking Raptor. He was getting desperate or punchy, he wasn't sure which.

"Okay, St. John I might give you—Ucelli's trademark way of doing business." Tim pointed his finger at Dante and worked his thumb, bang! bang! "That's our Eddie. But hell, chief, correct me if I'm wrong, but you've never turned up anything between Kreiger and Gounaris or Atlas Entertainment. St. John was attorney of record for Atlas, not Kreiger."

"Yeah, Skeffington St. John—who just happened to get his head blown open in L.A. this afternoon. Just enough hours after the gas pipe went up on Sixth Street for the same man to do it. Tim, there has to be a connection."

Tim broke in with his big belly laugh once again, and slathered on the extra mayonnaise he'd asked for before slamming shut his cheeseburger. He waved greasy fingers in the air.

"Only in your diseased brain, chief."

Dante had already admitted to himself that Tim was right, but he couldn't give up that easy. Raptor rode his shoulder like a hooded falcon waiting to swoop on its prey.

"Kreiger was in Vegas along with Gideon Abramson a week before Spic Madrid was hit. Abramson was in Greece in the fifties and staked Gounaris to his first freighter—"

"So what? If the Abramson connection was vital, it'd be his brains on the car seat, not St. John's. Drink your fuckin' decaf and go home to Mama, little fella's had a long day."

Which, in the end, Dante meekly did.

There was just nothing to tie the two deaths together. But he would take a good long look at Kreiger anyway. See if he was connected with any of the other principals besides the dead Lenington in ways Dante hadn't uncovered yet. But who were the other principals? He kept going around in circles, learning who was important only after their deaths made them so.

When he got home, there was a message from Raptor waiting. The voice was airy, British comedy stuff, actorish— perhaps even an American doing British.

"This is Raptor, old bean. Remember the line from that dreadful Thomas Hardy poem, 'The Dynasts'? 'One pairing is as good as another'? Fits quite nicely, don't you think? Cheers, tallyho, and all that rot."

PART FIVE

Late Triassic

208 m.y. ago

I am the family face;
Flesh perishes, I live on,
Projecting trait and trace
Through time and times anon,
And leaping from place to place
Over oblivion . . .
The eternal thing in man,
That heeds no call to die.

Thomas Hardy
"Heredity"

CHAPTER TWENTY-EIGHT

It is 6:30 A.M. and my car has paused at a Bay Area pedestrian crosswalk, because in California the pedestrian crosswalk is more sacred than the Trinity. So even though I am on my way to San Francisco to kill Otto Kreiger, I honor it.

I am startled by a sudden passage on my right: a jutting beak of white smooth-capped half-oval helmet which in profile extends several inches horizontally above the brows and nose of a passing cyclist. He is followed by a cluster of others on similar lanky many-speeded racing bikes, all in black midthigh racing tights and jerseys of varied bright colors, moving very fast in a bunch, in a silent breath, no jerkiness like walkers or runners because there is no stride, only turning wheels.

A herd of animals in motion, but what animal moves in such fashion? From my childhood comes a memory, almost a shock of recognition. Like most American children, at about six I become besotted with dinosaurs. What now flashes through my mind from those long-ago years is one of the coelurosaurs, the ostrich dinosaurs, named *Dromiceiomimus brevertertius. Dromiceiomimus,* if I remember my Latin correctly, means "emu-mimic"—the emu being an ostrichlike ratite bird of the Australian grasslands.

It is hard to see how a ten-foot-high dinosaur from the dying days of the Cretaceous could mimic a five-foot-high flightless bird that came into existence 70 million years later, but there you have the casual idiocy of science.

Dromiceiomimus, running in herds and having a jutting ostrichlike beak, is stirred in my memory by the jutting helmets of the bike riders; as he ran, his head would not have bobbed. My flash of recognition is of a dinosaur I have never met.

Most apropos, do you not think? I am on my way to kill a man whom I have never met, although I have followed him about for two weeks. Otto Kreiger, who . . .

Oh, no. You first want to know about St. John? Goddam your eyes, I want to talk about Kreiger; but *two* lawyers for the price of one makes me mellow and cooperative. So by all means let us look at the *finis* of Skeffington St. John, whore to the mob and nasty pedophile to little girls. He parks in the garage under his building, as he starts to get out a Jennings J-22 is placed against the bridge of his nose, *crack!* Instant lobotomy.

Where is the fun in that, the challenge, the drama, the mystery for Raptor, that sly and clever assassin? On my own, I probably should not have wished poor fool Sinjin dead, despite what he is, but should I weep? Should I mourn? He is not near my conscience; he did make love to that employment. So *sans* compunction, I consign him to the other whores of Hades. After all, I am not God, I do not control all things, I only do my job.

And the *Kreiger* kill is doing my job excellently. Excellent work, challenging work, more challenging even than Jack Lenington. Jack was more wary, a rogue male with every man a potential enemy, but it took only imagination and cleverness to separate him from his wariness. Then I had him.

But first I must eyeball Herr Otto, not easy because he has surrounded himself with bodyguards since Madrid's death. Kreiger takes Woodside Road home each evening; see that car with the flat tire? *C'est moi,* Raptor. See the florist, in brown uniform and peaked cap and bogus beard, who mis-delivers a dozen pink roses to Kreiger's personal secretary? Raptor.

Now I can recognize him, I must figure out how to have him. Herr Otto himself shows me the way, because he cancels his bodyguards and he has two dangerous habits: he likes to walk the city streets of San Francisco; he likes to gloat.

Several of his walks—with me half a block ahead in what private-eye novels love to call "front-tailing"—take him to an aged apartment house on Sixth Street he is getting condemned so he can build a commercial arcade in its place. He is always getting into intense arguments with one of the few—finally, the only—residents left, Mr. Adam Kreplovski.

I know that when Kreplovski is finally ousted, Herr Otto must be there to gloat. So I start my campaign of circuitous and baffling phone calls in my persona as corruption-minded Ed Farrow of the San Francisco Redevelopment Agency. Ed never *quite* comes out and flatly asks for a bribe to keep from stalling Kreiger's project, but he obviously has his hand out.

When Mr. Kreplovski sets himself up on the sidewalk in front of the building, I go to his emptied apartment and make my little arrangements with flint paper and match heads and ruptured gas line. To set the farce in motion, it needs only my gloved hand twisting the gas line stopcock which I had closed before holing the line, then my openly demanding call to Herr Otto so he will go there, irked beyond caution, at the perfect moment.

Mr. Kreplovski wanted to die in his beloved Sarah's apartment; but at least he has the pleasure of knowing that Herr Otto died in it in his stead. (One need not laugh at a farce, *comprenez-vous?*)

Over Irish coffee at the Buena Vista Cafe near the foot of Hyde Street, I have struck up an acquaintance with an out-of-work actor. He leaps at the chance to earn $100 by reading a few lines over the telephone to an answering machine in the plummy British accent that is his most prized thespian possession.

There is no way he, or anyone else, can think a Thomas Hardy quotation about pairings refers to the murder of a corrupt lawyer in Los Angeles, and the fake-accident murder of an even more corrupt lawyer in San Francisco. Only Stagnaro will make the connection. By now the joke will be wearing thin for him; but one must have *some* fun to keep killing from becoming a bore.

One other thing, *mon gar*. Because of my pledge to you of truthfulness, I must admit that after the message is delivered to Stagnaro's answering machine, I have another bad night. A horrible night, in point of fact.

Indeed, when that rather large piece of Herr Otto almost hits me in the alley, I toss chunks. Fortunately the police buy accident, else they might have ended up trying to DNA-type my *vomitus*. Farcical indeed—and now you may laugh.

Enough of that. My terrible night. Not a nightmare this time. Insomnia. And of the worst kind, insomnia laced with the blackest of thoughts about myself. Earlier I mention to you the little man at the hinge of my unconscious—my dwarf, my Rumpelstiltskin. On the right of the split in my personality is me, my conscious mind. On the left, my feminine side and my dark side, my subconscious. I am not always thus, I dare say, but it seems that now I can reach neither except through that ugly little walnut of a creature some part of me has placed on guard.

Sometimes he allows darkman or imperfect female to swarm across the split and fog me out. My reaction to events is dulled, blunted, so it is as if I playact the emotions other people actually feel.

At such moments, I am a fist that cannot smash through the barrier no matter how hard I try. The barrier on the other side of which is the other half of me. What can I do except act out of this wound? What can I do except kill?

Thus, I am only about Death.

Is there no way I can be about Life?

CHAPTER TWENTY-NINE

"Life!" exclaimed Will Dalton zestfully. "At last, life is appearing on earth!

"But it is the lowest, one-cell sort of life, so we often can't tell whether it is actually alive alive-o or not. Or if it is plant or animal. There is even evidence that some unicellular mites switch back and forth between plant and animal at will—or do so as if they had a will.

"Let's hear Genesis on this exquisite moment in the history of planet Earth: 'And God said, Let the waters bring forth abundantly the moving creature that hath life.'

"Actually, the Genesis writers, being devoted to a hierarchy, a pyramid of creation with man at the top—made at the end of the sixth day—thought grasses and herbs and fruit trees came before animate life. They had no way of knowing we are 70 percent seawater, and that the sea, the primordial soup, is mother to us all. As desert nomads, they would think life, of necessity, had to have begun on dry land.

"Even some gradualist evolutionists reject the fits-and-starts, contingency theory of Darwinism: they favor a direct line from most simple to most complex life-forms—in inexorable progression from primordial ooze to freeway gridlock. We've already addressed the error (and arrogance) of this while talking about the *randomness* of evolution, but let's explain it better.

"Since the biotic sophistication of life-forms has indeed

increased, single-cell life has been around longer than complex, multicellular creatures like ourselves. But countless different kinds of single-cell bacteria still exist. And algae. And yeasts. Indeed, many of the body's one-celled parasites are degenerated forms of more complex life-forms. So we are not the apex of anything. Just another, and probably quite surprising, step along the road, evolving ourselves even as I speak."

Listening from his post against the back wall, Dante kept on being amazed that he was understanding it. Maybe Rosie was right. Maybe he wasn't a total dummy. But he had to stay alert for Raptor. The assassin's time to act, unless he intended to wait until after the lecture was over, was growing short.

"Science sees life beginning a unicellular existence in the sea," said Will. "Single molecules, slow, careless, inefficient, whose appearance is relatively quick. Not in the creationists' twenty-four-hour day, but quick by earth science standards.

"The sun, remember, was born about 5 billion years ago. The earth as a planet we might recognize had shape about 4.6 b.y. ago. The magma ocean ended 4.4 b.y. ago.

"Many organic particles that form the elemental building blocks of life had been rained down from asteroids and worldlets and dusts and gases during the 400 million years our conditions fluctuated from sun-warmed eons—when the atmosphere was essentially clear of detritus—to freezing periods when impact ejecta obscured the sun. Our primitive planet seems to have been heavily dosed with the stuff of life: chains of carbon hooked to hydrogen, nitrogen, and other essential organic molecules.

"Anyway, sometime during this seesaw, the spark of life appeared (perhaps once, perhaps several times, perhaps a million times, to be snuffed and spark again), and the flame steadied and grew. Our earliest fossil evidence, sketchy and delicate as it is, suggests that life (or at least the first complex organic molecules) was here by 4 b.y. ago.

"What went on in the 3.5 billion years from the birth of these first molecules able to make crude blueprints of themselves, to the Cambrian multicellular explosion? Well, half a billion years after the molecules we had prokaryotes, the first unicellular life. By 1.4 b.y. ago, life was seeking complexity. It forced certain molecules to have accessory molecules, either to scour needed building blocks from the surrounding warm seas, or to act like DNA polymerase to midwife genetic instructions for change. These molecules evolved a trap, a sheath, a membrane to prevent other essential molecules from drifting away again. Nucleus-celled eukaryotes had appeared. There was no turning back.

"We would expect to find evidence of this in the fossil record, and we do. Among the earliest fossils are stromatolites, layered mats of organic sediment, often the size of a watermelon, sometimes the size of a football field. Stromatolites, dramatic proof of individual cells living together in harmony, are still being generated in the warm waters of certain sheltered tropical bays and lagoons by microscopic organisms—in Baja California, western Australia, and the Bahamas. Something modern man with all his technology cannot duplicate.

"Of course—and this is very important because it tells us something essential about life—even then some free-swimming single-celled microbes, instead of manufacturing food as the photosynthetic stromatolite communities did, ate other microbes. Eating food is less trouble than making it, so this laborsaving idea appeared early in the chain of life, and never disappeared.

"Six hundred million years after the eukaryotes, we had multicellular sponges and algae; a mere 2.5 m.y. later came the exuberant multicellular 'Cambrian explosion' of chordate life, so beautifully recorded in the Burgess shales of 540 m.y. ago.

"To me that certainly qualifies as God saying, 'Let the waters bring forth abundantly the moving creature that hath life.' I see no destructive friction between Bible and science.

"Another interesting parallel: Christianity says the one true God created all life on earth; science says that despite its fits and starts, all life on earth sprang from a single line.

Proof of a single source for all life does not depend on what either the Bible or the stones and bones tell us; we need only look to biological facts of medicine that work every day to keep us all (and scientists and creationists alike) alive.

"Basically, all organisms work alike. They're made alike, they're made from the same basic stuff, and their genetic blueprints and molecular constructions are extremely close. All species' DNA has the same essential architecture, all species hold many proteins in common. Everything that lives is kin to everything else.

"So those species fossilized in the Burgess shales that made it through the post-Cambrian mass extinction sprang from the same hereditary line as those species that didn't. They were all water-dwellers, and they were all invertebrates—none of them had backbones.

"'And God created great whales, and every living creature that moveth, which the waters brought forth abundantly, after their kind. . . . And God blessed them, saying, Be fruitful, and multiply, and fill the waters in the seas.'

"Whales are mammals, not fish, but the writers of Genesis couldn't know that. What about the fish that *were* fish? Well, the first primitive fishlike vertebrates appeared a mere 50 million years after the Burgess shales were laid down.

"If we'd been there we probably wouldn't have realized it had happened. We would hardly have recognized these first fishlike creatures grubbing sluggishly around on the bottom of the sea as vertebrates at all, since they lacked jaws, they lacked fins, and they had a barely detectable skeleton.

"But they were soon followed by other 'fish' that are still around in slightly modified form as sharks. Sharks are so ancient and primitive that, unlike other vertebrates, their skeletons remain cartilage, never turning to real bone at all.

"Descendants of two other early lines of these fishlike creatures have survived: 'ray-fins' and 'lobe-fins.' The ray-fins developed bony fins, light and strong and ribbed by spines, and had air sacs they could use to regulate buoyancy. About 100 m.y. ago they blossomed into fish as we know them today. Fish are the most numerous of all vertebrates, with thousands of living species and billions of individuals.

"Certainly they have followed God's exhortation: 'Be fruitful, and multiply, and fill the waters in the seas.'

"Instead of light, strong, spine-ribbed finds, the lobe-fins had stumpy knobs of flesh containing numerous little slabs and splints of bone. And their air sacs not only regulated buoyancy, they passed oxygen from the air they swallowed directly into the bloodstream. See where we're going here? Some branch of the now nearly extinct lobe-fins ventured or was driven up out of the water into the mudflats surrounding it, and could survive.

"In time, they became the first amphibians. Those little slabs and splints of bone in their fins became the amphibians' four limbs; those air sacs became, in time, primitive lungs. So they slithered about in the mud by bending their bodies from side to side like fish swimming, and by shoving mightily with the stumpy little legs their fins were turning into.

"Lucky for us; without them, we could not have been. But that belongs with the sixth, last, all-important day of actual creation in Genesis, which we will get to in a moment." Will paused and smiled around the room. "As soon as I come back from the john."

There was relaxed, almost relieved laughter at the break. Without apology, Dante preceded Will to check out the rest room across the hall. It was at just such a moment that Raptor might choose to strike.

He didn't. Will whizzed in peace and safety.

For the first time, Dante wondered whether anything would happen at all. Maybe this was not a night for dying.

CHAPTER THIRTY

"So Mendelson is dying," said Gideon Abramson. "He says to his wife, 'Call the priest, tell him I want to convert.' She says, 'But Max, your whole life you've been an Orthodox Jew. Now you want to convert?' And Max says, 'Better one of them should die than one of us.'"

Gid laughed heartily at his own joke, as he always did, and Martin Prince laughed with him, politely. Prince understood what he was doing, breaking the ice, smoothing the way.

Kosta Gounaris gave a weak chuckle, but Enzo Garofano's aged face was like some ancient, pitted ice floe. It had been a rough trip from Jersey all in one day for the old capo, even if done by Prince's jet to Vegas, then by limo here to . . .

"Whadda fuck you call this place?" he demanded abruptly. When he was tired, like now, and a bit disoriented, Garofano's Bronx beginnings would show through his veneer.

"The Furnace Creek Inn," said Gideon brightly. "First-rate accommodations and a great golf course over at the ranch."

Gideon and Kosta had rented both of the inn's $375-a-day luxury suites, with the king-size beds and the built-in Jacuzzis. The two-story, red tile-roofed, Spanish-style hotel of stucco and local travertine stone, built at the mouth of Furnace Creek Canyon by the Pacific Coast Borax Company in the 1920s, gave Death Valley its reputation as a stylish winter resort.

"They close for the summer months," continued Gideon. He had suggested Death Valley for the meet because it would be difficult for the feds to put the four of them all together here at the same time. "They just opened for the season last week."

"I think we should get down to business," said Prince. Gideon may have chosen the spot, but it was Prince's meeting, Prince's agenda.

"It is safe to talk here?"

"Swept an hour ago for bugs, Don Enzo."

The inn faced out across tan open desert toward the Furnace Creek Ranch a mile away, but the wings enclosed an extensive date palm garden with bubbling streams and placid reflecting pools.

"As for the windows, we've got a couple of men strolling through those trees. Anybody there trying to listen to us . . ."

The aged Enzo Garofano sank back into one of the massive leather-seated hardwood chairs. "Let us proceed," he said.

Prince was on his feet; the others were seated. He started softly, no passion in his voice. Gounaris wasn't fooled; Gideon had said the don was fuming.

"Over two years ago we made a decision to extend our new acquisition, Atlas Entertainment, from Los Angeles into the San Francisco Bay Area. It was a deliberate decision on my part . . ."

Prince began pacing between Garofano's chair and the couch where Gideon and Kosta sat.

"We have never had much influence in San Francisco, apart from that cheese merchant the feds busted a few years ago. The Italians up there are not *siciliani*. They're *genovesi, piemontesi* . . . hard to deal with, hard to control."

"North Beach is not Little Italy," agreed Gideon.

"So we moved Atlas Entertainment in, put one of our own in charge"—he gestured at Gounaris—"and what happened?"

Kosta hadn't spoken yet except for hello-hello: he had just met the legendary Enzo Garofano, survivor of New York's great mattress wars of the thirties, and was nervous about him rather than Prince. It was irrational, Prince was the one to watch, the one to fear. To Prince he sent weekly reports by hand-carry messenger. But he not only answered Prince's rhetorical question, he answered it a little bit smart-ass.

"We've shown a profit from the first week of operation."

The suave, imperturbable Prince suddenly shrieked, veins standing out at his temples, *"I am talking here!"*

Gounaris felt the blood drain from his face. He had heard of these sudden flashes of rage, like Bugsy Siegel was supposed to have had, but it was the first he had witnessed.

"I am sorry, Don Martin. I was just—"

"No matter." Prince gave a magnanimous wave of his hand.

The gesture was casual, but those cold eyes were murderous. Speaking up had been a mistake; why had he? Remembering the tough kid he once had been, the glory days when his nuts were big as bowling balls and belonged to him alone? Dammit, those days didn't have to be over!

"Last February," Prince continued, "after our meeting in Las Vegas, Spic Madrid was hit in Minneapolis."

Kosta felt cold again. What the fuck was going on? He was sure Prince himself had ordered the hit on Madrid, for opposing him at the Vegas board meeting.

"And less than four months later, St. John and Otto Kreiger were hit on the same day. Now—"

"Wait a minute," interrupted Garofano, "I understood the police and fire people were satisfied that Otto's death was an accident. Now you're telling me—"

"I'm telling you that he was hit," snapped Prince. Both of the capos were ignoring the usual protocol now. "Based on the police department lab forensic workup of the gas explosion."

"Are you suggesting, Don Martin," said Gideon, "that the same man carried out both hits?"

"I'm suggesting that the same man *ordered* both hits."

"I think Kreiger was responsible for St. John," said Gideon, showing more balls than Kosta would have credited him with. "He voted to have him hit at the board meeting at the Xanadu in February and was overruled. But the killer's M.O.—"

"It was not Eddie Ucelli," said Garofano quickly. "He would never hit one of our own without full board sanction."

"With all due respect, Don Enzo," said Gideon, "St. John was hardly one of our own. A paid employee—"

"Who was branching out into new areas without informing us," snapped Prince. By this time, they had all heard about St. John's nascent personal management company.

"Could it be someone in Atlas?" asked Garofano.

"Possible, I suppose," admitted Kosta. "But so few employees of the company know anything about . . . *us* . . ."

"The woman found out," said Prince.

"*Was trying* to find out," said Gideon in a soothing voice.

"Who else would have the guts to do it?" asked Gounaris, since protocol seemed to have been abandoned.

"Who indeed?" mused Prince. But his eyes locked with Kosta's for a long moment. "In any event, I want you to find out. Comb that company from top to bottom. Set people to watching other people. I want any word, any whisper, any *breath* about Otto's death. And Gideon, I want you to check with our Los Angeles people on this St. John thing. It has brought a lot of federal heat into that town. Our financial involvement in his firm is extremely well hidden, but we need this resolved as soon as possible. Be casual but thorough."

"It will be like old times!" enthused Gid.

The two Mafia soldiers looked like ravens in their black pants and their black shirts hanging out to hide the handguns on their belts. They patrolled the palm grove in a sort of figure eight, so nobody could point a shotgun mike at the windows of the suite.

Pale green fronds clacked overhead, laid lacy patterns of light and shadow over the faces and somber clothes. They stopped to chat between the almost red trunks of the date palms. One man was short, wide, sloppy, with black hair sprouting at his wrists and on the backs of his fingers and growing low and curly over his forehead. More hair sprouted

into the open V-neck of his black polo shirt. His Beretta 92
was considered a classic, but he couldn't hit anything with it
from over three feet away.

"Hey, Red, I'm gettin' fuckin' sick of walkin' around in
circles in the fuckin' desert," he said.

His partner was a very large redhead with an open face
and twinkling blue eyes and a boozer's complexion. His
drink actually was carrot juice and he could bench-press six
hundred pounds. On his hip he wore a Colt-clone .45 auto
loaded with subsonic rounds that made it effective yet remarkably quiet when fired. He was an excellent shot.

"Tell it to Mr. Prince," he said. "Hell, Tony, you're in here
under the trees, in an oasis—soft duty."

"This an oasis? So where's the fuckin' belly dancers?"

A bluejay-sized bird with a long beak soared into the palm
tree directly over their heads with a loud whistle. When he
flew, red patches showed on his wings. Tony went into a
shooter's crouch at the cry, straightened up sheep-faced.

"I didn't know there was any fuckin' birds in the desert
except them ravens and those big buzzards always soarin'
around."

"How long you lived in Vegas, Tony?"

"Three, four years."

"And you never see any birds?"

"Just ones with tits an' hair between their legs. Anyway,
what's eighteen inches long and makes a woman scream
when she wakes up in the morning?"

Before Red could answer, a man appeared, walking quietly through the trees, dark-haired and lean and moving like
an athlete. A pair of binoculars was around his neck, a canteen was on one hip, and a skinny paperback book was in
one hand.

Red slid over to confront him without seeming to, beam-
ing at the binoculars. "Those Zeiss-Ikon glasses?"

"Good Lord no, I got 'em at Eddie Bauer's!" The man
held up the slim glossy paperback. "I use 'em for bird-watch-
ing." At that instant the bird above them whistled again, then
arrowed away. "Did you see that? A red-shafted flicker!" He
opened the book to the back page and began writing in it

with a ballpoint pen. "I can add it to my Death Valley life list."

"I heard they were pretty common here," remarked Red.

"Not indigenous at all—a late-autumn visitor from the Panamint Range. There's almost three hundred species of resident and migrant birds in the Valley—"

"Fuck the goddam birds," said Tony in an aggrieved voice. "I'm tryna tell a fuckin' joke here!"

Red grinned and winked at the bird-watcher. "Okay, Tony," he said, "what *is* eighteen inches long that makes a woman scream when she wakes up in the morning?"

"Crib death!" crowed Tony.

"Crib death?" exclaimed the redhead in a disgusted voice. Neither man had laughed. "That's revolting."

"Hey, just fuck off, okay?" said Tony.

Red's beeper went off. The two buttons started away through the trees. When they had disappeared from view, the bird-watcher sought a point of vantage facing the inn.

Dante kept out of sight behind a palm tree while he glassed the windows of the suite the inn's front desk had told him was rented by Kosta Gounaris. Yes, people in there, but he couldn't see who. So he refocused on the inn's sweeping stone steps. Most of the front turnaround was taken up by a black stretch limo with a black-uniformed chauffeur lounging against the fender.

Tony was just a stupid button man, but with a couple of short and seemingly casual questions, Red had elicited why Dante had binoculars, that he actually could identify the bird flying out of the tree, and that he knew it was not a year-round resident at the Furnace Creek oasis. The redhead was canny and quick-witted, dangerous, which meant the man who paid him was also dangerous.

The chauffeur opened the back door, came to attention. Dante ground the glasses against his eyes; heat shimmers slightly distorted his view through the lenses, but he knew the four men coming down the wide stone front steps of the inn. Shaking hands with the two who obviously were depart-

ing was Gounaris. No surprise, since the fact he was flying
himself down here was why Dante had been here before him.

Dante had studied the second man's face ranging from his
1960 passport photo to an FBI surveillance picture taken a
week ago poolside at the Tallpalms Country Club in Palm
Springs. It was Gideon Abramson.

The other two were astounding. First, the legendary Don
Enzo himself, out from Jersey. Probably flown openly into
Vegas by private jet, then whisked out of some underground
garage in this anonymous limo and would go back in the
same way so the surveilling feds would think he'd never left
the hotel.

The fourth was The Man himself, Martin Prince. Marcantonio Princetti. Dante could recite the man's biography in his
sleep.

The limo disappeared around behind the hotel toward
Highway 190 which eventually would take it back to Vegas.
A cream Lexus followed, stuffed with Red and Tony riding
shotgun. Dante considered alerting the feds, rejected it; the
meeting was over. Nobody knew he was here, he wanted to
keep it that way.

Gounaris and Abramson were sitting down at one of the
tables on the inn's broad patio for a drink under a sun um-
brella. He'd have given a year's pay to hear what they were
saying, but he couldn't get close: Gounaris would see him,
and he wanted to be the one doing the viewing.

What was important enough to drag frail old Garofano out
here from Jersey? The doubleheader on Kreiger and St.
John? Was somebody within the Family trying to take down
its leaders one by one, grab control? Did Prince call this
meeting because these were the only men he could trust
within the Organization? Or because he thought one of them
was behind the murders?

Or was he playing some dangerous game of his own?

"I tell you he's playing a fucking game, Uncle Gid!" exclaimed Kosta Gounaris. He was drinking beer in the thin
dry desert air. Gideon was having iced tea.

"To what point, Kosta? He already has all the power."

"To set me up for unsanctioned killings he ordered him-self!" Gounaris mimicked, "'I'm suggesting that the same man *ordered* both hits.' He's just putting on a show for the old man so there won't be any heat when I get hit."

Gideon chuckled. "Who's the unhappiest man in New York?"

"New York? What the hell does New York—"

"A man with an Irish psychiatrist and a Jewish bartender." Gideon stirred his tea, sipped it. "Mr. Prince setting you up makes no sense. What does make sense is Kreiger having St. John hit, using Popgun. Ucelli is an old-timer, he would do it and deny it afterwards. And get away with it, because he's tight with Don Enzo and St. John was not a made man."

"Then who had Kreiger hit?"

"I fear Mr. Prince is starting to feel that perhaps you did. Out of ambition, a desire to move up . . . Let me tell you how he thinks. The killing was clever. You are clever. The killing was on your turf, San Francisco, where the Organization has very little influence. You fly your own plane, so he might even suspect you of Spic's murder."

"That's crazy! It's all crazy! *He* had Spic hit!"

"You know it's crazy. I know it's crazy. But Mr. Prince . . ." He shrugged. "In the morning—"

"I've got to fly back up in the morning, Uncle Gid."

"Then let's play a round of golf this afternoon."

With obvious relief, Kosta said, "I'll get my clubs."

Gid thoughtfully watched his protégé stride lithely across the patio toward his suite. So tough, so strong—but in many ways still so naive. Was his Kosta naive enough to be getting ambitious? Or was he maybe skimming, starting to panic and trying to cover it up with a little flurry of killings that would suggest a Mafia power struggle was brewing?

Or was Kosta right about Mr. Prince being behind the killings? The trouble was that Gideon didn't know enough about what was going on; so he would just stay here in Death Valley for a few days, tell jokes, play golf, until things got resolved. Gid was the ultimate survivor.

CHAPTER THIRTY-ONE

Dante watched them tee up, then set out to explore a little of Death Valley. He wouldn't have been there except that in collecting data on Kosta Gounaris he'd found out about the single-engine Mooney 250 turbo Gounaris had bought for over a quarter million cash in Los Angeles two years before.

The Mooney was tied down at Marin Ranch Airport, a private airfield off Smith Ranch Road just north of San Rafael. Dante had spent a couple of hours poking around the little field with its tin-sided hangars and tiny office. With a twenty-dollar bill he'd recruited the skinny, engaging youth who pumped aviation gas into the planes. At seventeen, he had braces still on his teeth and was a chain-smoker. He had told Dante that Gounaris wanted his plane serviced and checked out thoroughly because he was planning to fly down to Death Valley midweek.

Dante went to Zabriskie Point. It was only four miles down Highway 190 from the inn, and he'd loved the music in the movie of the same name. He turned right into the parking lot, climbed the short trail to the overlook. It was breathtaking. Soft layers of what looked like mud hills rather than rock stretched in every direction. Below the low wall of the overlook the bare tan dusty earth was crisscrossed with trails. Youthfully energetic hikers of all ages panted their way up them, dwarfed by distance.

A slight sun-blacked man in his seventies, dressed in baggy red shorts and leather sandals and whose black T-shirt read GRATEFUL DEAD—WORLD TOUR came panting up the path leading to the overlook. He stopped to wipe his face with a red bandana and grinned at Dante. His skull showed beneath his leathery lizard's skin like the Dead's logo skull on his T-shirt.

"Beautiful, isn't it?"

"Breathtaking—if I knew what I was seeing."

"You're seeing ancient lakebeds that have been upended and eroded into sandhills." He flung out a long skinny arm. "Those yellows and tans and browns are mostly from iron minerals that have been weathered by exposure to the air." He pivoted to jab a forefinger to their left, where the softly serrated hills ranged from gray-green to dark gray. "Those, the color comes from volcanic ash and ancient lava flows sometime between 9 and 3 million years ago."

"You seem to have spent a lot of time here."

"My favorite spot in the world. I'm a retired geologist. In Death Valley Mother Nature lifts her skirts and shows you everything she's got."

The little sun-dried raisin of a man headed down for the parking lot; Dante followed shortly. On his way back to the inn, he was surprised to see the old geologist walking along the shoulder of the two-lane blacktop. He stopped and opened a door.

"Hop in. It's too hot out here to walk."

The man slid gratefully into the car. "You're right, it's that afternoon sun. I parked at the foot of Golden Canyon, hiked up past Manley Beacon to the Point. Only about a mile and a half but mostly uphill. I do it every year. I tell myself that when I can't make it any more, I'll quit coming to the Valley." He stuck out a hand. "Charles Thornton. Everybody calls me Chuck."

They shook. "Dante Stagnaro. Tell me, what's the best thing to see if you've maybe only got one day?"

"The sand dunes, just before dusk. I'll show you."

The vast sloping floor of the valley was smudged with

cloud shadow. Harsh dark mountains rimmed it to the west, stretching up a mile or more into the stunning blue sky and reaching great hands of denser shadow out across the sunken valley floor.

"The Panamints," said Chuck. "Death Valley isn't the result of erosion, it's what geologists call 'basin and range' huckcountry. The same forces that cause the California earthquakes are pushing the Black Mountains higher in the air and tilting the Panamint Range higher up on its side."

"Dropping Death Valley down lower and lower in between?"

"Admirably put. Less than two inches of rain a year, evaporation a hundred times that, mean summer temperature readings the highest on earth. It's a true desert. Lowest point in the United States is Badwater, south down the valley a ways—two hundred eighty feet below sea level. Dante's View, straight above Badwater, is more than a mile *above* sea level."

"Dante's View because you're looking down into hell?"

Chuck grinned at him. "A minority opinion, I assure you."

They drove twenty miles north through the clear late afternoon light, with Chuck pointing out things they were passing.

"Gravel road to the left leads to the Harmony Borax Works. That's where the twenty-mule teams left from—eighteen mules and two horses, actually. Round trip to Mojave and the railhead was three hundred miles and took three weeks. The teams pulled two wagons and a water tank, total weight close to forty tons."

The road led across the lower slopes of alluvial fans spreading out from valleys in the Funeral Mountains to the east. The fans were dotted with desert holly, creosote bushes spaced out by massive ground-surface root systems stretching forty feet in every direction, and turtleback—great spreading bushes that looked much like their namesakes.

At Sand Dune Junction they went north. Here the Cottonwood and Grapevine mountains forced the winds to switch direction, swirl and slow enough to drop the load of sand they were carrying from their sweep across the valley floor.

"Hence, the Sand Dunes," exclaimed Chuck. "Fourteen square miles of moving, billowing sand that look like ocean waves—but aren't going anywhere. Oh, they shift around constantly, but because the winds turn on themselves here, the dunes never move far before getting pushed back."

Dante passed a little turnout to the right after Sand Dune Junction, blacktopped and with a single chemical toilet standing in lonely splendor. At Chuck's direction, a hundred yards further he turned left on a narrow dirt track toward the yellow-white amazement of the sand sea.

"Takes us to the original stovepipe well," Chuck said as they bounced along the sandy track pursued by their own dust cloud. "It was an important water hole on the old cross-valley trail in the days of the mining towns of Rhyolite and Skidoo, so they set up a way station. Long gone now. Park here."

Dante pulled up and stopped. Their dust overtook them, gritting between their teeth and in the corners of their eyes. Theirs was the only car in the little parking area. They got out, stretched, started across the level sandy desert floor toward the great sloping dunes that rose up suddenly ahead of them. Chuck stopped at a rusted capped-off pipe.

"Here's the well—they don't use it any more."

"Why stovepipe?"

"Used to be a literal stovepipe stuck down through the sand to the natural spring so they could get at the water. That rusted away many long years ago, of course." They started out across the billowing desert dunes. "Lucas shot a lot of *Star Wars* here in Death Valley. Used these dunes a lot."

Dante could see why. Fifty feet from the edge of the dunes, there seemed to be only sand for miles in any direction. Chuck said most of it was tiny fragments of quartz, buried, uncovered, reburied thousands of times as the sand shifted and flowed under the pressure of the wind.

The dunes themselves had an eerie beauty in the late slanting light. Long smooth sweeps of sand with crests like blunt sword edges, breaking suddenly to fall away in delicate blue-gold shadow toward the ground far below.

As they labored along one of these sword blades, Chuck panted, "They call this the cornice of the drift—it keeps collapsing under the pressure of more sand brought by the wind. That steep slope they call the slip face, with an angle of repose usually somewhere around thirty-five degrees. Come on!"

He started to run down it. Dante followed, sinking in almost to his knees at each stumbling, giant step. Sand whipped and stung his face. Each step splashed out a miniature avalanche of snowlike sand.

They collapsed in the cut between two massive dunes, to share Dante's canteen and the scraggly shadow of a creosote bush half-buried in drifting sand. Their faces were covered with sand stuck to their drying sweat.

The ground was a flat layer of dried mud, cracked by a summer of sun into patterns and shapes often unlike the usual triangular segments Dante expected. Here were circles and swirls, the edges eroded by wind so each segment looked like a miniature mesa. Other circle patterns looked like the dinosaur hide on the models at Marine World in Vallejo.

Around scraggly clumps of tough dry bunch grasses, poised for a winter rainstorm so they could shoot up, seed, and replenish themselves with dazzling speed, were circular drag marks where the wind had swept them against the sand.

"Tracks and sign," said Chuck. "Let me show you."

Both dried mud and sand carried wildlife tracks with great clarity, though Dante didn't know what he was seeing until Chuck pointed them out.

"Those sort of delicate ones with a pad and four toe marks are bobcat. Don't get too many in here."

"How can you tell it's not a coyote or a dog?"

"Retractable claws." He pointed. "*These* are coyote."

The tracks were larger but quite similar to Dante's untrained eye, except they indeed had made distinct claw marks in the sand. Running across them were delicate X-shaped tracks that went up over the lip of a shallow sand drift.

"Roadrunner."

"Beep-Beep?"

"You got it. And these—'Quoth the raven.'"

They looked somewhat like the silhouette of a swept-wing jet fighter, except the toes making the winglike marks pointed forward rather than back. Rather confusing spraylike tracks with a line drawn in the sand between them had been made by a lizard dragging his tail.

"Here's one nobody gets."

The tiny double row of endless pinpricks in the sand went from nowhere to endless nowhere. Running between the pinpricks was the lightest of pencil lines drawn in the sand.

"Stink beetle," said Chuck. "The line is drawn by its dragging abdomen."

Daylight was failing. They started back. Dante was hopelessly lost, turned around, disoriented.

"If the wind doesn't blow 'em away, you can always follow your own tracks back out in daylight. Or get to the top of a dune to see the mountains and most likely a road."

"I wouldn't know which mountains or which road."

"Don't matter so long as they get you out of here."

They crossed a vast stretch of low-lying dune that was rippled by the wind like the bottom of a stream rippled by flowing water. There were other wonders: the energy-filled bounds of leaping kangaroo rats; the delicate mincing trot of a big-eared kit fox; the talon marks of an owl dug into the sand where an unwary rabbit had died, surrounded by the giant brush marks of its wings beating predator and prey aloft again.

Most evocative of all was a series of long parallel scroll marks, each somewhat offset from the mark before it so the scrolls moved across the sand at an angle.

"Sidewinder," said Chuck. "Desert rattlesnake, you don't see them very often."

Not very often was fine with Dante.

They sat for a time in the car with the motor off, watching the sunset over the western mountains. The clouds turned first gray with gold foil edges, then golden, then an incredible bloodred herringbone pattern, finally fading off to delicate silver.

"Show's over," sighed Chuck at last. Dante started the engine. "Full-moon nights, sometimes I come out here and just sit on the lip of a dune and listen. You can hear everything that goes on, can hear yourself think." He paused. "Can hear yourself *blink*."

Dante's lights caught a tiny kit fox, great ears standing out in alarm, as he trotted into the sand dunes for the night's hunt. He looked gray in the headlights. On the way back to Furnace Creek, they saw a coyote loping away from the road into the rock-strewn desert.

A memorable day.

But still Dante couldn't sleep.

He had a hamburger and fries and berry pie at the Furnace Creek Ranch cafe, on his own time here, feeling a little guilty. He went to the front office and used the pay phone to call Rosa and tell her he was okay and that he loved her.

It should have sent him to bed relaxed and satisfied. But when he walked the dim roadway back to his room, the palm trees tossing and shivering against the full moon in the evening wind woke the familiar restlessness the full moon used to raise in him as a kid in San Francisco. Out his bedroom window he would go, to climb Telegraph Hill in moonlight, or run along the silent wharves of the Embarcadero, or race the night's final cable car up the California Street hill.

He returned to the little bungalow cabin and went to bed. The cabin was wood frame, built during the depression by the WPA after Death Valley had been made a national monument in 1933. Dante liked this old room with its feel of days gone by, when a motel really had still been a motor hotel. Linoleum floors, no phone or TV, just a clock radio, a desk and chair and twin beds set a prim distance apart. A joint front porch with the sister unit.

Dante tossed and turned like the ferny tamarind leaf patterns the moon laid across the windows. Tried to read a guidebook, put it aside, thought about his case.

Hymie the Handler had told him that Otto Kreiger's death had been managed. A section of gas line had shown a recent, deliberate rupture. A fragment of door frame had a strip of sandpaper adhesived to it. And a persistent but invisible Ed Farrow the San Francisco Redevelopment Agency had never heard of had phoned to demand a meeting with Kreiger in the condemned building just an hour before the explosion.

Ed Farrow was obviously Raptor. If Raptor was real. Raptor. A thought to murder sleep like who was it—Macbeth? He sat up and looked at the clock. Midnight. Moonlight.

Dante got up and got dressed, got his heavy jacket, found his way to the stovepipe well again. A zillion stars dimmed by an unwinking eye of moon. Back up at the highway, the lights of another car slowed, started the turn into Dante's dirt road, then disappeared. The wind kept him from hearing any sound of its engine if sound there was to hear.

He lighted his way into the dunes with his flashlight, stumbling and floundering and killing his night vision, a city boy in the open. The wind pulled at his hair, blew sand grit into his eyes, then dropped like a stone.

Sudden, total silence except for the hiss and slither of sand around his shoes, his panting breaths. Thirty feet up the side of a dune from a huge creosote with dozens of crannies between its half-exposed roots, the sand around it covered with tracks, Dante sat down and turned out his light. The sand was cold on his butt through his jeans. He shifted around for a comfortable position, quit moving to listen. And listen. No sound except for the creak of his jacket with his breathing.

Night blindness gone, he could see the creosote bush, see the dark scribbles of the largest tracks beneath it. He could have read his guidebook by the moonlight. Could hear himself breathing. Could hear his eyelashes coming together, the sound of the separate hairs meshing, parting. Chuck had been right. He *could* hear himself blink.

His head dropped and he slept.

In his dreams a scarred old coyote came trotting in from the flat ground around the stovepipe well, wary and clever and carrying Dante's upwind scent in its nostrils. It circled

him, sidled softly and sideways up to him, stuck a nose close
to his face to breathe in his strange scent.

Predawn desert chill awoke him. The moon was low on
the horizon; Dante needed the luminous face of his watch to
see it was nearly 3:00 A.M. He'd fallen asleep and hadn't
heard, hadn't seen a damned thing. Nothing at all. Except
something in a dream about a coyote.

He groaned and creaked his way to his feet. Something
yipped as it ran off from under the creosote bush. He started
down the dune, pitched forward on his face and slid down
the sand in the half-darkness, flailing and thrashing.

Dante swung around and sat up and turned on his flashlight. His goddam feet had gone to sleep, his . . .

Somebody had tied his shoelaces together while he slept.

A primitive dread shot through him. He remembered his
dad's tales of the Fiji Scouts in World War II, who would in-
filtrate the Japanese lines and slit the throat of one soldier in
a two-man trench, leaving the other alive. Untying and rety-
ing his laces, Dante knew how that survivor must have felt
when he awoke to the sight of his dead partner.

Chuck? No, the old geologist might have been capable of
moving that silently through the night, but he wouldn't . . .

When Dante stood up, something crackled against his
chest. He jerked around in a circle, beating at himself, terrified by thoughts of sidewinders slithering under his jacket
for warmth. But his spastic hands found only paper. Paper?

A note was fastened to his shirt with a safety pin.

Dante unfastened it carefully, his flesh almost crawling at
the knowledge that another human being had been able to get
that close to him in the night while he slumbered peacefully.

The note was on Furnace Creek Ranch letterhead. He read
the heavy ballpoint printing by the beam of his flashlight:

I DO NOT KILL

MY OWN KIND

RAPTOR

CHAPTER THIRTY-TWO

Kosta taxied his Mooney from his tie-down spot to the southern end of Furnace Creek's 3,000-foot paved airstrip. It was just after 8:00 A.M. and there was nobody except a pilot getting his Aztec filled with aviation gas, and the airport mechanic who was pumping it.

Kosta released the brakes and the plane surged forward, left the ground. He took off northwest, banked to the left, rising sharply to get over the saw-toothed Panamints toward Owens Lake. Below was the golf course where he had played eighteen holes with Gid the day before—losing about $500 to the old shark. It was emerald green in the slanting morning light, bounded by slim irrigation ditches and a small lake lined with weeping willows.

The engine's steady roar faded into longtime familiarity. He tuned to Castle Rock and asked Flight Following to advise him about other traffic in his vicinity. There was none; apart from private fliers like himself, the only planes that came into Furnace Creek were charter bush flights from Lone Pine or Vegas.

With the turbocharger he could have flown over the high mass of the Sierra lying between him and California's hot interior valley, but he chose to go up the Owens Valley and down the Tioga Pass. He liked the hazards of flying the passes: it challenged him more urgently than anything except sex.

Sex. Diana Pym would be waiting at Marin Ranch Airport with no panties on under her skirt, hungry for degradation in the back of his closed van. He would have liked her with him on this trip, but he hadn't wanted *any* of them, Mr. Prince or Don Enzo or even Uncle Gid, to be reminded of the fact that it was a woman close to him who had started this whole damned mess.

Not that he wasn't planning to get a great deal out of it, maybe even the brass ring with his dangerous game. Proving to himself he wasn't afraid of them? Simple greed? Lust for power? Those big balls of his youth again?

Anyway, there was Uncle Gid yesterday, almost believing Prince's suspicions about him. Was it just the usual Outfit paranoia, where everyone was always slightly suspect? Or was it something more concrete?

And then there was the cop, Stagnaro, showing up at the Greek Film Festival. Subtle harassment that couldn't be answered by a lawyer's cease-and-desist letter: after all, the man was just there with his wife, some Greek friends . . .

The plump pretty black-haired woman next to him would be the wife. For a wild moment, Kosta thought of seeking her out, getting her to fuck him and abase herself for him, as he did any other woman he wanted. But the fucking cop might shoot him in return. Still . . . she was there, desirable, that ever-potent hostage to fortune that made vulnerable all men who loved . . .

No. Dangerous and unnecessary. Dante knew nothing.

Dante had joined the two men topping off the Aztec's tanks just as Gounaris's plane had left the ground.

"That a Mooney that just took off?"

"Yeah," said the mechanic, wiping his hands on a faded red rag that looked greasier than his knuckles. "Turbocharger, cabin heater, the works. A beauty."

"Do you fly yourself?" asked the pilot.

Dante shook his head. "Can't afford to."

"I can't afford not to," grinned the pilot.

Dante had been up and around at first light, after a mighty struggle with his cop's instincts had called the inn and asked to be connected with Kosta Gounaris. But Gounaris had checked out. And was now well away and, for the moment, safe.

Because Raptor was here in Death Valley, given pith and substance for the first time by the note pinned to Dante's shirt. No longer just a series of sly phone messages on his machine, detailing the stalk of Dr. Death through the ranks of the Mafia.

Following him out to the dunes, turning into the dirt road by the stovepipe well, killing lights and engine, jogging in, picking up Dante's tracks into the dunes—an awesome bit of fieldcraft. And an act of either sheer bravado or sheer contempt, *letting Dante know that he was here!* Scorning him, showing him he was helpless against Raptor's omniscient ways.

But *was* he scorning Dante? I DO NOT KILL MY OWN KIND. Or acknowledging him as a fellow hunter? Raptor was Dante's prey; but who, here, was Raptor's? Not Dante; he could have had Dante out in the dunes last night. Not Gounaris, Gounaris was safely away. But Gideon Abramson was still here. Dante would warn him, then start the long drive home.

Death in Death Valley. Almost corny. Almost.

Gideon had finished his early-morning laps in the heated pool, now was on the terrace of the inn, drinking orange juice while waiting for his decaf and toast. A beautiful morning for eighteen holes of golf. He had slept like an angel despite the questions going around and around in his mind until his head had hit the pillow.

He regretfully put aside consideration of what to get his favorite granddaughter for her birthday—a five-foot stuffed purple Barney had the inside track at the moment—to return to the previous night's churning thoughts. He hadn't told Kosta that he secretly agreed Mr. Prince was probably behind the Madrid and Kreiger killings, because he felt that Mr. Prince *was* looking at Kosta as a possible threat somewhere down the road.

A pretty young waitress came with his toast and coffee. He watched her hips glide like oil beneath the oddly erotic uniform as she walked away. Could he possibly . . . No. He went to Vegas for that. Outside Vegas these days he was decidedly avuncular.

If Mr. Prince was not behind the killings, then who? *Could* it be Kosta? Could he have set up the hit on Moll Dalton with a phony fuck-up confession, so the rest of the killings could be seen to grow out of that?

Where should he stand should there be a confrontation between these two? *Gross Gott,* he knew the answer to that. Stand with Kosta, fall with Kosta. Gid planned to live forever: he had seen enough men die to know there was nothing worse than dying, nothing on this earth. If Mr. Prince gave him the order today to set up a hit on Kosta, by morning Kosta would be dead.

Not that Mr. Prince would. The man's mind was too subtle for such a gross challenge to human feeling and commitment. Gid would be the last to know—except for Kosta, of course.

A lean dangerous-looking Italian with a tired face sat down at Gid's table. He wore jeans and heavy hiking boots and a light baggy sport shirt outside his pants. Gid glanced involuntarily at the heavyset man alone at a table on the corner of the terrace.

"You won't need him. Dante Stagnaro. You want ID?"

"No. That explains the gun under your shirt."

"Sig-Sauer 228—a beauty." He pointed at Gid's pot of coffee. "Decaf?"

When Gid nodded, the Italian turned over the unused cup and filled it, added milk and Equal. He sipped, sighed in pleasure, leaned back in his chair and crossed his legs. The tables were set far enough apart so nobody could casually overhear them.

"I'm sorry, I know nothing about guns," said Gideon.

"Pity. I'm a fucking deadeye with it, I could shoot off your chauffeur's toes before he could stand up."

"You aren't quite . . . as I pictured you, Lieutenant."

"I get giddy when I talk to mobsters."

Gideon was starting to get into the spirit of it, starting to enjoy himself. He said, "Such a remark would be actionable in front of witnesses."

"But it's just between us girls." Dante leaned forward across the table, focusing his energies, and Gideon suddenly understood the reputation of this seeming buffoon. His first impression had been right: here was a dangerous man. "I think your life is in danger, Mr. Abramson."

That broke the spell. Gideon said, "So this woman goes in to buy a fresh chicken. She lifts a wing and smells underneath it; then she lifts the other wing and smells. Then she spreads apart the chicken's legs and sniffs again. She turns to the butcher and she says, 'You *meshugga,* this chicken is no good.' The butcher says to her, 'Lady, can *you* pass a test like that?'"

Dante didn't crack a smile. Instead, he said, "Meaning?"

"Meaning, you stink worse than the butcher's chicken. I suppose Mr. Prince is going to have me killed, so I must scurry to you as my passport into witness relocation."

"I don't know who wants you dead. I don't know who wanted Spic Madrid or Otto Kreiger or Skeffington St. John dead, either. But I know that the man who killed them is here in Death Valley. Gounaris is gone and he's not after me."

For a moment, Gideon was shaken. The man was very good!

"Then why don't you arrest him?"

"I said I know he's here, not who. He left me a note."

Dante laid Raptor's note on the table. Gideon leaned forward, scanned it without touching it. No fingerprints.

"'I do not kill my own kind. Raptor.'" He looked up at Dante. "Raptor?"

"It's what he calls himself."

The waitress was at his elbow. "Mr. Abramson?" He

turned. "You have a telephone call. Would you like me to bring—"

"No, thank you." It was probably some ploy the *meshugge* cop had set up, he wasn't going to give the man the satisfaction of listening in. "I'll take it at the desk."

"I'll have some more coffee while I wait," said Dante.

Inside at the phone alcove, Gideon picked up without hesitation; nobody would call him on business at an open phone like this. The voice was thick, heavy, Bronx-accented.

"This is Raptor, tell me one a ya fuckin' hebe jokes."

Anger swelled Gideon's chest. "*Hebe* jokes?"

"I gotta know I'm talkin' to the right guy here. I never met you, but you're famous for them terrible Jew jokes you tell."

This made sense. His fury dissipated. "Ah . . . okay. This Jewish mother is talking with her son's teacher, she says, 'My Gregory is very smart. If he's a bad boy, slap the boy next to him—Gregory will get the idea.'"

"Yeah, they're right," said the heavy voice. "Terrible. Now, ditch the fuckin' cop." This call was local. Somebody in the building—or down the road a half mile with binoculars and a car phone. A heavy chuckle. "I left him a note." Then he said, "I did them all." When Gid didn't answer, he added impatiently, "All of them. Starting with the broad. You're supposed to be next."

It was just so goddamned pat; another simpleminded gambit by the cop to either frighten him or compromise him in some way. But Stagnaro was not a simpleminded man. If he came up with a gambit, wouldn't it be a convoluted one, instead of children's games like the note, this phone call?

Could both note and call be genuine? Was he talking with the man who had hit all the others? Gid couldn't help it, he heard himself asking, "For whom are you supposed to do this?"

"I tell you that, I got nothing to sell."

"Why would I want to buy it?"

The caller gave a harsh chuckle. "To stay alive, pal. To stay alive." Gideon felt a finger of dread down his spine.

"Why would you want to sell it?"

"I think he's got me on the list after you." When Gideon hesitated, the voice added, "Make up your fuckin' mind, I gotta get somebody between me an' the light. You don't wanna play I gotta go to the fuckin' cop."

"No, no. I'm in the market. It's just that I . . . I need some protection, a place where I can feel safe."

"You think I don't? I want it flat and I want it wide open. I know all about you, Abramson. You'd fuck your dead mother so you could steal the pennies off her eyes afterwards."

He was truly, blindingly angry for a moment. Retired or not, nobody talked that way to Gideon Abramson.

"Men talk like that end up drinking a Drano cocktail."

"Twenty years ago, old man, maybe. Now you're just pissing in the wind. So we'll play this my way . . ."

CHAPTER THIRTY-THREE

When Abramson returned to the table, he paused just long enough to sign the chit and add a tip and his room number.

"Raptor?" ventured Dante. "Wanting a meet?"

Gideon met his eyes guilelessly. In the old days, many a cutter in the garment district had been seduced by the limpid honesty in those eyes, always to his sorrow.

He gestured to his chauffeur. "Gus." To Dante, he said, "Admit it, Lieutenant. Raptor is a figment of your overactive Latin imagination. I have a twosome scheduled, that was my partner on the phone. He's at the first tee and waiting."

Dante gave an elaborate shrug. "I warned you, that's all I wanted to do."

Alone, Dante poured the last of the coffee, doctored it to taste. He should have thought of the possibility that Raptor was here to make a deal, not a hit. The old mobster had been shaken by the Raptor note, had been a little scared when he left the table. To come back confident. Only a sellout by Raptor could make a canny guy like Abramson go to a meet backed up only by muscle like Gus.

It would have to be a mutually safe place. That meant no canyons to hide a sniper in the rocks above. No sand dunes—they would be an ambusher's dream. Someplace flat. Just about anywhere in Death Valley. The golf course itself? No. Flat and *isolated*. Abramson would have to leave by car, go either north or south—there were no east-west roads from Furnace Creek, and Abramson's Mercedes wasn't all-terrain.

Easy to tag along. There was traffic on the roads and Abramson didn't know Dante's car. He'd hang back, move in when the meet went down.

Gus had some kind of cannon under his arm, but Gideon had told Dante the truth: he didn't know much about guns. As a young, tough, brash enforcer on the Lower East Side streets of New York, his tool of choice had been a baseball bat.

Later, when he'd moved up to middle management, he'd stopped getting blood on his clothes. As a capo, he'd had his soldiers adapt the IRA's treatment for suspected informers: kneecapping by electric drill, not bullet. A drill was not a felony weapon, you couldn't go down for carrying one in your car.

But guns had their place, and Gus was damned good with his. So Gideon explained to Gus how he wanted it played while they drove to the meet. The place Raptor had chosen was exactly the sort of place Gideon himself would have chosen.

"You still have the extra piece clipped under the dash?"

Gus grinned. He had beautiful dentures; all his teeth had been knocked out during a garment district organizing beef.

"Don't leave home without it, Mr. Abramson."

"Good. I'm sure he'll make you put your gun down on the blacktop and return to the car while we talk. As soon as I have his employer's name, use your backup piece on him through the windshield. We can tell the garage at Furnace Creek something flew off a truck and hit us."

Twenty minutes later, Gus turned the heavy Mercedes sedan into the little blacktop rest area half a mile beyond Sand Dune Junction. It was deserted except for them, the plastic-stalled chemical toilet, and a litter basket. Gus got out leaving his door hang open.

"Check the toilet and the litter basket," said Gideon.

Gus did, the basket first, then the empty toilet stall's ceiling and corners, even down the hole, for explosives.

"All clear, Mr. Abramson."

Gideon got out, leaving his door open also. Gus opened the rear doors and the trunk lid according to Raptor's instructions. The first car since they stopped came by from the same direction they had come, but the lone man behind the wheel didn't even turn his head as he zipped by. The sky was achingly blue, unclouded. Far overhead, a pair of turkey vultures glided in silent circles, great wings spread to catch the updrafts, binocular eyes seeking the dead and dying.

Behind the pancake of blacktop the creosote-studded base of a broad alluvial fan sloped gradually up, narrowing toward the base of the series of flat-topped hills and deeply eroded canyons at least a mile away. No worry of sniper fire from there.

Gideon turned and looked the other way, across the road down toward the sand dunes. At least a thousand yards away. Otherwise, just the empty road. Desert flatness.

A good choice. Raptor was nobody's fool.

Neither was Gideon Abramson. Once he knew who had hired Raptor for all the killing, he would know where he stood, whether in safety or in jeopardy. And then Raptor would be dead, a threat erased, that insult about his mother avenged.

"Uh . . . whadda we do now, Mr. Abramson?"

"We wait, Gus. Give him a good chance to look us over. He's probably in that little parking area down by the dunes."

The parking area by the dunes, Dante thought as he drove right by Abramson's Mercedes, off the road with all four doors and the trunk lid open. He didn't even turn his head. Didn't want Abramson spotting him because he was inquisitive. The dunes parking area was where Raptor would be, checking out the site.

He turned down the little dirt road he was getting to know by heart. Raptor's car would be among those parked there.

He stopped, backed and filled to turn around a hundred yards from the highway, got out his glasses. Raptor would have to drive by him to get back to the turnout where Gideon waited.

A quick check through his glasses. Gideon and the chauffeur were both well clear of the car. When Raptor drove up, he could just circle it to see nobody was hiding within.

Now it was a waiting game.

A half hour later Gid said, "We'll give him fifteen more minutes, Gus."

This wasn't just some exercise in control, was it? Would there be a call on his car phone, trying to send him off to some other remote area of the Valley, and then another, and another?

Gid wasn't going to play. When he left here, that was it.

Unless it had been set up by Stagnaro to get him away from his room. Go through it, plant a bug? He chuckled at the idea. Gideon Abramson had never left anything incriminating, never said an incriminating word, in an unswept room in his life.

"It's a no-show, Gus. I'll take a leak, then we'll go."

Gid entered the hot little chemical toilet stall. Even out here in the desert it didn't smell very good. And it was hot as hell. Instant sweat broke out on his forehead, upper lip, and the backs of his hands as he unzipped and directed a good healthy stream down the hole. No prostate trouble for Gideon Abramson. He was going to live forever.

Maybe Raptor was booby-trapping his room while he was gone. Gus would check it out as Gid sipped ice tea on the terrace—

A huge bumblebee bit him on the arm with shocking power but no pain. It had come right through the plastic wall, leaving a small neat drilled hole through which sunlight poked. The air was full of bees. The plastic rattled and quaked with their buzzings. Gideon's dick dissolved in his hand into a gory splash of flesh. One bit him in the upper chest, knocking him down. His arm went down the hole. He started to scream. Struggled upright, shoved open the door, stumbled out . . .

A high-powered round went through the tendons at the back of his neck, burst his face outward like a ripe melon. Gus was down on one knee, seeking a target, but there was none. Just bullets to keep him pinned down and clip the car, smash a headlight, skip off the pavement. Two more drilled Gideon's body as he sprawled there on what was left of his face.

But Gideon Abramson had produced eight grandchildren. Biologically, he died successful.

Dante, through his glasses, saw the holes appearing in the walls of the chemical toilet, saw the thin plastic shudder and quake under the supersonic needle-sharp assaults. He was already ramming the accelerator to the floor by then, slewing up the dirt road toward the highway.

It was over by the time he got there. Gus was behind the Mercedes. Dante already had his badge in his hand.

"You got a phone in that thing?" he snapped, without waiting for an answer, added, "Try to raise the Stovepipe Wells Hotel—they're closer than Furnace Creek—"

"Took a round," said Gus laconically of the car phone.

Dante began slamming his fists down on the hood of the Mercedes and cursing. "Of all the goddam . . ."

He ran down. He hadn't even drawn his piece. Neither he nor Gus could even tell from which direction the fusillade had come. Just . . . somewhere up on the alluvial fan. Raptor obviously was a crack shot, he could lie up there in the creosote and cacti, three, four, even five hundred yards away, take a tripod or sandbag rest, set the elevation on his scope, wait for the right moment. If it didn't come, just fade back into the desert without anyone ever knowing he'd been there. But it had come.

Probably left his vehicle on the road that led up through Daylight Pass. Beatty was only twenty-five miles away, the Nevada border half that. Or he could have just driven sedately back to Furnace Creek to take a swim. Or gone hiking up some canyon. Nobody knew his car or his face.

What they had all forgotten was that the seemingly table-smooth barren featureless desert was as seamed and pitted as an ancient Indian's face, a maze of little washes and gulleys and dry runoffs that furnished impeccable cover. Hell, it's why they had called ambushing "dry-gulching" in the Old West.

Now it was *really* personal. For all the good that did.

It wasn't until the next morning that a Shoshone tracker, working from the angle of fire, found Raptor's place of ambush 403 yards from the rest area. The assassin hadn't made any mistakes. No spent brass, no rifle, on that flinty ground no footprints—just a few dried branches broken down to give a clearer field of fire and incidentally mark his position.

Dante stayed overnight to give and sign his statement. Of course Gus had a license to carry—hell, he was a deputy sheriff in Palm Springs! Mr. Abramson had received threats, etc. Dante knew more about the killing than Gus did, but only gave the locals that he'd been passing by. Gus didn't contradict him.

Dante got back to San Francisco in the middle of the night after a day of hard driving. As expected, Raptor's message was waiting on his phone machine.

"This Jewish mother is talking with her son's teacher, she says, 'My Gregory is very smart. If he's a bad boy, slap the boy next to him—Gregory will get the idea.'"

Gideon Abramson's voice. Raptor must have somehow gotten him to tell one of his pathetic goddam Jewish jokes over the phone, taped it for his message to Dante, making a joke of it.

PART SIX

End of the Cretaceous

65 m.y. ago

The Way of the warrior is resolute
acceptance of death.

Miyamoto Musashi
A Book of Five Rings

PART SIX

End of the Cretaceous

65 m.y. ago

CHAPTER THIRTY-FOUR

Murder is never a joke, I grant you—but what is all this darkside nonsense I spout when last we chat? I feel wonderful—Gideon Abramson, dead in such a comical way, no longer pollutes the world with his presence. Oh, what a sly fellow is Raptor!

Meanwhile, I have become obsessed with the intricate-puzzle aspect of my assassinations. Not the *fact* of the deaths, but with their psychological impact. What are they thinking—the remaining people on the list? And what did those already erased think in that flashing instant when they went down?

They can't stop me, but do they know I am coming? Do they know why? Do they refuse to believe it if they do know? Surely they must know I am coming after *somebody* next time around, but do they know it is *their* appointment in Samarra that draws nigh?

When I have executed boring old Will, when the list lies crumpled in the wastebasket of my mind . . . what then?

I cannot worry about that now. Until then, I kill, and that is enough. And it is time to go kill again.

But before I do, I must tell you about friend Gideon. He lives in Palm Springs, is a member of the Tallpalms Country Club. A membership card from a club in Scottsdale gets me a reciprocal guest membership at Tallpalms. The members' bulletin board gets me the information that Gideon is a demon bridge player. In the card room I get my first look at him—he has never seen me, there is no danger of recognition.

In the bar I hear he has somehow winkled ownership of a Mercedes agency away from a former club member, Charlie Hansen, that he drives a new S-600 Mercedes sedan that retails for $135,000, and that he has a penchant for terrible jokes no one dares find unfunny. Perhaps rumors of his former profession and current affiliations have filtered through the club like fecal matter through the baffles of a sewage treatment plant?

On the putting green, I learn that he will be leaving midweek to play golf at Death Valley. A call to Furnace Creek as Mr. Abramson's travel agent gets me his arrival date and that he will be in one of the two luxury suites at the inn.

I drive over ahead of him, get a modest cabin in the old section of the ranch, and reacquaint myself with Death Valley's possibilities for ambush. I have never planned an assassination there, but I know the Valley well and its splendid isolation suggests easier disposal of Gideon than on his home ground.

Imagine my surprise when I discover that he is here only peripherally for golf, primarily for a meeting with his Mafia associates. One of them is Gounaris. I observe from afar; some of the newcomers can recognize me. I do not worry about missing: from his booking, Gideon will stay behind when they leave.

I get a nasty shock, however, while wandering through the inn's beguiling date plantation; I come almost face-to-face with Dante Stagnaro, skulking about in the guise of a bird-watcher.

I save myself by turning away to contemplate one of the grove's clear bubbling streams, my face shaded by a long-billed fishing cap. His sleeve brushes me as he passes. I have made him dangerous to me by goading him as a picador goads a bull, doing everything short of taking his ear as a trophy.

I watch surreptitiously past the long bill of my cap as he is stopped by two obvious thugs because he has a pair of binoculars around his neck. They talk of birds. One of the pair is just a thug, but the one called Red is intelligent and probing. One of Prince's creatures, no doubt.

Paradoxically, I must now spend most of my time following Stagnaro about so I will know where he is and won't risk another face-to-face confrontation. I assume he is here because of Gounaris, and will leave Death Valley when Gounaris does.

Thus I am his shadow as he talks with the Mafia goons, at Zabriskie Point, at the stovepipe well, at the dunes. Returning to the ranch, I get my second nasty shock: by the grossest of coincidences we are sharing the same cabin! He the left-hand unit, me the right, with a common front stoop.

This unexpected proximity drives me to decisive—perhaps foolhardy—action. I have not yet figured out how to kill Abramson, so I decide to precipitate matters, as one precipitates a chemical reaction in a retort. I will let Stagnaro know that Raptor, Fantômas to his Inspector Juve, is here in Death Valley. If nothing else, I will learn much of Stagnaro; always valuable with a man so dangerous to my enterprises.

Will he see Gounaris, or Abramson, as my prey? Will he let them know he has them under surveillance? Will he alert local authority with its powers of search and seizure? Or will he do nothing at all, despite his policeman's *protect and serve* oath?

I filch a few sheets of stationery from the office after seeing him safely in the cafe for supper, return to my room and, wearing gloves so I will leave no prints, use a heavy marking pen to write on a sheet taken from the center of the sheaf:

I DO NOT KILL

MY OWN KIND

RAPTOR

I am about to shove it under the door of his unit when I see him returning. I barely get back into my own room in time. I could leave it under the windshield wiper on his car, but it is parked in front of his window. I must wait until he retires.

Through the thin walls, I hear him moving around. I can sympathize: as Raptor, I have many bad nights. But then, at midnight, he leaves again. What is he up to, driving off into the dark emptiness?

He returns to the dunes. I park my car up near the highway and follow on foot. Halfway up a dune I find him, sleeping like a baby. Death Valley's stark beauty seems to have given him profound tranquillity: I shall take it back.

My RAPTOR note still in my pocket, a safety pin in the compact first-aid/notion kit I always carry in the field, I think myself into my coyote-trickster mode for stalking game. He will not sense me. I approach, tie his shoelaces, pin the note.

I return to the ranch. Stagnaro returns at 4:16. He paces, paces, leaves again at first light. I follow. We both see Gounaris off. Perfect—our appointment will be at another Samarra, later. Stagnaro joins Abramson at the breakfast table; a man of honor indeed, I know how he hates all mobsters' guts.

In a flash I see my method of execution. I call Abramson on the phone, *tell* him I am scheduled to kill him next, admit I fear for my own life and will make a deal with him. I say a nasty thing about his mother, to enrage him and thus keep him from thinking clearly; emotion always clouds reason. I offer him a meet. He leaps at the chance.

The rest is mere execution. The site is admirably chosen. I have the necessary rifle and scope in the trunk of my car—I have been a hunter, a shooter, all my life. It is manufactured the year I am born—a Winchester center-fire Model 70 in .270, bolt action, which I can work in a blur because I have fired thousands of rounds through it. My scope is a Leupold 10X, my ammunition is Lake City Match M852s. I have come to shoot.

I am about to squeeze off the killing round when Abramson enters the toilet stall. To equate his death with his ultimate evacuation is too delightful to pass up. I lay down a barrage, take him out decisively, slip away when Stagnaro shows up.

Abramson's is the first killing I have actually enjoyed. Am I getting callous? Losing my soul? Or is it because this is long-distance rifle shooting, the kind of shooting I have been doing at targets and game most of my life? You are no longer man and rifle, it is no longer scope and target, it is spot-weld of cheek to stock, it is nonverbal, it is . . .

Or is it just that the colossal hypocrisy of Gideon Abramson's life makes his death—the sixth in the series—the most satisfying?

CHAPTER THIRTY-FIVE

"The sixth day of creation," said Will. "Tomorrow, the God of Genesis rests. Today . . . well, today is a long day indeed for Him. Tough to cram all that creating into twenty-four hours. In science's terms an even longer day, stretching from the late Paleozoic a bit over 300 million years ago to this evening's mighty reckoning in this little room."

Another hint, thought Dante, that Will had returned knowing Raptor was going to be waiting for him.

"Genesis: 'And God said, Let the earth bring forth the living creature after his kind, cattle, and creeping thing, and beast of the earth after his kind: and it was so.'

"That's it, folks. Shazam! Cattle, creepings things, beasts of the earth. *Everything* except His final creation, man, made and then instructed during the balance of the sixth day.

"But we need the fossil time frame, not a few minutes of a single twenty-four-hour day, to explain what went before to shape us with all our terrible and glorious complexities and contradictions.

"As vertebrates we had gained a bony skeleton, a jointed spine, muscle and nerve systems that oxygenated and circulated the blood. As amphibians we became tetrapods: air-breathers with no more than five digits on each of our paired limbs.

"The amphibians were most successful for their day, some getting to be a few feet long and shaped like a silly-looking crocodile drawn by a five-year-old. In less than 100 million years they developed into the earliest reptile, proto-reptile, what we could call the base reptile, so successful that the amphibians today have been reduced to barely enough frogs and newts, as William Howells notes, 'to keep a witch in brew.'

"By changing to proto-reptile, what did we gain over the amphibian ancestors we so closely resembled? We became amniotes. Only mammals, reptiles, and birds—which wouldn't appear for sure until the flying feathered dinosaur, *archaeopteryx,* in the late Jurassic 170 million years ago— are amniotes.

"Amniotes have their fetal development either in an egg or in a womb. The amnion, and other protective membranes, supply the fetus with food and oxygen.

"Successively more advanced models followed that base reptile of 300 million years ago. They became the first of four 'Megadynasties' that Robert Bakker, a maverick dinosaur guru who has stood paleontology on its ear a score of times, suggests have existed during the history of life on land.

"Megadynasty One, the proto-reptiles, had great staying power—these early reptiles ruled for 20 million years with two types of beasts. Big quick predators, dimetrodons—popularly, 'sail lizards' because of tall webbed spines on their backs—and big slow vegetarians.

"Near the very end of the Paleozoic era, maybe 260 m.y. ago, one line of these sluggish and decidedly cold-blooded proto-reptiles split into two basic new vertebrate life-forms. One, called thecodonts, became the modern reptiles, the dinosaurs, and their descendants, the birds.

"The other became mammal-like reptiles called therapsids—some call them *syn*apsids, although I doubt they had very many synapses to help them along—that formed the second of Bakker's Megadynasties. They dominated the thecodonts from the late Permian through the Triassic, ranging from early bone-headed proto-mammals to, at the end of their reign, very advanced dog-faced cynodonts just a knife blade away from true mammals.

"They had become warm-blooded—mammal-like bony palates separating the mouth and nose cavities in some of them suggest this—but the mass extinction 249 m.y. ago at the Paleozoic/Mesozoic boundary finished them. They already had spawned the true mammals, however, tiny mouse-like things that had to wait their turn because the reptiles moved first, evolved faster, to grab all major Mesozoic ecological niches.

"These Archosauria—true reptiles—the most successful early model being the so-called crimson crocodiles, were soon weighing in at a half-ton or so, and the third Megadynasty, the Age of Reptiles, was under way. Through the Jurassic and Cretaceous right up to the end of the Mesozoic 65 m.y. ago, dinosaurs and other reptiles reigned supreme. Their story is not our story, but they were a tremendous success.

"They ruled the earth as tyrannosaurs, as stegosaurs, as ceratopsians, as massive sauropods like diplodocus and brontosaurus who reached eighty tons in weight and a hundred feet in length. Truly thunder lizards. They reentered the sea as plesiosaurs, ichthyosaurs, and mosasaurs. Soared the skies as pterodons, pterosaurs, and pterodactyls, in sizes ranging from a robin to a jet fighter.

"Archosauria seemed destined to control the world forever. Why didn't it? Because of the infamous mass extinction at the K/T (Cretaceous-Tertiary) boundary 65 m.y. ago, often called the Great Dying. The dinosaurs went extinct not through bad genes, but through bad luck. Environmental catastrophe overtook them. Three-fourths of all living species on the earth, in the sea, in the sky, were abruptly terminated.

"The current Megadynasty Four, the Age of Mammals, was about to begin. At first it didn't look like much. During the dinosaurs' reign the mammals essentially were limited to two major sorts of what Bakker called little furballs: the rodent and the shrew. These little guys played out their tiny, apparently insignificant destinies down around the dinosaurs' toenails, but they bore the marks of the mammal—live birth, warm blood, flexible skeleton.

"Live birth means mammary glands—the young are nursed and receive maternal care.

"Warm blood means hair and fur, a four-chambered heart, two sets of specialized teeth (milk teeth to grow with, permanent teeth to live with) essential for true warm-bloodedness, with variously shaped hard enamel crowns adapted to the animal's diet.

"Flexible skeletons mean a free lumbar spine, and a unique bone growth pattern called epiphyses whereby the bone grows in the middle, not at the ends. It is this that gives the mammals their tight, flexible, very usable joints.

"Early rodent—let's call him proto-rat—had *very* big teeth to chew the roots and plants of the day: tree ferns, horsetails, cycads, conifers, sequoias, araucarias (monkey puzzle trees), and the spanking new flowering plants called angiosperms.

"And proto-rat used those sharp teeth on proto-shrew, forcing the little scuttler to become tree shrew by taking to the trees where proto-rat wouldn't—couldn't?—follow. Also, since nocturnal proto-rat controlled the night and the ground, tree shrew became diurnal and claimed the day and the trees.

"When the dinosaurs finally galloped and leaped and plodded off in the Great Dying, our little squirrel-like ancestors were waiting in the trees just as proto-rat's descendants were waiting on the ground. During 30 million years in their arboreal world, the tree shrews had evolved, had begun developing and coordinating our three major features—hand, eye, and brain. They had started to become monkeys.

"In the process, our eyes moved to the front of our heads, giving us the tremendous advantages of binocular and Technicolor vision. Our muzzles shrank as eye became more important than nose, the claws on the digits of our hands and feet became nails, and we developed opposable thumbs and friction skin (fingerprints) on hands and feet to help us grab useful things like tree branches or a piece of fruit.

"All of this new activity was making our brain bigger and

bigger in relation to our size and weight. Which, for some, kept getting bigger also.

"Some of the monkeys got so large and slow, in fact, that they had to confine themselves to lower branches that could support them. As we move to about 28 million years ago, remember that heaviness: it is forcing some of them to develop into . . . loud movie music here . . . *apes* . . ."

A lean, fast-walking man was passing across the windows on the walk outside. Dante quit listening. The man looked in, saw Will behind the podium, and faltered for a moment before going on. Dante waited, tense, until he had gone up the stairs to the Theological Union. It was a while before he settled back against the wall, and then he kept his hand close to his gun, in case that other fast-moving man should appear out of nowhere.

CHAPTER THIRTY-SIX

The P.W. appeared out of nowhere on the icy, windblown day after Thanksgiving, materializing out of a swirling snowstorm like a figure on a Polaroid photo gradually taking on definition once it has been pulled from the camera. He was walking as he would always walk, with his arms raised and bent at the elbows, his hands clasped behind his head in the traditional "surrendering prisoner" manner. Thus, P.W.— prisoner of war.

On that first late afternoon, with the light already fading and early snow on the ground, there was nobody to see him but Old Mose. Mose was seventy-eight, with a seamed chocolate face and frizzy hair white as the snow he was struggling with. When the Roadhouse had been one, Mose had played some mean blues piano in the lounge; but an irate customer, a made man—Eddie Ucelli (cool on the kill, a creep in his cups)—had taken care of that by repeatedly slamming the keyboard cover on Mose's hands because Eddie wanted *"O Sole Mio"* instead of "Hellhound on My Trail."

Mae had kept Mose on as handyman—a misnomer if there ever was one, seeing the state of his hands—so on this snowy afternoon he was outside painfully clearing the front walk, holding the shovel awkwardly in his more or less useless claws.

That was when the P.W. appeared between the eastern

white pines, crunching through the snow from the road that
had once been a highway. He took the shovel from Mose's
twisted fingers with his strong gloved hands, and started
shoveling vigorously.

"Hey, mister, ain't no call for you to . . ."

The P.W. paused to lay a gloved finger to his lips, then returned to his shoveling. Mose didn't have to shovel again as
long as the P.W. was there. He didn't have to tend the furnace, either, or the water heater, or carry in cases of booze or
crates of frozen steaks from Ucelli's meat wholesale company, or perform any of his other heavier tasks. The P.W., in
the same plodding manner he did everything, took care of all
of them.

It was hard to tell how tall or how heavy the P.W. was, or
even how old. His scraggly hair was mostly hidden by a
Navy watch cap he seemed to wear both day and night. He
had a matted beard he never cut, wore God knew how many
layers of clothes underneath an Army camouflage jacket and
baggy camouflage combat pants. The soles of his battered
Army boots were sadly run over on the outside edge. He
never removed his gloves.

Old Mose told the girls in a self-important voice that the
P.W. had confided he'd been tortured repeatedly by the V.C.,
and his hands were not something anyone would ever see
again. How much of this was real and how much Mose had
dreamed up because it seemed that's the way it *must* have
been, nobody ever knew, since the P.W. talked to Mose
damned little and to anyone else not at all. But anyway, it
made a nice story. And it made old Mose feel he had a co-
eval in the hands department.

The P.W. carried his head thrust forward on his neck like a
lily on a stalk, walking with a stooped shuffle that neither
slowed nor speeded nor turned aside. It seemed that if he had
needed to walk through the building, he simply would have
done so like a tank, trailing broken lengths of lath and up-
rooted wiring and odds and ends of plasterboard with him.

Nobody ever tested the impression, because Mose made
sure on that first night that he got some of the half-eaten

meals that otherwise would have gone into the garbage, and found a place in the basement by the furnace for him to lay out his grimy sleeping bag. The P.W. rigged a length of hose to fit over the overflow valve on the water heater, and thus could give himself a rudimentary shower—not that anyone ever saw him take one.

Mae didn't even become aware of him until the third morning after his arrival, when she saw him carrying in cases of booze from the Acme Liquors truck—an Organization firm, of course.

"Mose, just who the hell is that?" she demanded.

"He jes' show up t'other night, Miss Mae."

"But who the hell *is* he?"

"He jes' show up, Miss Mae," repeated Mose vaguely.

Delia Ann, a short sturdy black girl much in demand because she had a big butt but was very supple and inventive, said, "The girls have started calling him the P.W.—for prisoner of war."

"Why do you . . ." Then Mae saw him walking around to the back of the building to get another load, his arms in their invariable "I surrender" position, and she understood the name. So she changed what she had started to say, to, "I don't care what the hell you call him, just so long as you call him gone."

Old Mose said dolefully, "He be a pow'ful he'p to me roun' de place, Miss Mae."

"Be a sport, Mae," said tall, stately, redheaded Clarisse. She was also very popular with the clientele because she could get up on a tabletop, squat naked over a long-necked beer bottle, and pick it up without a laying on of hands. "Let him stay. He's harmless and a real gentleman."

"How can you tell?" asked Mae.

"He never ogles any of us no matter what we have on—or don't have on. He's like a horse with blinders."

So the P.W. stayed. His only idiosyncrasy occurred the first time he saw each of the girls, and never again with any of them. He would stop in front of her and peer intently into her face for a moment with his shocked, faded blue eyes behind a pair of women's lightly tinted sunglasses.

"Soo Li?" he would ask in a hoarse mumbling voice that sounded as if he either had vocal cord damage or didn't use his voice much any more.

Whatever the girl answered, and many of them never got a chance to answer at all, he would immediately put his finger to his lips in a shushing motion as he had done to Mose that first evening. Then he would shake his head and turn dolefully away, never to speak to her again.

Within a week he had gone through them all except Mae, who never let him get that close to her because he gave her what she called "the willies." Even so, he soon became as much of a fixture around the establishment as Mose or Dietrich, the massive and savage Rottweiler who guarded Mae's Place after hours.

Until the P.W. arrived, nobody was able to touch Dietrich, and only Mose even dared get near enough to throw raw meat in his direction once a day. He was a huge, silent, morose, and savage attack waiting to happen, let out to roam only at night after all the clients had departed, otherwise kept locked away in a cage under the cellar steps to which he was lured each morning by a slab of bloody beafsteak left in his food dish courtesy of Mose.

The P.W. had laid out his sleeping bag that first night after Dietrich had been released to roam. When the huge dog returned to the basement, it immediately rushed him, roaring and snapping, sharp fangs gleaming. The P.W. dropped to one knee as Dietrich sailed at him, somehow swayed aside, getting a gloved hand behind Dietrich's passing cocked front leg, and using the dog's own momentum, smashed his 180-pound body nose-first into the concrete-block basement wall.

After this happened three more times, Dietrich stood panting in the middle of the floor, nose bleeding and a little spraddle-legged, staring at the P.W. with puzzled eyes . . .

Then he *whined*. The stub of what would have been his tail if they had left him one started, very slowly, very tentatively, as if he had used it no more than the P.W. had used his vocal cords, to wiggle back and forth. Had it been whole, it would have been *wagging*.

The P.W. finished laying out his sleeping bag and got into it, totally ignoring the dog. After a long time, Dietrich shuffled over and lay down beside him with a huge sigh of what sounded almost like relief. Sometime through the night, in his sleep, the P.W. draped one arm over the dog's massive body.

After that, the P.W. always fed Dietrich, and together they patrolled the building and the grounds after hours, two silent primordial ghosts drifting in tandem through the icy darkness of the New Jersey night.

During the month before the P.W. arrived in Jersey, in San Francisco Dante's bone-deep rage and resolution at the almost scornful blowing away of Gideon Abramson in Death Valley had made him fess up to Tim about the Raptor phone calls. To do it, he took Tim out to dinner at the Salonika on Polk near Green.

Since the film festival, Dante had been accompanying Rosa to festivals sponsored by various Greek Orthodox churches around the Bay Area. He'd gotten to like the food, and knew it would appeal to Tim's gargantuan tastes. So he ordered a tray of *mezethes*—literally "starters"—to begin the meal. Sure enough, Tim was first enchanted with the *dolmathakia*, stuffed vine leaves, usually grape, and ate the whole plate of them himself.

"Delicious! What's in 'em?"

"Long-grain rice, pine nuts, onions, dill, mint, parsley, lemon, pepper . . . Rosie makes them, but she adds ground lamb, too. Hers are better."

So it went through the *melitzanosalata*—eggplant and feta cheese and a lot of herbs—the *soutzoukakia* of lamb and beef sausage served with pita bread, and a dynamite *tzatziki* of cucumber and yogurt that Dante fought him for.

"I know all this ain't out of the goodness of your heart, chief," said Tim, waving a greasy-fingered hand, "since we been eating forty-five minutes and haven't gotten to our dinners yet. So c'mon—talk to Daddy."

Talk Dante did, over *kefthes,* fried meatballs that released tantalizing aromas from the kitchen as they were cooked, and the *horiatiki salates* of tomatoes and cucumbers and black olives and onions and feta cheese topped with dried oregano, known to most people just as "Greek salads."

"So this guy has called five times—"

"I think it was him after Moll Dalton," said Dante, forking flaky-crusted *spanakopita*—spinach pie—into his mouth and talking around it, "but I didn't save the tape. By Hymie's voiceprints, all the others are different people. Raptor used Gideon Abramson's own voice as *his* message. Telling a Jewish joke."

"Recorded him off the phone, I bet," mused Tim.

Main courses were *kotopoulu fournou* for Tim, roast chicken with potatoes, and baked lamb with pasta, *giouvetsi,* for Dante. Over impossibly sweet *baklava* served with thimble-size cups of thick Greek coffee, Dante told about the note pinned to his shirt while he slept in the Death Valley dunes. Tim started to guffaw.

"That's one I would have liked to see, chief," he chortled. "It's only because of that note that I'm buyin' into the calls. Otherwise I'd be laughin' in your face while I'm readin' these." He was shuffling through the transcripts of the calls like a hand of cards. "None of them really say, bang, bang, I did it, do they? Uh-uh. But that note pinned to your shirt . . ."

"And doing Abramson from four hundred yards out."

"Whadda they got on the slugs?"

"Not much so far. The ones they could find are badly distorted. Since the killing occurred in a national monument, the FBI's involved, and you know their Forensics Ballistics lab takes its own sweet time to analyze and report."

"Four football fields away, so we know high-velocity, scoped . . ." Tim shook his head. "Near a fifth of a mile? That's shooting, it tells us stuff about him."

"Like what?" Dante had ideas of his own, but he liked to watch the big homicide cop's mind work.

"Probably a good ol' southern boy from Arkansas, Tennessee, like that. Maybe sniper-trained, maybe by the Marines in 'Nam."

"Lots of Marines in 'Nam weren't from the South."

Tim leaned back with a luxurious sigh, his belly out over his belt. "More than you'd think. And southern boys make about the best killers there are—of animals or men. Take one of 'em who really likes killing . . ."

"Yeah," said Dante, "with maybe some seasoning as a CIA spook or merc or somebody before going to work for the mob."

"I buy it—he's too methodical for a guy just poppin' caps 'cause he's got a hard-on against somebody."

"Somebody who knows Popgun Ucelli's M.O. and has Raptor use it on the close-in hits."

"All of a sudden you don't think Popgun did any of 'em?"

"Not if we have one man here—and I think we do, because of the Raptor messages and note. Popgun wouldn't be *bright* enough for the gas line trick, and from his federal rap sheet he sure as hell couldn't make any four-hundred-yard rifle shots."

"Unless this Raptor shit is just a smoke screen," mused Tim. "Multiple hitters . . ." He shook his head. "That doesn't make much sense, does it? Single perp."

Dante paid their bill with a 20 percent tip. They kept at it on their way down Polk Street toward the Hall where Tim had to pick up his own car.

"What can we maybe figure about who hired him?"

"Mob," said Dante instantly. "Prince . . . or old Garofano."

"Old, all right—old as water. Why'd he want to knock off a bunch of his compeers? He can't have too many years left."

"Maybe that's why."

"Go out with a bang? Maybe. How about your boyfriend?"

"Gounaris? I can see him hiring Raptor for the others, but Abramson was his mentor, his buffer with the big boys. If he screwed up and let Moll Dalton get too close to him, he'd need all the buffers he could get."

"But what if he's been skimming or something? If she nosed it out, that's why she'd have to go. Then Lenington dug it out . . . Spic Madrid . . . right up to Abramson and St. John. I read him as a guy'd hit just about anybody who threatened him."

"What about the calls? The note?" They were stopped for the light at Market. "If it's Gounaris, there's nothing I can do to confirm it; I'm gonna focus on Raptor. He's made himself my business."

CHAPTER THIRTY-SEVEN

Kosta thought long and hard about going to Uncle Gid's funeral. Myra would expect him to be there, she and Gid had been regular visitors aboard Kosta's yacht in the Gounaris Shipping years. The visits had ended when Uncle Gid had started grooming him as a front man for the Cosa Nostra. But still, Myra . . .

Now Gid and St. John both were gone, who could he talk to about Myra? He finally made a call to a safe number in L.A.; Prince called him back from Vegas on the scrambler phone.

"We all commiserate with you on your loss, Kosta," came Mr. Prince's heavy baritone, "but the funeral is out of the question. Too public. The value of Atlas Entertainment would be markedly reduced should our involvement be proven." His voice dropped several degrees in temperature. "What was that policeman, Stagnaro, doing in Death Valley? What does he know?"

"Stagnaro was in Death Valley?" Kosta's surprise was real.

Prince must have realized it. He merely said, "Stagnaro could get to be a problem for us. He gets around."

"Do you want me to—"

"No, I will initiate action if it seems indicated."

Kosta hung up uneasily, drove back to his apartment playing the conversation over in his mind. The way Prince had offered no comment on the man who had hit Uncle Gid suggested he had ordered the hit himself. Who would be next? Kosta?

Or *was* there an independent operating here, for his own obscure ends? As Kosta had been operating for his? He wasn't going to let Myra down in her hour of need. She was respected in the Family, might be useful to him in turn. He would go down to Palm Springs for the private service where they would sing *kaddish* for Uncle Gid. That would be for family only, not Family, so Mr. Prince wouldn't find out.

Martin Prince sat at his desk, frowning. Myra had been a good and faithful Organization wife, she would understand that Gounaris couldn't attend the funeral, and Gounaris would know that. Gounaris could have some agenda of his own, could have had Gideon hit, perhaps by some contract hitter imported from Greece.

There's been too much killing recently, and Gounaris was vital to Atlas Entertainment at present. But eventually . . .

And then there was Stagnaro. Just a little *mosca* buzzing around right now, but he kept turning up. When Moll Dalton had been hit. And Spic. Even St. John. And there he was on the scene in Death Valley. What did this guy know? Who did he report to? Was his superior reachable? Or maybe a break-in at his office, to see what he had in the way of hard evidence.

Maybe better, for the moment, just leave him alone.

Basta. He used the scrambler phone again to call Enzo Garofano back in Jersey.

"What is going on out there, Marcantonio?" came Garofano's ancient but strong voice. "Why are all these people dying? Do we have problems in the Organization? And why is this Stagnaro turning up all over? Do you think he is working with Rudy Mattaliano here in Manhattan? That could be dangerous."

"I'm looking into all of those things, Don Enzo," said Prince soothingly. He thought for a moment. "But just in case, it might be wise to make sure Ucelli is uncommitted so he can act for us on short notice if we need him."

"It is what he lives for," said Enzo.

Fuckin' life was good, thought Eddie Ucelli, sucking the flattened knuckles of his right hand. The punk on the next stool had called Eddie an old man when Eddie had told the bartender to switch off some TV shit called *Beavis and Butthead*. Eddie, a roll of nickels in his hand, had coldcocked him instantly, no warning, no preliminary discussion, just knocked him on his ass.

Eddie chuckled to himself. Peeler Paradiso—so called because he liked to hang somebody up on a meat hook and then use a knife on him—had always said, "Don't lead with your right, *stronzo*." But he had, smearing the guy's nose all over his face.

He jabbed a finger at the big-shouldered *fannullone*—literally, big do-nothing—who was just scrambling to his feet. Eddie's right cross had sent both him and his barstool flying.

"G'wan, getta fuck outta here, I look at your face I'm drinkin', makes me wanna puke."

The punk was holding a hand over his flattened nose.

"Lissen, you sucker punched me. How about I—"

"How about *I* kick you in the nuts so hard they end up in your cheeks, make you look like a squirrel?" Eddie was in great good humor. He licked his stinging knuckles, repeated, "Like a fuckin' squirrel," then added, "But I ain't gonna do that. I'm a gentleman. Harry—a round for the house, here."

"Sure thing, Mr. Ucelli."

Both Harry and he knew Eddie wouldn't pay for it anyway. But the blood that wasn't on the *fannullone*'s nose left his face.

"Uc . . . Ucelli?"

"That's me, kid. They call me Popgun 'cause I'm a pistol."

He laughed heartily at his joke. The men waiting for their free drinks laughed loudly with him. Through the front window of the bar with the backward red neon sign COORS LIGHT on it, snow could be seen swirling down from the gray December afternoon sky. Big soft flakes that would stick.

"Geez, Mr. Ucelli, I din't know . . ."

" 'Sokay, *fannullone*." He turned to Harry. "Set him up a beer. He's a okay kid. He takes a good punch."

He liked being known and feared in this neighborhood bar. He liked the sting of his knuckles from belting the *fannullone*. He liked still being able to knock a big kid like that down with one punch, even if it was, like the kid had said, a sucker punch.

He especially liked the phone call to Ucelli Meats from Mae's Place that had made it such a good day.

"Tell Eddie that we need some extra pork sausage out here for the holidays," the message had read.

They'd delivered some extra links to Mae's Place with the next delivery, just in case the fuckin' feds were listening in and decided to check the order. But he knew what pork Mae meant. The pork in his pants. Delivered to *her* place.

Which meant she had a phone message to relay to him.

Yeah, December 2nd, a Friday. An all-around good fuckin' day. And a good day for fuckin'.

That Friday in December was eight weeks since Raptor had assassinated Gideon Abramson in Death Valley, six weeks since Dante and Tim had worked out a tentative profile of the killer, two weeks after the FBI's forensics report on the slugs found at the scene of Abramson's death had been completed. But Dante hadn't seen it because he didn't get along with Jack N. Theobaux, the local SAC—nobody did. The Special Agent in Charge was a self-righteous prick even his own men called Jack-in-the-Box.

Dante had a good working relationship, however, with Special Agent Geoff Hoskins, a very tall, very lanky man with sorrel hair in a bristly brush cut, a delicate bony face with piercing blue eyes, long-fingered hands like someone in an El Greco painting.

Dante bought him a late dinner at the old Golden Spike on Columbus Ave, where his dad had said you used to be able to get all the spaghetti you could eat and dago red you could drink for two bucks fifty. No more.

They sat in the back booth with the ancient deer head on the wall, ate pasta, drank wine. Geoff told him about the report.

"We're taking this a little more seriously than we did before," he said, slurping minestrone. "The guy was a shooter. He was using a scope, ten-power or better, and target-quality ammo, not something you'd buy off a gun shop shelf."

"By target-quality I take it you also mean sniper quality?"

"Yeah. Lake City Match M852s, in .270 caliber. Forensics Ballistics says fired from a Winchester Model 70, the old bolt-action center-fire jobbies that long-range shooters seem to prefer. Plus that particular gun has another great advantage."

"What's that?" asked Dante.

"They were manufactured in the tens of thousands. They're a very common hunting rifle that would excite nobody's notice during hunting season. October is hunting season."

"It sure was for him," said Dante.

They checked the dessert menu, both ordered *cappuccino* and *biscotti*. Dante was about to ask the FBI for a favor, always a touchy, usually a demeaning, proposition.

"Tim Flanagan and I worked out a sort of profile of what sort of guy he might be. I'd like to run it by you . . ."

"You got no standing in this case, Dante, nor does your pal Flanagan, even if he is Homicide. It's *federal,* you know."

Even with Geoff, a certain ration of shit. "Sure, Geoff, I know that. But you can't blame me for being *involved.* I was right there when Abramson got it. I think it ties in with a homicide that *is* Tim's baby, a woman named—"

"Margaret Dalton—I did my homework. So go ahead."

Dante ran it down—probably a southerner, probably Vietnam vet, probably a sniper for some special unit, Marine or Army or CIA, probably would have been a mercenary after 'Nam, probably would have drifted into heavy lifting for the mob . . .

"Were you in Vietnam?" asked Hoskins. He would have been in his teens when that particular brushfire war had ended.

"I was just a kid," said Dante. "Just a grunt. Shoot and get shot at. But it took me a year or two to get back to normal after they shipped me home. If I could see your computer files on ex-Vietnam, ex-mercs who have kept up their skills—"

Geoff was truly shocked. "You've got to be kidding!"

"Just guys fit the profile who have records that might suggest they had gotten involved with organized crime . . ."

"Jesus Christ, you don't want much for a plate of spaghetti." Then he chuckled. "But what the hell?"

A few days later, Dante got his printout. A month after that, fifty-seven names had become three, and on this Friday, the second of December, between the work the city of San Francisco was actually *paying* him to do, Dante eliminated the last of those. And decided he just wasn't going to get at Raptor that way.

There was still the enormously complicated world of gun nuts and hand-loaders and shooting enthusiasts, but it was a million-to-one against turning him up there. Tim had been right—it was an appalling task. Raptor had not struck again, and nothing he had done so far was going to expose him. What Dante needed was little dancing men to spell out answers for him like in one of those Sherlock Holmes mysteries on the A&E channel.

CHAPTER THIRTY-EIGHT

Fucking Miss Pym had developed into an ever-changing mystery over the months. It was ten in the morning and right now she was on her knees, bent over the bed, arms out wide and twisting the top sheet in her passion as Kosta crouched over her from behind. When he'd exhausted every orifice she had, and all the casual cruelty at his command, she laid him back on the bed to work on him for one last serving of dessert.

Kosta wasn't sure whether he had corrupted or been corrupted by her. He certainly had uncovered in her a hidden passion for both degradation and domination. It was as if the sixties had returned, when everybody took their sex seriously and orgasm ranked right up there with Zen archery as a topic of serious discussion. He had been struggling with his shipping line then, married to a stern Greek woman whose passion was business, so he'd missed the revolution.

Miss Pym had blasted Moll Dalton right out of his sexual consciousness, made him wish he'd never heard of Moll Dalton, made him glad Moll Dalton was no longer around. Miss Pym knew nothing of Atlas Entertainment business, but she was shrewd in her suggestions for besting his enemies.

Right now she was sprawled sideways across his thighs in utter exhaustion and abandonment, her pale hair lank with sweat.

"Champagne," he snapped. She leaped up, he watched her

bottom wobble-flex across the room. As she went through the open doorway to the hall, he yelled after her, "Hypothetical!"

"Hypothetical" was a new game between them. She kept going without response so that tomorrow he would chastise her for ignoring him. She liked to be chastised. He liked the sixties a lot, even on rerun. But he was not obsessed by Miss Pym.

Oddly enough, his new obsession centered around Dante Stagnaro. He knew it was all projection, the guy was just another fucking cop, for Chrissake; but he couldn't shake the feeling he had to *do* something about the man before Stagnaro somehow got into the Atlas Entertainment books.

He couldn't have Stagnaro taken out, Mr. Prince had spoken. So he had to diminish him as a force. As a man.

The guy's wife. Do something to her, that would cut his nuts off, geld him. Well, ever since the random thought about screwing her had entered his mind, he hadn't gotten it out. He doubted he'd have much trouble seducing her, he seldom did with women. But there was that fucking Stagnaro lurking around like a leopard in the bushes.

But he had a plan. That's why he was here with Miss Pym today. To check out his plan with her. At this sort of thing, she was excellent.

She returned with two fluted glasses and an icy bottle of Cordon Rouge put in the freezer an hour before. Sitting naked and cross-legged on the bed, he stripped the foil and untwisted the wire, gripped the cork as he turned the bottle beneath it. The cork came out with a dull *thunk!* and no spilled champagne. He poured them each a glass. They tinked.

"All right," she said, eyes alight. "Your hypothetical."

"There is a business rival a man is having trouble with."

"Personal or professional?"

"Both." He drained his flute, refilled. She drained hers, held it out for more. "His business associates have ruled out physical recourse . . ."

"So, no direct attack. What does he hold dear?"

Kosta held up a hand, three fingers open, marked off the possibilities. "Job, family, wife. Job, he *could* be compromised, but it would be difficult. His reputation is good. Even if well done, it might not stick."

"Family?"

A second finger was folded down. "A son at home, a daughter in her first year at Cal."

"Berkeley can be a very dangerous place," murmured Miss Pym, her rather horsy face serious with thought. She licked her lips. They were dry and chapped from the various uses she had been putting them to during the last two hours.

"I believe our businessman was thinking more along the lines of his rival's wife," said Kosta.

"You want to fuck somebody's wife!" she burst out.

"Not me. Hypothetical. And not just fuck. Our hypothetical businessman wants to *rape* somebody's wife."

She was frowning in concentration. "One sort of man would blame the wife . . ."

"Not this man," said Kosta.

She met his gaze. "But . . . should he and his wife get an endless series of naughty phone calls afterwards, spelling out in precise detail exactly what was done, and how . . ."

"Excellent, Miss Pym!" Kosta cried. He fell silent, picturing it, all of it, his gaze turned inward.

"May I watch, then?" she asked, her eyes gleaming like a wolf's by torchlight.

"All of this is hypothetical, remember?"

"I insist you describe it to me afterwards, in detail."

"Why—since it's hypothetical?" he asked. She smiled almost shyly, and put her hand between her own legs. "Yes, of course." The thought of watching her while he told her about it was exciting to him.

"Will it be soon?"

"Soon." He could have told her *tonight* but didn't.

His member was stiffening at the thought of what he would do tonight. Miss Pym gave a low throaty laugh and tossed aside her champagne flute to reach greedily for Kosta's flute.

*   *   *

Martin Prince was getting a massage also, but it wasn't sexual. The masseur gently pummeling him at the Xanadu's health club was a black ex-NFL linebacker who had blown out his knee in a divisional game against Dallas three years before.

"A little on the backs of the legs if you could, Troy."

Troy laughed and bobbed his head. "Overdid it on the thigh-curling machine today, Mr. Prince."

"I can't hide anything from you, Troy."

"What I'm here for, Mr. Prince. What I'm here for."

Prince relaxed, let his mind drift.

Half his Family's income was legitimate these days; companies like Atlas Entertainment gotten for money-laundering purposes had proved to be income-producers in their legitimate guise. There would be more money to launder in the new year also, with the upsurge in heroin, dust and crank usage. The Latinos had no foothold in those areas.

Nothing more on the Gideon Abramson matter, and it had been two months. Myra had called to tell him that Gounaris had gone to Gideon's wake or whatever the Jews called it, after Prince's strict orders not to. Significant. But since no Family people had been there, Atlas Entertainment hadn't been compromised.

But even so, now that Gideon was no longer around to keep him in line, Gounaris was a loose cannon. The cop, Stagnaro, less of a one. But still bothersome. Sounded like he was smart and got on good with the feds. Maybe . . . maybe he was a problem Prince didn't want around any more. After the first of the year he'd have to make hard decisions about both of them.

Meanwhile, in another two weeks he would be in Hermosillo, dove hunting. Where he went, there were no bag limits. You stepped out of the plane, threw fifty pairs of sneakers on the blacktop beside the plane, local kids rushed in to grab them. Then you killed until your shotgun felt red-hot. Fifty, seventy-five, a hundred a day—it didn't matter. The kids, in return for those sneakers, flushed the live birds, collected the dead ones. He went every year, he loved it. Maybe he'd buy a new shotgun for it.

Then, La Paz to meet the new governor of Baja, pay his respects. His seventy-eight-foot powerboat *Tosca* would take him from La Paz to the little sport-fishing hotel Pez Grande, forty miles north of Cabo, where he always spent the week between Christmas and New Year's fucking and fishing while *Tosca* waited for him at Cabo. Last year he'd boated a record blue, had made the sports section of the *L.A. Times* standing in front of his huge strung-up fish with *Tosca* in the background.

Time to send Red Grant to L.A. to make sure the boat was ready and then take it to Cabo as he did each year.

Finally, back to Vegas the first week of January to start the new year of work. Maybe he should make those hard decisions now, so his holiday season would be a carefree one. With the shift in emphasis, maybe this would be the last time he'd have to resort to such old-fashioned remedies . . .

His mind drifted off as Troy pummeled gently away.

It was 10:00 P.M. and Greenwich Street slanting down the side of Telegraph Hill was silent and deserted. The night was clear, cold. Kosta, dressed in black and with a black ski mask rolled up on his head like a Navy watch cap, was waiting in the deeply shadowed entryway of the three-unit apartment building uphill from the Stagnaro house. Stagnaro rented this building's garage for Rosa from the Chinese landlord, street-parked himself.

Kosta had broken the bulb over the inset door so it was dark. If anyone entered or exited the building, he would abort, but everybody was in for the night. Lights in the Stagnaro house, too. The boy, Tony, home studying. On Monday nights Rosa was out until ten, so Stagnaro caught up on paperwork at the Hall of Justice. Got home an hour after she did, steady as clockwork. A devoted husband.

Which was why this would work.

A car turned uphill from Stockton; Kosta scrunched back a

little deeper in the inset doorway when the turn signal went on. It was Rosa. He felt her in his groin. He pulled down the ski mask to cover his face.

Her lights swept across the entryway as she turned in at the garage of the building where Kosta waited, but their probing eyes couldn't quite reach into his angle of wall and door. She stopped the car crosswise over the sidewalk, killed lights and motor as she took her keys to unlock the garage door.

Kosta suddenly realized he really wanted to fuck *her,* not just to take Stagnaro out of the equation, but because he wanted to rip her panties off and open her legs cruelly wide and . . .

She fumbled her key into the garage lock, turned it. He tensed. When she pulled the counterweighted overhead door open, he would move. He had rehearsed it in his mind a thousand times.

Dart forward, shove her into the garage, pull the door shut. Leave the car where it was, on these San Francisco hills where parking was at a premium, many residents left their cars across the sidewalks all night.

Thirty minutes of doing anything he wanted to her.

The door creaked up. *Now!*

And Kosta Gounaris slammed himself back into the blackness of his little alcove.

A car coming down Greenwich from Grant had stopped behind Rosa's. The driver called across to her through the open window.

"You leave your car there like that, lady, I'm gonna have to ticket it."

"You're home early!" exclaimed Rosa in delight.

"Just wanted a little extra time with you," said Dante. "I'll go find a place to park."

Kosta stayed crammed back in his little triangle of darkness. The fucking bastard, somehow he'd known! Had known, had come home early.

Kosta watched Stagnaro's taillights disappear down the hill, watched Rosa, unaware, drive her car into the garage.

What if Stagnaro's intuition went further, centered on him as his own fucking obsessions had centered on Stagnaro, gotten him into this mess? Maybe he needed another hypothetical with Miss Pym. Maybe he needed to kill Stagnaro no matter what Mr. Prince said.

"It ain't gonna kill you, suck my dick a little make it hard," Eddie said to Mae in an almost plaintive voice.

"He's gonna call any minute," she said. She was astride him in her queen-size bed upstairs over Mae's Place, both of them nude. "He said he'd call about one."

"But afterwards," insisted Eddie.

"Afterwards you won't need it," said Mae with a wink.

Oh, she'd given plenty of head in her day, nobody in her line of work hadn't, it just had never been her favorite fuck.

The phone rang. "Yessir, Don Enzo, he's right here."

She handed it to Eddie, took his flaccid cock in her hand. It was pointing at her bush like a flabby little sea slug.

"Eddie," said Eddie into the phone.

He listened to the squawks from the other end of the line. Mae began flexing her fingers expertly. Eddie put his hand over the phone mouthpiece.

"He's gonna patch me through to Mr. Prince!" he whispered to her in hoarse, awed tones. It was like being introduced to royalty. His cock was stiffening just in anticipation.

"Yessir, this is Eddie, yessir . . ."

Mae lifted herself so that Eddie's now-hard member could slide inside her. She started to rock almost dreamily on top of it as Eddie listened to his instruction.

"I gotcha, Mr. Prince! Both of 'em! Yessir! It'll be a pleasure, Mr. Prince . . ."

Eddie, his call finished, had shut his eyes, going to work on her in earnest, starting to groan in anticipation. The door opened silently and the fucking freak, that P.W. guy, came shambling into the room! What a fuck of a time for him to do his google-eyes act on her! The asshole didn't even seem to see Eddie, just kept staring at Mae in that intense, puzzled way he'd done with each of the girls in turn.

"Soo Li?" he asked her in his broken voice.

Eddie heard, opened his eyes, snarled, "Who da fuck—"

But the muzzle of a Jennings J-22 like the ones that had killed Moll Dalton and Spic Madrid and Skeffington St. John was already against the bridge of his nose. It said *pop!* as it spit another of those hypervelocity hollow-point Remington Viper rounds through Popgun's brain and out the back of his head.

At the same time, the P.W.'s other gloved hand gently covered the mouth Mae opened to scream. He dropped the Jennings onto Eddie's chest and then put the forefinger of that hand to his lips in the shushing motion Mae had seen so often, shook his head sadly, backed out of the room and was gone.

Mae started to reach for the telephone, then jerked back her hand. The man was a psycho, probably standing outside the door listening right now. She crawled heavily off Eddie's corpse. The pillow was a red halo around his ruined head.

Eddie, deflowerer of her youth. Dead in her queen-size bed. Dead before they'd finished. The sight of Eddie dead excited her in a perverse way. Well, what the hell, he was gone and she was still here, and it was going to be a long night what with the cops and all that. So Mae, being *au fond* a practical soul, finished herself off before calling the Organization and then the cops, in that order. It was her best in years.

The sheriff found the P.W. gone, along with his sleeping bag. He found nothing else. No fingerprints; for the weeks he'd lived in Mae's cellar, he'd always worn his gloves. No usable description apart from what the girls told him: big, shambling, blue eyes.

They kept at Old Mose until dawn without result, never thinking to inquire after Dietrich, the massive Rottweiler. When somebody did notice that Dietrich was gone, Old Mose said he'd run off two days before by hisse'f, yassuh, he mos' surely did, dam' fool dog run off into the night, yassuh . . .

Dante got Raptor's phone message alerting him to the fact that another one had died before he even knew who. He only got Eddie's name later, off a routine FBI printout.

The message was a quite creditable impression of Marlon Brando as Terry Malloy in *On the Waterfront*.

"I could've had class," said Brando's voice. "I could've been a contender. I could've been somebody. It was you, Eddie. You was my brother. You should've looked out for me a little bit . . ." A heavy, thuggish laugh. "I looked out for him tonight, Dante." That laugh again. "Like I looked out for good old Gid in Death Valley . . ."

Hymie the Handler said it was yet another new voice.

PART SEVEN

Mid-Pleistocene

200,000–50,000 years ago

Whosoever you be, death will overtake you,
although you be in lofty towers.

The Sacred Koran

CHAPTER THIRTY-NINE

To start, I know only Popgun Ucelli's name and that he resides in New Jersey. I spend a day in a Jersey City library, checking the state's phone books. No Ucelli listed, thus, no way to get him at home. I can hire a private investigator to check his driving and auto registration licenses through the New Jersey Department of Motor Vehicles, but then there will be a record of my search. Not acceptable.

But I also know he is a purveyor of wholesale meats. Yes. Ucelli Meats, with an address in Orange. Now I face the same problem as with Herr Otto: how to identify Eddie Ucelli himself?

Très simple. I check the company parking lot for the space with his name stenciled on the wall in front of it. He drives a new Cadillac Eldorado. I observe from afar. A squat, wide, hairy man. I follow, also from afar, only part of his route home each day so I will not be observed, until ultimately I watch him go up the drive of his upper-middle-class house.

A wife. A Puerto Rican housekeeper. Sometimes surly sons come visiting, looking like made men themselves. Not good. But at irregular intervals, Ucelli goes to an old-fashioned roadhouse some twenty miles away, with girls upstairs, called Mae's Place. Sometimes he goes with his wife, sometimes alone. When alone, he stays several hours. A liaison, then. But with whom?

For several months my hair and beard have been flourish-

ing; they are easily made unkempt. A surplus store provides
the rest of the P.W.'s ex-military persona, especially the
gloves he is never without. No fingerprints will be left behind.

The approach, the entry, the acceptance by Old
Mose . . . and the waiting. The listening. Waiting for another
of the sexual couplings between Popgun and, as I have
learned, Mae, empress of the establishment. Finally, he
comes alone. And dies.

This death has made me decide, straight out, to tell you
why I kill. I know, I say that before; but no games this time.

Following my senior year in college I go backpacking in
Spain for a summer and find myself in Madrid. This beautiful old city has the Prado, one of the greatest of all art muse-
ums, available for a few pesetas admission. I plan to haunt its
galleries, to spend countless hours with Goya, Velázquez,
Bosch, Murillo, El Greco, the Breughels (father and son), Fra
Angelico, Botticelli, Dürer, Rubens . . . the list is essentially
endless.

But on my first day there, as I am studying Goya's twin
masterpieces, *The Naked Maja* and *The Maja Clothed,* a female voice says to me in English, "Which do you prefer?
Naked or clothed?"

She is an American about my age, barely into her twenties, breathtakingly beautiful in a fragile way, gleaming
black hair in a smooth waterfall halfway down her back, a
heart-shaped face, huge dark eyes with long lashes and unknown hurts lingering in the corners of her glances. Willowy
and warm, with an appealing inner dignity.

"Naked," I say, "because her face is more demure."

She claps her hands. "What a wonderful answer! When
she is naked, a woman to survive must be more demure, no
less!"

I tell her I am hitchhiking across Europe, she tells me she
is a touring art history major with a month each in some of
the great gallery cities: Madrid, Rome, Paris. It is the first
high adventure of her young life. Despite her tiny budget
she already has one American, in Madrid studying the guitar

sleeping on her couch. If I need a floor to throw a sleeping bag on . . .

I assure her I am here just a few days, and have a room.

If she cannot give me accommodations, at least she can begin my art education. And she does. With, oddly—because I am a sunny chap in those days—the museum's darker, more brooding works. El Greco's *San Sebastian* with the murderers' arrows buried deep in the naked saint's flesh; Bosch's grotesque *Lust;* Pieter Breughel's macabre and frenzied *Triumph of Death* . . . What does she see in me, even then, that I do not see in myself?

And, of course, she shows me Goya's "black paintings." I cannot tear myself away from *Saturn Devouring His Children:* an aged, naked, demented figure with mad and terrified eyes, a flying mane of white hair, cramped, twisted limbs, screaming even as he bites the head off his own nude daughter.

"Saturn is the symbol of time," she tells me. "He devours his children—us—because he is our fate, our melancholy."

I find this, from this untouched and lonely girl, almost unbearably poignant. In Buen Retiro Park a short distance from the museum we share a half-bottle of red I supply, a carefully wrapped ham sandwich she brings from her handbag. The park has tall plane trees lining footpaths where nurses push rich people's babies in prams, and old men who probably fought in *la guerra civil* rake up the leaves to put into wheeled receptacles. Around this little oasis the traffic grumbles and honks.

This becomes our pattern: we meet each morning in front of that day's painting to be analyzed, lunch each day in Buen Retiro on wine and that inevitable ham sandwich. Her presence makes of Madrid a pure and wondrous adventure. I am half in love without ever having touched her or even knowing where she lives.

On the Friday I become aware of a man standing very close behind me. I turn quickly; in Spain are many Gypsy pickpockets.

"She is not coming," he says.

I know him instantly, though she has never described him: the student of the guitar who sleeps on her sofa. He is as tall as I but bulkier, with brown and curly hair, a fleshy chin, a strong, almost hooked nose. His face is round. Without the chilly blue eyes he would be the Pillsbury Doughboy.

So sure of him am I that I ask, "Flamenco or classical?"

He looks surprised for a moment, then sneers, "Oh. Pillow talk. Classical. I am the next Andrés Segovia."

"I doubt that. Why is she not coming?"

"I told her you'd found someone else to fuck. I knew she was dicking someone so I followed her, saw you two together." His fleshy face darkens. His heavy brows draw down. His skin flushes. "Dicking you and she won't even give me stink-finger."

What says Cyrano?

Oh, my friend, I seemed to see
Over some flower a great snail crawling!

"Every night she makes the next day's fucking ham sandwich. I got up early this morning and opened up her sandwich and jerked off into it and wrapped it up again." He gives a sneering laugh. "Now that's what I call mayonnaise! She's probably eating it right now. Eating *me* right now. Maybe I should have waited until after you'd had lunch with her to tell you about it so—"

I knock him down. Had I been Raptor at that time, I would have slain him where he stood. A woman is running for the guard, her shoes echoing on the marble floor. I stand over him.

"If you return to her apartment, even to pick up your guitar, I will kill you. Do you believe me?" I know in that moment that I am speaking true matters, and I can see the belief in his face also.

I walk away, out of the Prado and out of Madrid and out of her life forever. I wait long enough to see him leave the museum and entrain for Barcelona. Perhaps there he will buy a new guitar. Now my path to her is clear, you say; but to what end? In truth, I cannot bring myself to see her without telling her how he has violated her; but to be told it will destroy something within her it is essential I preserve.

In a world where such horrors occur, as Raptor I find in myself a violence to equal them. Need more to be convinced? I have more—*la vérité, toujours la vérité*, remember? It can be found in Colin Wilson's *A Criminal History of Mankind,* the chapter titled "The Psychology of Human Violence":

> *They found them [the habitual violent criminal] amazingly skillful at self-justification—suppressing any material that might lose them sympathy—but the real problem lay in the criminal character. They lied as automatically as breathing. . . . Most criminals have developed a psychological "shut-off mechanism" to push inconvenient thoughts out of consciousness. . . . This meant that responsibility, too, could be shut off. . . .*

It seems to eerily echo my own dark nature, but surely, I tell myself, this is not me! These men are true psychopaths. But then I have a terrifying thought: is it possible that I also have no capacity to understand what truth is? Is this why I constantly seek the origins of things—especially in myself? If I know it from the beginning, must it not be true? So I always compulsively demand, Why did this happen? To whom did it happen? What are the consequences?

But in the last analysis, does it matter? You see, he has jerked off into her sandwich and she has eaten it. Telling her about it will not change it, only destroy her. And now I know that Raptor, not yet named or acknowledged, lurks within me.

Thus, when the current need arises, I become him. Ah, what relief! As Raptor, I can let the discarded shards of myself pierce the barrier. And afterwards . . . Well, afterwards, I need only activate my shut-off mechanism to be pleased at the cleverness with which I have slaughtered, is it not so?

Rather than suffer any afterthoughts, bad dreams, sleepless nights?

Aha, say you, but Raptor has such insomnias, regrets, nightmares. What if you have rent the temple veil from top to bottom, have left the fabric of your life tattered around you? What then, murderer?

But that is nonsense. I *am* my profession. To prove it, I go now to kill again. After that will be time to stop.

If I can.

CHAPTER FORTY

"If I can," said Will, "I want to stay with the great apes. The first one known, thirty-pound *Aegyptopithecus* (28 m.y. ago), once was believed to be ancestral to all living monkeys and apes. But we now know the hominoid line began about the same time he did, rather than descended from him: some twenty-two pithecoid species, scattered over Africa, Europe, and Asia, now are known. Yet only the line of *Dryopithecus* (12 m.y. ago) survived—by devising a whole new way of getting around.

"Brachiation.

"Brachiation means swinging beneath the branches by the arms, rather than running around on top of them on all fours. Evolutionists call brachiation 'utterly adaptive'—which means that if you were an ape, you learned to brachiate or you died. In a world of shrinking forests, brachiation gave us new function and anatomy to go with our innate primate playfulness.

"Function: developing amazing gymnastic skills to swing through the trees, to hang by an arm while reaching out to the tips of branches for ripe fruit. This required *judgment*—how far away is that next limb—and *concentration*. Lose your concentration, misjudge, you miss your grip and fall. And die.

"Anatomy: the torso is straightened, the arms and upper body are strengthened, the hands and wrists become fluid, the pelvis begins its adaptation for eventual upright walking. The ape could retain his bulk while expanding his brain and remaining in the trees where, for the time being, all the fun was.

"This is most important: there is the same joy in an ape's swift flight through the forest as there is in a bird's soaring flight over it; and it was this sense of fun, of adventure, that helped certain hominoids walk out into that unknown veldt.

"Between those Miocene pithecoids we have been talking about and the modern apes we want to talk about, the fossils showing homin*oids* becoming homin*ids* are, as William Howells says, 'no more than mutterings in the dark—a piece of jaw here, a piece of arm bone there.' We hear not even mutterings about the ancestors of gorillas and chimps, except a single bone from the Samburu Hills in Kenya some 6 to 9 m.y. ago.

"The gibbons and siamangs are the most joyful, perhaps the brainiest of the surviving great apes. But by one of those double whammies of which Nature is so fond, they 'chose' a life of wondrous dexterity and delight in the tops of the trees—thereby removing themselves from this discussion.

"The orangutan's direct affinity to us is tenuous: he packed his bags for Borneo about the time *Proconsul* (22 m.y. ago) appeared in Africa. But he is a hominoid, and when we talk about our direct ancestors we find some of his ways suggestive.

"The basic orang social unit is blood-related females who stay together in a single area. Once a young male is driven away from the band, he rapes any female he runs across. It is true rape, by the way—she is not ready to receive him.

"When he is full grown, he seeks females who *are* receptive, mates with them, and *then* leaves. He is solitary and his relationship with all other males is antagonistic: meeting, they invariably fight until somebody backs down or is seriously hurt.

"Gorillas, in their mountain habitats in Central Africa, are different: they travel in fairly stable social groups of females and infants led by a dominant 'silverback' male. Most immature males, as they mature, are driven off as the young male orang is. The young gorilla loner also will grab any females he can find, but his intent is very different. He keeps them to form his own harem—thus establishing a new basic social group.

"Big daddy silverback defends *his* harem against such seducers with violent displays in over 75 percent of the encounters, with actual physical battle 50 percent of the time. He must, because a low-ranking female often will run off with one of these traveling salesmen: in his new harem she will have the status she lacked in the old.

"Chimps and gorillas have a shared morphology that suggests species closeness; the complexities connected with knuckle-walking are even more compelling. Nobody but chimps and gorillas do it, and both species do it exactly the same. So . . . a shared common ancestor well after the human line had split off?

"Not so, says DNA-structuring and amino-acid analysis: almost identical human/chimp DNA suggests their split was only about 5.5 m.y. ago, while our single ape fossil from the Samburu Hills suggests the gorilla split off 6 to 9 m.y. ago.

"The basis of chimpanzee society is a male kin-group with one or more alpha males; it is the females who are the strangers. If the band splits up, there is no bond among the females; they disperse until they find new male bands. And they mate with as many of the males in their community as they can so the males, never knowing if they are the father of any given infant, will usually be solicitous of all.

"Chimps live mainly on fruit, so they have to travel in small bands of four to eight because the availability of ripe fruit dictates how often they get together. Separation can be for several weeks, and upon remeeting they have elaborate reunion reactions—hugs, kisses, back-slapping . . . sound familiar?

"Nobody can see anything much in a rain forest, so basic communication is by the so-called pant-hoots PBS specials have made so familiar to most of us. Every voice is unique—chimps can recognize each other over long distances of forest. These calls are usually territorial or to announce a major food source.

"Males travel with other males, aggressive to protect against aggression. They view their environment as hostile and patrol the peripheries of their territory in stealth and in numbers, always ready for war.

"So here we are at long last, at the edge of the trees with the chimps and the direct hominid forerunner of Lucy whom many anthropologists picture as a timid plant-eater forced from the trees by bad weather and bad neighbors. Sure, the Pliocene was dry after the wet Miocene, and the forests were shrinking; but anthropologist Owen Lovejoy targets bipedalism as an absolutely enormous anatomical change, one not for the faint-hearted.

"So was it the weak, or the strong, who crept down out of trees into the unknown—and survived? Common sense gives us the answer. For those who don't believe in common sense, the chimpanzee is here as a prime source about our earlier selves, because he is so close to us, and because he obviously has changed less than we since we shared the edge of the savannah.

"Only a third of a century ago, Robert Ardrey could write with a straight face: 'Every modern primate, whether gorilla or macaque, chimpanzee or vervet monkeys or gibbon or baboon, is inoffensive, non-aggressive, and strays no further from the vegetarian way than an occasional taste for insects.'

"Ardrey was wrong about the chimps. The chimp, so close genetically to man, is a hunting ape, the *only* hunting ape apart from ourselves. He does it for fun, not necessity; for pleasure, not for profit. He does not need the protein supplement to his diet to survive. So, why hunt?"

Will drank water, and Dante realized with a start that he had been so caught up in the story that he had again forgotten his central function of looking out for danger. Of being constantly alert like a chimp patrolling the perimeter of his territory. This lecture hall, right now, was Dante's territory. He had better be ready to defend it against Raptor.

"Bloodlust? Dudley Young believes, and I agree, that the

chimp's hunting is at once something much simpler and much more profound. He hunts for the hell of it. Because it is *fun,* because it wards off boredom. That chimps get bored and hatch convoluted political and domestic plots within the troop is well known. That they are clever is undisputed: given an electronic board in place of their unevolved vocal apparatus, some chimps use large vocabularies, even create simple sentences.

"Is his hunting behavior shocking? Probably, when we consider that he is the brainiest and most affectionate, and the closest to us of all the primates. Certainly his behavior on hunting forays is decidedly at odds with the way he lives the rest of his life—which in my fieldwork I have found to be subtle, complex, even touched with a sort of refinement.

"Yet hunting troops seem to hunt twice a month, usually successfully. 'Success' is relative: the killing is inelegant at best. They kill infants often snatched literally from the mothers' arms. About half the kills are monkeys, the rest infant baboons, baby bushbuck, squealing bushpiglets.

"They bite their victims on the head or neck, they flail them to death on rocks, they stomp them to death, they dismember them, they disembowel them. Eaten first is blood, then brains, if the skull can be cracked open so they can be swabbed out with finger or leaf. Next, viscera, flesh—all is fought over, and there are politics involved. Though male chimps are tremendously more aggressive than females, the females are surprisingly keen and vicious hunters, vociferous in their demands for their fair share of the spoils.

"Indeed, these hunts cause a veritable contagion of aggression—biting, screaming, crapping, mounting, groveling, embracing . . . Young likens it to the Dionysian frenzy. As if the chimps know they are doing something *forbidden,* almost shameful. Schizophrenic, Dr. Jekyll one minute, Mr. Hyde the next. Their brains, biologists tell us, are neither large enough nor complex enough to hold such concepts; yet anyone who has ever loved a dog knows that dogs understand all about shame and forbidden acts—with a brain a lot smaller than a chimp's.

"While there is violence in the other primates' lives, it is genetically ordained and ritually contained; in the chimp during his hunting forays it is not. Why is the chimp so different? Why is his violent behavior so out of control?

"Because he has no genetic or ritual guides to curb his hunting behavior, and, like us, is not physically designed for it. No claws, canines not a whole lot better than ours, and, most importantly, he is not *au fond* a predator like lions, leopards, wild dogs or hyenas. So he carries no genetic imprint of how to do it.

"Predators hunt for a living. There is certainly enjoyment in a good stalk; there is no anger at a failed one. Disappointment, perhaps, but not rage. It is their profession, after all. Chimps gather fruit for a living. It is an orderly and ordered activity without loss of control, though there might be a scuffle or two over some choice fig or banana.

"But when the chimp hunts, it all changes, because he is not 'tooled up' for predation. Though he uses behavior adapted from his range of daily domestic aggression—charging displays, shrieking, baring the fangs, occasionally biting or striking—he goes outside the limits of his genetic triggers. In the hunt he does not stop, he goes on, he maims, he kills.

"For the unarmed, fear and rage accompany the act of killing. The nonpredator cannot be moved to violence without these emotions. The chimp is not afraid of the baby monkey, this tiny mite cannot harm him; but fear there is. Of what?

"I believe it is fear *of the act of killing itself*. The chimp knows he is out of control—but that is precisely why he seeks the state. To experience the unknown, to know the nasty pleasures of the forbidden. Do we see Adam and Eve foreshadowed here, eating of the forbidden fruit of the tree of knowledge?"

CHAPTER FORTY-ONE

Armand "Red" Grant swung the cream-colored Lexus off Marina del Rey's Via Dolce into Tahiti Way where *Tosca* was docked in Marina B. *Tosca* was a seventy-eight foot all-weather motor yacht custom-built for Mr. Prince by Hattaras for a million-two; RADAR, SONAR, a thousand-mile cruising range, slept a dozen people in luxury.

Red parked between a BMW and a Mercedes in the designated lot, went down the dock toward the locked gate protecting the moored yachts from vandalism, robbery, or casual rubberneckers. He was dressed in white topsiders and an aloha shirt with short sleeves that showed his massive arms. Above him gulls keened and swooped, around him bright blue water sparkled in the California sun. He breathed salt brine deeply into his nostrils.

Vegas was the vein of gold that never ran out, but Red dreamed of Mr. Prince moving his center of operations to L.A. He was sick of twenty-four-hour neon, casinos without clocks, people who never slept, the constant ringing bells and cascading coins of the jackpots, the faces, gray with shock as they hocked their watches to get back home, of the losers without jackpots.

Vegas, Death Valley, Palm Springs—maybe it was the depleted ozone and global warming and the greenhouse effect, but there seemed to be a hell of a lot more deserts around than anything else these days. Except oceans. Ah, oceans.

Now you were talking! That's why he loved the holiday season each year, he got to *cruise* ahead of Mr. Prince down to Baja on *Tosca*.

Red often thought he had the soul of a poet. Flying fish flashing across the waves in the mornings, whales blowing white spouts on the horizon. Once a whole school of orcas, the so-called killer whales, had raced *Tosca* for over a mile like sportive dolphins. He'd never forgotten it. He'd also killed two men, one with his .45 and one with his bare hands, but that had been in the way of business for Mr. Prince.

He used his key on the heavy, boxlike steel lock and went through the thickly barred gate, whistling. His shoes made hollow *thunks!* on the boards of the dock; he was a big guy, six-six, weighed 250. Last night he'd attended a postmodernist opening at the Los Angeles Museum of Art. He'd enjoyed every minute of it, much more than he'd enjoyed the *pro forma* sex afterward with the pretentious blonde who'd accompanied him.

A lanky brown-haired man was hosing down the dock just beyond *Tosca*'s proudly curved prow. He was dressed in jeans and a polo shirt and Nike Airs; his hair was cut so close to his head it looked like a boot camp Marine's. Red was instantly alert; Mr. Prince had enemies and this guy was only a few feet from Mr. Prince's boat and looked like he could make things happen.

When Red approached, the guy gestured at the wet planks.

"Can you believe? Some idiot left fish guts and scales all over the dock, somebody could slip and break their neck."

Red could see the washed-away offal floating in the water below the dock. He asked, "You have a boat here on the pier?"

The guy waved a vague arm down the line of moored yachts. "I've been staying on a friend's ketch, I quit my job to paint." He stopped, frowning at Red in a quizzical way. "I know you."

"No. I'm not from around here." Red spoke curtly.

"The art opening last night! It's your height. Well, just your overall size, and the red hair. You're hard to miss even in a crowd, and the blond lady with you looked like a movie star."

"Not a lady, not a movie star, not a real blonde." Just for a moment, Red envied this guy: on a boat, alone, quiet hours just painting, doing art instead of blondes with I.Q.'s to match their bust size. "What'd you think of the opening?"

"Superb work, superbly mounted." He gestured at *Tosca,* said wistfully, "Talk about superb . . . yours?"

Red chuckled. Here he was envying this guy, and the guy was envying him. What a strange world!

"I just get to ride on it. Just a hired hand."

"Must be nice. No responsibility. Looks all ready to go."

"Tomorrow, down to La Paz to wait for the boss."

The lanky guy spread his arms wide. "The Jade Sea," he said. "Three years ago, we drove down to the bay where the whales go. You can go out among them . . . Once in a lifetime."

He gave a small almost sad shrug, a smile similarly sad, with a wave of his hand went away down the pier.

Red thought he'd sort of like to see some of the guy's paintings. But, leaving tomorrow. Maybe he'll take some art classes in Vegas after they got back. Fine art, not commercial; like the lanky guy who'd been at last night's opening.

A week had passed since Ucelli's death. Driving to Mae's Place from the Newark airport, with a stop in South Orange to get a motel room right along 510, Dante Stagnaro was feeling guilty about Rosie. Here he was, on his own money and leave time he could have spent with her, poking around in the Ucelli hit, leaving the burden of Christmas preparations on her shoulders.

At least he hadn't left his two Organized Crime Task Force inspectors in the lurch. Yesterday they'd broken a ring of Asian car boosters who had been plaguing the malls during the last-minute Christmas rush. The Asians stole Christmas presents from parked cars and returned them to the stores where they had been purchased to get cash refunds. If the store refused to refund, they kept and later fenced the goods.

A cruising Danny Banner saw two of them crowbar an auto trunk at the Stonestown mall, was behind them when they were refused cash for their plunder and went to store the stuff. He called Dante, baby-sat the drop house until Dante got there with the warrant.

When they went in, they got five of the ring, with more to come as the busted ones started to sing. A major coup for his task force, and after getting back from the raid, Dante had been up to his ears in processing paperwork until just before his mad dash to SFO for the eleven-thirty red-eye to Newark.

Now he was turning up the snow-covered drive to Mae's Place, yawning with fatigue but driven by the same obsession that had sent him to Minneapolis after Spic Madrid had been killed. His tires spun briefly on the ice-slick surface; the coating of new snow over everything was kind to the joint, but it still looked tawdry in the bright cold December sunshine.

The local police had long ago come and gone, the feds had come and gone; none of them had found a damn thing giving them any lead to the identity of the man whom Mae's girls had dubbed the P.W. Dante was there only on sufferance, because of a phone call to the local feds from Rudy Mattaliano, his convention-buddy federal prosecutor in Manhattan.

Mae turned out to be a blowsy overblown perfume-drenched broad with glittering fingers, glittering eyes, and a chest you could eat lunch off of. Dante was talking to her in the bar of her roadhouse, a funky ornate intimate room with red plush on the walls and lushly painted nudes of surprising quality above the bar. She was so hostile he knew it had to spring from fear; he could see it glinting in the depths of those glittering eyes.

"You know I don't have to tell you a fucking thing, cop!"

Dante made a great display of checking around his belt. "Shit," he said, "I left my rubber hose back in San Francisco."

She cracked a little grin in spite of herself, jerked her head toward the back of the bar.

"I got coffee—nothin' stronger while we're closed down."

Around them the roadhouse was silent as a tomb. He was sure the girls were moving around upstairs, but he couldn't hear them. Mae, he knew, would soon reopen. Such sops to public conscience were bad for business, and she obviously had something heavy on the local power structure.

Dante made the thick black coffee blond and sweet, took a big gulp. "Why the red carpet for me all of a sudden, Mae?"

"You're the first one didn't look at me like I was shit on a stick." She gave a big belly laugh that reminded him of Tim's. "I'm insulted they didn't try'n' look down the front of my blouse while they were trashin' me."

Dante looked, bugged out his eyes. "Wow! Dolly Parton!"

Tears suddenly came into her eyes, impatiently wiped away with the back of a bejeweled hand. "Thanks, even if you're shittin' me. I miss the little fucker, is the thing."

"You guys go back a ways?"

"Christ, almost forty years."

"Then you just gotta have a few ideas who wanted him dead." He added almost diffidently, "It ties in with a dead woman I got out in San Francisco that I figure maybe Popgun did."

"Listen, he was retired from all that stuff years ago! He was an old man, for Chrissake! He sold wholesale meats!"

Dante stopped her with a palm-out traffic cop hand.

"Hey, Mae, I gotta ask, he was the best in his day. I was just hoping you knew how he stood with the boys these days."

"Hell, top of the heap! Why the night he got it . . ."

Mae stopped herself abruptly. Dante didn't even try to follow up on it. He didn't want to let her know he had caught anything significant in her stifled sentence.

"So there was no reason for them to put out a hit on him."

"Not a fuckin' reason in the world."

"Somebody from years ago, getting even?" mused Dante.

"Trouble with that, the guy was so damn *patient*. Waiting around two, three weeks—"

"Fuckin' freak, is what he was!" she burst out bitterly. "Comin' around with his Soo Li shit . . ."

"Soo Li?"

She told him about the P.W.'s coming, his strange habit of seeing if each girl was some lost love named Soo Li.

"He scared me—and now see what he's done!"

Leaving, Dante went downstairs to find Old Mose in the basement, tending a water heater that didn't need tending.

"Don't want to talk to me, huh, old-timer?"

"Jus' doin' my job, boss," said Mose vaguely. "Yassah, dat's de troof, jus' doin' Old Mose' job. Pow'ful lotta work."

"Ashcan the Amos and Andy, Mose. I know you liked the guy. But he's a bad dude, going around killing innocent people—"

"People like Popgun Ucelli?" The Stepin Fetchit was gone from Mose's voice. "Then I say, give that man a medal!"

He had Dante there. They chatted for half an hour about the great old blues men of Mose's youth whose 78s Dante had grown up on because his grandfather had been a "race record" fan. Pegleg Howell, the Atlanta street singer who made twenty-eight sides between '26 and '29; Jaybird Coleman out of Gainsville, eleven sides in about the same years; Blind Willy Johnson, thirty sides, the best bottleneck guitarist of his day . . .

Mose extended one of his shattered claws to shake Dante's hand when they parted, then called after him.

"Whatever that fat woman upstairs tell you, that Popgun was still doin' people." The faded brown eyes suddenly blazed with joyous light. "I'd wish you luck, Mist' Stagnaro, but that wouldn't be the truth. P.W. done me a mighty big favor." Mose held up his claw. "Was Popgun Ucelli did this to me, nearly thutty years ago."

Old Mose shuffled closer.

"Thutty years, then here come that P.W., take care of that little chore for me. When they laid Popgun to rest, I be taken me to the cemetery, had me a little dance on his grave."

CHAPTER FORTY-TWO

Dante drove back toward South Orange's urban sprawl through the bleak, snowy landscape. What was he to make of Mae's slip of the tongue, old Mose's insistence that Ucelli had still been working? Had Popgun aced all of them? None of them? Some? Why was he hit? To keep him from talking about what he had done? Or to keep him from talking about what he *hadn't* done?

Dante had no idea of how to get to Raptor, even less idea of how to get to who had hired Raptor, but he was starting to get a pretty good idea of why. Somebody in Martin Prince's arm of the mob wanted to move up or was trying to keep somebody else from moving up. As Tim had surmised, Moll Dalton had known something, probably unwittingly, that had placed her in the way of that grand design. If Lenington had been used in setting up her hit, he would have been a potential danger to be eliminated.

By this scenario, the first real target had been Spic Madrid. Solidly ensconced in four northern states, ambitious, ruthless, building a power base. Had just gotten elevated to the board. Had he let his ambition show too much at the Vegas meet?

Dante stopped at a truck stop called the Highway on the outskirts of South Orange. A low flat building with gas pumps out in front, the slush-covered blacktop lot crowded

with semis from all over the country, some puffing diesel
fumes into the cold morning air.

Inside, Mel's Diner come to life; counter straight ahead,
booths by the windows. Full of moisture from wet overcoats
and windbreakers, the smell of grease and coffee, loud
voices and cigarette smoke, the linoleum floor wet with
muddy bootprints.

He was ravenous, ordered eggs over easy, sausage, bacon,
hash browns, white toast and coffee. Real coffee. With cream
and real sugar. He'd be traveling the rest of the day anyway,
the caffeine would be gone by nightfall. Maybe he'd send
Tim a postcard describing his breakfast.

After Madrid, Otto Kreiger. Same reason as Madrid. A
man with empire-building in his head. Out there on the edge
of the Organization, almost in exile in San Francisco where
his mob affiliation was little more than honorary: his real income was from defending scuzzballs and making astute real
estate investments. But wanting to move into the center of
power?

If so, Raptor had moved first.

St. John was easy. The reason Dante himself had advanced
to the degenerate attorney and had explicated to Rosie. The
man was a deviate whose sexual preferences would not only
be distasteful to the mob, but dangerous; Dante had been
close to breaking the man himself.

The middle-aged waitress came by to pour more coffee
into his cup. She had impossibly orange hair, thick ankles,
wrinkles on her face, and a junior version of Mae's formida-
ble bosom. A trucker grabbed her butt as she went by.

"Hey, Carla, when you gonna let me into your pants?"

"What for? I already got one asshole in there."

Dante ignored the byplay. Gideon Abramson was a
tougher call. While still just as vicious as in his garment-
district days, he really had retired. From the FBI reports, his
ambitions had lain with the grandchildren he had doted on,
his golf and bridge, his swims and dry toast in the mornings.

On the other hand, he had delighted in Byzantine intrigues, plots, counterplots. After World War II he had chosen to operate in Greece and Turkey, where profits were large but risks equally large—and slyness the way to success. And there he had befriended Kosta Gounaris—which might be the key. Abramson might have had a fatherly impulse; no ambitions for himself, perhaps, but he might have had them for Kosta.

The Ucelli hit, on the other hand, made perfect sense. He could tell the authorities, if put in a real squeeze, who he had eliminated, and for whom. Or, perhaps even more dangerous for whoever had hired him, who he *hadn't* eliminated.

Leaving, in that arm of the Mafia, who? Only Martin Prince and old Enzo Garofano. Prince, a ruthless, powerful man with the kind of subtle mind that could come up with the idea of using intertwined hitmen to mask his purposes. He could very well be the man behind the Raptor name and phone calls. Could even have scripted them. Garofano, *old* was the operative word. Too old to take Prince down, and Prince would know it.

Finally, if Dante's beliefs about Atlas Entertainment were correct, Gounaris. If Prince was behind the killings, did he dare stop until Gounaris was also dead? Gounaris was potentially dangerous. Eliminate him, all threats were gone.

Dante knew his reconstruction was shaky, but he still felt he'd better make some phone calls. Just in case.

He slid out of the booth, found the pay phone on the wall between the rest rooms, got out his calling card. A man in a dark blue overcoat wearing a Russian-style hat with fur earflaps folded up over the top of it came in the back door, bringing an icy blast of air with him.

By luck, Dante caught Rudy Mattaliano at his office over in Manhattan. Rudy hated the Mafia with a fervor born of obsession, it was one of the things that gave him such a good record as a prosecutor, and it was why he was always willing to help Dante out. But this time he sounded hurried and not too interested.

"Listen, Dante, I'm due in court in ten minutes, so have a good flight home and—"

"I have something for you."

"What?" Mattaliano was instantly focused.

"Ucelli was still making hits for the wise guys. If you check Mae's phone records at the roadhouse, I think you'll find that she was Ucelli's cut-out. That's why you could never get anything off the phone taps at his house and meat-packing plant. I think he got a call from somebody big the night he died—maybe Garofano or even Prince."

"How in Christ did you get this stuff? The FBI worked Mae over pretty good and got nothing but skinned knuckles. You ever want to get a real job, let me know."

"I wouldn't last in the Feebs for a week. I'd tell the SAC to go to hell and that would be that."

"Especially if he was Jack-in-the-Box," said Mattaliano with a laugh. "Hold off a day on going back, I want to talk and I'm willing to buy you one of the best steaks in Manhattan so I can do it. Eight o'clock at Morton's, Fifth Ave at Forty-fifth."

Dante agreed, then called his task force office in San Francisco and told Danny to reinstitute the loose tail on Kosta Gounaris. "I think somebody might try to take him out, and that's the guy I want."

"So let's grab him *after* he does Gounaris."

They hashed over the loose tail a bit more, Dante got updated on the Asian carboosters, gave Danny his motel.

It was after 10:00 A.M. when Dante clawed his way up out of sleep. His eyes felt as if there were lead weights on the lids; he hadn't gotten back to his chain motel in South Orange until three in the morning. He and Mattaliano, a stocky hard-bodied aggressive man with deep-set brown eyes and thinning curly hair and political ambitions in New York, had closed up Morton's after Dante had eaten the best porter-house he'd ever tasted.

Then the prosecutor had insisted they catch old-time jazz great Mal Waldron at Sweet Basil in the Village. The aged black musician had slumped at the piano as his massive hands scooped music from the keys and hurled it around the room with casual genius and indifferent abandon.

"I put my people right to work on those phone records, Dante," Mattaliano said over the applause for Waldron's forty-minute set. "I think they're going to pan out. There was a whole interconnected nest of calls to her number from various pay phones in Jersey—and a couple from Vegas. We're checking them against the dates of the list of hits you gave us . . ."

Dante showered, shaved, packed, went down to the office to check out. Mattaliano could push ahead on the Ucelli case, try to trace the labyrinthian ways through the phone lines to further taps on further phones so they could eventually come down on Mae and make her spill her guts to a grand jury, but, Dante suddenly realized, he was out of it.

If Atlas was a mob front it was beyond his powers to prove it. And apart from Moll Dalton, who had been getting killed here? A bunch of fucking mobsters. What did he care? He should be applauding. Time for him to get back to the Job, and to Rosie for Christmas.

"A fast-mail overnight package came for you." The old clerk had despairing eyes and arthritic fingers. He handed Dante a small mailer. "From San Francisco. I peeked."

Dante sat on the edge of his unmade bed to open the packet from the task force office. There was a small manila envelope inside with, THIS CAME TO YOU AT THE OFFICE. THOUGHT IT MIGHT BE IMPORTANT, scrawled across it in Danny's back-slanted hand.

Inside was a bent and dirtied Christmas card with two gorgeous stamps on it—an elephant emerging from a thicket of tall trees, and a tall graceful crane or stork or something with a beautiful fan of feathers on its head that looked like a crown.

Inside was written: "I gave this to the *duka* owner in Fort Portal to mail when I was there to pick up supplies . . . I plan to be back earlier than first planned, mid-January in fact . . . if so, maybe you can catch me up on what—if any-thing—you've learned about Moll's killer . . . Regards . . . Dalton."

Dante sat in the cheap motel room across Jersey 510 from a HoJo's festooned with Christmas lights, a resigned look on his face and a sinking feeling in his gut. Will Dalton, damn the man, was bringing himself back into the target zone months before Mattaliano's RICO investigators would un-tangle the twisted skein of phone records. With Popgun dead, they would have to be extremely sure of the links in their chain of evidence before they could drag Mae up in front of a federal grand jury and exert enough pressure to make her crack.

Mattaliano was too good a prosecutor to take a weak case into court. He wasn't going to get more than one chance, even if his team could put the jigsaw together correctly. And as soon as Mae started talking, her life would be at risk.

As could Will Dalton's as soon as he returned, Dante was afraid. Dalton's card had aroused all of his unease again. When Raptor had hit Moll, Dante was sure the man had fully expected her husband to be at Bella Figura with her. What if Will *did* know something? Maybe even something he didn't know he knew?

Of course Tim didn't agree with Dante about possible dan-ger to Dalton, and Tim was a hell of a good homicide cop. Tim had to outthink the bad guys ahead of time as well as sweep them up afterward. Tim's opinion had weight.

But could Dante take that chance with Dalton's life?

Moll was gone. Her father was gone. Her mother had been squeezed dry. Dalton's parents in Wyoming were the only

people left to whom Dalton might have confided some part
or all of whatever Moll had sent him in that mailer.

He sighed and called the airlines. More damned snow and
wind and cold and blow for Dante.

people like us who in Dallas night have chartered some yacht to all of whatever Nick had sent in for that matter.

He went into the surface. More ruffled wave had wind and odd and blow for Dallas

CHAPTER FORTY-THREE

Dry and still and sunny and hot all at the same time. The road twisted north out of La Paz along the cup of bay that Steinbeck had written about so movingly in *The Pearl*. Tony was behind the wheel, sitting beside him their Mexican guide in an ill-fitted, sloppy uniform with a lot of brass and braid on it. Red Grant sat in back with Mr. Prince, who he knew was worried about Popgun getting popped like that.

La Paz didn't look much like the novel's descriptions any more. No little palm-frond huts: the poorer people of La Paz had beaten-out five-gallon kerosene tins for roofs; commercial developments and funky fast-food joints lined the highway. Rich houses with red tile roofs dotted the higher ground, and they passed a large resort hotel complex with wrought-iron gates ablaze with bougainvillea set between ornate concrete and stucco balustrades. Still had nice sandy beaches, though.

Five minutes later, the guide said in slurry, heavily accented English, "Turn left. Up here. Next left."

Tony slowed the heavy Chrysler, turned in at the sharply angled driveway. Gravel crunched under the tires. The heavy steel gates were open, with a single armed guard on either side of them. Branches brushed the top of the car as they passed.

"Sorta lax security," said Tony in barely veiled contempt.

The thick tropical foliage abruptly ended as the drive

widened into a broad parking area. On the right a number of small buildings spread out over the open grassy ground. There were a black Mercedes, a red Ferrari, a chunky olive-green Range Rover, a Cadillac Fleetwood sedan, a Corvette.

"You park here," said the guide, his voice surly.

Several men in civilian clothes lounged about by the cars, eyes watchful. One was wiping down the sparkling Mercedes: a fully auto Ingram MAC-11 was lying on the fender he was polishing. The man working on the red Ferrari had a mini-Uzi on a leather strap worn bandoleer fashion over his shoulder and across his chest. Red got out, his hand hovering by the tails of the brightly colored sport shirt he wore outside his slacks. When he nodded, Tony opened the rear door for Mr. Prince.

The way led through an arbor and on the other side was the mansion. The heavy perfume of tropical flowers swept over them. It was immense, Spanish style, set on a knoll overlooking the bay. They were greeted by a tall lean distinguished-looking man with a beautifully barbered white goatee and flowing white hair.

"Señor Prince, you honor my household."

Ignoring Tony and Red, as was proper, he shook Prince's hand. Mr. Prince returned his slight bow.

"You honor me with your hospitality, Governor."

At the front of the mansion, a cool breeze was blowing up across the face of the low bluff from the achingly blue bay. Below were sparkling waves sweeping up to break upon a creamy white sand beach with gentle thuds before sliding back down to mate with their following clone.

Sandpipers on spindly legs were tiny moving dots at the lip of the advancing and retreating waves. A little girl in a blue one-piece swimsuit was rushing in and out of the water, shrieking with distant laughter sweet as birdsong. A small black and white dog ran in and out with her, yipping to her laughter.

"My daughter," said the governor with pride in his voice.

"She is very beautiful," said Mr. Prince.

"I am pleased that she takes after her mother."

A tall elderly woman in a one-piece cotton dress was standing on the beach watching the girl. She seemed to be alone. Tony nudged Red's arm.

"Lousy security," he said.

"Look by the big boulder."

Two soldiers in uniforms were lounging against the rock with AK-47s. The girl looked up and shaded her eyes and saw her father and waved extravagantly. The governor's aristocratic face was wreathed in smiles. The smiles drew sharp crinkles at the corners of his eyes and etched lines in his lean cheeks. His eyes were almost black, with warm depths. He waved back. So did Mr. Prince. Their little group returned to the house.

"I am sorry my wife is not here to greet you. She is in Mexico City. Last-minute Christmas shopping. Shall we go in?"

The mansion was dim and spacious and quiet and cool. Everything gleamed, from the red waxed tile floors underfoot to the crystal chandeliers overhead. The carpets were thick and handwoven in bright Indian colors.

"I understand your election was very successful."

"It was what you North Americans call, I believe, a landslide?" He raised an eyebrow quizzically as he spoke. Mr. Prince nodded. "Of course we are a poor country, but with NAFTA we hope to steal some shipping from Oakland and San Diego . . ."

In the living room, every wall was covered with paintings, the polished antique furniture had beautifully worked Mexican silver and ceramic artifacts on the surfaces. The chairs were of rosewood with spindly legs and hand-crocheted seats. There was a marvelously handmade model sailing ship five feet long on a davenport table behind the couch which faced the sea through tall front windows.

"I understand your Las Vegas has the fastest-growing economy in the United States," said the governor.

"It's got everything," bragged Prince. "Weather, access to California, cheap labor, entertainment . . ."

"And the gambling."

"The backbone, of course," agreed Mr. Prince seriously.

Red stood with his back to the wall, his head on a swivel. A hell of a lot of firepower around this place, casually displayed. It worried him, a little. Tony, as usual, was out of it, a fucking tourist, walking around touching stuff; Red could see the governor keeping a wary eye on him. Bull in a china shop.

None of the furniture looked as if anyone ever sat on it. To one side was a grand piano with ranks of faded family photos marching across its polished top in silver frames. A grandfather clock tolled the seconds with a pompous pendulum beat.

"Shall we have some breakfast?"

The dining room had a very long polished hardwood table and two walls of glass looking out on the spacious grounds. Red half expected to see strolling peacocks. The other walls were of polished hardwood. There was a museum quality to the mansion, as if nobody lived there.

Tony was already in the kitchen, chowing down with the help. Red took his stance just inside the door, his back to the wall, his hands laced in front of his stomach. The butt of his gun was only inches away.

The governor said to him, a trifle sharply, "There is no threat of danger here, young man."

"It's my job, sir," said Red in his low soft voice.

"I see." The governor paused, then jerked his silvery head in a little nod. "Yes. Your job. Quite admirable."

The breakfast was bountiful, beautifully served on fine china and solid silver cutlery. Papayas with limes, eggs done Mexican style with chiles, hot tortillas and warm rolls, juice, coffee in silver pots. The napkins were lace, hand-embroidered, as was the antique tablecloth, its ivory color maintained by washing it in tea.

"The gambling is the backbone, you say, Martin?"

"It makes the rest possible. The house never loses money, its percentage is built right into the odds."

"A marvelous source of income . . ." Red finally understood why the governor had invited Mr. Prince to breakfast. "If we here in Baja California *de sud* should locate a casino in La Paz to bring added revenue for needed government spending . . ."

"I'm sure you would find our industry supportive," said Mr. Prince smoothly.

"And the necessary technical knowledge . . ."

"Would be forthcoming."

For a percentage, of course, thought Red, and understood why Mr. Prince had *accepted* the invitation. A small percentage; but a toehold here in Mexico! Fun in the winter sun—with gambling! Dynamite.

The driveway in from the main road had been plowed, snowbanks stood four feet high on either side of Dante's rental car. He fought the wheel; even with chains *crunk-crunk-crunking* against the insides of the fenders he could end up in a snowbank. The sky was deep blue, the sun off the snow dazzled the eyes.

The drive curved across the open rolling ground, he saw the long low single-story ranchhouse. There were barns and outhouses and even a bunkhouse with smoke drifting up from a stovepipe through the roof. It looked like a Christmas card.

Off to the left was a corral with three horses inside, blowing white plumes into the air as they trotted around in a circle. The snow under their hooves was churned and muddy. A cowboy who looked Mexican was sitting on the top railing watching them while he rolled a cigarette with one hand.

Dante heard the dog barking before he heard it thudding against the bunkhouse door. He was glad it was latched; his taste in dogs ran to mutts who waggled all over and licked your face, not ones who wanted to bite it off.

The door of the ranchhouse opened and a tall lean man with silver hair stood there in his stocking feet. Even at a distance and with the white hair, Dante could see Will Dalton in the older man's features.

"Mind your manners!" the man yelled at the unseen animal.

The barking reduced to snarls, a grumble or two, ceased. Dante went up to the house.

It was cherry pie à la mode, wonderful after a venison stew loaded with big cubes of meat, carrots and potatoes and onions, all in a thick rich gravy. Served with home-made baking-powder biscuits. As he forked rich cherry filling and flaky crust into his mouth, Dante felt that at any minute he and the old man might go outside and start chopping at that tree stump with the huge roots in front of the house like Alan Ladd and Van Heflin in *Shane*.

"Another piece of pie, Lieutenant?"

Dante patted his belly sadly. "I couldn't, Mrs. Dalton."

"Please. Marjorie."

She had insisted, over his objections, that Dante stay for lunch. Western hospitality. She was a woman in her fifties with frankly gray hair and glasses and a kind strong face. She looked as if she still rode, with strong wrists and a sturdy body under jeans and a sweater.

"I saw a cowboy out in the horse corral," said Dante. "Do you have much work for them in the winter?"

"Must have been Alfonso. Been with us forever. Taught Will how to ride and how to break horses." John Dalton shrugged. "About half our men are Latinos these days. Hard to find Anglos will work for the wages we can pay. So we find work for our *vaqueros* all year 'round. Works for them, works for us."

He leaned forward, big hands clasped in front of him. His hard-bitten face was tranquil. His son's resemblance to him was remarkable. He had refused all discussion until after they had eaten, but pie and coffee seemed to fall outside the ban.

"Now, then, you said on the phone you had some questions."

Easy and direct, so Dante could be the same.

"How long since you've heard from Will?"

"We got a Christmas card," said Marjorie.

"I did too," said Dante. "He told me he was coming back in maybe mid-January—anyway, sooner than expected."

John nodded. "Something about a report of his findings, the funding of his grant . . ." He paused with a shrug in his voice. "He wasn't too explicit . . ."

"I think he might be in danger when he comes back, because of something Moll left him. I can't get hold of him where he is. He wouldn't tell me anything before he left. So I thought . . ."

John chuckled again. "You figgered we might tell you things he wouldn't?"

"Will always pretty much keeps his thoughts and feelings to himself," said the mother thoughtfully. She stood up, went to fetch the big enamel coffeepot. "He wouldn't have told us anything he didn't want to get out."

"But you told him you didn't like his wife," said Dante. "He didn't ask you to her funeral."

"Wasn't that we didn't like Molly—we did, a lot. We just felt she wasn't the right woman for our son," said the rancher easily. "We don't have secrets among us, but there's plenty Will just don't talk about."

"We always felt she'd bring him a lot of grief," said Marjorie. Her eyes looked damp behind her glasses. "She did."

"Got a little herself," said Dante sharply, "getting—"

"Before," she said. "Being unfaithful and all."

"You knew about that?"

"Always suspected it," said John. "We could see it in the way she looked at men. There was a . . . hunger in her eyes. Would have felt sorry for her if she hadn't been married to Will."

Dante probed about the package he was sure Moll had mailed to Will shortly before her death. They had never heard of it. He had a hunch they wouldn't have told him about it if they had. He didn't really blame them. These were tranquil people, aware of their own worth and dignity. Self-sufficient, lived on the land, with the land, molded the curve of their lives to the curve of the seasons across the land.

There were worse things than danger, even death, in such a life. Such as betrayal of those rhythms of the earth. Such as dishonesty and dishonor. They wouldn't lie to him. They just wouldn't tell him anything they didn't want him to know. Or that their son wouldn't have wanted him to know.

He finally left, unsatisfied. A little wary. There was something he was missing, some signpost in the right direction; he just wasn't sharp enough to see it.

It was five days later. *Tosca* held her position off, while Red ran Mr. Prince in to the short plank dock at the Hotel Pez Grande in the rubber dinghy. Miguel was waiting, his ancient seamed brown face split into a huge grin of pure delight.

"We get the big one, señor!" he called to Mr. Prince. "We got four, five hours to dark."

"If not today, then tomorrow, Miguel," said Mr. Prince in great good humor. He loved it here. And he had a whole week, as he did every year, where nobody knew where he was except Red and the crew on the *Tosca*. And none of them stayed here with him. Here was no danger from the outside.

The only dangers were from the sea, when they were far out on it in a small fishing boat. He welcomed the sea's dangers. They challenged his sense of himself as a man.

When they came in, the walks would be outlined with little paper bags full of sand holding lit candles the Mexicans called *farola*. There would be hymns, the candlelight procession from the hotel to the nearby *iglesia* for midnight mass. Afterward, there would be carols in the upstairs bar, and dancing, and playing darts, and margaritas with salty rims.

Tomorrow, blindfolded children with sticks would flail away to break *piñatas* and shower everyone with candy. And the *padre* would bless the hotel. This was Mr. Prince's yearly vacation, he was dying to get to it.

CHAPTER FORTY-FOUR

It was Christmas Eve in San Francisco, too. For the third night in a row the man bent on murder stole the car he would use in the killing; the owner was back east for the holidays. He had taken the key off the hook in the parking garage where he also parked; when the boy was off shagging someone else's car, he simply drove out in it. Would return it when he was finished.

Third time lucky. His target was a good Catholic, the man was bound to go to midnight mass at Saints Peter and Paul.

He was obsessed with the killing urge. He had to do it. He knew he would have no rest until he did.

On a dark side street, he stopped, opened the trunk, got out the Domino's Pizza delivery sign he had stolen a week ago, with gloved hands fastened it to the top of the stolen car.

Nobody ever looked twice at a parked pizza-delivery car.

In Cabo San Lucas, the man bent on murder settled himself deeper in the short-legged deck chair dug into the sand in front of the little Mexican fast-order cafe, ate tortilla chips. The sun was almost set and the swimmers and sunbathers had departed, but the sand was still warm around his bare ankles.

Out in the harbor the Christmas lights strung on the masts and bodywork of the dozens of yachts and cruisers were coming on. The yachts rocked slightly at anchor, the colored lights laying wavering shafts of color from the boats to him, the rocky hillside that was the very tip of Baja forming a black velvet backdrop behind them. It was a true fairyland.

The man bent on murder had spent most of a week wandering around the clubs, the waterfront, innocuous, friendly, his Spanish quite fluent and serviceable, even if of a workingman sort. How he loved to talk. But he loved to listen even more. His dark eyes missed little, his ears missed no fact, no nuance.

Hotel Pez Grande. During the week between Christmas and New Year's. Hotel Pez Grande. Alone.

So this was his third evening here on this beach, in the sagging canvas deck chair, sipping beer he didn't want and eating Mexican junk food he didn't need. Waiting.

He straightened up. A huge motor yacht whose silhouette he knew was coming in with the last rays of the sun, water purling gently below its cutting prow.

Tosca.

He arose, threw the paper plate in a trash can set in the sand beside the cafe, shook the sand out of his shoes, went back up to the slanting earth street where he had parked his ancient battered yellow VW bug. There were no streetlights but it was not quite full dark yet. He was obsessed with the killing urge. He had to do it. Forty little miles away.

Tomorrow Dante's folks were coming up from Modesto, Rosie's coming over from the Marina. Julie was home from school for the holidays, out with her friends. Tony was out with his. The in-laws were due at noon tomorrow. The tree was up, he and Rosie were doing the preliminaries for the big holiday dinner.

Dante always made the stuffing, roasted the turkey, did the gravy, the mashed potatoes. Bread stuffing made with ground round and sausage and a lot of herbs and onions, moistened with the stock the giblets for the gravy had been cooked in, then left to stand overnight. He'd browned the flour for the gravy, too.

The women did everything else, but these were his. He'd be up at six-thirty in the morning to salt the bird down, inside and out, stuff it, dot it with Crisco, cover it loosely with foil, pop it into the roasting pan breast-up at 325 degrees.

"This is the mother of all turkeys," he said to Rosa as he manipulated it back into the fridge where they had taken out one of the trays so it would fit. "Twenty-two damn pounds! I won't be turning this baby in the oven tomorrow."

She was dressed in a red dress for Christmas and was pulling on her red winter coat. She wore red Christmassy earrings, too. "Will it be done by three, Dante?"

"Done by two-and-a-half," he grinned. He noticed her coat as he turned from the fridge. "That time already?"

"If we aren't there by eleven-thirty, we'll have to stand all the way through mass."

He'd put the stuffing down in the garage when they got back. There wasn't room for it in the fridge and it had to be kept cold. He clipped his gun and holster to his belt without conscious thought; it was what he did when he left the house. Put on his topcoat; he'd just put the lining in it last week. He remembered just in time Rosie'd been to the hairdresser's.

"Your hair looks wonderful, Rosie."

"Do you really think so?" She checked herself in the small wall mirror beside the front door, touched the hair gently.

"It shows off your earrings, too."

She gave him a little kiss, he opened the door, they went out. He pulled it shut, checked that it was locked. Used the key to shoot the dead bolt home. They started down the concrete stairway; it was wide enough so they could go down arm in arm. A car was parked across the street with the motor running, a lighted pizza-delivery sign attached to the roof above the open driver's window. Rosie gave a disdainful little snort.

"Who wants to eat pizza on Christma—*Dante!*"

She yelled his name in outrage as he shoved her back against the concrete steps and fell on top of her, even as the pistol his conscious mind hadn't even seen yet started firing. Bullets were ricocheting off the concrete, whining through the night. His only thought was to shield Rosie with his body. Something struck him a terrific blow on one cheek, jerked his head around. Rosie cried out beneath him as the pizza-delivery car accelerated up Greenwich for the left turn into Grant at the top of the hill. Rosie's face was smeared with blood.

Oh dear God, no! "Rosie, are you—"

"I've run my new panty hose," she said, and started sobbing. Then she saw Dante's face. She shrieked. "You've been shot—"

"Concrete chip." He had realized the blood on Rosie was his own, from the cut on his cheek.

They clung to each other there on the stairs, safe on Christmas Eve. Dante thanking God with some part of his mind, thinking with another part, some cop. Didn't get a round off. Didn't get a license plate. Didn't get a look at the shooter. Didn't even know for sure what kind of a car it was.

Hey, a hell of a cop at that. Rosie was unhurt, wasn't she? Merry Christmas.

Hotel Pez Grande—literally Hotel Big Fish—was a quarter of a mile in from the highway on a sandy road barely wide enough for two cars to pass. The adobe main building holding the dining rooms and bars and offices was set facing the bay, its back to the parking area. The living units were in double rows down the slope to the beach, each with a concrete patio in back for sunbathing out of the wind.

There was horseback riding, a pool, but Pez Grande, as the name suggested, catered to serious deep-water fishermen; the dining room walls were covered with trophies, and the menu always featured that day's fresh catch. Their summertime "biggest fish" contest drew anglers from all over the United States.

Now, in December, the wind was gritty with sand from the shore, blowing hard and cold up the hill. Anybody wanting to sunbathe in that during the day was out of their skull. But Hotel Pez Grande gave Prince his only true vacation each year during this jolly week between Christmas and New Year's. Thing was, the Feebies had no legal jurisdiction down here, and now that he and the governor had come to a meeting of the minds, their clout would be even less. The DEA had a little juice, but they were after drug-cartel Latinos, not vacationing Mafia dons.

So they left Prince alone down here.

He and Miguel had brought in a good marlin; after it had been strung up by its tail from the block and tackle on the dock for that purpose, and photographed, it had been laid in the back of Miguel's pickup to be taken up the hill and cleaned. Part for the hotel kitchen, the rest was to be sold at market the next day. Mr. Prince was widely known and liked by the locals because of his generosity with his catches. A true *caballero*.

Midnight mass was finished, Prince was sitting in Pez Grande's upstairs bar with most of the rest of the hotel guests, having a few postprandial jolts. It was, after all, Christmas Eve. There was even a tree. He raised a beckoning forefinger at the lean Mexican behind his array of bottles and gleaming glasses inside the horseshoe-shaped bar.

"A Christmas drink for everyone, José, *por favor*."

José had been a bartender for two years in San Diego before La Migra caught up with him and shipped him back home. He affected a drooping gunfighter mustache, sideburns an inch below his ears, and red suspenders.

"And a Merry Christmas to you."

"Thank you, Mr. Prince."

José got busy with the drinks. Prince was at a table by one of the front windows, where he could look down the lighted walkways to the darkness of the water. No lights showed out on the bay. At the far end of the room was a TV getting a country music video show by satellite from Memphis. Tomorrow it would be showing an NFL game Prince planned to watch.

Tex came limping in; Prince gestured and the hard-bitten old cowboy sat down across from him with a sigh. Tex had been a rodeo rider of some note until he had retired, semi-crippled, down here in the sun.

"You still have that big black stallion—"

"Mean as ever," chuckled Tex. Prince was an excellent rider and could control the brute, and the old horse wrangler appreciated it. Most of the horses were for women or kids, but he kept a few feisty ones for guys like Mr. Prince.

"How's the hip, Tex?"

Tex gunned his shot, jerked his head a little to one side and winked his faded blue right eye as the whiskey hit home. "Better here than up in *el Norte*, that's a gut."

The jukebox was playing, people were dancing. Talk was difficult. They played a game of darts; Prince won honestly, he was always a competitor. Tex said he thought he would turn in.

Restless, Prince drifted down the interior stairs to the main floor, to a shadowy alcove between the two dining rooms where there was always hot coffee. He poured himself a thick white ceramic mug full, drank it black, thinking.

Eddie Ucelli had been hit at the very instant Prince himself was giving him a pair of assignments. Which meant both men were still alive, but, more importantly, the timing *couldn't* have been coincidental. Somebody inside the Organization had been sending a message to him. *Him*. Martin Prince. That fucking Gounaris. Had to be.

Well, there were other hitters around, and tomorrow he would reach out for one of them. Even if it was Christmas.

Laughter and singing and music were coming through the ceiling from the bar above. He heard giggling voices, stepped back further into the shadows. Two women, Anglos, had appeared on the tile patio beyond the windows. Obviously mother and daughter. They began dancing arm in arm to the music, laughing and tossing their heads. The mother was slender, with a deerlike grace. The daughter had a beautiful athlete's figure and all the right moves, she had to be a professional dancer.

Even for a man like Prince it was a magic moment. He

watched briefly, then slipped away so they wouldn't know
they had been spied upon.

He walked out into the sandy parking area. With no moon,
the stars were huge and bright and close. He had a sense of
impending adventure, as if something momentous was coming in his life. The lot was filled with cars, some rentals,
some the cars of Americans who had houses down here. One
was a battered yellow bug. His first car had been a VW Beetle. A long time ago.

He walked down the slanted walk toward the beach. The
wind was cold on his face, sand gritted against his teeth. He
stood facing the wind as it whistled up off the water, stood
thick and blocky against it, tasting it, feeling its power, letting it feel *his* power, his immovability.

Out at the end of the dock was the three-pole tripod with
its block and tackle, waiting patiently for its next upside-
down marlin with glazing eyes and fading colors. Even on
the dock, Prince could feel the thud and roar of the surf
through the soles of his shoes.

He heard Tex's uneven footsteps on the dock behind him,
turned. In the starlight, he could just make out the tall Tex-
an's lanky form. He chuckled.

"I thought you were off to bed, Tex."

Tex didn't answer until he had come up within a couple of
feet of Mr. Prince. He wasn't Tex.

"Look at this," the man who wasn't Tex suggested.

Mr. Prince looked down involuntarily. The man's hand, itself indistinct, held a huge glittering knife that faintly caught
the starlight.

As Prince's eyes locked on it, widened, the hand slid the
wide, heavy blade into Prince's gut. He felt slippery cold,
felt the guard thump on his stomach, knew belatedly that the
whole ten-inch blade was *inside* his thick trunk.

The hand ripped the blade upward, to his sternum. The
man's eyes watched his face with interest; they seemed to
gather light from the darkness. He pulled out the blade,
stepped back.

Prince's hands couldn't quite keep his own hot, steaming,

jumbled intestines inside him; they spilled out over his wrists.

"I . . . they . . . *mama* . . ."

He was a fetus lying on his side on the rough spray-wet planks. His legs jerked and kicked. A great darkness was behind his eyes, a great terror . . . He knew . . .

"*Ave Maria . . . piena di grazia . . .*" His sweet mother's prayer, to the sweet Virgin . . . it was important. "*Il signore è teco . . . tu . . .*" He couldn't hang on. He was going into fatal shock. "*Sei . . . benedetta . . .*"

A final sigh . . . the soul leaving the body . . .

"What soul?" said the man who wasn't Tex. He spat into the sand, wiped his knife on Prince's shirt, sheathed it. Then he bent and grabbed Prince's ankles, and with no trace of a limp began dragging the dead man along the dock.

It was the day after Christmas, no work for most because the holiday had fallen on a Sunday, but Dante was in his office reading the reports of the shooting attempt. He had a small neat square of bandage on his cheek where the chip of concrete had struck him; rage still coiled through him like a snake.

A .38, a wimp's gun in this era of Glocks, Magnums, and hypervelocity bullets. But it could kill you just as dead. Would have, if the guy had been any kind of a shot. No cars reported stolen in the appropriate time frame. No leads, no suspects, no witnesses who had seen the car racing away, no clues, no evidence, no nothing . . .

The lousy shooting took Raptor out of it, even if the Death Valley note hadn't: I DO NOT KILL MY OWN KIND. No, had Raptor been behind the .38, he and Rosie would now be dead.

Which meant Prince had hired himself a new shooter. Well, Dante was going to get on a plane to Vegas, go to the Xanadu, go up to that motherfucker's suite, and tear his guts out.

The door opened and Tim's stomach came in followed not

too closely by Tim. He ambled over to one of the desks and hoisted his big buns up on the edge of it with a sigh.

"Way I ate yesterday, they oughta let me hibernate for a week or so," he said. "I got a little something for you."

Dante tensed up. He knew that tone of voice.

"Martin Prince. Christmas Eve. At a little fishing hotel in Baja called Hotel Pez Grande. Somebody gutted him like a fucking shark and hung him upside down by his ankles off one of those big-game-fish block-and-tackle arrangements. Guess a couple of early-rising honeymooners sort of lost their breakfasts when they found him."

Tear his guts out. All of Dante's theories were turned upside down once again. And when he got home . . .

"Our text today is from Ernest Hemingway's *The Old Man and the Sea,*" said the obvious English lit professor's voice on his answering machine. "'Those who had caught sharks had taken them to the shark factory on the other side of the cove where they were hoisted on a block and tackle, their livers removed, their fins cut off and their hides skinned out and their flesh cut into strips for salting.' There will be a spot quiz on the meaning of this passage in the morning."

Then the man laughed a whinnying English-professor sort of laugh, and hung up.

PART EIGHT

25,000 B.C. to the Present

Death is the evaluator. . . . Death stalks the fish eggs, the seedlings, the foetuses. Death is a leopard that sees in the dark. Death is a goshawk, a glacier, the serpent; a wind from the desert, a dispute among friends, a plague of locusts or viruses, a tiring of species. . . . We should all be lost in the wilderness of chance had not death, through a billion choosings, created the values of the world I know.

Robert Ardrey
African Genesis

Part Eight

25,000 B.C. to the Present

CHAPTER FORTY-FIVE

Well, sir, talk about your savagery! I let myself get carried away in the matter of Mr. Prince, don't I? Yet what am I to do? I plot brilliantly to arrange an unexpected *tête-à-tête* with that *capo di tutti i capi* where I have surprise on my side and a weapon besides, and he has only empty hands. When I have it, I indulge myself. Is this *fair*—is this *sporting*? No. But it is prudent. I wish to gaff the shark, not be his meal.

And gaff him I do.

I start out knowing only three things for certain about Martin Prince: what he looks like, thanks to congressional hearings into organized crime; that he is a Mafia don; and that his center of operations is the Xanadu Hotel on the Las Vegas Strip. Oh, I know one other thing about him. His personal security will be state-of-the-art and of the highest quality.

How am I to get next to him to eventuate his demise in as nasty a way possible? Long-range rifle, as in the case of Gideon Abramson? I would have to hang about resort hotel rooftops for weeks, even months, to catch him entering or leaving the Xanadu. This means I will last two or three hours if I am lucky, before being spotted by some of his bodyguards and suffering the fate I have been dealing out to his compeers.

A pistol shot, a similar problem: He is seldom seen in public, and when he is, he is surrounded by sharp-eyed men versed in the use of their weapons.

Explosives? I have only a stump-blaster's knowledge of dynamite, would probably blow myself up with pure TNT, wouldn't know how to get C4.

So it must be in close and personal—and that is the way I prefer it with this man. I want him to know he is dying. Already the savagery is surfacing in Raptor, is it not so? Up close and personal means somehow isolating him, or discovering him when he has isolated himself, from his protective minions.

I begin with newspapers and periodicals, and thus learn an interesting fact: he is a big-game fisherman of some note, and indeed his photo with a dead fish is in last year's *L.A. Times* sporting section. Taken in December on a plain wooden pier with a huge motor yacht in the background. Taken where? In Mexico. Where in Mexico? Where they catch big fish. That takes in much of the Mexican coastline. Small help.

Examination with a magnifying glass of an 8 by 11 glossy of the original art sent to the paper gives me, however, the name of the motor yacht: *Tosca*. He is sport-fishing in Mexico in December from a boat named *Tosca*.

December. I am beginning my workup on Prince in October.

I instinctively know that security will be more relaxed around that boat than it is in Vegas. So I can try to find where the boat is moored, and wait by it until he arrives; but even if my search is successful, my wait could be months in duration.

I do not have months. Dante Stagnaro is nipping at my heels, even if he doesn't know it yet. I must complete my list before his synapses complete the circuits within his skull. So I must find a way to trace Prince to his boat rather quickly.

In such an endeavor, I have one hidden asset. I know that one of his personal bodyguards is a very big and very smart man called Red. I watch him casually question Stagnaro in a Death Valley date grove. If I can tag Red in Vegas, and keep him in sight, can Prince be far off? I know him; he does not know me. An auspicious beginning.

I go to Vegas, play slot machines at the Xanadu for days, pulling those bandits' single arms with as much mindlessness as I can muster, morning, noon, and night, giving myself a zombie face, before I finally spot Red passing through the casino. Then, gradually, by judicious observation, I learn where his apartment is. I learn when he works out, and where. I learn where he parks his cream-colored Lexus. I never let him make eye contact with me; I am reserving my options.

In all this time I have not yet seen Prince himself—he leaves from and returns to the hotel garage where security is too fierce for me to venture. I occasionally see smoked windows passing by my point of observation, with Red's Lexus behind. So choosing Red as my point of contact is sound.

Red's parking garage has only locked-doors security, so on a day in mid-December, in midmorning, from behind a pillar I observe him getting off the elevator, suitcase in hand, and opening the trunk of his Lexus. I follow discreetly when he leaves. He drives south and west out of town on I-15 in the brilliant desert sunshine.

Decision time. He might just be going on vacation. But I know he is one of Prince's trusted men. I know that last year Prince was on his motor cruiser *Tosca* in Mexico in December. I know that the I-15 freeway is the direct motor route to Los Angeles. And I know that Los Angeles is the logical place for a man who lives in Las Vegas to berth his expensive power cruiser.

So I follow Red. Freeway tailing is easy, especially when the subject has no idea he is under scrutiny, and is in no hurry. Los Angeles it is. Then Marina del Rey. And *Tosca*. He moves aboard the yacht; there is enough sporadic activity by the permanent crew to suggest the craft will soon be in use.

I hover. A couple of evenings later, Red and a blonde attend a postmodernist art opening at the Los Angeles County Museum of Art. Being indifferent to postmodernism, I enjoy the life-size prehistoric mammals stuck in the adjacent La Brea tar pits. Red stays overnight at the blonde's apartment in the 600 block of Grant Street in Santa Monica; I drive to San Pedro.

At dawn I buy fish heads and offal from returning fishermen. At Marina del Rey, I again gain access to the locked pier at which *Tosca* is moored—nautical clothes, a nautical face, call a cheery, "Hold it a second, will you, I've got my hands full," at someone entering or leaving the dock.

When I see Red's Lexus driving up, I dump my fish heads and intestines on the dock close by *Tosca*, am angrily hosing them off when Red arrives. How thoughtless some people are! He agrees.

The rest is child's play. We talk art, Red lets slip that Prince will be joining *Tosca* in La Paz, capital of Baja *del sud*. I fly to Cabo, rent a battered old yellow Volkswagen Beetle at the airport, spend a couple of days familiarizing myself with Cabo and environs.

I am in La Paz with good 10X glasses to see Prince in the flesh for the first time. Learn over a waterfront beer that *Tosca* will be sailing for Cabo next day. I am there first, continuing my quest, eventually learning where Prince does his December fishing—at Hotel Pez Grande, forty miles north.

I see *Tosca* safely to its mooring on Christmas Eve and, on the assumption that she left Prince at Pez Grande, drive there. I have a beer in the upstairs bar at the hotel, courtesy of Martin Prince when he buys a Christmas round for the house. I watch him play darts with Tex, observe Tex's handy limp.

It is as if Prince seeks my blade. He goes down to the beach in the darkness, all souls alone, then out onto the fishing pier. I walk with Tex's limp to get close enough for handwork.

This obscene man dies with the Virgin's prayer on his lips.

I am in a plane to Los Angeles by the time his body is discovered, strung up on the block and tackle like one of the hapless marlin he took so much delight in stringing up himself.

CHAPTER FORTY-SIX

Kosta Gounaris was going over the preliminary operating cost estimates for the year just ended when Diana Pym called him on the intercom, not using the speaker so his words could not be heard by anyone in her office.

"Lieutenant Dante Stagnaro is waiting to see you, Mr. Gounaris. He has no appointment."

"Let him sweat until I tell you to bring him in."

Kosta stood, walked to the window, stood looking out and down at the human ants far below, hands thrust in his pants pockets. He felt like whistling, or doing a little *zembeikiko* there in the window.

What a difference three weeks made! On Christmas Eve he had tried to assassinate Stagnaro, result of another hypothetical with Miss Pym, and had missed. He'd been sure Stagnaro would uncover him as the shooter, had been even more sure Mr. Prince would find out he'd been skimming the Atlas profits.

Stagnaro didn't come after him. And on that same Christmas Eve, Prince had been gutted and strung up like a dead fish at some little pisspot hotel on the Baja coast. Kosta's whole life had changed. Now there was no chance of his skimming from the Atlas profits being uncovered. And he was the fair-haired boy who had gotten a toehold for the Mafia in the rich San Francisco Bay Area where they had previously been only a shadow presence.

Nothing to fear from Stagnaro, either. He probably had never had anything to fear from him. He buzzed Miss Pym.

"Send him in and leave the key open so you can listen in."

He was immersed in paperwork when Stagnaro entered. Kosta glanced up, pointed a careless finger at a chair on the other side of the desk, went on with his study of the file. He made a couple of notations on the accounting sheets, finally put down his pen and looked up.

"Lieutenant. You caught me on a busy morning."

"Can the crap. I had a tail on you Christmas Eve."

For just a moment, Kosta's blood froze; then he relaxed. If the man had anything he could make stick, he'd have had Gounaris down to the Hall of Justice long before now.

"Then you know I spent the evening with Miss Pym."

Dante was on his feet. "I know that you tried to hit me outside my house on Christmas Eve. I've found the car you used, it was in storage in the same garage where you park. So—"

"You know, Lieutenant," interrupted Kosta, standing himself and coming out from behind the desk, "I believe that cease-and-desist order forbidding the SFPD—and you specifically—from harassing me is still in effect." He chuckled. "I'm going to break you, Lieutenant—right down to uniformed patrol."

Stagnaro seemed unperturbed, but he had to be seething.

"We had the mistaken idea that you might be in danger, Gounaris. I thought you were probably next on the hit list."

Kosta couldn't help asking; he really wanted to know. "But you were wrong?"

"I think it was *your* list." He stood up, started for the door, turned back. "If you ever come near me or my wife again, Gounaris, I'll kill you. And fix it up afterwards to look like self-defense. 'Til then, keep Raptor away from Will Dalton."

Kosta kept his face straight. "What is a Raptor?"

Stagnaro left, Miss Pym came in with that look on her face.

"I have Charlene covering your calls," she said. She

locked the door. "Rather exciting, hearing you talk to that policeman."

"Show me," said Gounaris. She did. Afterwards he told her to take the rest of the day off to buy some lingerie. "With open crotches. Be wearing it when I come over tonight."

Power. *Power!* Jesus, there was nothing like it. What had Henry Miller written? Living in the land of fuck. The gold ring was within his grasp. Nothing could stop him now.

Dante, feeling depressed, stopped for a cup of decaf in the lobby coffee shop. How many ways could you blow one interview? He'd planned it all out in advance, and it had been a dud. The loose tail on Gounaris had lost him that night. He'd gone into his parking garage after work, hadn't come out. Hours later they caught up with him at Diana Pym's apartment on Telegraph Hill. He'd been loose during the vital time.

And a man who had left his car garaged there while gone for the holidays had found a Domino Pizza sign in his trunk—the kind that clips on the top of a car. The kind that Dante had seen on the top of the shooter's car just before the bullets had started flying.

He had thought the information about the car would shake Gounaris; the man had just laughed at him. And Diana Pym was giving him an all-evening alibi; she was completely in the thrall of the tall Greek, just like Moll Dalton before her. Even Rosa had thought Gounaris was a handsome devil.

Dante's eyes found the lobby pay phone Gounaris had used to call Gideon Abramson in Palm Springs, back in the days when he'd had Gounaris on the run. Now Gounaris was on top of the world. He'd been involved somehow in Moll Dalton's death. He'd been able to eliminate everyone in power between him and a position of high importance in the mob. He'd gotten the Mafia a toehold in San Francisco. And, although Dante didn't know why, he'd tried to kill Dante and had gotten away with it.

And Dante couldn't prove a damned word of it. Accuse

him, Gounaris could sue him and the department. Tim was right. Let it go. Gounaris just wasn't his problem any longer. Probably never had been.

His problem was that tonight Will Dalton planned to make a speech over in Berkeley at the Institute of Human Origins, detailing his fifteen months in Uganda studying chimpanzees. And hadn't returned Dante's calls urging him not to.

Will Dalton, whose wife had left him *something,* a computer disk maybe, that might shed light on the riddle of Kosta Gounaris. Dalton, who had brought himself back into the danger zone months before he was scheduled to return.

Dante wanted to *stop* Raptor from killing, not put the cuffs on him after Will Dalton was already dead. If Dalton spoke, Raptor would be there; Dante could feel it in his bones. So he had to be there, too. Alone. Nobody believed him that Dalton was in danger. Except for Raptor. And probably Kosta Gounaris.

Kosta was at his desk, thinking about Will Dalton. Fifteen months ago he had wanted Dalton dead. Had wanted revenge on him, in a weird way, for Moll's death. Now Moll and her passionate lovemaking had paled to insignificance next to Miss Pym's delicious perversions of body and mind.

The phone rang. Charlene said, "There's an Inspector Flanagan on line two, Mr. Gounaris."

"Tell him I've already left for the day."

"Gee, I'm sorry, Mr. Gounaris, I said you were still—"

"Oh, all right, put the bastard on."

"I'm already on."

That fucking Charlene was out of a job, as of right now! Not closing down Flanagan's line while she buzzed him . . .

"Can't blame me for trying, Inspector," said Gounaris. He heard Charlene hang up. At least the stupid cunt had gotten that right. "Your friend Stagnaro was sniffing around all morning, I'm sick of the stink of cops."

"Yeah? Tough titty. Somebody whacked Diana Pym in her

apartment an hour ago. I just got here, I'm waiting for the tech boys now. I want you to get your ass over here."

A huge hand seemed to seize Kosta's heart. "Diana? Dead? But that can't be! She was just—"

"Dead. And she didn't die easy. Like maybe whoever did it was trying to get some information out of her."

"I don't . . . know what to say . . ."

There was a heavy bray of laughter over the line. "Just say she was a great piece of ass and move on to the next one." The voice suddenly hardened. "I want you over here right now, Gounaris. There's papers and shit all over the floor, and she's naked except for some Victoria's Secret underwear without any crotch in it. Whoever did this liked his work . . ."

It was nearly five o'clock, dark out. The light drizzle that had fallen early in the afternoon had ended; the pavement gleamed in the streetlights but the air was clear and crisp. Gounaris was lucky enough to flag down a cab just as he emerged from the Atlas Entertainment building.

"Kearny above Broadway," he told the driver.

Vivid sexual images shot through him. Going down on Moll Dalton, finishing off in her mouth . . . And an hour later . . . Diana Pym, going down on him so he finished off in her mouth. And now, a few hours later . . .

Stop it, goddam you, he thought. There wasn't time for that. Moll was gone. Diana was gone. As the cab threaded its way through the stalled, angry, honking rush-hour traffic, he knew he had to think, think hard and quick. It wasn't over after all! It hadn't died with Martin Prince! Maybe that Raptor mentioned by Stagnaro . . . *She didn't die easy . . . trying to get information out of her . . . whoever did this liked his work . . .*

Think, goddammit! What had she known that could be dangerous to Kosta Gounaris? He relaxed fractionally. She had known nothing about the things the mob would want to know: whatever might cost them money or endanger their operations.

He remembered Flanagan now, fat, red-faced and deliberately stupid. Even so, he could be a problem, might think this gave him a right to dig around in Atlas operations . . .

"Here you are, pal."

Kosta shoved some bills at the cabby, got out, almost slipped crossing the wet-slick, steeply slanted sidewalk toward the gaping street door of Diana's second-floor apartment. Flanagan's unmarked sedan was parked at an angle halfway up across the sidewalk, the driver's door hanging open.

Gounaris ran up the interior stairs, his shoes echoing on the old hardwood risers. The door to her apartment at the head of the stairs also stood open. Bright light came through from the living room beyond the hallway. He went in, faltered. He didn't want to see Diana . . .

"In-Inspector? I—"

The wire garrote was looped around his neck from behind. The big predator coming out of the hall closet gave a grunt of effort as he jerked the wire tight with its two handmade wooden handles, ramming his knee into the small of Kosta's back for leverage.

"Die . . . you . . . fucker . . ."

Gounaris did. Almost immediately. But not before he had been spun around to face the hallway mirror so he could see, through dimming eyes, Raptor's ferocious and triumphant face reflected over his own shoulder.

CHAPTER FORTY-SEVEN

I want something special for this one—the savagery unleashed last time seems to be growing. Something up close and personal. The gun? I've used that already, more than once. The bomb? If you will allow a directed gas main explosion to count, I've used that too. The knife? Prince of darkness. Which leaves the club or the garrote.

The garrote it shall be. Up close and personal. Easy to fabricate out of piano wire and two pieces of dowel for handgrips. Gloves at all times, of course. And I want it to be at Miss Pym's apartment—somehow fitting, don't you agree?

I go in two days ago using the old telephone repairman ruse. Cap, jacket, a phone to hang off a thick leather belt . . . Lovely view of the Embarcadero, the piers, the Bay Bridge from her front room window. She has a telescope—for watching the ships, she tells me. Spare bedroom fixed up as a home office; fax machine, filing cabinet, speakerphone, copy machine . . .

Outside, the view is equally delectable. A breathtaking panorama down Kearny and across Broadway to the financial district, dominated by the towering white golf tee of the Transamerica Tower. A similar view, in fact, to that from the late Moll Dalton's penthouse apartment, visited, thoroughly scouted, many times by Raptor before her demise.

I have been tracking Gounaris for two weeks now, I know his patterns, his habits. I see Stagnaro visit him today, I watch Miss Pym depart, follow her shopping, home, activate my plan. When the time is right, I go up to her apartment, do what I do, call Gounaris. Impersonating fat Tim Flanagan over the phone is easy; Gounaris has not spoken to the man for fifteen months.

I leave my Hertz car—the epitome of an unmarked sedan—parked at an artistic angle across the sidewalk, door agape. I leave street and upstairs door to the apartment open, flood it with light to make it subliminally seem a crime scene.

I wait in the closet. Gounaris arrives. Sees himself die.

I arrange the scene further, drive to my Berkeley motel room; I have two hours to wait before the Will Dalton *finis*. Or my own. I don't know how that will go, not with Stagnaro lurking around. I lie down for a moment, fall asleep, dream.

I have completed an assassination in a strange city, rent a cheap hotel room for the night. It is high-ceilinged and boxy, sparsely furnished with a neatly made double bed and an almost napless carpet on the floor.

In the night I come half-awake with a warm heavy weight on top of me. At first I think it is my dog, he weighs as much as a person, but when I put my hand down to pat his head, I encounter soft human flesh. I feel an arm, a female breast, I jerk my hand away. A woman is lying asleep on top of me.

At first I think, My beloved! But then I remember that she has no way of knowing where I am or what I am doing.

"You have come to the wrong room," I exclaim, very puritanical, shaking the sleeping woman awake. "You must leave."

She mumbles something and rolls aside so I can jump out of bed. I find the light switch, but the fixture in the high ceiling has a very dim pink bulb, so it furnishes ambiance but little illumination. The woman is tall and comely, her body beautifully shaped under a filmy blue negligee. Because of the dim light, however, I cannot see her face as she comes toward me.

She slides the negligee down off her shoulders to bare for my ecstasy her beautiful breasts, nipples erect with sexual anticipation, and I realize she *is* my beloved! I put my arms around her hips and crouch to bury my face between those breasts, my own sex already thrusting out stiffly in its excitement.

"One need only be faithful unto death," she murmurs in an astounded, suddenly fading voice.

And I am crouching in the middle of that strange barren pinkly lit hotel room with a ridiculous hard-on, clutching only an empty blue negligee, the texture of my beloved's departed flesh still burning my lips. I hear mocking male laughter dissipating into thin air above my head.

Lips burning. Face wet. I think with tears, but when I bring down my hand it is stained with something dark. I stagger into the bathroom, look in the mirror. My face is smeared with blood like the face of a vampire.

End of dream. I awake in my Berkeley motel room, heart pounding, fearing I have missed the next murder, fearing I have slain my beloved. I sit on the edge of my bed, face buried in my hands. I bring my hands down. They are red with blood. I run into the bathroom, look in the mirror. My face is smeared with blood like the face of a vampire.

The bed is bloodstained, too, but . . . empty. Void take me, my beloved is not dead by my hand after all! I merely have had my first nosebleed since I was a child.

I have checked out and am driving toward Will Dalton's assassination, feeling confused, when I recall that departing male laughter above my head. God's laughter—God, in Whose existence, you will not be surprised to hear, I have very little faith. Suddenly I am enraged at this God I do not believe in.

"Why do You do things like this to people?" I demand, but reasonably at first. "They pray, they try to live good lives, they give love to other people . . . and then You destroy them."

No answer. He never answers, as those of you who engage in the futile exercise of prayer well know. You must take it on faith that some cosmic ear is up there listening. Louder now.

"What do You get out of it? You claim to be all-powerful. Why do You need the humiliation and destruction of human beings? Of all living things?"

No answer. I wait. Louder again. I am pounding my fist on the steering wheel by this time. My face, caught in the rearview mirror, is contorted with rage.

"WHY? DOES IT MAKE YOU FEEL GOOD? DO YOU ENJOY THE SCREAMS OF HUMAN PAIN? DOES IT MAKE YOU FEEL ALL WARM AND TOASTY INSIDE? DOES IT MAKE YOU FEEL LIKE A BIG MAN?"

No answer. I am at a stoplight. The woman in the next car is looking over at me. She cannot hear me through our closed windows, so perhaps she thinks I am singing along with some operatic aria—with Rome's sinister chief of police, Scarpia, let's say, plotting Cavaradossi's murder in the church of Sant'Andrea before cynically falling on his knees to pray.

I shriek, *"ANSWER ME, GODDAM YOU! OR DON'T YOU HAVE THE GUTS?"* No answer. The light changes. Traffic moves. I scream: *"ALL RIGHT THEN, FUCK YOU! I'LL KILL YOU TOO, YOU FUCKER, SO YOU CAN ROT IN YOUR OWN HELL!"*

No answer. Because there is no answer He can make.

And God has the balls to claim He created us in His image!

CHAPTER FORTY-EIGHT

"'So God created man in his own image, in the image of God created he him; male and female created he them. And God blessed them, and God said unto them, Be fruitful, and multiply, and replenish the earth, and subdue it: and have dominion over the fish of the sea, and over the fowl of the air, and over every living thing that moveth upon the earth.'"

Will paused and looked around the room full of scientists, most of whom had little sympathy with the Genesis story of the beginnings of life. But the room was still, almost tense.

"So there we have it, folks. The creation of man. And woman. And dominion over the earth. But *when* did we become us? How far back were Adam and Eve? We left our hominid ancestor, Lucy, with our cousins the chimps at the edge of the savannah, venturing out of the forest into the open. Why? Well, remember the dinosaurs rushing to fill the niches left empty when the proto-reptiles went extinct? Remember the mammals rushing in to fill the dinosaurs' niches after the Great Dying?

"For the chimps and their siblings, the hominids, failing rainfalls and shrinking forests meant new challenges to be met, new ways of life to test out there in the grasslands, had one the courage or sense of adventure to go. Including the meat-eating way of life. Can we seriously contend that we, unlike the chimps, shrank from the challenge of hunting other animals?

"Yet that is what most scientific thought holds today. This is partially in reaction to the hunting hypothesis that held sway from the mid-sixties to the mid-eighties, until 'Hurricane Lew' Binford pointed out that a three-and-a-half-foot creature weighing ninety pounds, with no claws, no fangs, no weapons and a negligible brain, could not have been much of a hunter.

"But could it have had the beginnings of an imagination?

"Lucy, or at least her descendant *Homo habilis*, lived some sort of scavenging/gathering way of life. The astonishing fieldwork of such ecological archeologists as Rob Blumenschine and his student, John Cavallo, certainly suggests it. But the belief in scavenging, and only scavenging, is now in danger of becoming as doctrinaire as the hunting hypothesis was in its day.

"*No* hunting for *A. afarensis* or even *H. habilis*? Can we really believe that Lucy's kind, and more especially *habilis*, already a meat-eater, would not have snatched up any small or weakened animals they chanced upon, would not have figured out some way to kill and eat this helpless prey? Do we truly believe there was no envy and admiration, to go along with their fear, of the mighty predators whose kills they scavenged? No attempt, in their own negligible way, to copy them? To *ape* them, in a word?

"The human psyche is the result of evolution; we come by our genocides honestly. Our propensity to kill—especially to kill our own species—is one of our evolutionary heritages. But not . . . *not* from our hominid ancestors. It *predates* Lucy. It comes from our *primate* heritage.

"We'll probably never know for sure what Lucy and her kin thought or felt or imagined. But the chimp, sharing 99 percent of his DNA with us, who came out of the trees with us and has rituals of dominance and submission like other mammals that keep him short of violence against his own kind, *contemplates* killing. So we must consider the possibility that he is not far from contemplating murder. Because his codes—taboos—seem to crack under the pressures of hunting and those territorial games we call, in chimps and in ourselves, war.

"Yes, war. The chimp does what no other animal besides man does: he wages war—for three years in one known instance, for ten years in another—with adjacent bands of chimps. My troop at Kibale doesn't, but they have no contact with other chimps. The war ends only when the adversary males are dead, the females seized, and the enemies' territory annexed by the victors.

"My observations suggest the chimp also contemplates death—or at least wonders about it. He returns to an animal he has killed, pokes it, prods it, studies it, *thinks* about it. I believe he does this because he has a vivid imagination, and the power to create symbols. Can we believe less of Lucy's people?

"Poor discredited Ardrey actually had the right idea—man is a creature innately dedicated to violence. Ardrey just had the wrong mechanism. He thought little fruit-eating Lucy and her kind were killer apes. No. They had the genetic capacity to be so, but not yet the conditions, personal or environmental, to trigger it.

"I believe *habilis,* the first true human, was a hunter, not just a scavenger. The groundbreaking studies of Kathy Schick and Nicholas Toth show that many of the flake tools that *habilis* created were used not only to break open bones for their high-protein life-giving marrow (a scavenger's technique), but to remove the meat from the bones of quite large animals (Schick and Toth butchered a dead *elephant* using only *habilis* flake tools!). Scavengers have only hunters' scraps to process; hunters have carcasses with enough meat on them to require butchering.

"Whatever his way of life, meat and marrow fed his big brain so it could grow bigger yet, more complex. *Habilis* probably was developing a rudimentary language (perhaps not sentences but sounds that indicated concrete things—tree, fruit, wildebeest, perhaps even *you* and *me*). Eventually he evolved into *Homo erectus. Erectus* almost surely could speak, surely had fire.

"Part of our nature is to hunt other animals to live. We are, after all, omnivores—we will eat almost anything. By the time of that true *Homo sapiens,* Cro-Magnon man, some forty thousand years ago and virtually indistinguishable from us, we had become the most deadly hunter the world had ever seen. Crossing the land bridge into the Americas, we decimated vast herds of big-game animals, driving most of them to extinction.

"But now let us go beyond hunting and killing to the next logical step, in imagination, at least. We know Lucy evolved into *Homo habilis* probably through the hominid *Australopithecus africanus.* But other australopithecines, called variously *robustus, boisei, aethiopius,* or *paranthropus*—seed and grass eaters with huge jaws and enormous grinding molars (but no canines)—were contemporaries of *habilis.* They disappeared from the fossil record just when *habilis* was becoming *erectus.*

"What happened to them? What happened to Neanderthal? What happened to all of the other 'archaic' humans who were around when the *Homo sapiens* explosion occurred?

"We are told that these various early human species were 'absorbed' by modern man. Mated with us, we fed into the gene pool. But there is no shred of DNA or other scientific evidence to show this is so. Indeed, the latest studies, based on links between language patterns and genetic traits in European populations, posits a single, probably African, origin for all modern humans. These scientists are confident that Neanderthal had nothing significant to do with modern human evolution.

"Of course there is no evidence to show earlier *homos* were annihilated by our line, either. Species can decline below a 'survival line' and go extinct all by themselves. But modern man has a great genetic capability for violence against his own kind, up to and including genocide on a massive scale. The chimps show we've had this capability since we were apes. Can we really just dismiss as nonsense the possibility that we got here, alone, because we killed off our relatives along the way?

"Crime statisticians can draw a picture of the *average* jump-out-of-the-bushes rapist with remarkable accuracy. The profile cuts across race, nationality, country of residence. Our rapist is predictably mid-twenties, not married, already involved in other criminal or antisocial activities, and a socioeconomic wreck. He usually stops raping by the age of forty.

"Remember the young rapist orang? Unmated. Equivalent in age to mid-twenties in humans. No economic base. And he stops raping and starts mating when he reaches full maturity.

"The murder statistics are comparable. The perpetrators are in the same age group as rapists, already criminal, from a lousy socioeconomic background. Murderers and rapists have several other things in common. Most are criminally inclined *before* and *after* committing their rapes or murders. They have a record of criminal offenses. They want something they aren't getting. They operate outside the controls of their societies.

"Males kill their own kind forty to one over females. Among apes, among men. If a human female kills, it is usually her spouse.

"Ape males kill the infants of females just joining their troop; the female, deprived of her infant, immediately comes into heat again and is impregnated by the males who thus 'know' the offspring is theirs. Human stepfathers kill infants seventy to one over blood fathers (in the U.S. it is one hundred to one). The killings usually occur when a male—ape or man—is recruiting a new female.

"If a female kills her own infant—ape or human—she is usually young, unmated, and her resources are limited. A female with an infant—human or ape—has less of a chance to mate and reproduce than the same female without an infant.

"Finally, war. Since we left the hunting way of life to hold land and till the earth, which led to permanent shelters and then towns and finally cities, war has been our central preoccupation. Once there was something to be taken away from someone else, we began doing it on a massive scale.

"War is ordered by alpha males, in chimps, in men, and is always fought for the same things: resources. Chimps, led by their alpha males, set out to annihilate another chimp community—wage war upon it—because they think they can win territory, wealth, and females for reproductive purposes. *Nobody* starts a war he *doesn't* think he can win.

"Rape. Murder. War. They are in our blood, in our genes, from long before we started to become man. Until we accept this, we cannot hope to make progress against violence.

"The chimp's ability to wage war against his own kind grows out of his imagination—he can imagine doing it, so he does it. But imagination is positive as well as negative. Sometimes, as the evening light faded in the Kibale Forest, my troop of chimps, each one in its own nest in its own tree for the night, would begin to hoot softly into the gathering darkness, and would begin drumming, with its hands. Chanting, and thoughtfully drumming.

"Prayer? Not likely. But *some* aesthetic is at work here, probably to announce one's self and also one's solidarity with those around one. Comfort, perhaps. African tribesmen drum to the darkness; soldiers play 'Taps' to the sunset; we used to chant Evensong, Vespers, and Angelus. Why all these? Comfort.

"At the outbreak of huge thunderstorms, I have seen my male chimps charge up and down forested hillsides, hooting wildly, grabbing up fallen branches and striking the trees with them just as the wind and rain are doing. Huddled in the trees above are the females and children, watching the display. It is defiance of the storm. It is theater. It is also a rain dance.

"I have seen my troop start walking around a lightning-shattered stump in the center of a moonlit glade. First walking, then marching, then trotting around and around the stump, in rhythm, stamping hard with one foot, lightly with the other—in unison. Dancing.

"Could their dancing grounds be the first faint stirrings of reverence for the sacred? Must not Lucy and her kin have danced beneath the full moon in the same way? With no thought of deity yet, of course, but perhaps with an . . . *unease* at some faint glimmering of something beyond the leaf, the rock, the fig, beyond the pain and the pleasure of the now.

"Out on the edge of the unknown. How frightful and how exhilarating, all at once! It is for us. How much more so for a chimp, a Lucy, a *habilis*, without a brain big enough or complex enough to spin a tale about it and so master it.

"We certainly know that Lucy's descendants danced; around the campfire, once we had fire; around the hearth, around the threshing floor. Learned how to drum, how to sing, how to re-create the day's events. Then came the solo dance—the alpha male leaping into the center of the circle, his performance incarnating (literally, making flesh) the spirit of the prey.

"To Dudley Young, the dance became a dialectic of energies, love and hatred, expansion and contraction of the spirit. Until once, sometime, that alpha male in his pride in the center of the dance *slipped, fell*—and was fallen upon by the other dancers in their frenzy. And torn apart. And devoured, because he had *become* the prey whose spirit he previously had only represented.

"And man had holy communion. Frenzy, with remorse only later, when the frenzy had passed. All of it haunting echoes of the chimp hunting—and ritualistically devouring his prey.

"Since I am expert only in our primate brothers, and in our earliest hominid selves, I can only speak of who we were and of what we did in those earliest formative years. But I do know this about *Homo sapiens sapiens*: somewhere we have gone astray. We have written *dead end* across myth's guidelines, forgotten their psychological truths. We have killed all the old gods of the spirit, embraced the gods of the material. But science now says the material is not real, it is merely a fistful of energy.

"I think Teilhard de Chardin was right, our evolution now is as social and psychological beings. This evolution is going on at a bewildering rate, each new complexity spawning a geometric progression of complexities. Perhaps this is how we can return to ourselves, find out who we were. Know that, and we can know who we *are*. Know *that*, we will know why we act as we do.

"Why we, with our big brains, cannot control our violence, is the wrong question. We should try to understand how we, with our big brain exaggerating all our natural genetic tendencies, are able to control our violence as well as we do."

Will Dalton paused, a strange look on his face. To Dante it seemed a look of surprise, as if what he was going to say next was not what he had intended to say. It could even have been regret; or even fear.

"Anarchy stalks but does not rule our world. It is only the beginnings of a start, but I can only believe that as a species we are just at the threshold, not about to be swept out the back door of extinction by our own hand. I believe that by looking backward as well as forward, we can control our genetic heritage. I believe we are in a race with our own destructive nature, learning, evolving ways to cope with our own violence, and I believe that we will win that race. I believe that we, as a species, are that smart.

"Thank you for your attention here tonight. I will take questions . . ."

As an enraged female voice in the first row began, "How can you possibly suggest that . . ." Dante tuned out. Nothing had happened. Dante had miscalculated.

CHAPTER FORTY-NINE

He waited patiently at the back of the lecture hall for almost half an hour as a core of hardy dissenters circled around Will like wolves, vociferous and finger-waggling as they disputed points of his thesis. Dante's hand was on the automatic in its hip holster, but he was already quite sure that Raptor was not going to strike within this hall tonight. Why should he? Raptor need only trail Will Dalton back to the big old empty echoing house he had just moved back into . . .

Will finally broke free and came down the aisle between the folding chairs. Dante took his upper arm. "Now it's my turn."

"Not another critic, I hope."

"Just a bodyguard. I'm going to follow you home."

"I'm too tired to argue."

They walked out to the now nearly deserted parking lot, Dante with his hand on the butt of his Sig-Sauer. Nothing. He swept his pocket flash under the 4Runner, in the backseat, before letting Dalton get in.

"Lock your doors. I'll be right behind you."

The big old rambling house was warm and homey; Dalton obviously had slipped in and turned the heat on even though ducking Dante all day. Homey, but empty. Waiting for the voice it would never again hear, the footfall it would never again feel on its polished hardwood floors. A fire was laid;

Will crouched before it, lit the newspaper under the kindling, stood up, brushed off his knees.

"Cognac good, Lieutenant?"

"Cognac is fine." Dante wandered around the living room, looking at books on the shelves, touching artifacts from Will's travels. "I saw your folks last month."

"They told me."

"They didn't tell *me* anything. Not even when I said your life was in danger." He accepted the brandy snifter from Will's hand. "Do you think your life's in danger?"

"No."

Will reached into the inside pocket of the sports jacket he had worn to his lecture, brought out a 3.5" floppy disk. He laid it on the coffee table in front of the couch where he had been sitting the last time Dante had been in this room.

"There's the disk that got Moll killed, Lieutenant."

Dante stood looking down at it, forgotten brandy snifter in hand. "Now you give it to me," he said bitterly. "If you'd done this before you left, a lot of people would still be alive—"

"Moll wouldn't. And now you can shut Atlas down. That's your job, isn't it, Stagnaro? Organized crime? Not murder?"

"Hard to tell the two apart sometimes," said Dante.

His beeper went off. Will moved his head slightly, almost as if he had been expecting it.

"The phone is there."

The police dispatcher said she'd patch Dante through to Tim Flanagan. Tim's big voice boomed over the phone.

"Gounaris is dead at his tootsie's place."

"His tootsie?" Dante's own voice sounded strange to him.

"Diana Pym. They were gonna have a party, but when she got home from Victoria's Secret with a lot of fancy underwear without any crotches in it, a fax was waiting for her." There was some paper-rattling, then Tim read to him: "'GO TO MY APARTMENT AND WAIT FOR ME THERE. DO NOT CALL ME AT THE OFFICE. THE POLICE HAVE BEEN HERE AGAIN.' So she goes there and waits, about

an hour ago she gets pissed with waiting and comes back
here . . ."

He stopped. Dante said, "And?"

"Gounaris was here. Strangled with a wire garrote, pulled
so tight it almost severed his neck. Then he was draped over
an easy chair with his pants off, so he'd be the first thing she
saw when she got home."

"Nasty," said Dante in his strange voice.

"Typical." Tim gave his big laugh. "I think he spent a lot
of time that way. His office log shows the killer got him up
here with a phone call—"

"From Raptor?"

"From me. Musta been a good impersonation, huh?" His
braying laugh. "Pym's takin' it a little hard, but what the
fuck? Maybe Raptor'll die of old age before he kills us all."

He hung up. Tim was finally pissed off about Raptor—fifteen months too late. Dante returned his own receiver to its
hooks.

"Gounaris is dead. Murdered. With a garrote."

Will was meeting his eyes. "You want tears?"

Dante began, "If I didn't know it wasn't possible . . ." then
trailed off.

"Anything's possible, Lieutenant," said Will with sudden
decision. "In fact, if I were a betting man . . ."

Dante grabbed up the phone again, jabbed out the number
he knew best. Rosie would still be at Greek Dance, or at coffee afterward. He added the code to activate his phone-
machine playback. There was a single call.

"Remember the end of *Hamlet*," said the voice, "when
everybody's dead and only Horatio is left to tell the tale?

   " . . . *let me speak to the yet unknowing world*
   How these things came about: so shall you hear
   Of carnal, bloody and unnatural acts,
   Of accidental judgements, casual slaughters,
   Of deaths put on by cunning and forced cause. . . .

"Just ask me, I'll tell you. This is Raptor."

It was Will Dalton's voice.

Dante automatically pressed the combination to save the tape, hung up. He began in a hushed voice, "But your . . . the Raptor message after your wife's . . . after Moll was murdered . . ."

"I'd deciphered the disk by then. It told me who was involved in Atlas Entertainment, and I knew they'd murdered her. You'd told me she'd been promiscuous for our whole marriage . . . I was crazy with grief and love and hate . . . and guilt. If I'd been there on time she wouldn't have died. If if if . . . I had to *do* something. Had to . . . " His voice was anguished. "I had all the money coming from Moll's life insurance to spend, the name Raptor just came to me, so I used it . . . He was a sort of shorthand . . . Somebody who could do what I couldn't do myself . . ."

Dante remembered giving Dalton his card on that other visit to this house, his card with his unlisted home telephone written on the back. He was still struggling with belief, assimilation.

"But . . . Tim and I talked to you on the phone. In Kenya. After Jack Lenington was hit . . ."

"I'd just gotten there the day before."

"I put you on the plane myself—"

"To L.A. I didn't fly on to Africa until after I'd killed Lenington."

"I checked the plane manifests."

"Kampala, not Nairobi. Uganda, not Kenya."

Dante hadn't moved from his place at the phone. He had only to pick it up, call for backup. His gun was on his belt, Dalton—Raptor—was relaxed in the leather easy chair.

"You flew back again to do Spic Madrid?"

"Not mine. Not involved in Moll's death." Will was on his feet, suddenly pacing, gesticulating, as if everything he had bottled up inside was bursting out after fifteen months. "I was still in Nairobi, saw a filler about it in the international *New York Times,* got a priest at a mission down the road from where I was staying to make the phone call."

"The fucking dog!" Dante exclaimed suddenly. "That was what I missed at your folks' place! The dog! He was the one at Mae's Place that disappeared after . . ."

"I couldn't leave him there. He'd come to depend on me."

"Then your folks knew that . . ."

"That I was back from Africa some months ago, that's all. What they might have guessed beyond that . . ."

"The fucking code of the West," said Dante bitterly.

"The genetic code, more likely," snapped Will. "My father killed men in the war. He said it never bothered him for a moment. He always felt that's what soldiers did. I was in a war, too. They'd swatted Moll like a fly. To protect their fucking empire. So I pulled their empire down any way I could."

"Just like that," said Dante softly. He'd spent his whole professional life trying to do just that; Dalton had done it in fifteen months. *Let me speak to the yet unknowing world . . . of carnal, bloody and unnatural acts . . .* "Of course you killed a lot of people in the process . . ."

"People?" Will paced again, gesturing, face distorted. "Yes. Of course. You're right. They were people, weren't they? After Lenington I quit. I couldn't stand it. I'd never known that killing another human being would be so . . . so *hard . . .*"

"But you got used to it," said Dante coldly. He was waiting for the wave of hatred, of revulsion for this murderous bastard to hit him, but it hadn't yet. Maybe now it would.

"I spent three months in the Kibale Forest. The nightmares stopped. I was getting immersed in my work. Then a female came into estrus. Chimps . . . they were all . . . All I could see was Moll . . . with Gounaris . . . with all of them . . . And I knew I had to come back, keep going until all the men who had killed her were dead."

"Why Moll's father?"

"Not me—I'd say it was Ucelli acting under orders from Otto Kreiger. But when I heard about it, on the same day I killed Kreiger, I just used that Hardy quote about pairings . . ."

"How'd you know about Ucelli? He wouldn't have been on this disk."

"You told me—remember?"

Dante remembered. Right here in this room. He could see it all now. How Dalton had worked it. Once everyone believed he was in East Africa, nobody would look in his direction again.

How he had done it, yes. But that he'd been *able* to do it . . . Such a sustained rage, such a . . .

He remembered his secret contempt for Will when he'd heard the man was going to run off to Africa, leave his wife's death unresolved. Remembered his own blustering thoughts about what he would do if someone did to Rosie what they had done to Moll . . .

Would he have done any different?

"If we weren't here, if you hadn't told me about this . . ."

"I'd go back to Uganda." His eyes had, for a moment, an almost peaceful look. "Eventually, publish my findings. Keep looking for answers about us . . ." He met Dante's gaze directly. "It's important. After all of this"—he waved an arm—"I know just *how* important. How could I do it? Yet I'd do it again. *Knowing* it was wrong, *knowing* we have to find other ways to react to loss and pain and rage if we are to survive as a species, knowing all that I'd still do it all again. Because whatever has been driving me is in all of us. We have to understand it or we're doomed."

Dante thought of the Raptor messages. The lecture he had heard that night. The impossibility of getting evidentiary proof of any of the slayings Raptor had committed—he still couldn't think of the assassin as Will Dalton. The Raptor tapes meant nothing, even those that could be shown by voiceprints to be in Dalton's voice—just a man reading quotes from literature . . .

Will burst out, "Don't you see it, Stagnaro? Young primates in the ghettos, forming bonds like chimpanzees on the *veldt* . . . Pockets of nationalism or race festering until they split open and spew violence . . . Spouses beating spouses, stepparents killing children . . . Me murdering the men who murdered Moll . . .

"We can't escape our animal nature, it's like cholesterol in the blood—in times of stress it's going to come out. But still we ignore the myths that told us who we were, where we came from. We try to live the myth of man, shiny and new, apex of life, different in kind, not degree. It doesn't work. Our only hope is to recognize who and what we are, hope that we're still evolving, that we still have time—just barely—to save ourselves and the world. Otherwise . . . "

He stopped, rubbed his eyes wearily. Dante took his hand from the phone, where it had been all of that time, crossed to the coffee table, picked up the disk. Dalton hadn't been asking for absolution; just understanding. And not for himself. Just for . . . *us* . . .

Will Dalton spoke softly, almost indifferently.

"So what happens now?"

Dante wasn't God. Just a cop. A cop who'd have a hell of a time proving anything he'd heard here tonight in a court of law. He hadn't even read Dalton his Miranda rights. And for the moment, all his own enemies were dead. He put the disk in his pocket. He'd erase the message on his answering machine.

"What happens now? Atlas Entertainment goes in the toilet, my organized crime squad looks like champs. The Mafia'll probably have a big war over who grabs Vegas now that you've taken Prince out, and the Feebies'll think they're gonna save the world. You'll have to learn to live with what you've done—I, God help me, will have to learn to live with what I'm doing."

He knew he'd tell Rosie. Eventually. And he knew she'd approve. Eventually. He'd never tell Tim; he wouldn't approve. Or maybe he would. Dante wasn't so sure about anybody any more.

"Not with a bang but a whimper," said Will Dalton softly.

"Whatever the hell that means," said Dante.

Neither man offered to shake hands. As he shut the door behind him, Dante heard Will Dalton, for the third time in his adult life, start to cry. Moll was still dead, and Raptor was gone. Will Dalton was truly alone.

But he had avenged his dead wife, and could begin to grieve for her. After all the hatred and spilled blood, wasn't that a human achievement of sorts?

AND AFTERWARD . . .

It is the height of folly for a mystery novelist who writes escapist fare to take his work too seriously. On the other hand, what is escapist fare? Must it always be the latest bodice-ripper from the romance writers? The latest mindless sitcom or TV talk show parading moral cripples before us like county fair carnival freaks? In a 1944 essay for *The Saturday Review of Literature*, "The Simple Art of Murder," Raymond Chandler wrote:

"*All* reading for pleasure is escape, whether it be Greek, mathematics, or astronomy. To say otherwise is to be an intellectual snob, and a juvenile at the art of living."

Menaced Assassin is a mystery novel that happens to examine man's origins, his nature, his relationship with the world around him, and the wellsprings of his almost unremitting violence against his own kind. It does so deliberately, by weaving these questions into the plot, so I have listed below those books from which I stole shamelessly during the writing. They have amused, astounded, delighted, educated, and excited me for countless hours, *entertained* me beyond measure. I list them here so they can give like pleasure and excitement to you. Any scientific accuracy is theirs; any theorizing, any errors, mine alone.

Ardrey, Robert. *African Genesis*. New York: A Delta Book, 1961.

Bakker, Robert T., Ph.D. *The Dinosaur Heresies.* New York: Zebra Books, 1986.

Eldredge, Niles. *The Miner's Canary—Unravelling the Mysteries of Extinction.* New York: Prentice Hall Press, 1991.

Fisher, Helen E., Ph.D. *Anatomy of Love: The Natural History of Monogamy, Adultery, and Divorce.* New York: W. W. Norton & Co., 1992.

Ghiglieri, Michael P. *East of the Mountains of the Moon.* New York: The Free Press, 1988.

Gould, Stephen Jay. *Wonderful Life: The Burgess Shale and the Nature of History.* New York: W. W. Norton & Co., 1989.

The Holy Bible (King James Version). Nashville, Tenn.: The Gideons International, 1967.

Howells, William. *Getting Here: The Story of Human Evolution.* Washington, D.C.: The Compass Press, 1993.

Jacobs, Louis, Ph.D. *Quest for the African Dinosaurs.* New York: Villard Books, 1993.

Johanson, Donald; Johanson, Lenora; and Edgar, Blake. *Ancestors: In Search of Human Origins.* New York: Villard Books, 1994.

Raup, David M. *Extinction—Bad Genes or Bad Luck?* New York: W. W. Norton & Co., 1991.

Russell, Dale A. *The Dinosaurs of North America.* Minocqua, Wis.: NorthWord Press, Inc. 1989.

Sagan, Carl, and Druyan, Ann. *Shadows of Forgotten Ancestors.* New York: Random House, 1992.

Schick, Kathy D., and Toth, Nicholas. *Making Silent Stones Speak.* New York: Simon & Schuster, 1993.

Tattersall, Ian; Derlson, Eric; and Van Couvering, John, eds. *Encyclopedia of Human Evolution and Prehistory.* New York: Garland Publishing, 1988.

Young, Dudley. *Origins of the Sacred.* New York: St. Martin's Press, 1991.

*   *   *

Also I must acknowledge:

Foremost, and forever, my wife, Dori, lover, friend, unequaled editor, a remarkable woman who has puzzled with me over the nature of man for the twenty years our lives have been intertwined.

Robert Ardrey, whose *African Genesis* dragged me into the maze of man's origins and nature, and the countless other writers and scientists and naturalists, not cited above, who work in a bewildering array of disciplines and have been my guides through the labyrinth for over thirty years.

Jamie Frazier-Page, for invaluable information on weapons, ammunition, and the lethal effects of gunshot. Again, the expertise is his, the errors are mine.

Bill Malloy, my editor at Mysterious Press, who fought for this novel's place on the fall list despite the fact that I was unconscionably late in delivering it.

Finally, Henry Morrison and Danny Baror, my agents, who have hounded me over the years to be the best novelist I can be, and who understand the necessity of a living wage for writers daily facing their own mortality on the blank page.

Joe Gores
San Anselmo
May 20, 1994